Praise for
CHRISTINA DODD
and Her Novels

"Christina Dodd's talents continue to grow and readers
are guaranteed pleasure and true enjoyment."
—*Romantic Times*

"Christina Dodd just keeps getting better and better."
—Debbie Macomber

"Memorable characters, witty dialogue, steaming
sensuality—the perfect combination for sheer
enjoyment."
—Jill Marie Landis

"*Outrageous* is bodacious!"
—Susan Wiggs on *Outrageous*

"A beautiful, sensual love story filled with mystery,
intrigue and adventure. . . . A book to curl up and enjoy."
—June Lund Shiplett on *Treasure of the Sun*

"A very special romance—heartbreaking and
heartwarming, original, beautiful, compassionate, and
well written. It is a story you'll never forget. . . .
Ensures Christina Dodd a place in readers' hearts."
—*Romantic Times* on *Candle in the Window*

"A great hero, a gripping plot and all the color and
excitement of the Middle Ages. Christina Dodd is a joy
to read."
—Laura Kinsale on *Castles in the Air*

ATTENTION: ORGANIZATIONS AND CORPORATIONS

Most HarperPaperbacks are available at special quantity discounts for bulk purchases for sales promotions, premiums, or fund-raising. For information please call or write:
Special Markets Department, HarperCollins Publishers Inc.,
10 East 53rd Street, New York, NY 10022-5299.
Telephone: (212) 207-7528. Fax: (212) 207-7222.

THE GREATEST LOVER IN ALL ENGLAND

CHRISTINA DODD

HarperPaperbacks
A Division of HarperCollinsPublishers

HarperPaperbacks
A Division of HarperCollinsPublishers
10 East 53rd Street, New York, NY 10022-5299

This is a work of fiction. The characters, incidents, and dialogues are products of the author's imagination and are not to be construed as real. Any resemblance to actual events or persons, living or dead, is entirely coincidental.

ISBN 0-06-108561-8

HarperCollins®, 🔥®, and HarperPaperbacks™ are trademarks of HarperCollins Publishers Inc.

Cover illustration by Doreen Minuto

First HarperPaperbacks printing: December 1994
Special edition printing: February 1999

Printed in the United States of America

Visit HarperPaperbacks on the World Wide Web at
http://www.harpercollins.com

❖ 10 9 8 7 6 5 4 3 2 1

With thanks to Carol Bortner
for letting me work at
Carol's Book Corner,
for teaching me about reps and returns,
and for giving me some of the best times of my life
with the best customers in the world.

I

All the world's a stage,
And all the men and women merely players.

—AS YOU LIKE IT, II, vii, 139

1

England
Autumn, 1600

> *"Catch them two* whoreson actors!"*

The shouts of five men-at-arms propelled Sir Danny yet faster. The mud of the squalid London streets splashed to his knees, and he cleared a garbage-eating pig in one leap.

"Catch 'em an' th' earl o' Essex'll reward ye!"

Curious spectators turned to watch as Sir Danny and his ward skidded around the corner, but no one stepped between the soldiers and their prey. With every stomp of their boots, with every shout and every curse, the men-at-arms proclaimed their intention to commit murder most foul.

Sir Danny loved the drama of it. When watered with intrigue, he grew like a mighty oak, and he thrived on life's tumult. Responsibility was for lesser men; Sir Daniel Plympton, Esquire, lived to laugh, drink, fight, swive—and act. Seeing the crowd of beggars, drunkards, and prostitutes gathering in the doorways of the tall, ill-kept taverns and tenements that lined the street, he slowed and pointed one hand skyward. Pitching his voice to reach the farthest member of his audience, he proclaimed, "Damn yon brazen sun! Would God that wispy London fog might cover o'er its bright and erring face, and so conceal us from our enemies—"

"Shut your maw and run."

His ward planted one firm hand on his back and shoved him along the sunny lane. Dear Rosencrantz, Sir Danny thought, always so worried about him, always sure that this adventure would be their last. Didn't Rosencrantz realize that in his fifty years on this earth, Sir Danny had not yet fulfilled his destiny? That audiences still waited to be thrilled by his thespian endeavors? That Queen Elizabeth's reign had not been defended by him?

That he had not yet resolved Rosencrantz's own fate?

"In the alley. Quick, Danny. Quick!"

He chuckled at the panic in Rosencrantz's voice, at the slender shoulder shoved into his spine.

Spurting ahead, Sir Danny darted into the dark, narrow lane, overhung with the eaves of two-story hovels. He raced past the massive washerwoman hanging sheets on the line, ignored her furious cry, and ducked beneath the dangling white canvas.

Still playing to the crowd left behind, he announced, "Oh, stinking mud beneath our feet which even now reminds of us of our mortality! The stench of death hangs heavy o'er our fair city—"

Between the flapping sheets, the washerwoman seized Rosencrantz and yelled, "'Ere now, ye young oaf, ye'll not be fer ruinin' me laundry."

"Let me go!" Rosencrantz sounded panicked.

When Sir Danny poked his head back, he saw the youth captured by the beefy washerwoman.

Rosencrantz struggled, but the washerwoman lifted and shook Sir Danny's ward. "This is *my* alley, an' no lickspittle goin' t' come through lessen *I* say so."

Rosencrantz's feet kicked in midair. "No, m'lady, but yon soldiers'll murder us."

"Yon soldiers?" The washerwoman put Rosencrantz down hard and faced the entrance to the alley, blocking the meager leak of sunlight with her girth.

Using the damp line of laundry like a theater curtain, Sir Danny warned, "They come. They come! The ungodly heathens even now curse us with their hot breath, and fair Jupiter himself—"

Ducking beneath the sheet, Rosencrantz grabbed Sir Danny's hand and pulled him aside even as Essex's men thundered through the gap.

"Begone, ye leadenpated lug-loafs!" the washerwoman roared. "This is my alley, an' no—"

They shoved her so hard she landed in a puddle. Her broad beam created a wave that left a tide mark on the side of the building, and she shrieked out oaths to make a lord blush.

The soldiers ignored her, slashing the clothesline with their swords and trampling the sheets beneath their boots. Both Sir Danny and Rosencrantz tried to dart toward the far end of the alley, but the sharp and shiny edge of a blade blocked that way—and then every way. Helmeted heads obstructed the scant light, and the faces within sneered.

"Like maddened dogs," Sir Danny said. "Your visages proclaim your lineage and your temper."

"Danny. Don't . . . don't . . ." Rosencrantz could scarcely speak for terror. "Don't provoke them."

Sir Danny looked at the men towering over him. He

looked at their leather armor, their scars, and their swords, and, for the first time, fright possessed him. This was no drama, no imaginary threat which brave words would vanquish. He'd done the worst thing a common man could do. He'd proved himself a menace to a nobleman, and regardless of the justice of his cause, he would die for his insolence.

But Rosencrantz would not die. By the gods, he—Sir Daniel Plympton, Esquire—would not allow it.

Calling on his theater art, he softened his bones and weakened his muscles. The dynamic fifty-year-old transformed himself into an easy victim. With more conviction than pathos, he said, "And so my prayer is answered, and the sun sets upon this life lived too long in the bosom of the blessed earth." He nudged Rosencrantz away from him, wanting his dear ward positioned for flight. "Yet youth slips away between the bandy legs of threat and rises again for better times."

Rosencrantz understood, of that Sir Danny had no doubt. But answering him in kind, Rosencrantz moved closer and denied him firmly. "Youth and age will die together, and so entwined, give life to that blessed earth."

Sir Danny abruptly lost his eloquence. "Dammit, Rosencrantz, if these clots discover—"

"Clots?" The chief man-at-arms, a hulking soldier with a single eye, grabbed Rosencrantz by the long tail of hair. "Ye aren't talking about us, are ye?" He twisted the unkempt brown locks until the youth sank into the mud with a moan. "Are ye?"

"Nay. Nay!" Sir Danny observed, horrified, as the bully grabbed the long, white throat exposed by his brutality and squeezed. "I meant no disrespect, kind sir. Brave, brawn sir." He poked at the soldier's arm and professed amazement at the muscles he found, while ascertaining that mere wool covered those muscles. A hardened leather vest protected the soldier's chest and back, and a padded leather trunk hose shielded his hips from slashing blows, but the rest of his body was vulnerable.

Vulnerable? One-Eye stood a full foot above Sir Danny, and grinned with the relish of a butcher about to dismember a lamb. Tearing his ruff loose, Sir Danny pointed at his exposed throat. "Only look at my neck and know how this better suits your purposes."

"But we like th' pretty lad. Yer son's head'll look fine decoratin' a spike on London Bridge." He tightened his grip again, and Rosencrantz clawed at him, choking.

"Better than this ol' man's." Another soldier thrust Sir Danny against the wall and poked the displayed throat with the point of his sword.

He was going to die. *They* were going to die, and with them all his dreams of glory. Silently, he prayed for deliverance. He promised to reform, to give up drinking to excess, smoking tobacco, plowing wild cunny, acting. Well, perhaps not acting. Nor the cunny—he did love women.

But anything else. Anything else he would do to be delivered . . . or, better yet, to have Rosencrantz delivered.

But deliverance, when it came, didn't smell like deliverance. A splash of warm piss came flying from the open window above, accompanied by a lady's shriek. "That'll teach ye boofheads t' mess wi' Tiny Mary!"

A second deluge followed the first. Astonished, the men-at-arms released their hostages.

Looking up, Sir Danny saw females in various stages of undress protruding from every window.

"Ye'll not knock that doxy around again," another woman cried.

Sir Danny laughed aloud.

Fool. Fool! Now he recognized this lane. Now he recognized the mighty washerwoman. He and Rosencrantz had stumbled to the best-known brothel in London, and the soldiers had attacked the best-loved madam in the business.

The now-damp men-at-arms danced as they tried to avoid the odious contents of the chamber pots. They never saw Tiny Mary pawing the ground like an infuriated nanny goat. She charged, and three soldiers went down like bowls hit by a wooden ball. Two remained standing, but staggered, spitting and cursing.

The harlots screamed encouragement, and Sir Danny screamed with joy. They were saved. He knew it! The heavens watched over him, for only he could rescue Her Majesty Queen Elizabeth from the nefarious plot against her. Only he could return Rosencrantz to a proper place. Sir Danny laughed again, and One-Eye stiffened and wiped his eyes.

"Stupid," Rosencrantz muttered. "Stupid old actor."

When the chief man-at-arms headed toward him, sword out, Sir Danny almost agreed.

In Rosencrantz's hand, metal glinted. His ward held an eating knife. An eating knife! Against a fully armed soldier!

Lowering his head, Sir Danny rammed into his attacker's groin. The chief man-at-arms doubled over, but he took Sir Danny down with him.

He rolled over on Sir Danny, holding him down with his body. Sir Danny flopped like a beached fish and tried to bite. Then the hand holding him suddenly loosened. The body above him exploded into action. Surfacing, he heard a man screaming in a most unmanly way. Rosencrantz dragged Sir Danny to his feet, urging, "Run. We've got to run!"

Stumbling, Sir Danny tried to catch his breath. No

more would he laugh at fate. For now, he would clasp escape to his bosom.

At the corner of the alley, he glanced back. Metal chamber pots showered the two standing soldiers. Tiny Mary sat on two more men, holding their heads and stretching their necks in her elbows. And One-Eye writhed on the ground, emitting that awful screaming.

At a loss for perhaps the first time in his life, Sir Danny stammered, "What . . . ? What . . . ?"

Rosencrantz glowed with grim satisfaction. "I shoved the point of my eating knife up under his trunk hose and into his—"

Sir Danny clutched himself. "My God!"

"Aye," Rosencrantz said. "He'll not come after us any time soon."

Wiping her muddy hands on her apron, Tiny Mary grinned down at One-Eye. "Got ye in th' family apples, did she?"

One-Eye stopped examining his privates and glared at the immense woman. "There's no permanent damage."

"Wouldn't have been any permanent damage if she'd cut 'em right off."

Furious and wounded, One-Eye snarled, "I've still got th' goods t' take on a butt-peddler like ye."

Flinging back her head, Tiny Mary laughed. Her merriment boomed back and forth against the walls; her body jiggled with glee. "That feeble little root couldn't make a dent."

The women above joined in her laughter, and the recovering men-at-arms hid their heads and sniggered.

One-Eye covered himself and leaped to his feet, groping for his sword.

"Looking fer this?" Tiny Mary dangled it from one fat finger. "Ye lost it when th' little woman stabbed ye."

Flopping back against the wall, One-Eye groaned and held himself.

"Looks like he lost more than 'is sword when she stabbed him," one of the harlots said.

"Hey, Tiny Mary, do ye know her?" another asked.

"Nay, but with an arm like hers, she could fight on me team anytime," Tiny Mary answered.

"Ye stupid ol' whore." Blood dripped down One-Eye's leg. "That's an actor. He plays women's parts, but he's no woman. Ain't no women actors. Ain't proper."

"Ye stupid ol' footslogger," Tiny Mary mocked. "That's a woman. I know th' law says there ain't supposed t' be no women actors, but I seen me share o' bodies in me day, an' that actor's got all th' equipment t' live on th' distaff side o' th' street." Observing the stunned soldier, she laughed again, and her ladies laughed with her.

A woman? A woman had half-gelded him? A woman had defeated him? "'Tisn't possible," One-Eye muttered.

"A padded doublet covers a lot, but even a fool like ye ought t' recognize she ain't got no spindle-shanks beneath them trunk hose. Not t' mention"—Mary minced in a circle—"I've seen Papist monks wi' more worldly wisdom. Haven't ye?"

Recalling the narrow, beardless face and wide brown eyes, he knew the uncomfortable truth. He *had* been defeated by a woman. He, who had raped and murdered more women than a Hun on a rampage.

Blood rushed to his brain, and he forgot his injury. Shrieking "Rosencrantz!" he ran full tilt toward the alley's exit.

A man stepped in his way. One-Eye skidded to a stop and reached for his sword, but it wasn't at his side. He pulled his knife and prepared to gut the stranger, but—

"Ye." One-Eye jerked his arm backward, although the man before him made no move. "Ye! I know ye. We fought together."

"Long ago."

The deep, guttural voice held a trace of accent and no trace of emotion, and a chill touched One-Eye's back. Dressed like a civilian, this former soldier exuded menace in his stance, in his steady, challenging gaze, in the stillness of a battle ready wolf. One-Eye tried to remember the man's name while remembering all too well the stranger's ruthlessness. "Remember when that Frenchie burned th' hut around our ears, an' broke yer knee? Remember how we tracked an' captured him? Remember how he screamed when—"

"Nay."

One-Eye squinted through the dim light. "Th' fire didn't scar ye much."

The stranger didn't answer, and One-Eye said, "If ye'd step aside, I'm after a bitch named—"

"Rosencrantz?"

Uneasy still, although he didn't understand why, One-Eye agreed. "Aye. Rosencrantz."

"Then"—the man's hand shot out, a shiny blade clutched in his hand—"you must die."

Astonished, One-Eye saw blood spurt from his own throat. He fell to his knees, breathless, in pain.

Yells of fear penetrated his fog; screams of fright and sounds of battle. He risked one glance up, and observed a seemingly disembodied sword dispensing death. With relentless efficiency, the stranger murdered every soldier in the alley.

A living barrier, Tiny Mary spread herself over the door that led to her brothel, but the stranger stalked toward her. She lifted One-Eye's bright sword; the stranger lifted his bloody blade. Tiny Mary shivered, melting like a jelly on a hot bakestone.

Even now, One-Eye wanted that strumpet dead, and he croaked, trying to lend encouragement to the stranger. The stranger's head swiveled; for one moment their gazes met. Memories of ruthless laughter and crimson knives passed between them. The stranger smiled coldly and in slow increments, he withdrew his sword. "Go inside, fat woman," he instructed, and Tiny Mary sprang through the door with fear-endowed agility.

The stranger stalked across the alley, listing back and forth like a sailor on a stormy deck. With sword poised, he said, "I don't like people to remember my past, but you've a grievous wound, my friend. Let me cure you."

Terror spurted through One-Eye's veins.

Lifting his sword high, the stranger plunged it deep into his former comrade, then jerked it free. With the edge of One-Eye's cloak, he cleaned the blade and glanced in the direction of the theater. He would go there next.

To take care of Rosencrantz.

2

Mischief, thou are afoot,
Take thou what course thou wilt.
—JULIUS CAESAR, III, ii, 262

"*Sir Danny Plympton's* in the house. Stop the play." Uncle Will waved one arm at the actors on the stage of the Globe Theater and clutched the script with the other. "By great Zeus's lightning bolt, stop the play at once! He'll memorize it and produce it himself before we can make a pittance."

The performers ground to a halt while Rosie sagged against one of the columns of the ground floor gallery. Her joints shook, her muscles were flaccid with exhaustion. She constantly scanned the round, three-storied, open-roofed structure, examining every bench in every tier. She watched the entrance, listened for the tramp of heavy feet outside, and tried to convince herself she and Sir Danny were safe.

She flexed her dirty fingers and watched the movement with weary fascination. She'd incapacitated the captain with her knife thrust, but she hadn't killed him. Maybe if she'd had a long, sharp knife. Maybe if she'd stabbed harder. Maybe if Sir Danny would stop rushing to meet trouble with open arms . . . She laughed, a rusty, choking laugh, and then a sob caught her by surprise. Rubbing her eyes with the back of her wrist, she knew that as long as Sir Danny was Sir Danny—exuberant, flamboyant, outrageous—they would never be safe.

"Hey, Rosie!"

Dickie Justin McBride hailed her, and she jerked her hand down. She didn't dare let the Chamberlain's Men see her in tears. Every one of them had been with Sir Danny's troupe at one time or another. Every one of them believed her to be a man, and a few of them scorned her as a craven. Nay, she didn't dare let them catch her crying.

"Hey, Dickie!" she yelled back. She had despised the handsome actor when they were youngsters, and she despised him now. He had an ugly tendency to pick on those less muscled than he—mostly Rosie, and mostly when they were alone. He had made her life a terror. Now he jumped down from the raised stage into the dirt yard from whence the standing-room customers watched the plays and swaggered toward her.

"I haven't seen you that dirty since you fell into the pigsty when you were eight." He flashed a grin at the actors who fell in behind him. "Good fellows, circle 'round and let me tell you the tale of how Rosie squealed louder than the pigs."

They advanced toward Rosie, and she recognized the tactics. Gather a gallery of rogues, bring them in a circle around her, then taunt her with jeers and contempt.

She was almost glad when Dickie swerved away.

"Whew! Haven't you washed since you fell in that pigsty?"

All the men waved their hands in Rosie's direction, making elaborate gagging noises, and her sweaty palms slipped down the column. Aye, she stank, although she and Sir Danny had run to the edge of the silver Thames and splashed the worst of it off.

With a flourish of his extended arm, Sir Danny proclaimed, "'Tis a sad day in Londontown when the worms of the earth mock the rose. The silver showers from the heavens will wash the rose and it will again be the noblest of flowers. But when the silver showers wash the worms, they will still crawl on their bellies through the dirt."

"Aye, and if these worms don't take their supper break now, their stomachs will wonder if their throats have been cut." Script in hand, Uncle Will glared at the actors as they changed courses, heading for the entrance and jostling each other as they fought their way out. Uncle Will turned to Sir Danny. "They're gone. What do you want?"

"What makes you think I want something?" Sir Danny asked.

"You never come unless you want something."

"Suspicious bastard," Sir Danny said.

"Pernicious knave," Uncle Will replied, and reached out to ruffle Rosie's hair. "At the risk of being called a worm, I must say you *are* more bedraggled than usual, my lad. Isn't this reprobate treating you well?"

"This reprobate almost *did* get his throat cut." Rosie cupped her hand under Sir Danny's elbow as if he were about to faint and wished someone was doing the same for her. "We've got to bandage him."

Sir Danny snatched his elbow away from her, clearly offended. "It's nothing, I tell you! And you were nigh onto choked yourself." He pushed her collar aside. "The bruises stain your skin like wine stains an ivory cup, and your youth would be more mourned than this old carcass. When next I tell you to escape, do so."

"I didn't understand you."

He shook her slightly. "When I tell you to escape, do so."

"Not without you," she said stubbornly.

"When I tell you to escape—"

"I can't!" She pulled away and turned her back to him. New pain and old panic mixed, and she fought to control them, pressing her hands before her face in an attitude of prayer. "I can't let you go again, Dada."

Sir Danny rubbed her back. "Look at me and listen, Rosencrantz."

"Nay. You're not going to look at me with those big eyes and wipe my fears away as you do when one of the troupe to you with a toothache or a gallstone. No tricks with me, Sir Danny. I'd rather die *with* you than to live alone."

"And I don't understand that," he said softly.

Sometimes even she didn't understand the terrors that captured her with clammy fingers, yanking her from the real world into a terrain stony with menace. Usually the specters broke through only at night, but occasionally the phantasms confronted her in broad daylight.

Like today. Swinging sharply away from his touch, she muttered, "I will not listen, Dada, and I will not let you go."

A moment of silence, then Sir Danny cleared his throat. "Modern youth is insolent, is it not, Uncle Will?"

"I would my son still lived to be so loyal to me," Uncle Will said.

Rosie rubbed her arms, up and down, up and down, trying to disperse the fear that chilled her.

Uncle Will studied her, then guessed, "You're in trouble again?"

"Aye," said Rosie.

"Nay," said Danny.

"Aye, then," Uncle Will decided.

"Some cowardly folk might say, 'Aye.'" Sir Danny looked severely at Rosie, then muttered in an undertone to Uncle Will, "But send a message to Ludovic."

Uncle Will shuddered. "Ludovic? Better to call him Lazarus. He moves like one raised from the dead."

Sir Danny pressed a perfumed handkerchief to his nose. "But he has been ever loyal to me since I engaged him seven years ago."

"As I remember," Rosie said, "he made that decision."

"He is a forceful man," Sir Danny admitted. "There are times when I would have dismissed him, but for the suspicion he'd refuse to leave."

"You!" Uncle Will pointed at one of the stagehands. "Seek you Sir Danny's manager and instruct him to bring Sir Danny's troupe, wagons and all." To Sir Danny, he said, "You can ride inside the wagons to escape the city. Come into the box office. We can be private there."

Still not totally convinced of Sir Danny's good health, Rosie followed close behind the men to the tiny room where the receipts were kept. What seemed to be rivalry and distrust between Sir Danny and Uncle Will rested on a solid foundation of friendship. Not for the first time, she thought they resembled David and Goliath. In wit they were well matched; in size, the physically powerful, balding Uncle Will overshadowed the small-framed, dapper Sir Danny. Yet Sir Danny's aggressive nature formed a counterpoint to Uncle

Will's thoughtful melancholy, and it was to Sir Danny that Uncle Will ran for inspiration when he wrote his more bellicose characters.

Taking a large key off his belt, Uncle Will opened the door and ushered them inside. "Who wants to cut out your heart now?"

"Oh." Sir Danny tapped the money box. "Nobody much."

"Just the earl of Essex and the earl of Southampton," Rosie said bluntly.

Even in the dim light of the little room, she could see Uncle Will lose his ruddy color. "Southampton? My God, he's my patron."

Sir Danny jumped like a flea in a circus. "He's a damned traitor and deserves execution at the least."

"And Sir Danny told him so in Essex House with Essex sitting hard by," Rosie informed Uncle Will.

Uncle Will fell backward against the wall, clutching his chest in a gesture honed to perfection in countless theatrical performances. "This is disaster. Southampton knows we're friends!"

"That's how it began," Rosie said. "He called us in from the street and asked us to bring you a message."

Uncle Will placed the script on the table. "What message?"

"Southampton wants you"—Sir Danny glared—"to perform *Richard II*."

Puzzled, Uncle Will pulled at his scrawny beard. "Why? 'Tis an old play, and not popular, dealing as it does with a monarch deposed."

Sir Danny grabbed him by the doublet and shook him with all the aggression of a rat terrier baiting a bear. "That's why he wants it performed. With no shame—with no discretion, by God—Essex spoke of an insurrection."

"An insurrection?"

"A revolt. A rebellion. A revolution."

"I know the meaning," Uncle Will said in irritation. "But I don't understand."

"You don't understand?" Hand on hip, finger pointed skyward, Sir Danny stood like a monument to indignation. "They wish you to perform *Richard II* to perpetuate an atmosphere of unrest, and bring about a mutiny against the very captain who guides our island ship through the turbulent waters of war and peace!"

"Against the queen? You are mistaken." Uncle Will appealed to Rosie. "Isn't he mistaken?"

"Would God he were." Rosie wandered to the table and looked down at the sheaf of papers. "But as you know, Queen Elizabeth is not pleased with Essex, and has cut off his income."

Still flabbergasted, Uncle Will said, "But insurrection? Essex was her favorite. He would have to be mad to think it would succeed."

Sir Danny nodded. "The queen has spoiled him with her favor, and that combined with his good looks and wealth has turned his head. He spoke of our gentle monarch in such agitation of spirit, I thought him mad. He cursed his poverty, and claimed"—he lowered his voice—"that the queen's conditions for curbing him were as crooked as her carcass."

"She'll have his head." Uncle Will clutched his own throat.

"I do so pray." Sir Danny paced across the dim, tiny room, a whirlwind of emotion that stirred the dust. "He spoke of rousing London, capturing the queen, and forcing her to do his bidding."

"He said this to *you?*" Uncle Will questioned doubtfully.

"Vehemently," Sir Danny replied. "I told you I thought him mad."

Rosie rubbed her forehead and left a streak of dirt. "You told Lord Southampton, too. You told them both we would repair to Whitehall Palace and inform Queen Elizabeth of their plans."

"Do you not agree that is what we should do?" Sir Danny asked.

"Aye, I do. But the basest intelligence tells me, also, that we should have performed the deed first and orated about it later."

Apparently unmoved by Rosie's aggravation, Sir Danny said, "We *do* need to get out of London."

"As soon as possible." Uncle Will turned on him savagely. "But this isn't what I wanted."

"I know what you wanted." Sir Danny flicked invisible dust particles from his sleeve. "We've already discussed it. 'Tis impossible."

Uncle Will picked up the script and dropped it with a thud back on the table. "I wrote this part with you in mind."

"Let Richard play it," Sir Danny said.

"You're a greater actor than Richard Burbage. You know you are. If you'd play this part, you'd receive acclaim and wealth. But you can't, because you slew yourself with your own jawbone again—"

"Are you calling me a jackass?"

"—And have to go into exile in the country."

Sir Danny shrugged. "I like the country."

"You hate the country," Uncle Will corrected.

Dropping her head, Rosie wished she were somewhere else. She didn't want to hear about Sir Danny's skill, for she knew it was true. When Sir Danny trod the boards, men sobbed and babes listened with rapt attention. Women found him irresistible, and the queen herself would applaud him. But he never remained in one place long enough to receive the acclaim he deserved.

And she was the cause.

How could he remain, when they both feared her masquerade would be revealed by extended familiarity? The waste of his talent sickened her, yet she knew of no steps she could take to end his exile.

She could have wept easily. Too easily. She looked at the script Uncle Will had dropped. Leafing through the pages, she squinted at the ink scrawls that writhed across the paper like worms. They sought some destination, they formed some organization, but she couldn't decipher them. Sometimes it seemed she could remember the letters. Sometimes it seemed she had learned to read a few words.

But mostly, she guessed, she had only imagined a time when she had a tutor and a home and a father whose face she could not recall. It was all part and parcel of her desire to read, and she was too old for dreaming.

"I used your name in this play," Uncle Will said.

She glanced up, and he was looking right at her.

"That's right. *Rosencrantz.* It's not a big part, but it's deliciously wicked, and you could play it."

Pointing to the script, she asked, "Where is it?"

"Your name?" Uncle Will flipped through the pages much as she had, but unlike her, he had a clear comprehension of the writing which so puzzled her. Pointing, he said, "There."

She bent over the page and stared.

He spelled it aloud, then laid his finger below a large, looping squiggle. "That's an '*R.*' It's the first letter of your name, and it makes a growling sound."

He rolled the sound across his tongue, and she imitated him. "R," she repeated. "R." She stared again, committing the squiggle to memory.

"Sir Danny, look at him." Uncle Will gestured, and she shrank from the two men who gazed at her so intently. "He stands there and stares at the pages and wants more than the life you've given him. A bright lad like him should be able to read."

"Why does he need to read?" Sir Danny asked. "He has a memory the equal of mine. I can memorize anything the first time I hear it."

"Aye, aye, and you can recite the whole Bible—backwards. But don't, because I've heard you do it before, and once proved a veritable bounty of holy script."

Sir Danny combed his shoulder-length hair with a comb he pulled from the purse at his side. Whatever happened, his vanity survived.

"But Rosencrantz is not an actor. Not like you are." Uncle Will shook his head sadly. "I know you don't want to face it. I know you don't want your protégé to be less than magnificent, but he has never progressed beyond playing women's roles."

"Rosencrantz has his magnificent moments," Sir Danny argued.

"Followed by some terrible half hours. But if he could read, he could become a clerk. He'll never learn if he continues to travel with that provincial touring company."

"That's *my* provincial touring company," Sir Danny reminded him.

Uncle Will wrinkled his nose with scorn. "With wagons to move you from town to town and a scaffold for a stage. Perhaps you long for nothing more, but Rosencrantz has been with you for fifteen years—"

"Sixteen." Sir Danny removed his short cloak and slapped the drying mud off the threadbare velvet.

"And he must be nigh onto eighteen years old."

"I'm twenty-one years," Rosie insisted.

"A delicate-looking twenty-one." Uncle Will sounded as if he didn't believe it.

Rosie lifted her hairless chin. "Sir Danny said I was four or five when he found me, so I am twenty-one."

"Hm." Uncle Will looked her up and down. "Obviously, traveling doesn't agree with you, or you wouldn't be such a scrawny boy." Displaying a fine-tuned intuition, he coaxed, "Rosencrantz, I'd teach you to read myself if you'd just remain in London."

"We can't." Sir Danny took Rosie's hand and squeezed it. "I lost my temper and we've got to go."

Impatient with him, Uncle Will demanded, "Why didn't you think of the lad for a change, rather than your egotistic emotions?"

Sir Danny took on the role of noble defender, his depiction made compelling by his sincerity. "I *was* thinking of the lad. Do you know what would happen if the government was overturned? Queen Elizabeth has guided this nation for forty years and two, and brought us peace and prosperity. What life would there be for my Rosencrantz if our Good Queen Bess were stripped of authority?"

"Aye, what life?" Grudgingly, Uncle Will concurred with Sir Danny's assessment.

"Someone must take action," Sir Danny said, "and that someone must be you. You must warn the queen. I would do so, but I dare not show my face on the streets."

"Aye, I must warn the queen, and when I do, I'll have lost my patron." Nervously, Uncle Will dislodged the few strands of hair that covered his scalp, providing a clear view of the shining pate he so carefully concealed. "Pray God, Sir Danny, she listens without prejudice to an actor and playwright, and ignores the notorious reputation our fellows have begotten."

With a wry twist of his mouth, Sir Danny said, "Speaking of Ludovic, do you think he's arrived yet?" He jerked open the door and stumbled backward.

Rosie gasped. Ludovic stood there, tall, broad, and as motionless as an adder basking in the sun.

Of sturdy stock, Ludovic had been born in some foreign country and smashed on the shores of England by an unruly fate. He'd proved himself to be indispensable to the acting troupe—and he'd proved himself incapable of making friends. No one liked Ludovic. No one bested Ludovic. Although he'd never resorted to violence, everyone feared him. Something in the slant of his cruel mouth and the scars that marked his back and chest dissuaded a challenge.

"Ludovic!" Sir Danny caught Rosie's hand and squeezed it.

"Sir Danny." Ludovic's low, deep voice contained a slight accent, and it seemed thicker now. Had he been listening at the door?

Recovering from his shock, Sir Danny decided to brazen it out. "I sent a boy for you. Did he find you?"

"I'm here, am I not?"

"Good." Sir Danny walked forward, Rosie's hand still clasped in his own, and Ludovic yielded. Sir Danny and Rosie strolled back out into the afternoon sunshine that warmed the standing room area. "I am anxious to travel with my"—Sir Danny sounded sardonic—"*provincial* touring company. Ludovic, have you brought the wagons?"

"The wagons? Nay." Ludovic followed. "But I will get them."

He bowed and backed away, staring at Rosie with his slightly bulging eyes, and Sir Danny shouted, "Begone!"

Ludovic glared, then limped toward the exit.

"Sir Danny," Rosie remonstrated, "why did you yell at him? You've offended him and you know we need him."

Sir Danny contemplated the place where Ludovic had disappeared. "He's been with us a long time. Perhaps too long." He glanced at her, then shouted, "You can come out, Will. He's gone." Uncle Will stuck his head out and looked both ways, then slipped out. Eager to be rid of them now, he said, "I'll assist you within the limits of my poor abilities, but I haven't any money so—"

Sir Danny pounced. "So you'll let us hear your new play?"

"Nay!"

"But we'll be in the country," Sir Danny coaxed. "Far from your London audiences. None will know when we perform it first."

"Nay." But Uncle Will was clearly weakening.

"Dear old friend." Sir Danny threw his arm around Will's neck. "Such a small favor for those whose lives were almost forfeited for Her Majesty and God's own England. What do you call it?"

"I call *it Hamlet.*" William Shakespeare kicked the dirt in disgust, then capitulated. "And I call *myself* a fool. You may listen, but once." He held up one long finger. "Once only. Then you must go before Southampton inquires of you here. And where will you go?"

As coolly as a brigand, Sir Danny answered, "We're going to an estate not far from London."

Shocked, Rosie jerked her hand from Sir Danny's grasp. "Nay, we are not."

Sir Danny ignored her. "We have an invitation to perform for Sir Anthony Rycliffe and his guests at a house party."

"We're not going there."

Puzzled, Uncle Will asked, "Why don't you want to go there, Rosencrantz?"

She shoved Sir Danny with a violent motion. "Because Danny has taken leave of his senses."

"We're going to make our fortune there." Sir Danny smiled.

"I can almost see the feathers protruding from between your lips," Uncle Will marveled. "What do you plan to do?"

Sir Danny gave a cultivated flutter of his fingers. "We'll escape the confines of London, travel to Lord Anthony Rycliff's estate, breathe the fresh country air, eat well, drink deep—"

Rosie interrupted. "And blackmail Sir Anthony out of a goodly sum."

3

O mistress mine! where are you roaming?
—TWELFTH NIGHT, II, iii, 40

Sir Anthony Rycliffe staggered, knocked from his passionate exploration of Lady Blanche's full, pouting mouth by the tip of a cane jabbed into his side. Lifting his head from the kiss, he glared—right into the eyes of the girl's indignant father.

"I'm going to pretend I didn't see this." Lord Bothey obviously wanted to rip Tony to pieces with his bare hands for kissing the lovely Blanche, but two things stopped him—his girth and his reluctance to offend the master of the Queen's Guard.

So he lifted his gaze to the treetops and signaled to his daughter to come with him, out of the gardens and back to the other aristocrats who danced in the long gallery of Odyssey Manor.

Blanche ignored her father. She smiled up at Tony

and drew her tongue slowly over her lips, still wet from his kiss.

It was an invitation few men could have resisted, but Tony took the girl's wandering hands off his shoulders and tried to straighten his ruff. "Go with your father, sweetheart. I'll see you . . . later."

Her eyes glistened ever brighter from the tears that filled them, and she blinked, using her eyelashes the way a señorita used a fan. "But, Tony—"

As if she were a pet, he tapped her nose with his finger. "Later."

"But you promised—"

He had promised her nothing, nor would he until he'd made his choice. Every one of the girls at his house party longed to be the woman in his arms, and quite a few had been. He'd been experimenting—a kiss here, a clasp of passion there—trying to decide which of the noblewomen would be his bride.

It wasn't the act of an honorable gentleman, but Tony prided himself on being neither honorable nor a gentleman. He still smiled as he handed Blanche over to her father. "I would love to continue our discussion, sweetling, but the audience grows." He waved a broad hand at the two older ladies who stood tapping their feet in the manicured grass. "My sisters await me."

Lord Bothey snatched Blanche by the arm before she could protest further, and marched her away.

"Tony, have you run mad?"

He shushed Jean and waited until the lagging Blanche turned to look at him. He blew her a kiss, wiped her from his mind, and said, "If I marry Blanche, she'll learn to keep her kisses for me. She's too free with them."

"You won't marry her," Jean said.

"Probably not. Her father's only a baron, and with his uncouth ways he's likely to offend the queen. I can't have that in a father-in-law." Graciously, he agreed. "You're right, Jean, I won't marry her."

"That's good," said Ann, his other sister. She beamed at him from beneath heavy brows. "I'm glad you're showing some sense."

"Is he?" Jean knew her brother well, and so never believed the best of him. "Is he indeed?"

Tony smiled his winsome smile.

"Don't give me that disarming look," Jean said. "You're going to be scolded."

"Scolded?" He wrapped each of his diminutive sisters in a bear hug. "Why would you ladies want to scold me?"

"Because you have run mad. You've been kissing every maiden here." Jean struggled out from his clutches to shake her finger at him. "Their fathers are threatening to leave."

"You're causing a scandal." Ann unwrapped his arm from around her neck and skipped in front of him down the path. "No one knew why you'd invited half of the nobles in England here for a party, but they're wiser now. Every family you invited has a marriageable daughter."

"True." He lifted an amused brow and allowed Jean to tug him to a halt.

"And like a codpiece, you're trying on every one for size."

"A crude analogy." He tried to sound severe.

"You're a crude man," Ann answered. "The parents of these maidens are frightened."

"But the maidens aren't."

"Oh, no." Jean snorted with disgust. "They're twittering like a flock of starlings every time you pass."

He dredged his soul for modesty, but he had never

learned the art of self-deception. He had a way with women, he knew, especially when he chose to exert himself. "I'm twenty-eight. 'Tis time I took a wife."

"We have no argument with that." Jean pushed him down onto a marble bench. "'Tis the suggestion we've been making since you came back from the Continent. If you had done so when you returned, bathed in Her Majesty's praise and loaded with her rewards, you could have had any woman in the kingdom. But Tony, that was five years ago."

He contrived to look hurt. "Is memory so short?"

"Don't play the innocent with us." Jean's eyes narrowed. "You're master of the Queen's Guard. Her Majesty granted you the Sadler estate, no small plum, and the income from that extinct family's lands. If you would but reach out your hand, you could have any widow in the country."

"Widow."

He repeated the abhorrent word, but Jean paid no attention. "Instead you are offending every nobleman with a maiden daughter."

He arched his back and flexed his arms, then locked his hands behind his head. "They could leave."

Sensitive Ann watched him and read the menace in his gesture. "They're afraid of you."

He moved over and patted the bench beside him. "Sit, sweet sister, and tell me why they should be afraid. If they left, what could I do? I'm not likely to take a sword to all of them."

With a sweet, sarcastic edge to her voice, Jean said, "Nay?"

Ann sidled over and perched on the edge, her skirt a rigid circle around her. "You have the queen's favor."

"I am currently out of favor."

"Currently!" Jean snapped. "Temporarily is a better

term. No one doubts you can sweet-talk your way back into her good graces."

"You flatter me."

"You've proved yourself a dangerous man with a sword when a lord is quick with an insult."

"You exaggerate."

Jean lost her temper with him. "Don't patronize me, Tony Rycliffe. I disciplined you from the time you were a babe and I'll discipline you now if it'll knock some sense into you."

Tony didn't laugh. If Jean chose to take a stick to him, he'd take the beating and not complain. He owed her so much. He owed them both so much.

Leaning back against a tree, he studied his sisters. He'd seen Jean angry often enough, and she was angry now. Her swarthy complexion flushed and glowed from the tip of her nose down to her chest. She tugged at her neck ruff as if it choked her. She'd always been his disciplinarian.

Ann. Now, Ann wasn't angry. She was distressed. As dark as her sister, she had brown eyes that filled easily with tears, and they were filled now. She didn't like to see her siblings at odds, and she wrung her hands and murmured soft noises.

Tony could resist neither Ann's distress nor Jean's anger. Perhaps he owed them an explanation, an outline of his grand scheme. "I want to start a noble dynasty."

Ann laid her gloved hand on his arm. "You're part of a noble dynasty."

Picking up her hand, he stripped the glove away and examined her fingers. Not a callus, not a mark to show she had ever done a day's work. And she hadn't, of course. She didn't understand, and for her he bridled his impatience. "That's not *my* dynasty. It bears the name of my father and my brother."

"But you're my brother, too," Ann wailed.

"For that I thank you. And you." He nodded at Jean, who understood him so much better than the gentle Ann. "But found the Rycliffe dynasty I will, and for that I must take a maiden to wife."

"But a maiden has a father who will decide her fate, and no father . . ." Ann groped for words.

"Will have me?" Tony concluded.

Embarrassed, Ann looked down at their entwined hands, but Jean rallied. "You've gained a reputation for fighting good noblemen and seducing good noble wives—"

"And I'm a bastard son."

"—and if it weren't for Elizabeth's favor, you'd have been assassinated years ago."

"And I'm a bastard son," he insisted.

"That is perhaps the reason." Jean surveyed him, as stiff and pale as if the chill marble had penetrated his bones. "But feeling as you do about your legitimacy, you must understand the fathers' objections."

"Oh, I do." He stood and grinned, showing all his white teeth. "I just don't care."

He didn't care about the objections, because no one dared make them to his face. Jean was right. In the last five years, he had taken a sword to every nobleman who had dared to mention the circumstances of his birth.

Abandoning her attempt to make him show compassion, she went to work on his male pride. "Why do you need a maiden? Are you afraid your bedroom technique might not bear comparison?"

The bright orange-and-yellow leaves quivered beneath the blast of his laughter. "Nay, for if you'll remember, Father always said I had a natural seat."

Ann tittered. "He was talking about your horsemanship."

"One skill is much the same as another, and I'll keep my wife besotted with me until the day she dies."

"While you find your pleasure where you will?" Jean snapped.

His amusement died a painful death. "Nay to that, also. I'll make no bastards for my wife to care for."

"Mama didn't mind," Ann assured him.

"Your mother was a lovely woman," he said. "And she gave me no less love than she gave her own children. I thought she was my real mother. She *should* have been my real mother."

The memory of their mother, crippled and weak as death crept upon her, brought tears to Ann's face and sent Jean searching for her handkerchief.

He gave them a moment, then explained. "I'll have a noble maiden who's young enough—not more than seventeen—to bear me many babes. I must have a fecund woman for breeding purposes, and it's well known that young mares throw more colts."

For the first time in her life, Jean appeared to be speechless, but Ann was not. She struggled to stand, wrestling with her heavy farthingale, and when he would have helped her, she knocked his hand aside. On her feet, she said, "A young mare would perfectly suit you, Tony, for you are nothing but a horse's ass."

Jean and Tony stared after her as she stalked toward the house, then Tony turned to Jean in confusion. "What did I say?"

Jean opened her mouth, and shut it. After a turn about the clearing, she came and stood in front of Tony. "I had forgotten that Ann could see the truth of a situation so clearly, and speak her mind so succinctly."

Astonished, Tony asked, "You agree with her?"

"You're due for a fall, Anthony Rycliffe." Her already-deep voice deepened with relish. "And I hope you don't break your leg when it happens. I'd hate to see you put down. But that's not why I need to speak with you. I promised Lady Honora Howard I would act the part of her father and propose a match between you and her."

He burst into laughter, expecting her to join him.

She did not, and his laughter faded.

He examined his sister, but she appeared to be serious, waiting for his amusement to die. "You jest."

"I do not."

"Lady Honora wants to marry . . ." His voice failed him as the absurdity of it struck again, but without the humor this time. "Lady Honora must be forty if she's a day."

"We are of an age," Jean admitted.

"And if she were to take off her corset, I fear for the vegetation at her feet."

"She has a large bosom, but her figure's very fine. She was a beauty in her youth, and her face is still sculpted—"

"Out of ice!"

"She is not free with her emotions, but that should make her all the more attractive to you."

He thought of the restrained gentlewoman who gazed upon the world from her lofty status and judged her peers with such superior precision. "Why would that frigid woman be attractive to me?"

"Because she chose you using the same cool logic you've used to winnow the grain of your marital candidates."

Detecting a hint of triumph in Jean's demeanor, he narrowed his eyes and stepped closer. "Why me?"

"She wants a child, and believes you to be the most vigorous stallion in England."

Amazement gripped him, buffeting him from emotion. "But I've taken care not to father any bastards."

"She has faith in your ability, when you apply your-self, and she's a woman who fulfills almost all your requirements."

Then fury broke, and he reacted like a man who knows his worth, yet finds himself valued as nothing more than a breeding animal. How could anyone seek a mate for no other reason than fertility?

The specters of his matrimonial prospects rose in his mind, and he flushed. But their breeding ability was not important now. What was important was to escape this trap.

Like the serpent in the Garden of Eden, Jean dan-gled an irresistible lure. "She's wealthy."

He tugged at his suddenly tight ruff. Indeed she was, very wealthy, and he prayed for the strength to resist the temptation of her money.

"She's the queen's dearest friend, and she's still, er, fecund as a mare."

Impatient with inaction, he stood and walked away, skirting the hedges and leaving the garden. Jean fol-lowed, matching his long steps, and when he reached the expanse of lawn that sloped away from the front of the house, he swung on her. "Lady Honora's buried three husbands and has no children living. You call that fecund?"

Jean glanced toward the marble edifice, but no guests were in sight. "The first two husbands were cho-sen by her father for their connections, influence, and wealth, and he scarce regarded their inbred weakness. They gave her no children, and lasted no longer than her teens. The third she married in a fit of passion, and he was all any woman desired in a man. He gave her a child, and should have given her more, but he spread his seed among the female population and mocked her when she tried to rein him in."

He'd heard too much of this comparison to horses. "Do all women think of men as stallions?"

"Nay, some are geldings," she mocked, "but not you, Tony. Stop champing at the bit. You wouldn't be so insulted, except you feel the cold hand of fate on your back."

A shiver ran up his spine. Jean was right. Beneath his indignation and outrage lurked a very real sense of doom. What Lady Honora lacked in humor she made up in determination.

His search for a wife had become a race against time.

"I won't marry her," he said firmly. "I hold Lady Honora Howard in the highest esteem, but never could I think of her in the carnal sense."

Jean laughed, clearly unconvinced. "You'll have to explain that to *her*."

"Jeannie, dear sister." He put his arms around her. "I'm only a humble man, no good with words. Surely you—"

"I'm not telling her."

"—could find a way to spare her feelings."

"It would take a runaway stallion to flatten her feelings." She grinned at his ire. "Besides, I've known Lady Honora all my life, and never have I convinced her of anything. You're doomed, Tony, doomed, and I can't say I'm unhappy. Lady Honora is the perfect wife for any man, and especially you. You'll no longer hear a word about your bastardy. No one would dare face her down."

"But I don't want my wife to be the source of all respect directed at me. I want to earn that respect myself."

"You have already earned it, except with fools, and in your own eyes. If you had already made your choice, perhaps Lady Honora could be persuaded to abandon her mission, but—"

"But I have!" He glanced around, desperate for escape.

"My bride has just arrived. I've been fighting the attraction, but she's here."

"Where?" Jean glanced at the traveling acting troupe. Camped at the edge of the expanse of lawn before the manor, they unloaded the scaffolding for their stage, preparing for their afternoon performance. "Where?"

"There she is!" He almost collapsed in relief when he saw a girl. The only girl within sight. She stood apart, nervously shifting from foot to foot. Hunching her shoulders, she stared at the manor and muttered words that were lost to him in the distance. She would have to do. "She's standing beside that painted wagon."

Following his gaze, Jean saw her, too, and squinted. "*Her?*"

"Do you know her?" He hoped not.

"I've never met her before, but she looks"—Jean cocked her head—"familiar. Who is she?"

"She's the portrait of perfection." A perfectly vague answer.

"In that garb?" Jean shook her head. "Better rein yourself in, Tony. She's no wealthy, influential virgin."

Even from this distance he could see that her clothes were odd, and her red wig towered in stiff curls above her face. How had he got himself into such a trap?

Recalling Honora's upright figure, he answered his own question.

Desperation. Sheer desperation.

He said, "For her, I would give up my shallow desires."

Jean continued, "I do know she shouldn't be tarrying by the wagons. Actors are not savory company."

"I'll go rescue her." And hope he could persuade— or seduce—her into helping him with his own rescue attempt.

4

To have seen much and to have nothing is to have rich eyes and poor hands.

—As You Like It, IV, i, 22

Dada, don't leave me here. I'm tired and it's too far to walk.

The lawn undulated like a flying carpet, soft green and pale gold, carrying the massive manor like an honored passenger.

I picked these pretty flowers. Don't you like them, Dada? I picked them for you.

Like a white lady with arms spread to embrace all comers, the wide-winged manor shone in the sunlight. The autumn-frosted trees bent protectively around her; the ever-green shrubbery decorated her.

I didn't take it, Dada. Don't leave me alone. Dada, please, I'm frightened. I'm scared, please, Dada please Dada please—

"You're a lovely lass."

Rosie jumped so hard her nosegay flew into the air. The confusing vision that had filled her mind swirled away. She snatched at it as if trying to recall a dream, but it left as quickly as it had come.

The big man caught the flowers deftly as he stepped around the edge of the wagon.

With a charming smile and a flourishing bow, he presented the flowers again. "My eyes are drunk with your beauty, my lady, so I scarcely know my own name, but I would swear I have never met you ere this moment."

"Who? Who?" she stammered, pressing her hand to her chest, trying to contain the thump of her heart.

"I am Sir Anthony Rycliffe."

She stared, still agitated and lost.

"Your host," he prompted.

"Oh." Oh. He was Sir Anthony, and she . . . she was . . . was . . .

She shook her head, trying to dislodge the images.

She was Rosie. Rosencrantz. Sir Danny's daughter and part-time son. She was facing Sir Anthony Rycliffe, their employer. Searching for her decorum, she bobbed a curtsy. "I'm honored, sir."

Overwhelmingly masculine, overweeningly confident, their host picked up her hand and kissed the back as delicately as if she were the queen. "You speak so softly, but there's no need to be shy, lass. If you'll but tell me your father's name, I will go to him at once and beg him leave to court you, for you are as fresh as the spring breeze, and as appealing to me as . . ." He hesitated, like an actor who has forgotten his lines, and shrugged his massive shoulders in a movement she would have called sheepish. "Tell me your father's name, and I'll court you as man has never courted a maiden."

Her mouth dropped open, and although she knew

she looked foolish, her astonishment proved too much for her control. "You jest with me, sir."

"I would not jest about a gift of the gods, lest fair Jupiter himself should snatch her out of my reach. Tell me your father's name, so I might prove my good intentions."

He didn't realize who she was. He thought she was a woman.

Which she was, of course, but most men penetrated her disguise and saw what they expected—a disreputable youth, a vagabond, an actor.

Did this man see less than most men, or more?

Large and blond, sunny with charisma, overwhelming with welcome—what did he want of her?

His smile never wavered. Indeed, it deepened the dimples in his cheeks and brought a bright twinkle to his blue eyes. "Lass, you act as if no man has given you his heart, and I know your charm must have overwhelmed even those more wary than myself."

Instinctively she recognized his swaggering intent. He was a man intent on a maid who had struck his fancy. More than that, he was a man no maid ever refused.

"Sir Anthony," she began.

But he pressed his finger to her lips. "Call me Tony."

She freed herself with a jerk of her head. "Respected sir, I dare not speak to you with such familiarity."

He leaned one elbow against the wagon beside her head. "Then call me Anthony. Or dearest, or lover, or sweetheart, I beg you."

He loomed over her: too tall, too broad, too brash, too masculine. A cape of crimson velvet hung around his shoulders, so bright it hurt her eyes. His cutwork silk stockings and ribbon garters showed off legs rippling with muscle. His black doublet glittered with an embroidery of golden thread, and in the middle of his broad chest hung a heavy gold pendant—a pendant that proclaimed him master of the Queen's Guard.

He reminded her of Essex's men-at-arms, who would slay her with their swords.

Yet Sir Anthony Rycliffe's sword was blunter, a weapon to be used on women only, for their pleasure and his own. But she had never had a man look at her with knowing eyes, or woo her aggressively, or want her. It frightened her. "I can call you none of those things. Your rank is a barrier."

"I would not have my affianced wife place any barrier between us. Not words nor"—his gazed delved the depths of her bodice and heated her flesh—"clothing."

She placed her hand over her cleavage to hide it. But he would have none of that. Again he took her hand and kissed it, but this time his lips caressed her palm. He curled her fingers over the caress and whispered, "Keep that to remember me when I am not near. Open your hand and place my kiss upon your cheek, your lips, your body, and imagine that I am with you. For in truth, I will be."

Amazed and uncertain, she wondered at her identity, at his objectives, at this estate that confused her. It seemed he waited for some sign which she should give, but indecision crippled her, and instinct warred with habit. "Dear Lord," she whispered, and he took that as permission.

"Call me not lord," he whispered as he bent closer, boxing her in between his arms in one direction, between his body and the wagon in the other. She stared at his lips as they moved with his speech. "I am Tony."

Too wide for beauty, his mouth promised pleasures forbidden her before. Now, as he nuzzled her chin, her cheek, and shut her eyes with a flick of his tongue, the promise became reality. Breathless, she waited, strained, wondered.

"Say it," he instructed. "Say my name."

"Tony," she whispered.

A reward for obedience, he layered his mouth on hers. The kiss, her first, should have been a lesson he taught her, but it was not. He listened to her body's signals. He deepened his advance only when she craved it, touching his tongue to hers and withdrawing, enticing her to follow his example. She did as he wished, for curiosity's sake.

It had to be for curiosity's sake. Nothing else could explain this madness.

Yet like flint striking against metal, her curiosity and his patience brought a spark to life, and he laughed softly as that spark jolted her.

"That's it," he murmured against her mouth. "That'll warm us."

Had she marveled at his patience? he wondered. The growing flame obliterated any trace of his control.

"Give me," he demanded, greedy as a child. "Give me."

His kisses forced her head against the wagon. Her wig slipped, and he pushed it off and flung it away. A single long, thick braid tumbled down, and he untied the string that held it in place. She winced at the tug when he combed his fingers through, loosening the weave that kept the rich brown hair tidy, and he kissed her in apology. He kissed her again as he created his own weave—his fingers, her hair, tangled to hold her in place for him, keeping her as if she might run away.

"More."

As if she could run away. As if her knees could even

hold her up. His other hand lifted her ruff and roamed her neck, then delved below the steel corset of her bodice and filled his hand with her. She moaned when his thumb rasped across her nipple, and he murmured, "That moan. The serenade of a lover. My lover."

His tone drenched her in his satisfaction, and his satisfaction worked on her like a splash of cold water. What was she doing? She opened her eyes, and humiliation slapped her to consciousness.

Brilliant sunlight illuminated every bit of their surroundings, and in turn illuminated them. Anyone could see.

"No one can see." Tony read her mind, and his rich voice smoothed to a seducer's croon. "I've used my body to block the view of any busybody who might glance this way."

His glib assurance only launched her outrage. "Used your body?" she choked. "Aye, you've used your body, right enough. The body of a yeaforsooth knave, a foul and beetle-brained rascal." Desire mingled with fury— or were they one and the same?—and she slapped at his hand. "Remove your leprous paw from me, ere I use my knife to remove it at the elbow."

Although his broad chin firmed, he chuckled. "Rest easy, sweetling, my intentions are the best."

His amusement convinced her. She'd behaved like a drab from the docks. Doubling her fist, she punched at his throat.

He flung his head back and the blow struck his shoulder. The padding of his sleeve deflected the force, but impatience and amazement struggled for supremacy on his countenance. "'Tis marriage I wish, I tell you, and this delectable irritation which plagues you"—his fingers stroked her breast—"is easily cured."

She dislodged his impudent hand, and again rolled

out from under his shadow. He followed, hand outstretched, as she snatched up her wig.

"Which room have my servants given you?" he asked. "If you will but confess, I'll find you tonight and bring you such satisfaction that Apollo's loves themselves will envy your good fortune. Come, lady."

His persistent palm thrust itself beneath her nose, and such was his allure that she wavered even while her anger grew.

"Place your hand in mine, and we'll seal our fates, one to the other, for eternity."

"Madness! You're stricken with moon-madness and know not what you say."

The blow deterred him not at all, and he matched her step for step as she stalked away. "Moon-madness? Nay, love-madness."

"Brain fever," she countered.

"Love fever."

"You're a lunatic, fit only for Bethlehem Hospital." She clapped the wig on her head, not caring that her own hair straggled beneath and around as if she were the lunatic she declared him. "I don't know who you think I am, but I assure you"—she rounded on him, and found his palm again extended—"that you'll be horrified"—his fine eyes cherished her countenance as no man had ever done—"when you discover"—his fingers flexed invitingly, and she stared at that hand. Stared, and wished he hadn't ignited that spark within her. For it burned still, warm and tempting, and she knew not what would douse it.

But she suspected that he knew.

With an incoherent cry, she fled, running across the stubble of lawn, sure that he would pursue.

He did not.

Subduing his predatory impulse, he watched her

run and laughed aloud, then turned and waved at Jean.

She lifted a wary hand, and he swaggered toward his manor. It was an impressive structure, with three stories of pale stones, built in the shape of an E. The railed terrace jutted out along the whole length of the front, and chimneys, statues, and arches decorated the roof. A fine house and a worthy home for him and for his lady.

Would it be the little wren who'd run from him?

Perhaps it would be. Her appearance had been uninspiring from a distance, and worse upon close examination, but she kissed like a dream and displayed such a sweet confusion he'd been charmed. After all, her youth proved her greatest ally, and her clothing was easily improved.

Aye, he would enjoy pretending she was his true love. He'd enjoy setting her on fire, and teaching her how to set him on fire, too. He shifted uncomfortably.

Set him on fire *more*. His canions fit him well, he'd seen to that. The shaped, short breeches had been sewn by the finest tailor in London, for his position in the Queen's Guard occasionally required him to dodge an assassin's knife or fight in Her Majesty's defense. But nothing could ease the strength of his arousal, and he wondered at himself.

Did he need a woman so badly? Or did that plain girl have that special gift, the one that set foolish men ablaze with passion?

He looked again in the direction she'd run, toward the stage that the actors had set up. He'd have to find out, wouldn't he?

The play had begun, a quick, comic piece to entertain the gentlefolk, to lure them to the later, longer performance. A quick glance around verified that the girl had vanished. No more than he expected, for she would try to avoid him, and he would let her—until he needed further defense against Honora.

Taking his place at the edge of the crowd, Tony looked neither left nor right, smiling politely at the eligible girls as they beckoned.

"Anthony!" Honora's precise voice spoke close to his shoulder. "Come and sit with me on the front row. I reserved a place for you on the bench."

He jumped as if he were guilty.

Damn Jean for mentioning that diabolical union. He'd been one of the few men who'd been able to treat Lady Honora with equanimity. Her lush body and equally lush estates attracted many an unwary man, but her unsmiling countenance, her erect posture, her lack of humor propelled them into the arms of younger, poorer girls. He hadn't realized the tragedy of it until this moment, when he faced the prospect of Lady Honora across a breakfast table, her flat voice instructing him on his duties. Or worse, the prospect of Lady Honora laid across a bed, instructing him on his duties.

The woman was so convinced of her own superiority that she intimidated lesser mortals, and she now intimidated him. Ironically, the very characteristic which presumably had attracted her had proved his downfall. "Lady Honora, I am comfortable when I stand."

"Nonsense!" With a grip unfashionably strong, she jerked him sideways. "You are the host. It is your duty to stay where your guests can observe you. You will allow me to guide you in this matter, as you will allow me to guide you in the matter of your marriage."

"My marriage?"

"To me." She rested her narrow hand on his sleeve. "Jean told me of your trifling objections, but you're a logical man, and I feel sure you'll soon see the good sense of my ways."

Looking down on the jeweled cap which covered her fall of blond hair, he wondered if he stood a chance against Lady Honora's determination and his own need for affluence. Then he remembered the mystery girl and how he would use her. He had only to keep her at the forefront of his mind, and Honora's schemes would be for naught.

Lady Honora inspected him as if he were a peasant recruit in Her Majesty's army. Without care for those listening to the play, she spoke in a normal tone of voice. "You look quite odd, and you will of course wish to decide that our marriage is your idea. A man does like to believe he is the master of his destiny. But in the meantime, do your hostly duty and sit in the place I have procured."

Bursting with indignation, he snapped, "Damn my hostly duty, and damn—"

The audience turned as one and hushed *him,* as if *he* were the only one inhibiting their enjoyment of the play, and the actors raised their voices and their eloquence to reclaim the attention due them.

With her own unique interpretation, Lady Honora said, "You see, I am right. They wish you to sit with me."

She tugged at him again, and he gave up. After all, what did it matter where he sat or stood or thought? The play would unfold, but its plot could never compete with the plot that filled his mind.

With many polite murmurings, he worked his way through the crowd, following in Honora's wake. In some distant part of his mind, he appreciated the laughter the two players dragged from the spectators. He was glad the actors kept his company entertained with their passionate moaning for a heartless lady, Earlene.

As if his thoughts had conjured her, she appeared—the woman he'd kissed, the woman he'd lusted after, the woman he would perhaps court. She walked onto the stage, and her appearance was greeted by a roar of appreciation from the audience.

Did they know her? He glanced around eagerly. Was she some noblewoman who strode the boards as a jest?

But no, the audience's appreciation was coarse and impersonal, caught up in the play and waiting eagerly for the next line. What did it mean?

He looked at her again, and saw her with new eyes. He'd assumed her to be a poverty-stricken, lacking-in-taste noblewoman. But now . . . his gut tightened. Leaning toward Lady Honora, he murmured, "Who is she?"

"Who is who?" Lady Honora asked, her tone precise and austere.

"Who is"—he nodded at the stage—"she?"

Puzzled, Lady Honora followed his gaze. "She's the wife who cuckolded her husband."

"No!" He scrubbed the back of his hand across his lips and tried again. "I mean who is she, really?"

"Really?" Lady Honora turned to face him. "Really? She's an . . . *he's* an actor, one of Sir Danny's troupe. Why are you—"

The rest of her words were lost to him as he staggered to his feet. He never heard the cries to sit down or felt the jabs from the people behind him. He knew only one thing.

He'd kissed a boy. He'd kissed a *man*.

5

It is not so; thou hast misspoke, misheard.
                    —KING JOHN, III, i, 4

But had he really?
Lord Bothey kicked Tony's knee from behind, and he collapsed back onto the bench.

Had he really kissed a man?

The mere thought made him want to spit, to leap up on the stage and knock that Tom-farthing buttercup into next week. But something stopped him. Something niggled at him. Some evidence, some disregarded clue . . .

He looked at the declaiming actor in woman's clothes, and unable to bear the sight, he stared down at the ground. His elbows rested on his thighs, his hands hung between his legs and his hands were cupped. Cupped in the shape of a woman's breast. Cupped in the shape of . . . he looked back at the stage.

Cupped in the shape of *her* breasts.

Her breasts. That was no man posturing and proclaiming.

That was a woman.

A woman.

Lady Honora whispered, "Why are you holding your chest and sighing?"

Tony had fought in Her Majesty's army, then commanded Her Majesty's guard for many a year, and if there was one thing his worldly experience had taught him, it was that men had hairy chests and women had bumpy chests, and a damned pleasant difference it was.

Lady Honora poked him with her fan. "Why are you smirking like that?"

Yet what was a woman doing playing a man playing a woman? His eyes narrowed as he watched the actor muddle her lines.

Lady Honora poked him again. "Why are you frowning now?"

The girl couldn't have succeeded in this masquerade on her own. Someone had to know her secret, but who? That young buck? Or that posturing old scoundrel? Was she the troupe's meretrix, or the hidden mistress of one happy man?

Lady Honora pinched his arm until he winced. "Why are you mumbling? It's not natural."

She didn't have a wealthy father. She didn't have a dowry, she wasn't as young as he'd imagined, and she certainly couldn't be a virgin.

Even if she proved to be one of those women who set a man on fire, who kept him enthralled with her body, he couldn't have her to wife. He couldn't have children by her. He couldn't sleep with her, eat with her, talk with her, for if he wed an actress, he'd be a laughingstock. All his care to build his name and reputation would be for naught. The queen would discard him like a used handkerchief. The nobility would look down their noses, and say, "Blood will tell." The old tale of his illegitimacy and those years of misery would once more surface, and he'd be pitied.

God, how the pity made him cringe.

"You look quite ill." Lady Honora placed her hand on the back of his head and pushed. "Put your head between your knees lest you swoon."

He looked at Lady Honora, his sister's crony, the woman who could buy him his dynasty, and he shuddered.

He looked up at the woman on the stage.

He didn't even know her name.

Lady Honora removed her hand and inched away. "You're burning with fever. Are you ill?"

He'd lusted cautiously his whole life, never allowing physical circumstances to overpower his good sense. He'd laughed at men who languished for a woman. No more and no matter. He would take that actress away from whoever kept her and keep her himself.

And if he had children with her—the muscles of his throat tightened, and he could scarcely breathe—if he had children with her, he'd be condemning them to the same hell that had blistered and hardened his young hide.

He couldn't have her. No matter what, he couldn't have her, and his piercing sense of loss stunned and bewildered him.

"Sir Anthony." Lady Honora rose and shook out her skirts. "If you can master yourself enough to rise, you should do your hostly duty, for the play is over."

He was staring at the stage, he realized, staring at the woman who now bowed, one hand held by the old fart, the other clasped by the suave, smiling, slimy man who looked as if he knew his way around a knife and garrote.

Embarrassed and mortified, Rosie tried to recover her hand from Ludovic's sweaty palm, but he clutched her tightly. She tried to recover her hand from Sir Danny's cool fingers, but he clasped her firmly. She tried to turn away from Tony's cutting gaze, but he wouldn't release her.

Tony looked furious. Furious! His blond brows met over his nose, his pinched nostrils turned white, and his full lips had thinned into a single line. When she stepped from the stage, he would be on her like mold on week-old bread. She had to warn Sir Danny. She had to tell him.

Again she tried to free her hand from Ludovic, but he hung on, twisting her fingers until it turned painful, and she glanced at him.

He smiled, but not at her. He watched Tony as closely as Tony had watched her. Tony rose from the bench in a fluid motion, flexed his shoulders, placed his hand on the knife at his belt. Ludovic grinned and copied the gesture. Laughter rippled from the aristocrats who observed the exchange, and Rosie used the distraction to jerk her hand free at last.

Ludovic turned to her with a hiss, but Sir Danny led her away and assisted her off the stage. He had to. Her knees were shaking so badly she feared a fall. As always, the troupe had gathered at the back of the scaffolding, but Sir Danny didn't pause for their accolades, and the funereal atmosphere confirmed Rosie's worst fears—she had been dreadful. Worse than dreadful. Worse than customary.

She hurried after Sir Danny as he strode toward the manor.

A muscle twitched in Sir Danny's cheek. He tried

twice to speak, and finally snapped, "What happened?"

"I just"—Tony's accusatory gaze swam through her consciousness—"I panicked, I suppose."

Sir Danny walked faster, threshing the grass with each kick of his feet. "But why?"

"I don't know." She did know, at least a little, but she didn't want to explain. Sir Danny complained that she feared emotion, and she did. She feared that if she let it loose, even on the stage, it would prove stronger than her resolve, and it would possess her. And Sir Danny had been watching her since the moment their wagons crossed the boundary of the rolling estate, watching as if he expected just such an outburst.

What knowledge told him of the emotions that simmered within her and threatened to burst forth? Even the trauma of her first kiss paled beside her reaction to this property, this manor, this *place.* Not wanting to give too much away, she confessed, "Odyssey Manor makes me shudder."

"Odyssey Manor?" Sir Danny stopped and gazed around him. "But it's beautiful."

Reluctantly, she, too, looked about her. The lawn had been scythed at the end of summer, and it extended around the manor in a swirl of dry gold and pale green. Oaks, both large and small, were scattered randomly to provide shade in the summer, and off to the side of the manor rose the hedge which fenced the formal garden.

A spring day, a meal spread on a cloth, a laughing deep-voiced man. Garlic sausage, crushed grass, lilac blossoms. Bark scraped her hands, a hand steadied her as she climbed.

Catch me, Dada. Catch me when I jump.

"Where are you, Rosie?" Sir Danny asked.

His voice jerked her back to the moment. "Here. I'm here." Her heart hurt, and she tried to ease the ache with the massage of her palm on her chest. "This place bothers me because of our plan to blackmail Sir Anthony Rycliffe, I suppose. Or maybe I'm having a premonition."

"You've never had one before." The chill in Sir Danny's voice matched the chill of the wind.

"This place seems familiar."

Sir Danny visibly thawed. "Familiar?"

"Like I've been here before." She tried to laugh, but instead she looked at the manor, her gaze drawn to the harmony of stone and glass. "We haven't been here before, have we?"

"The troupe has never been here before." He stooped until he came into her line of vision. "Of course not. How could our plan work if we'd been here before?"

She shook off the eerie sense of intimacy created by the garden, the house, and her own imagination. "Our plan is not such a good idea. Tony . . . Sir Anthony is not a man to be trifled with."

Sir Danny withdrew from her a few steps and considered her as a master would consider a painting. "Sir Anthony?"

A gruff voice interrupted his scrutiny. "Our Rosencrantz holds *Sir* Anthony in awe, don't you think, *Sir* Danny?"

Rosie whirled around, and found herself facing Ludovic, who said, "Why don't you ask our Rosencrantz why this Sir Anthony merits such respect?"

"I don't know what you mean," she said.

"He kissed you." It was an accusation.

"He kissed you?" Sir Danny's shaggy eyebrows drew together. "Who . . . he?"

"Our handsome host." Ludovic spit on the ground, then wiped his hand across the back of his mouth. "I saw him. He kissed the fair Rosencrantz."

"As a man kisses a woman?" Sir Danny asked.

Ludovic wiped his palms down the sides of his jerkin. "Most certainly."

"Rosencrantz, is that true?" Sir Danny asked.

She cringed. She hadn't wanted to tell him. She hadn't wanted to tell anyone. Something—a fear they would point fingers and laugh, or accuse her of inviting intimacy, or just a sense of maidenly privacy—prohibited her confession. "Sir Rycliffe mistook me for someone else."

"Someone he could kiss? I'm quite confused."

And Sir Danny did look confused, as confused as ever Rosie had seen him, but delighted, too.

"Confused?" Ludovic asked. "Why confused? Sir Anthony Rycliffe obviously saw what few have guessed."

Sir Danny's confusion and delight seemed to melt away; he assumed the suave facade he habitually wore. Rosie tried to take her cue from him, but she had to hide her suddenly trembling fingers behind her back.

"What is that?" Sir Danny stepped up and measured himself against Ludovic and came up ridiculously short. Sir Danny seemed not to notice, and ordered, "Speak, knave. What is it you think Sir Anthony has seen?"

"Do you think I have no eyes?" Ludovic glared at Sir Danny.

"Nay, I think you have no brain," Sir Danny said.

Rosie said, "For pity's sake, Sir Danny—"

Danny's voice only strengthened. "Sir Anthony saw nothing. Nothing!"

"He did, too, and I know what it was." Ludovic stared pointedly at Rosie's bosom.

With a flamboyant gesture, Sir Danny gestured toward the road that led away from the estate. "I tell you now to go. Take your lies. Leave us, leave the troupe. We don't need you, so get you gone."

Ludovic stood, his hands dangling at his side, as he

gazed first at Sir Danny, then at Rosie. He looked like a man fighting a battle with himself, a battle lost in the flames of a primeval fire. In a lightning swift move, he plucked Sir Danny off his feet by the front of his padded jerkin. Rosie grabbed for Ludovic's arm, but neither her grip nor Sir Danny's kicking feet swayed the battered giant.

"Unhand me, sir!" Sir Danny demanded, and Ludovic shook him like a terrier with a rat.

His steel muscles flexed beneath Rosie's fingers as she dug them into the flesh. "Put him down. Now!" Fear made her voice shrill. "Put him *down*, Ludovic." She stomped one heeled shoe into his instep, and he cried like a beleaguered wolf and slammed his elbow onto her shoulder. She collapsed onto the ground, arm numb, collarbone pulsating from the impact, and Ludovic dropped Sir Danny.

"You . . . you're . . . did I break it?" Ludovic knelt beside her and reached out, but she scooted back with a whimper.

He froze, then stared at his hands, and he turned them over and over, like joints of meat on a grill. "Can you still see the blood on them?"

Ludovic had been a fanatic about keeping his hands clean, and she'd never understood. Now she feared she did, and both pity and fear roiled within her. "Blood? Nay. Your hands are washed."

One of his hands hovered close to her cheek, and he almost touched it. "You've always been so untouched. I like that." Rising, he towered over Sir Danny, crumpled in the grass, and tried to become the stoic actor who saved his emotions for the stage. "Whatever it is I haven't seen, you'd better hope no one else has seen it, either, or there'll be trouble, and when it comes to trouble, I deal it out with a vengeance."

Rosie watched him stride away, watched him enter one of the gypsy wagons, then stared as Sir Danny dusted himself off and said, "Well! I certainly taught him a lesson. He'll not be so insolent again."

But she noticed he didn't stand, and she wondered if his knees were knocking as much as hers. Flexing her shoulder, massaging it, she worked until tingles of feeling returned to her arm. "He knows."

"I fear so."

She plucked the brittle lawn beneath her fingers. "It's a miracle no one else has noticed."

"Not a miracle, but good planning. Always I've trained new actors, then promoted them to the London stage. We've had the best because of our success, but we've had none of them with us long enough for suspicions to form. All except Ludovic." Sir Danny smoothed her throbbing shoulder. "You'll have a nasty bruise. 'Twill be our excuse to keep you off the stage."

"What?" Crushing the handful of grass in her fist, she demanded, "Why?"

"Isn't it true what Ludovic said? You looked so guilty, I assumed that Sir Rycliffe had, in fact, kissed you."

She covered her mouth as if to hide the evidence, then realized her mistake as the dry bits stuck to her lips.

Sir Danny chuckled as she sputtered, trying to remove the straw. "Did you like it?"

"The grass?"

"The kiss."

"He thought I was a noble maiden."

"And then he saw you on the stage." Sir Danny nodded thoughtfully. "No wonder he stood upon your entrance. No wonder he glared so balefully. He thinks he kissed a boy."

The memory of a warm hand cupping her breast jolted her, and she muttered, "He may know of our masquerade." As the implications sank in, she brightened. "He does know our masquerade!" she repeated. "We'll have to leave at once."

"Why?"

Sir Danny's question first dumbfounded, then amazed her. "What do you mean, why? Because he knows I'm a woman. Remember? We don't want anyone to know? We're breaking the laws and traditions of England? If anyone else finds out, we'll be imprisoned, dunked, put in stocks, whipped through the streets?"

He glanced around. "There aren't any streets here."

"There aren't any . . ." Words failed her.

"We'll have young Alleyn Brewer play the women's parts."

"But I want to do them!"

He patted her hand. "I'm saving you for a much bigger part. Remember? That part of the missing heir."

"The heir was a boy."

Sir Danny stroked his flowing mustache and contemplated her.

"Wasn't he?"

"Wasn't he what?"

"Wasn't the heir a boy?" she insisted.

"You'll wear men's clothing from now on."

She shouted, "But Tony knows."

He didn't remark on her easy use of Rycliffe's first name. "What I want from you is your best, your finest acting."

"But he felt my teatie!"

Waving a dismissive hand, Sir Danny said, "'Tis no great thing, this teatie of yours. Now if it were Tiny Mary's, we'd have our hands full." He cackled. "Hands full? 'Tis a jest most appropriate." Observing her concentrated glare, he hastened on. "Everyone must believe you a young man. Parade yourself in front of Sir Anthony. Become his best friend. Spy out his secrets. Swagger, strut, court the women—"

She pronounced judgment in heavy tones. "Sir Danny, you've gone quite mad."

He smiled, the sweet smile he reserved only for her. "Have I ever misjudged a situation?"

Ticking situations off on her fingers, she said, "Insulting Ludovic seems an error, when I look back on it, as does threatening Essex and Southampton. And that was just this winter. Last summer, you got caught by that innkeeper husband and almost found yourself a gelding. Then you—"

"I meant, have you ever worried that I would betray you by word or gesture?"

"Never."

"Have I ever asked you to do anything for me before?"

Her reply came more slowly this time. "Nay."

"Then trust me and do what I ask. Edward Bellot, Lord Sadler, and his heir disappeared years ago, and Rycliffe got the estate. He's only the bastard son of a nobleman, and no more important than we are. He can afford to share some of the wealth."

She shook her head. She'd never heard Sir Danny talk so recklessly. He had been the man who taught her charity by giving their dinner to starving children, then making light of their own hunger. He had taught her honesty by being honest himself, respect for others by praising their accomplishments. He had anchored her, and now she floundered, awash with confusion. "But to claim that I am the inheritor to this estate, and ask to be compensated for not claiming the property and his ownership in doubt."

"A clever scheme, I thought. You're exactly the right age to be the heir."

"Sir Anthony doesn't seem the type to pay us for such a flimsy claim. Besides, he knows I'm a woman, not the boy who disappeared."

"Rycliffe will do as he's told. I investigated him, and he'll do anything to keep this estate. Anything." Sir Danny's dimples flashed, but she must have reflected her disappointment in him, for he broke out, "Oh, think of me for a change! This will provide for you if something happens to me, but more than that, it will be a nest egg for my old age. There's nothing more pathetic than a shriveled old actor begging on the streets."

"That'll never happen to you," she protested. "You're Sir Danny Plympton, Esquire, the greatest actor of all time."

He tossed his head, and his dark hair swept around his shoulders. "Aye, that I am, and this part will be my greatest." He stood and dusted off his rear. "You'll do as you're told?"

Unhappy, yet obedient, she nodded.

"Good lass."

He strode quickly away, and Rosie shivered in the cool sunlight. She'd thought Tony's knowledge would free her from this tangle, but Sir Danny displayed a remarkable lack of concern. Was she really so flat?

She peeked down her bodice.

It didn't look like any man's chest she'd ever seen, but she hadn't seen many. In the ramshackle world of the theater, Sir Danny had made sure she'd remained apart. She'd remained in their wagon, alone much of the time, while the others had gathered for evenings of drinking and wenching. She'd chafed at the restraint, but life with Sir Danny proved to be thrilling enough to fulfill any dreams of adventure.

Surely that was why she felt a prickle of apprehension when faced with the prospect of remaining in this place. She wanted to get away from Tony and that sweet, secret longing he inspired, but more than that, she wanted to get away from Odyssey Manor, away from the house that welcomed her.

Welcomed Rosie.

Welcomed her home.

Uncle Will wrote about people like her. People who hovered on the edge of madness, who fled their plebeian lives through the tortured mazes of their minds.

All her life, she'd wanted to live a role. She'd wanted to make Sir Danny proud. She'd imagined the roar of the crowd as she moved them to laughter and to tears, to a sense of their own mortality and a sense of their own immortality. It was her favorite dream, one that normally absorbed her.

But now it could not compete with the fevered nostalgia that assailed her like a fantasy come to wicked life.

As she remained at Odyssey Manor, her sense of recognition grew rather than diminished. It dominated her mind, and frightened her more than the stage fright that assailed her before a performance.

"Hey!" A man's shout roused her. "What're ye doin' here? We don't allow no good-for-naught actors so close t' th' house."

She looked up to see a gray-haired man bearing down on her at a great rate. He wore the warm cloak of a trusted servant, and beneath it she caught glimpses of a leather jerkin. His arms swung in circles as if he longed to use his fists, and she warily tried to scramble to her feet.

"Forgive me, good man." The French farthingale she wore under her skirt caught her heel, and she worked frantically to free it. "I'll leave at once."

"Do it!"

"I'm trying!"

Freeing her heel, she tried again to stand, but her heavy petticoats hindered her.

"Fer God's sake!" Hostility bristling from every pore, he caught her hand and pulled her up. "Now, get ye gone afore—"

Her head came up, she looked him in the face for the first time, and—

Don't leave me alone with him, Dada! Please, I'll be good, don't leave me alone.

With a cry, Rosie took to her heels, running for refuge, running away, running blind.

Her horror would have intensified if she'd looked back, for the grizzled man raced in the opposite direction, and the likeness of her cry echoed on his lips.

6

You a man! You lack a man's heart.

—As You Like It, IV, iii, 118

What was the girl up to now?

Tony watched Rosencrantz sneak around the outside of Odyssey Manor, then followed her with a stealth of his own.

Not that he cared what she did. He ought to tell everyone of this nefarious masquerade she'd been perpetrating for the last five days, except she was so amusing as she strode around the grounds in a youth's costume. The current fashion for padded doublets gave a man the desired peasecod-bellied profile, but they also hid a woman's attributes. Rosencrantz took advantage of that, as she did the fad for large soft caps that slithered around the face, obscuring first her left eye, then her right, and always protecting her countenance from complete surveillance.

Not that he wanted to see her face.

But why was Rosencrantz jumping up, trying to peek in the windows? He'd inquired about her, subtly, of course, and she had never set foot in the manor. If she were so interested, why didn't she just enter? Did she imagine someone would catch her and toss her out by the scruff of her neck?

After he'd had a firm discussion with Hal, his steward, he'd allowed the actors to commandeer the lower regions—specifically, the kitchen, where they ate constantly. Those cold years in his mother's home had taught Tony openhanded hospitality, and Tony found it offensive that this Rosencrantz seemed to think his home contained a plague which affected only her.

He'd left no special instructions about her, although he should have. Any wanton who kissed a man of his experience and convinced him she was a virgin was a marvelous, even dangerous, actress. Who knew what mischief she could persuade others to do in the name of innocence?

That's why he studied her. To protect his guests and his household. Otherwise, he wouldn't ever even notice her.

Of course, it did amuse him when she spoke in deep tones, used wide gestures, and belched after every drink of beer. Yet her impersonation of a youth close to his majority fell short. She was, as Tony had observed in the play, a dreadful actress. No one should believe her to be a man, but no one paid her enough attention to doubt her. Even Jean, after casting him one amused and knowing glance, dismissed Rosie from her mind.

In fact, if Rosie wasn't careful, she would catch one of the serving maids she'd been eyeing. That might prove amusing.

He glanced down at his cupped hand, the hand that had cupped her breast, and thanked God for his own inquisitive impatience. If he hadn't been so bold with her, he'd still be in hell, believing he'd kissed a boy.

Why was Rosencrantz sneaking up on the stairs that led to the gallery?

He watched as she tiptoed up the stairs, taking such care no one could possibly hear a footfall, then stopped four risers short of the top. She hesitated, swaying back and forth. She wanted to go in, but she didn't.

And why not? Why was this woman, this Rosencrantz, so afraid?

Tony mounted the steps. He moved as he always did, with a firm tread, but Rosencrantz still stared up at the door. As he stepped close behind her, she shook her head and he heard her mutter, "A fool you are, and a mad fool, too. Begone before the gods strike you down."

She wheeled so abruptly that he started. Taking one look at him, she missed the step. He reached out to catch her, but she swung her arms wildly, falling back.

She hit the step, and he heard a bone crack. She loosed one sharp scream, and the color slid from her face.

"Don't move," he ordered.

But she grabbed her arm and curled up in agony.

"Let me." He tried to take the affected limb, but she hugged it close to her body. He'd seen that reaction before on the Continent with the army. Soldiers in pain, yet fearing more pain.

And she feared for a reason, he knew. The arm would have to be set. He'd done it before, but it was a miserable procedure. Binding it after would ease her, but first he had to get her in the house. Taking her chin in a firm grip, he held her gaze with his. "Are you hurt anywhere else?"

She whimpered.

"Tell me," he insisted. "Does your back hurt? Your neck?" Carefully he rolled her head. "Your ribs?"

He tried to probe them, but she flinched, then moaned.

"Do—your—ribs—hurt?" He spaced each word so she could understand, and she shook her head.

"Hold your arm." Positioning himself beside her unharmed side, he slowly worked her into his grasp. She shook in a palsy of pain, and when he picked her up, she yelled again.

"Sorry. Didn't mean to—"

She choked back another scream, and he ached for her. Maneuvering through the door, he strode into the manor and down the gallery, bellowing, "Hal!"

A serving maid raced to get the steward, and Tony shouted after her, "Have Hal bring bandages and splints."

Another servant ran in front of Tony, opening doors. Out of the gallery, up the grand staircase to the bedrooms. There Tony hesitated. All twenty-seven bedrooms were occupied, both the large standing beds and the low truckle beds that slid beneath them. None of his guests would thank him for lodging an actor in their midst. More than that, Rosencrantz would need privacy for her personal functions—more privacy than other young *men* would require.

Little cheat.

The only place he could put her would be in his antechamber, and he had no desire to have the harlot underfoot. He'd take her to the kitchen and set the bone. From there Sir Danny could fetch her.

Then he noticed a wetness soaking his velvet collar. Rosencrantz had turned her face into his doublet, hiding her pain-racked countenance and shedding her tears like an embarrassed child.

Tony found himself laying her on the mattress of his own bed. "Hal!" he yelled again.

"I'm here, Master. What's yer pleasure?"

Tony never even glanced up as he disengaged the fingers of her good arm from their grip on his ruff. "One of the actors broke his arm, and I need you to hold him down while I set it."

A silence followed, a silence so long Tony turned to the doorway where Hal stood. "Come on, man, he's suffering."

"An actor?" Rosencrantz had pulled the blankets over her face, but Hal stared at the bed and snarled, "Don't dirty yer hands wi' him. I'll put him in th' kitchen an' th' other servants'll take care o' it there."

Tony dismissed the suggestion as if he'd not thought it himself a few moments ago. "I'll do it here."

"I'll get th' barber-surgeon t' do it." If Tony didn't know better, he would have said Hal was frightened.

Arranging a pillow to support her arm, Tony answered, "I'll do it myself."

"I'll get th' barber-surgeon t' help ye, then." Hal extended his hands, splints and bandages spilling from them. "I'm only a clumsy ol' ostler, an' I'll—"

"Then you've seen plenty of broken bones, and I want *you*." Amazement made Tony sharper than he should have been, but he'd never seen Hal dither. Strict, surly, yet devoted, Hal did what he was told when he was told, never avoiding work and never questioning orders. His tenure predated Tony's arrival at Odyssey Manor, but fanatical devotion to the estate and to Tony had earned Hal the highest position any common man ever obtained on the estate. Tony knew he could depend on Hal for anything, even to keep a secret. And Hal could very easily discover Rosencrantz's secret when they set the bone.

"Is it that actor they call Rosencrantz?" Hal's usual gravelly voice sounded almost breathless.

"For God's sake, Hal!" The crying from the bed had become whimpers, and those whimpers wrung the last drop of patience from Tony. "Bring those splints over here and let's begin."

Shuffling forward, Hal laid the supplies on the table beside the bed and muttered, "'Tis God's vengeance on me fer me sins."

"I'll give you vengeance to fear if you don't—" Tony took a breath. "I'll care for the broken limb, and you restrain the rest."

Hal stood and looked at Rosencrantz helplessly, as if he didn't know how to start.

"Get on the bed and sit on him," Tony instructed.

With first one knee on the mattress, then the other, Hal inched onto the bed. None of Tony's admonitions could hurry him. His hands hovered over her legs for long moments, moving up and down their length like birds unsure where to light.

"Here!" Tony took Hal's wrists and placed them on her knees.

As if it were a signal, Rosencrantz threw back the covers. Her blotchy cheeks were swollen from crying. She took one look at Hal's face and shrieked. Chills ran up Tony's spine when she cried, "He won't stay, Dada. Don't leave me alone."

A fit? Tony stared at her. What madness was this?

Transfixed by her fury, Hal didn't move, and she struck at him with her uninjured arm. "Get away from me, bad man. Bad man, go away!"

Hal sprang at her. Tony roared and jumped forward, but Hal didn't accost her. Instead he placed his palms across her mouth and said, "I'm goin' t' help ye now. Understand? I'll harm ye not." Her wide eyes watched Hal with suspicion, and he repeated, "I vow I'm goin' t' help ye."

Slowly, he lowered his hands, waiting for an outburst. The print of his hands shone white on her reddened skin, and she took deep breaths, like someone deprived of air. Yet she tilted her head regally and considered him for a long moment, and consented. "You may help me, and then never come near me again."

"Psst. Rosie! Are you awake?"

She tried to ignore Sir Danny, tried to cling to slumber, but Sir Danny was known for his persistence.

"Rosie, how do you feel?"

Without opening her eyes, she asked, "How should I feel?"

"Well, with the broken arm and all, you might be too sick to tread the boards." He peered at her. "But not sick enough to mourn it, eh?"

A broken arm? Rosie opened her eyes, looked around at the luxurious bedchamber, and groaned.

Well, she'd done it. She'd tried to sneak into the manor house, and got just what she deserved. A broken arm and a shredded pride. The last thing she remembered was vomiting into a basin, her head held by the honorable Sir Anthony Rycliffe. Now she lay on a bed, the most comfortable bed she'd ever inhabited. There were so many pillows piled at the head of the bed, she'd slid down and now lay crooked on the mattress. The fireplace glowed, gorged with flames that heated the room. Everywhere stood branches of candles. Not cheap, smelly tallow candles, either, but wax candles that gave off such a pure light it distressed her to think of the expense.

Beside the bed stood Sir Danny, looking as anxious as when she'd had the sweat as a child. "Does it hurt?"

Hurt? Everything hurt. Her shoulder hurt where

Ludovic had smashed it, her back hurt from the impact on the stairs. Her legs ached, and her throat hurt from crying. There'd been some screaming, too, although surely it hadn't been her. And her arm—Od's bodkin, her arm throbbed.

Hurt? Aye, she hurt, but that only made a falsehood more necessary. "Not much."

"Can I get you anything? Wine, ale, water?"

"Nay, I just want to go home. With you," she added hastily, when he seemed about to object.

Rocking back on his heels, he tucked his fingers into the braids on his doublet. "What home?"

"The wagon," she answered eagerly. When he didn't reply, she continued, "We could pack up and go to London. I'd hide out and you could perform *Hamlet* for Uncle Will. You'd make almost as much money as if we blackmailed—"

"They'll take better care of you here."

"No! I can't stay here."

"If Sir Tony says you can, you can." Sir Danny smiled and patted her gently, treating her like an invalid for the first time in her life and frightening her into the next fortnight. "It's not every day you get to sleep in the master's chamber."

"This isn't the master's chamber." Ignoring the muscles that almost creaked when she moved, she pointed with her good hand. "It's next door."

"Nay, that's the antechamber."

"Nay, that's where the master sleeps," she insisted. "Don't you remember? When . . . "

When what? What made her think that was the master's chamber? She'd never even been up here before. Her conviction must be part of the madness—or was it premonition—that seized her? "Nothing," she said. "Worry not. I've been dreaming." *Dreaming that I have explored every inch of the manor.* "So can we go now? *He* set my arm and tied it all up, and it scarcely aches."

"I can make any pain go away," Sir Danny said in his soothing voice. "Would you like me to do that?"

She would. Aye, she would, but she was suspicious. "Would you take me back to the wagon afterward?"

"If you feel better."

She always felt better after one of Sir Danny's treatments. "Please."

He picked up her hand and stroked it. "Look at me. Think of how, with sleep, the pain will slip away. Imagine your bone, whole and strong, and how rest will knit it together."

Looking into his eyes, she did as he instructed. She thought about sleep and rest, then imagined the broken bone healing. Relaxing under Sir Danny's spell wasn't as easy as it had been in the past. She was suffering, and in a strange place. But gradually her familiarity with him and the routine conquered her, and her lids closed as she listened to his soothing voice.

Lightly touching her face, he murmured, "Sleep rocks you in its arms, holding you close and safe, bringing you relief and contentment. You'll doze here until morning, and when you awake—"

Too late she perceived the trap. He promised to take her away if she felt better. But how could she tell him she felt better if she were asleep? Struggling, she threw off the spell of his voice and tried to sit up, but when she moved, every muscle objected. She fell back and two sets of hands caught her.

Sir Danny's. And Tony's.

She looked at Tony, noting the intelligence that sharpened his features, then closed her eyes. Maybe if she pretended he wasn't there, he would disappear. Maybe he wouldn't have heard her ramblings, and maybe he wouldn't remember her disgraceful illness. More important, maybe she could forget that determined expression on his face, so similar to the expression he had worn right before he kissed her.

Hands lifted her and stuffed pillows beneath her head, and she asked, "Sir Danny?"

"Do what Sir Anthony tells you."

His voice sounded farther away, and her eyes sprang back open. Wretched Sir Danny slid toward the door, leaving her alone. Alone with *him*, just because he thought she was too sick to stay in their paltry, puny gypsy wagon.

"Don't go!"

"I'll be back to see you tomorrow, Rosie. Be good." It was an admonition for a child. "And don't cry."

"I never cry!"

Sir Danny shut the door, leaving her with this person who frightened her. Frightened her in every way.

Since the moment she had walked offstage, Tony had behaved with consummate indifference. Yet it seemed that had all changed. Now he observed her with an infectious grin as he lounged back in a chair beside the bed. He'd disposed of his ruff and doublet, and his fine linen shirt gaped at the neck. A sheen of chest gold caught the light of the candles and rippled over skin and muscle.

"It seems we must cleave together," he said.

She wasn't sure how to respond. The cool stranger of the past days seemed to have vanished, as had the confident seducer she'd first met. In fact, the seducer had vanished so completely, she suspected he would never return—thank God.

"I like your Sir Danny. He's wholly a scamp, isn't he?"

"He has a good heart."

"Oh, the best." Tony appeared to be cheerful and

not at all accusatory. "And he loves you as if you were his own. He watches over you, too, for he found us even before I'd finished setting your arm. He's been hovering over you for hours. I tried to tell him sleep was the best thing for you, but as soon as I turned my back, he woke you."

That meant Tony had been there while she slept, too.

He rubbed his hand through his close cropped hair as if puzzled by her gravity. "He calls you Rosie."

"It's short for Rosencrantz."

He nodded solemnly. "I suspected that."

Realizing how silly she had sounded, she was tempted to respond to the twinkle in his eye. But she resisted. Who was this Sir Anthony Rycliffe, anyway? Was he the dashing lover, or the aloof aristocrat? Or was he this bluff man who, she feared, hid a shrewd intelligence behind a genial facade?

"I would never have thought to give my son such a noble moniker." He cocked an eyebrow. "You *are* his son?"

"Aye, his son." She repeated it for emphasis. "His *son*."

He tilted his head and frowned. "Odd. I thought you were adopted."

"Ah." So he wasn't questioning her gender, only her bloodlines. It seemed safer, for some reason, to claim Sir Danny as her birth father, but hadn't Tony already noted the truth? She tried to remember. Hadn't he made some comment about Sir Danny, how he loved her almost as if she were his own? Confused, in pain, she glanced out the window into the darkness.

Before she could ask, he said, "It's twelve o' the clock. The witching hour."

He said it with such deep emphasis that she again glanced outside, half expecting to see the devil's countenance leering through the glass.

"It's too bad of me to keep you awake when you should be swinging in the arms of Morpheus. Would you like me to sing you a lullaby and help you on your way?"

Embarrassed, she shook her head.

"Ah, you've heard me sing."

He surprised a giggle from her, and she clapped her hand over her mouth as if to call it back.

Standing, he began to blow out the candles, then paused. "Sir Danny says you're afraid of the dark."

Sir Danny said too much. She didn't want Tony to know of her vulnerabilities. She didn't want to *have* any vulnerabilities. "Men aren't afraid."

"Nay." Moving about the room, he extinguished all but one light—the night candle that fit on a sconce carved into the great headboard. "Men aren't."

The fire in the fireplace flickered like dragon's tongues, sucking the light away and transforming it into shadows. The cold, hungry November dark huddled close, and Rosie tugged the covers around her neck.

Tony seemed unaffected by her unease. "My cook, Mistress Child, brought an infusion of willow bark and poppy juice to ease your pain, and she'd take a switch to me if she knew I'd let you suffer."

Again a giggle burst forth, and Rosie realized she must be more tired than she thought. But the thought of the tall, dignified woman paddling Sir Tony! "That gives me reason not to drink."

"Wicked," he approved.

He loomed over her so suddenly she started. The light of the single candle touched his golden hair and turned it to silver. His eyes shone like polished amethyst, and his lips glistened like two smooth stones she'd collected in the brook and treasured ever since. He murmured with concern, like the mother she'd never known, then he chuckled like the father she couldn't quite remember.

Had she expected to see the devil outside?

Foolish woman! The devil was inside the chamber with her, transmuting himself to precious metals, precious memories, precious expectations of a girl who could never grow into a woman.

"Drink this," he urged.

Above the golden growth of his beard, his cheeks shone like two rosy peaches, perfect in their symmetry. His ears were shaped like two oysters with a coating of pink pearl shell. His breath hinted of mint and lemons, and his fine-meshed skin looked like honey.

"Drink this," he said again, "and I'll get you some broth. You're looking at me as if you could eat me."

With a start, she realized it wasn't that Tony was so tempting, it was that she was so hungry. That explained her fascination. That explained why she wanted to lick his skin and see if it tasted as good as it looked.

He placed the cup at her mouth, and the stench struck her just as the liquid lapped at her lips. She tried to jerk back, but he held her neck and she swallowed it all, not because he wanted her to, but to escape his touch.

His touch burned her, like the fire, and again she thought of the devil.

"Awful, isn't it?" he said, and she wondered how he knew.

But he was talking about the potion.

"I'll get you the broth at once. It will help wash the taste away."

He slipped from the bed and she shivered. Why, if his touch burned, did the absence of it chill her? Was his fire like an addiction, seeking disciples with its beauty?

"How came Sir Danny by his honor?" he asked.

"Honor?" He arrived carrying a steaming bowl, and she focused on his hands, broad-palmed, long-fingered.

He was a big man, yet his hands seemed oversize, capable of charity, but intended for tyranny.

"Sir Danny Plympton, *Esquire*. Who so lauded him?" He leaned his hip on the bed and fed her a spoonful—a big spoonful.

When she could catch her breath, she answered without thought. "He made it up."

Tony gave a shout of laughter. "Aye, I do like your Sir Danny."

Another big mouthful, and she wondered if she could wrest the spoon from him. Did he feed himself in such a manner, or was this for the youth she pretended to be?

"How did it come about that he adopted you?"

"I was left alone by the roadside." Funny. Admitting that—for it was the truth—made her lose her appetite, and she pushed his hand firmly away. "When I was about four."

"Do you remember?"

Did she remember? Only in her dreams, and those dreams hurt so much. "I remember nothing."

"Not your parents?"

"You call them parents? What kind of parents would leave a child to starve?"

He seemed to meditate on that question. "What kind of mother would steal a child from his beloved home?"

What did he mean? Dared she ask?

"Sure you're done?" He waved the bowl beneath her nose.

"No more." No more questions—not for her, not from her.

He didn't hear the meaning beneath her words. "You called Hal *Dada*."

"Hal?"

"The man who held you while I set the bone."

Hal? Aye, his name was Hal, and something about

him frightened her. Something she hadn't the strength to face tonight. "I don't remember."

"Come now. I'd believe you don't remember your parents, but 'twas just a few hours ago that we set the bone. You must remember why you called him *Dada.*"

Maybe she'd never have the strength to explore these mysteries. Maybe she wanted to go to sleep and not wake until she had the strength to fly from this place. "Why don't you ask Hal?"

Tony examined her face, then whisked the bowl away. He puttered about the room while she closed her eyes and wished he would go, because he frightened her, and stay, because she was afraid without him.

"Rosie?"

Just *Rosie,* but when he spoke her name she could almost smell the first rose of spring and see the blush of its blossom. His voice, so close against her ear, enticed her to open her eyes, turn slowly, and look at his face. He watched her, his blue eyes glowing, his lips parted slightly, his tongue just touching the corner of his mouth like a boy intent on a delectable blancmange.

Her own lips parted. She remembered her one lesson in kissing and wanted another. He leaned forward; she leaned forward. He put out his hands; she put out her good hand. He wrapped her fingers around something cold and heavy, and whispered, "I'll give you some privacy to prepare for bed."

He slipped away and shut the door while she stared stupidly after him. Then she looked down at the gift he'd given her.

A chamber pot. He'd given her a chamber pot.

7

This fellow's wise enough to play the fool;
And to do that well craves a kind of wit.

—TWELFTH NIGHT, III, i, 61

A chamber pot! Tony shut the door with a click. He'd given Rosie a chamber pot!

His head thumped back on the solid oak door so hard he winced. Where had the suave seducer of yesteryear fled? The old Tony would have never given a chamber pot to a woman he wanted. But the old Tony had never met a woman like Rosie. A woman who wore a woman's garb and attracted him, then wore a man's garb and attracted him.

He'd always liked women. Loved women. Loved to watch them in their skirts as they minced down the streets. Loved to use his height to peek down their bodices and see what beauties he beheld. Loved to imagine what lay beneath their body-altering stomachers and farthingales. Loved their crimped wigs and their high-heeled slippers and the charcoal they used on their lashes and the perfumes they smoothed over their limbs. He'd loved them because they behaved like women—women who lived to attract him.

Now he was finding that his appreciation of Rosie wasn't because of the things she did or the things she wore, but was for Rosie herself. Rosie swaggering like a youth. Rosie in pain with a broken arm. Rosie in male clothing.

Why, he'd like her if she wore nothing.

He groaned. He would *love* her if she wore nothing.

And he'd given her a chamber pot as a token of his desire—because he didn't want her to suffer the discomfort of having to ask, of having to eject him from the room so she could use it. What kind of man so thoughtfully provided for a woman?

He thumped his head against the wall, then rubbed the abused flesh with his fingers. Cotzooks, was he becoming that most pitiful of creatures, a sensitive man?

He leaped away from the door as if it were heated and straightened his shoulders. Sensitive? Certainly not! He'd prove it right now. He'd find a few of the men-at-arms, drink too much, laugh too loud, and make vulgar bodily noises. He'd take the best horse in the stable and ride too fast, and then he'd find himself a buxom barmaid, toss her skirts around her ears and—

"I'm going in there."

"Madam, you are not."

Lit only by night candles, the short hall carried the conflict to Tony's ears but hid it from his eyes. He strained, looking toward the stairway that led downstairs, but he could see no one. The owners of the voices must be in the stairwell, and the darkness that cloaked them cloaked him also.

"I demand to know why Sir Rycliffe has been in his room all evening."

Tony recognized the attitude, if not the voice. Lady Honora.

"By what right do you make such a demand?" It was Sir Danny.

"I am Tony's betrothed." Lady Honora again.

Tony's jaw dropped.

"Really?" Sir Danny sounded thoughtful.

Tony took a step toward the stairwell.

Lady Honora's answer stopped him. "Perhaps I was premature with that announcement. I am to *be* Tony's betrothed."

Tony staggered back. Lady Honora? Telling a falsehood, getting caught, and admitting it? What was wrong with her?

"You had better make other plans," Sir Danny said, and he sounded more noble, more scornful than even Lady Honora could.

"What do you mean by that?"

Tony echoed Lady Honora's question. Aye, what did he mean by that?

"Only a fool would betroth herself to Sir Anthony Rycliffe now. And you, madam, are no fool."

Haughtily, Lady Honora commanded, "Explain yourself."

Hugging the shadows, Tony advanced, every sense alert.

"Sir Anthony Rycliffe's existence as the queen's favorite is in jeopardy, his claim on his lands exists on her grace only, and rumors of the return of the true heir to Odyssey Manor fly through the nobility."

Tony froze.

"The return of the true heir?" Lady Honora sounded huffy. "I have heard no such rumor."

"Perchance you should make some inquiries," Sir Danny replied. "In a matter of such importance to your future, it would be wise to have all the facts."

The silence that followed was more eloquent than any words. Lady Honora did not quite believe, perhaps, but she heeded. Tony slipped back as she appeared, holding a single candle. She stopped outside her chamber door and looked back at the place where Sir Danny must be, then went inside and shut the door behind her.

From inside the stairwell, Tony heard a triumphant cackle, then the rhythmic thumping as Sir Danny descended the stairs.

It was a good thing Sir Danny had left, Tony reflected grimly. If he had stayed, Tony would have taken him by his scrawny neck and wrung it until he squawked like a chicken.

Who was this Sir Danny Plympton? Was he truly an actor, as he claimed, or was he a spy for the queen?

Or worse, a spy for the queen's enemies?

Or was he an opportunist of the worst kind, a lowlife who plotted to make a profit from a dead man and his dead daughter?

Tony faced his door, and grinned with his teeth clenched so hard his jaw cracked. Did that explain the woman who occupied his bedchamber? Was she the key to this mystery?

Because if she were, it would behoove him to keep a close eye on young Rosie. Keep a close eye and a restraining hand on the woman who played a man who played a woman . . . who played an heir?

"Tony."

Tony glanced around the terrace where the breakfast spread lay cooling. The breeze barely ruffled the white tablecloth in this protected place, the salt and silver glistened in the midmorning sun, and the servants stood with knives and spoons, waiting for the late-rising guests to come and eat.

He'd made a point of ordering a delectable feast as soon as he'd heard Sir Danny's scurrilous exposition about the missing heir. He knew how fast gossip spread, and knew also that Lady Honora would conscientiously take Sir Danny's advice and inquire about any rumors. Yet surely she wouldn't have done so. She wouldn't have had time overnight, and no one else had heard—he hoped.

"Tony."

He heard it again, a hiss from the bushes. Strolling over, he parted the branches of the prickly holly and saw the tearstained face of one of his many candidates for marriage.

What was her name? Ah, yes. Blanche, the one with the delectable pout and the too-ready smile. "Lady Blanche, what are you doing, skulking there?" He extended his hand. "Come and eat."

"I can't. We're leaving. I just came to tell you"—her chin wobbled—"I don't believe a word of it. And even if it's true, I'll always love you."

The hair lifted on the back of Tony's neck. Not already. It couldn't have got around already. "What don't you believe?"

"That story." She lifted a bit of lace and dabbed her swimming eyes. "About the heir."

The air seemed thinner suddenly, and he had trouble getting a full breath, but he smiled with all his charm. "The heir?"

"The true heir to Odyssey Manor. I told Daddy it was just a rumor and the queen still loved you—how could she not?—and that even if it were true, I could marry you and my family could provide for us, but he wouldn't listen."

She wailed like a babe deprived of its teat while Tony patted her hand and plotted. Plotted with the speed and efficiency of a general faced with a battle that altered even as he observed.

He broke into laughter. Hearty laughter, amused laughter—forced laughter, but Lady Blanche didn't realize that. "Is that old story making the rounds *again?*" Placing his fists on his hips, he roared with laughter—the kind of laughter that attracted attention. The kind of laughter that brought his guests out of hiding to watch and listen. "Who is the heir this time?" He whooped. "My dairymaid? An impoverished noblewoman? Or some bit o' skirt from London who's heard the tale and plans to earn a pound with it?"

Guests began to seep out of the open doors, attracted by food and explanation.

"Good morrow, brother." Jean greeted him with a kiss on the cheek. "You're jolly this morn."

"Aye, I've heard my favorite fairy tale." Surely she'd come to him because she'd heard the murmurs. Grateful for her support, he hugged her heartily. "Again."

"Good morrow." Lord Hacker strolled out, stretching and yawning just as if he hadn't been lurking behind the tapestries. "Are you telling fairy tales, Tony?"

"Aye, 'tis the tale of the missing heir. Would you like to hear it?" Tony walked over and picked up a plate. "I've heard it so many times I can recite it by heart."

Two couples wandered out, followed by a gaggle of Tony's candidates all dressed in traveling clothes. Had all his guests planned to sneak out without a word?

"It *was* a tragedy, Tony." Jean took a plate, also, and shot an instructive glance at the fascinated servants. They sprang to attention, holding their spoons like sol-

diers brandishing muskets. As they dished out eggs and
cut ham, she said, "Lord Sadler and his small daughter
fled their London town house when a footman fell
dead from plague, didn't they?"

"Aye." Tony presented Lady Cavilham with a plate,
a bow, and a smile, and he was relieved to see her
unwillingly smile back.

Good. He at least hadn't lost his charm overnight.

He continued, "They left quickly, planning to return
here, taking only the essentials in a traveling coach"—he
paused dramatically, drawing the rest of the guests outside—"and disappeared, never to be seen alive again."

"I remember." An older woman whose face reflected
a long life, Lady Caustun-Oaks nodded. "The coach was
later found, was it not?"

"Stripped of its accoutrements and without its
horses, with the decomposing bodies of Lord Sadler
and the little girl's nursemaid inside, and the coachman
not far away." The grim facts wiped all shreds of self-
interest from Tony's mind.

The gaggle of young women whimpered.

"I beg your pardon," he said solemnly. "Such a reflec-
tion of our own mortality is not breakfast conversation."

"Were they murdered?" one girl asked.

"I remember, too," Jean said, nodding at Lady
Caustun-Oaks. "'Twas the plague which killed them,
and how anyone had the nerve to go into that den of
contagion to steal the luggage, the money, even the
jewelry off the bodies, I will never know."

"The queen was grief-stricken at the loss." Lady
Honora stepped onto the terrace, correct and erect.
"Lord Edward was one of her favorite courtiers, and
she wanted his ring—the ring she'd given him—to
remember him by. But it was gone, gone with the thief
who took the rest."

"May his soul be damned to hell." Tony meant it in a way he couldn't explain. True, the thief had taken a tragic story and made it into a mystery that would vex Tony for the rest of his life. But more than that, the soldier in him despised anyone who would loot the corpses of the honored dead.

"Did they find the little girl?" It was Lady Blanche, finally drawn out of the bushes and into the conversation by the same gruesome curiosity that held the others.

Tony handed her a plate. "Better eat before your journey, Lady Blanche." She accepted it with a wavering smile, and he said, "Nay, the child was never found, nor even her body. It was assumed she had wandered off and died."

Jean shook her head. "'Twas the thief's fault. I knew that child. She adored her father, and he adored her. She would never have left his side, not even when he had died. The thief must have stolen her."

"Why?" Lady Blanche's big eyes bulged, and she invested the single word with horror.

"Perhaps she wasn't ill, and he took her to sell her into prostitution." Lord Bothey stepped out the door, glaring at his daughter. "That's what happens to girls who don't obey their fathers."

Lady Blanche lost color, but Lady Honora drew herself up to her full height. "I obeyed my father when I married, and I might as well have been sold into prostitution." The company gasped, and Lord Bothey's eyes looked like his daughter's, large and shocked. "So don't try to frighten the girl with that threat, Freddie. It's just your nasty bully tactics."

"Too true, Father." Tossing her head, Lady Blanche said, "So I'll stay here."

"You will not!" her father roared. "We're leaving at once. If the orphan-heir has returned, this upstart Tony will be out of his estate and I'll be saddled with an indigent son-in-law."

The company looked from Lord Bothey to Tony, and Tony didn't disappoint them. "Lord Bothey, you're forgetting a few things."

"Eh?" Knowing he had overstepped his bounds, Lord Bothey turned the color of the scarlet embroidery on his shirt and glared.

"One servant returned alive from London—my steward, Hal. He was left in London to bring back the horses, and he says when Lord Sadler and the child left, the child was ill already. Even if she might have recovered—and we all know how unlikely that is—she couldn't have recovered without someone's care. Her father died, her nursemaid died, the coachman died, and no one would have stolen the girl if she were ill of the plague. No one is that mad, and so the fate of the child is a mystery." Pausing, he let that sink in, then added, "Our gentle queen was indeed grief-stricken by the loss of Lord Edward, and she ordered a search for him that did not falter for years. For five years, Lord Bothey. The manor was empty for fifteen years in total. Not until Queen Elizabeth's deepest uncertainties had been laid to rest did she remand this property to me. To imagine the existence of an heir is to doubt the wisdom of our queen."

"I say," Lord Bothey sputtered. "I say!"

"For that reason"—Tony stepped as close to Lord Bothey as Lord Bothey's unpadded, protruding stomach would allow—"and through no fault of her own, I cannot beg your daughter to be my wife. An upstart such as myself dares not ally himself with a family whose patriarch lacks confidence in the monarchy."

There was one collective hiss as the company sucked in their breaths, and Lord Bothey turned white. "I never . . . I don't lack confidence in our blessed queen! I never mentioned that no woman should sit on the throne of England, that it was against the law of God and man. I never suggested such a thing."

"Oh, Daddy." Lady Blanche moaned in despair.

"If I were you, Lord Bothey," Jean said, "I would repair to London at once and assure our blessed sovereign of your confidence in her. She will not be pleased when she hears of the resurrection of this rumor, and need I remind you, you are *not* her favorite courtier." *And my brother is,* she added without words.

Tony looked around at the shocked noblefolk. "Come, let us eat and wish Lord Bothey and his family Godspeed. The rest of you, I assume, will be staying?"

Everyone nodded in unison, like dumb sheep who dared not oppose their shearer. He had squelched their flight with guile and fear, for none would dare risk Elizabeth's wrath by giving validity to the talk of the heir's return. But he couldn't keep them here forever, he knew. One by one they would invent excuses and slip off, wanting to see him fall yet anxious not to be involved.

This damnable rumor had blossomed fast. Too fast. Had it been making the rounds the last few days, or had it spread like wildfire from Sir Danny's single mention of it last night? Was Sir Danny repeating what he heard, or was he the instigator of the tale?

The house party might be coming to an end, but the acting company would have to stay. Stay until Tony reached the bottom of the matter, and that might mean a fortnight, a moon . . . he thought of Rosie lying upstairs in his bed, and smiled. A twelvemonth.

"Good morrow, all! Shall we feast while our appetite is keen?" Oblivious to the undercurrents, Ann stood in the doorway and beamed on the company.

"We shall indeed," Tony agreed. "And my appetite, I find, is most keen."

Although not for food. He thirsted after knowledge, and would not Rosie be the best way to obtain that knowledge? Wouldn't he, in his own best interests, have to interrogate the one he suspected of being the pivot of this whole plot? And if she proved impervious to subtle interrogation, might he not have to torture the truth from her?

Oh, not literally, of course. He didn't physically torture women. He persuaded them with the weapons he had on hand. And in this case, the best weapon he had on hand might be . . . his hands.

He looked down at his fingers, and again they were cupped in the memorable shape of Rosie's breast.

8

There's rosemary, that's for remembrance
—HAMLET, IV, v, 174

"*I don't understand* Ophelia. She's a pitiful woman." Rosie crossed one arm over her belly and held it as if she eaten too many green apples. "I want to do Laertes."

"Laertes is an important role in *Hamlet*, but Ophelia is a pivotal role. The troupe needs you to be Ophelia, just as you've been Beatrice and Hermia." The warm sunshine caressed Sir Danny and his student as they sat on the terrace, but his explanation didn't ease Rosie's defensive posture, and Sir Danny corrected himself. "We need you to perform with more passion than you did with Beatrice and Hermia. 'Tis easy to convince an audience that you're a woman when you are a woman in truth. 'Tis even easy to elucidate correctly, to make the grand gestures and capture their attention, but you say you want to make them laugh and cry."

"So I do."

"They'll cry for Ophelia. The prince she believed loves her rejects her most brutally, then kills her father. *Feel* her emotions—despair, anguish, uncertainty."

She stared at him solemnly, listening, trying to absorb his knowledge of acting, yet resisting the very root of its lore. It frustrated him, like trying to pour his wisdom into a closed container.

Moving closer so their knees bumped, he cupped Rosie's face. "It's so easy, Rosie, for you of all people. Don't you remember when I rescued you from—"

"Nay!" Rosie jerked her head away from his hands.

"—from that pestilent carriage wherein—"

"Nay!" Rosie jumped and strode to the edge of the terrace. Her arm remained in a sling, but she clasped the rail with her free hand and stared out across the fields. Most of Rycliffe's guests had slipped away in the past three weeks, propelled by the rumors Danny himself had started, and the quiet was almost oppressive.

He could hear the rustle of each leaf as it dropped to the ground, and the birds as they mourned its downfall. Rosie mourned, too, he thought. Mourned a way of life that was now ending. She knew it, although she didn't admit it, and only Sir Danny, the great, the magnificent, understood how that change would take place.

He hated to hurt her. He'd always hated to hurt her, and that's why he'd let her slide along all these years, having nightmares while he pretended he didn't know what caused them. He'd thought they would get better as time went on, and they had, but they still existed for her, hovering on the edges of her memory, creating shadows in her eyes. Returning sometimes with such intensity she screamed out.

They'd been coming more often lately, ever since the troupe had arrived at Odyssey Manor. Her acting had worsened, too, as if she feared the demons in her mind might take over her life.

He'd come to think that maybe, just maybe, the demons she imprisoned also imprisoned her, and they would have to be released before she would be free.

There was more at stake here than just acting. Her life was at stake now.

"Rosie." He went to her side and hugged her shoulder. "Let's talk about Ophelia, shall we?"

"I know the story."

She'd never been so curt with him. It might be that her arm was paining her, but he didn't think so. More likely it was an acute apprehension brought on by her first brush with desire. He smothered a grin. God might yet see fit to punish Sir Danny for his sin of neglect, but it relieved Sir Danny to know God had not visited any great misfortune on Rosie.

Oh, she might think so when Tony watched her with smoldering intent. Feminine instinct, no doubt, told her the reason for her uneasiness. But Sir Danny had protected her from men and their designs as valiantly as—Sir Danny tossed his hair back and arched his neck—as valiantly as the great Zeus himself might protect his own daughter. So Rosie believed him when in desperation he'd said that Tony's gropings didn't necessarily mean Tony had realized then that she was a woman.

Tony knew. Tony wanted her. But for reasons of his own, Tony had not revealed her. Not to anyone. Which meant Tony played a game of his own.

Lesser men than Sir Danny might be concerned about Tony's intent, but to Sir Danny, the uncertainty only added to the pique. How enlightening to see how

Tony thought! How stimulating to gamble with a master competitor!

Of course the knowledge that he held the trump only added to his satisfaction.

"Ophelia is the daughter of Polonius, the king's minister," Sir Danny said. "She loves her father, and she also loves Hamlet, the prince."

"Loving has made a jest with her," Rosie said.

"Verily, it has." Sir Danny turned his back to the scene and slid onto the railing, sitting where he could watch her face. "Prince Hamlet turns on her when he discovers his mother has wed his father's brother and murderer."

"Typical man," she muttered. "Blaming one woman for another's perfidy."

Sir Danny perked up. "Do you speak of anyone I know?"

"Nay." She traced a vein in the marble. "Do all men smile with their mouths and not their eyes?"

"Why say you so?"

"It seems that Sir Tony and Ludovic do so when they are together—at least when I am with them."

"Ah, Ludovic." Ludovic had proved to be a complication. Sir Danny gambled with Tony, but Ludovic was wild, the unknown factor in the deck. He hadn't been invited to play, but he made his presence known, and he made his knowledge known, also.

He knew Rosie's secret, and he wanted her. That had been the suspicion that drove Sir Danny to do what he should have done so many years before. But the time had not yet come to reveal what he'd discovered, and Ludovic thought Rosie available to him.

She was not. She would never be available to Ludovic. She was fine and pure, so far above Ludovic he might as well have tried to snare a star. Ludovic knew it, too, in his saner moments, but Sir Danny had begun to brood about Ludovic's sanity, or at least his single-mindedness. Ludovic's hostility to Tony might result in a battle.

Tony was a big, well-muscled man, bursting with health and in a position of power, but that didn't mean he would prevail against a ruthless warrior like Ludovic.

Ludovic, as Sir Danny knew, fought to win. So did Tony.

Picking his words carefully, Sir Danny said, "Ludovic wishes to protect you from any threat. Tony wishes to be your friend. Ludovic doesn't understand that it might be possible for you to be a friend of Tony's so he is wary of Tony's intentions."

"Like Ophelia's brother?"

Her intuition startled him sometimes. "What?"

"Isn't Ludovic like Laertes? He cautions Ophelia not to believe Hamlet's protestations of love. Ludovic has told me that aristocrats like Tony only pretend to have a friendship with an actor." She peered at him. "Isn't that true?"

"Not always." Sir Danny brightened. "As you know, the earl of Southampton is a friend to Will Shakespeare."

"He's his *patron*," Rosie replied. "And he definitely patronizes Uncle Will."

"Aye, well." Sir Danny scrambled for some other example, but could think of none. "Do you think you should be wary of Tony? He seems to me to be the depository of all virtues."

"That's what worries me."

"Hmm?"

"He seems that way to me, too."

He turned his head away to hide his hopeful face. "I

think mayhap Tony feels a responsibility to you after setting your arm. The time you spent in his room allowed his affection for you to take root and grow. He is an admirable gentleman. Don't you agree?" If all Sir Danny's brightest hopes for Rosie had been brought to life, they would have molded Sir Anthony Rycliffe in the flesh.

But Rosie shook her head. "I don't know. He's very refined, but beneath that facade I sense a different man. Tough as dried meat and twice as hard to swallow. He's nobody's fool, Sir Danny. He's like Hamlet, who knows of the murderous plot which killed his father, yet keeps his counsel to catch the perpetrator."

"And are you like Ophelia," Sir Danny probed, "torn between your love for Hamlet and your love for your father?"

"I do not love Tony—"

Sir Danny observed her befuddlement, and thought, *Trembling on the verge, my dear.*

"—but I do love you, and I tell you, if you insist on carrying out this blackmail scheme, Tony will be more like Hamlet than I would like."

"You mean, he will kill your father as Hamlet killed Ophelia's father?"

"I fear for you."

He couldn't doubt Rosie's sincerity, but divine destiny herself protected Sir Danny Plympton, Esquire. "And will you go mad because you cannot reconcile your love for your father and your love for your father's murderer?"

"I told you, I don't love—" She took a calming breath. "If we must perform this wicked blackmail, then why not do it at once and get it over with? Once we've been tossed off the estate by Tony's guards, we'll be able to patch ourselves up and return to a normal life."

Why not do it at once? A movement caught Sir Danny's eye, and he watched, immobile, as three women, two dark and one blond, strolled across the lawn and entered the garden.

"Danny?" Rosie sounded a little breathless, a little confused.

He reassured her. "We'll do it soon."

"How soon?"

"Soon." He hopped off the rail and took her hand. "As soon as you can do more than *recite* Ophelia's part."

She jerked her hand away. "I don't want to practice anymore now."

Wheeling, fuming, Rosie ran down the steps, and, from the garden, Tony watched. Tony watched, and she seemed to be totally unaware.

Tony didn't like that. He wanted her to be aware of him all the time.

It seemed only fair, after all. His servants had instructions to report her every move, yet without being told, he knew her approximate location at all times. He had only to lay eyes on her, and he knew her mood, her thoughts, and he liked it all. Admired her character, respected her mind, lusted after her body, and liked *her*.

Except for his sisters, he didn't know another woman he liked.

Dangerous, to couple admiration, respect, and lust.

"Tony."

He glanced back at the ladies seated in the garden. His two sisters and Lady Honora stared at him as if he were an interesting specimen of beast imported from the New World, and he stared back. "Aye?"

"You've been skulking through your own manor and across your own estate like an uninvited guest," Lady Honora said.

"Do you fear the rumors of the heir's return?" Ann inquired.

Jean's swarthy brow darkened yet further. "For you've chosen a sure method of convincing all of your detractors of your dubiety."

Separately, each one of them was a formidable woman. Together, they formed a fair representation of the Greek Furies, and he didn't want to hear their prophecies of doom. He began edging away, anxious to pursue Rosie.

"Why haven't you returned to London and the queen?" Lady Honora demanded.

"Because the queen forbade him to appear in her presence until she called for him." Jean answered for him.

"When has Tony ever heeded the rules?" Ann asked. Then, "Where is he going?"

Faintly, he heard Jean say, "He must be trailing after that actor again. The acting troupe has been the catalyst for his odd behavior. They will have to go, don't you agree, Lady Honora?"

He strained his ears, but heard no reply.

"Lady Honora?" Ann sounded puzzled.

Curiosity urged Tony to linger, to discover what falsehoods Sir Danny had been spewing in those "chance" meetings with Lady Honora. Sir Danny, too, had been under observation.

But Rosie walked quickly. She seemed to know where she was going, although this was the first time she'd been far from the manor. He followed her up a rise, down a hill, and along a faint path. It wound over grass well cropped by sheep, across the stepping-stones of a brook, and into a wood bare of leaves. She lost the path; she found it without a qualm.

And he now knew her destination.

A waterfall. A pool. A place where magic happened.

The waterfall shivered in the chilly breeze, and broke the sunlight into individual rainbows. Rosie skipped forward as if she could catch the rainbows by extending her hand. She smiled as she dabbed her fingers in the pool, spoke to some unknown entity, and then listened.

Did she receive a reply?

None that Tony heard, but Rosie drooped. Then, subdued, she nestled against a sunlit boulder, absorbing the warmth.

He didn't like the tenderness she evoked in him. If she was to play the role of heir—and he almost hoped she would, so he could loose his revenge on her—he shouldn't be observing her vulnerabilities, and he positively shouldn't be touched by them. A lesser man might find himself in the throes of some inappropriate passion. But not him.

He stepped out of his shoes and placed them beneath an oak. Careful to be silent, he stripped off his doublet. Nay, not him. He was a bastard, and a ruthless one, but he never forgot his principles. He wouldn't use her as he wished and father another bastard who sold his soul for respectability.

Puffing above his head, the wind provided a humming accompaniment to the splatter of water on the flat rocks.

He would entice her instead. When her mind whirled with confusion and she'd revealed the plot which threatened his property, he would free her from the masquerade which shackled her.

He would be doing her a favor. He untied the string at the neck of his shirt. Her situation confused her. Sometimes a woman, too often a child, she provided Tony with endless entertainment as she struggled to reconcile her feminine instincts with the role of young man, which had been assigned her. But he wanted to banish the youth and encourage the child to grow up. He wanted her to notice him. He wanted her to think of him as a man. He wanted her never to look at him without seeing a lover—because of the plot, of course.

His hands on the hem of his shirt, he hesitated. Could he resist her if she saw him as a lover? If she wore a woman's clothes, smiled at him with a woman's smile, flirted like a woman in love . . .

He ripped his shirt off and tossed it aside. The wind nipped with a touch of autumn's chill, but it cooled him.

He was too hot.

Moving forward, he touched her shoulder. "I'm going in," he told her. "Want to join me?"

She jumped up with a shriek. "Sir Anthony!" She caught her breath. "I didn't hear you approach."

"I wasn't quiet." He rotated his shoulders to ease the tension of the past few days and to show off like a peacock strutting for his peahen.

"I must have been in another world."

As he suspected.

But she wasn't in another world now. With both feet planted—literally and figuratively—in the dirt of Odyssey estate, she stared, wide-eyed, at the broad expanse of chest he displayed. She watched each inhalation with fascination. Her gaze traced each muscle, and he found himself sucking in an already-tight abdomen.

Without ever looking up at his face, she said, "I suppose I should go back to the manor."

"Why?" He pressed her back down beside the rock, and she sank as if her knees had pudding where the cartilage should be. He allowed himself a triumphant grin as his hands went to the ties of his garters.

In his lifetime, he'd used his charm to get his way and his strength to win his battles. It was gratifying to know he could use his body to enravish a woman—or at least this woman.

"Gracious, look at the sun!"

How she could see the sun when her gaze remained bound to his every movement, he didn't know.

"I promised Sir Danny I would would rehearse my part, and I'm late already. If you'll excuse me . . ." She half rose.

By God, she wasn't leaving until she'd seen the best part, and so he asked, "I find myself unable to decide—where do women fit in your scheme of life?"

She collapsed back down. "Women?"

"It has occurred to me that you're a young man with no outlet for your natural drives. You haven't vigorously pursued the maids, for which I am grateful. Yet perhaps you would be pleased to have a more intimate acquaintance with the fair sex, without the disturbance of involvement?"

"The disturbance of involvement!" Rosie blurted. "What did you have in mind?"

"A visit to the brothel in London. I have not been there for too many months myself and I have a very experienced lady waiting for me. I feel sure she can find an equally experienced and lovely lady for you. It was in this house that I gained my first knowledge of a woman's secrets, and it was good." He had vanquished not only the shadows from her eyes, but also the ability to flee. Consternation and anticipation held her as surely as if he'd tied her. "What is wrong, little man? You look as if you have never had a woman before." He had trouble restraining a shout of laughter at the stark panic on Rosie's face, and in simulated amazement said, "You have never had a woman before!"

Nodding, she agreed vigorously. "You are right! I have never had a woman before!"

"Didn't Sir Danny take you to a whorehouse?"

"I honestly do not believe the thought ever crossed his mind," choked Rosie.

"Then I'll take you." He almost felt sorry for her as he peeled off his stockings, but not sorry enough to stop. He had her attention now, her full attention, and he meant to keep it. "I assure you, Tiny Mary runs the finest brothel in London—nay, in all of England."

"Tiny Mary?" With an astonished half grin, Rosie admitted, "I've been to Tiny Mary's."

"Have you?" Damn, when had that happened? "That must have been most interesting."

Her smile disappeared. "Oh, it was."

"Tell me about it."

"It made my blood race."

He didn't want to know. "Well, when I was thirteen, my father paid for the whole night with a hot-blooded Spanish woman." That much was the truth. "She laid the groundwork I have built on ever since. What pleasured me, what pleasured her, how to build a woman's impatience, how to restrain my own. I have used every means she taught me and I think I can say, without bragging, that my lovers have been well serviced."

He reminisced for a purpose. He reminisced to construct a picture in her mind, and from her restless reaction, he knew he'd achieved his purpose.

"It was an unforgettable lesson. So it is settled!" He slapped his knee with resolution. "We will visit Tiny Mary's. At once! On the morrow!" He waggled his brows suggestively and wondered how the inventive woman would get out of this.

She didn't disappoint him. "I have no money."

"I will pay," he retorted. "I insist. It is an honor to pay for an initiation for our beloved actor."

Ah, but even this bit of reprisal tasted sweet, and he hopped from one foot to the other as he stripped off his canions, leaving only his brief—very brief—braes. "Are you sure you won't join me in a swim?"

She could barely shake her head and touched the sling of sticks and white linen. "My arm," she whispered, then dropped her gaze to her hands. Digging her fingers into the dirt, she created a road that wound through the drifts of early-fallen leaves.

The scent of rich humus rose in waves from the earth as it basked in the sun's last foray, and it made him think of the pleasure in planting a seed and seeing it grow. He'd never had that pleasure; coitus interruptus had been effective for him. Would it be effective if Rosie were the woman who moaned beneath him?

The image almost brought him to his knees before her. It would be so easy here in this secluded place to steal her clothes and her defenses and make her his. It would be revenge and pleasure all in one.

But coitus interruptus, he knew, did not always work. Too many babes had been created by couples who never even got to enjoy the ultimate pleasure. Yet if he and Rosie made a babe—a thrill shivered through him—he would have to wed her.

He looked again at her bent head. He noted the motley clothes, the grime around her collar and at her wrists. He remembered how she mixed the high-class English she'd learned as an actress with the lower-class accent of the London streets, and how she occasionally dropped into some obscure dialect from the provinces.

Wed Rosie. A nobody. Worse than nobody, an actress. A woman who dressed as a man. He'd be the laughingstock of London, and a furious Elizabeth would reclaim his lands with the justifiable comment that he was crazed.

His lands. Everything he'd worked for.

No, he couldn't make a babe with her, and he certainly couldn't wed her.

Besides—he chuckled at his self-deception—if he ever got inside of Rosie, he would never leave.

Her head jerked up at his laughter, and he examined the wide eyes and softly opened mouth. No, with Rosie there'd be no control.

As coyly as a barmaid enticing a customer, he stroked off his braes. "Ahh." He stretched, every last bare inch of him displayed in the broad sunshine. She blushed beautifully. "How did you find this place?"

Curiosity as well as compulsion raised the question. A jewel hidden on the estate, the waterfall cascaded into a pool deep enough to swim in and clear enough to pick pennies off the sandy bottom. It had taken good instructions and the better part of a day for him to find it the first time, yet she had walked right to it. How did she do it? What instinct carried her through Odyssey Manor and its environs with such foreknowledge? And why did her insight constantly seem to surprise her?

"Rosie?"

"I just"—her gaze examined him above and below—"knew it was here."

Maybe this wasn't such a good idea. She sat; he stood. She gawked; he preened. She wondered; he wanted.

"As you just knew"—he coughed, clearing the lust from his throat—"that my antechamber used to be the master's chamber?"

"The master bedroom. 'Twas a natural mistake to think the master"—her gaze flashed to his in what might have been feminine challenge—"would be big."

Dumbstruck, he realized that this was the woman she

would be if she were allowed: pert, bawdy, flirtatious, and more desirable than a temptress in the shadows.

"Damn." With an alacrity he hadn't planned, he walked a straight line into the cold brook. He'd planned to show himself to her, display his wares for the unwilling shopper, but his wares had grown to such a great size, he deemed it likely he would faint from lack of blood to his brain.

Such a shame he needed his brain. "Have you any soap about you?" he asked, as he splashed into the water up to his waist, and waited for its icy embrace to take effect.

She mumbled something, then pulled it from the purse at her waist. "Here." She tossed it toward the creek and he scrambled to catch it. "Give it back when you're done."

"You throw like a woman," he grumbled, lifted the misshapen bar to his nose. It smelled of carnations, and he sank beneath the surface under the effect of its seduction. Such a lady's scent would betray her at once if she used it, but the fact that she carried it revealed much.

So much, in fact, that he swam inside the frigid water until he could break the surface and sing soprano. "I love a bath," he called, scrupulously regulating the deep tones. "You ought to come in, too. It would rid you of that musty smell." He scrubbed his hair with the bar of soap and sneaked a glance.

She cautiously sniffed her clothing. "It's a manly smell," she said stoutly.

"Nonsense," he answered. "I don't smell. Am I not a man?"

In total control of himself, he stepped up to the edge of the pool, water at his knees, and spread his arms wide. Her gaze fixed, pasted to him like some housewife's concoction.

"You . . . don't stuff your canions with a sack of beans," she said.

He leaned his head into the water to rinse the soap from his hair, to hide his grin, and incidentally to give her an uninterrupted view of his backside. When he had his amusement adequately contained, he stood and called, "Give me your cloak as a towel."

No one answered him.

She was gone, and on the hill where she had been sitting, only a circlet of crushed grass remained. Only the crushed grass, and the memory of her amber eyes, alive with shock, unwanted curiosity, and the beginnings of a woman's awareness.

9

The strawberry grows underneath the nettle.

—HENRY V, I, i, 60

Sir Danny stood on the step leading into the wagon that was their home and peered inside the dim, crowded interior. "Rosie?"

"I'm in here."

"Remain, Ludovic," Sir Danny instructed, then edged inside. Two short, narrow beds piled with blankets took up most of the room, with a narrow walkway between. Hooks in the walls held props and costumes, and pieces of scaffolding crowded the one available foot of floor space. Rosie sat on her bed, absorbed in some task, and he asked, "Where have you been?"

"There aren't enough beans in my bag." She picked up another handful of broad beans, awkwardly stuffed them in, then with her uninjured hand exhibited the sack to Sir Danny. "Is that more realistic, do you think?"

Sir Danny looked as puzzled as she'd ever seen him. "What are you talking about?"

Realizing Ludovic stood on the ground just outside, she hesitated. Should she proceed? Should she provoke Sir Danny while his infinitely more dangerous lieutenant listened? But aye, she should, for always before, she knew she could depend on Sir Danny's unerring fatherly instinct. Yet he had been different lately, and she thought that if she baited Sir Danny in vain, Ludovic would provide the added incentive to move, to leave, to proceed with their plan or proceed with their travels. She wanted action, she wanted it now, and she would cold-bloodedly incite Sir Danny to perform or pack up.

Of course, they couldn't return to London. The earl of Essex wouldn't have forgotten them so soon. But they could travel the provinces. With an innocence that should have fooled no one, she said, "You should have told me my man-root was undersized. I'd have taken care of it before."

Sweat suddenly sheened Sir Danny's brow. "It never occurred to me to discuss . . ." He glanced over his shoulder at Ludovic, crowding in close. "Why do you think your, uh, man-root is undersized?"

"Tony's is a lot bigger than this." She jiggled the sack. "But I can't fit any more in."

Sir Danny took a sudden step forward. "Tony's what?"

"His man-root."

"I heard you!" Sir Danny snapped.

Behind him, Ludovic growled.

Ludovic's ferocity seemed to recall Sir Danny to himself, and he said, "It's a mistake, Ludovic. Don't make trouble." Taking a breath, he rubbed his chest like a man calming a fractious horse. "Rosie, you startled me. For a moment, I thought you had actually seen his man-root, when actually you just observed his canions."

"Tony took me swimming."

Sir Danny's cheeks turned maroon, his whole figure inflated like a puffball after a rain, and his shout swamped Ludovic's reaction. "I have never strapped you before, but I will now unless you tell me true—you went swimming with Sir Anthony?"

"It was Tony a few moments ago," she observed.

"You removed your clothing?"

"I didn't."

He sighed in relief.

"He did."

His eyes narrowed. "All of it?"

"All of it."

Sir Danny slammed his fist into the thin wall. Outside, she heard a litany of foreign curses, and one mighty thump as Ludovic imitated Sir Danny.

She watched with a simmering excitement as Sir Danny paced along the tiny aisle. It wasn't acting that whirled him around the wagon, it was fury, and his honest recoil gave her hope.

Tony's presumption infuriated Sir Danny, but Sir Danny's indecision had infuriated her. Adding fuel to the flame, she said, "On the morrow, Tony says, he'll take me to Tiny Mary's."

Shaking his injured hand, Sir Danny said, "Tiny Mary's? The madam's? For what?"

"In sooth, for my first experience with a woman."

"With a woman? He's taking you to swive a woman?"

"That is his intention."

With a scream of fury, Sir Danny launched another attack on the wall, battering it with both his fists before slamming the door in Ludovic's face. Diving for the trunk under his bed, Sir Danny dragged it out.

Rosie poked a few more beans in the bag and watched curiously as he tossed aside his shedding fur cloak, his scepter covered with bits of broken glass, and wrapped in kersey, his gilt crown. His most precious possessions, these—the props that turned him from a vagabond actor to a king.

But he ignored them as if they were tawdry in his eyes and dug to the bottom.

"What do you seek?" she asked.

"This." He lifted a yellowed paper from the lining of the trunk.

"And what will you do with it?"

"This." He grabbed her hand and jerked her toward the door.

The bag spilled beans in a great cascade over the floor, and she cried, "Wait! I'm not ready to perform."

Stuffing the paper into the gap of his doublet, he inquired, "Do you really think Sir Anthony is going to be looking for your man-root?"

So they *were* going to see Tony. "Well, actually, aye." Sir Danny jerked open the door and dragged her down the step. "He never seems to look at anything else."

"Like he's looking for something?" Sir Danny turned to face her so abruptly she bumped into him. "Or nothing?"

She met his fury with a fury of her own. "I don't understand why you're so angry. You told me to behave like a cocky youth, and I've done as you instructed. Tony so strongly believed me to be a cocky youth that he bathed in front of me."

The cords in Sir Danny's neck stood out, and the skin over them stretched taut. "I'll kill him."

"Nay." Ludovic's voice sounded thick as porridge. "*I'll* kill him."

They had forgotten he stood there, but he looked like some foreign hardwood tree, feet rooted in the soil, soul sucking strength from his anger.

Sir Danny laid claim. "It's my task."

Ludovic scoffed. "A little man like you against that Tony lecher? Leave him to me."

Rosie could have groaned at the challenge to Sir Danny's virility.

Taking Ludovic's tunic in his fist, Sir Danny said, "Mayhap you've never heard the old English saying, Ludovic, but let me enlighten you now." Sir Danny stood on tiptoe and glared into Ludovic's face. "If you stick your man-root where it's not wanted, you'll likely have it shortened. Now"—he gestured widely—"get back to work."

Ludovic steamed like a kettle on the boil. "I will work as I please."

Cocky as a miniature rooster, Sir Danny said, "You will work as you please when I am dead."

Looming over him, Ludovic replied, "That can be arranged."

Rosie stepped between them and cried, "Blast you both! Stop fighting. You!" She pointed a finger at Ludovic. "Start the troupe packing. One way or the other, we're leaving this place."

Ludovic hesitated, and she gestured again. With a bow, he went.

"And you!" She pointed at Sir Danny. "Come with me. We have blackmail to perform."

"Have you been managing me, Rosie?" She didn't answer, and Sir Danny grinned. "Why, I didn't think you had it in you. 'Tis the season for revelations, it seems." Grabbing her by the wrist, he pulled her across the lawn at a great rate. They almost ran up the steps and into the house. "We must beard Sir Anthony

Rycliffe in his den." He beckoned a servant. "My good man! Can you tell me where we may find Sir Anthony?"

The servant bowed, a little uncertain. "He's in the study. If you would wait here, I'll get someone to show you."

He walked toward the end of the long gallery, but Sir Danny sniffed contemptuously. "He'll go guard the silver. Well, I'll not wait for permission to visit my vengeance on that yeaforsooth knave. Come, my dearest." He tucked Rosie's hand into his arm. "Let us find Sir Anthony ourselves."

He started toward the opposite end of the gallery, but she stopped him. "The serving lad said the study. The study is here." She pointed at a tall door set in the paneled wall facing the outside door.

"Nay," Sir Danny said. "Why would the master put his study where he's bound to get a draft?"

"He likes to know who comes and goes," she answered, flinging the door wide.

A sarcastic "Enter," proved they'd found Tony.

She cast one triumphant glance at Sir Danny, then thought, *Just get it over with.* There was nothing here that could harm her, and they couldn't leave until they'd done this, so just get it over with.

"Enter!" Tony called again.

She sailed in—and stopped.

Hiding in the dark desk kneehole, hugging herself and listening while they all searched. "Where's Rosie?"

"I don't know. Mayhap she went to London to see the queen."

"Where's Rosie?"

"I don't know. Mayhap a fairy kidnapped her and she's dancing under the moon."

"Where's Rosie?"

Popping out into the candlelight. "Here I am!"

Strong hands lifting her high, a beloved face smiling, a deep voice crying, "Here she is. Here's my girl."

"Come on, my girl." Sir Danny grabbed her arm again as he swept into the room, dragging her forward. Tony sat, pen in hand, behind a desk piled high with correspondence. "Sirrah, we have business to discuss."

Plain speaking with a vengeance. Sir Danny must be truly angry to so ignore the forms of elegant phrasing, but it wouldn't last. He'd been imagining this scene for months, Rosie knew, writing and rewriting his mental script, trying to assure he had an answer for every possible variation.

He trusted her to do no more than remain silent, and that she willingly did.

Tony leaned back in his carved wood chair and studied them. His clean white shirt and black doublet gave him a Puritan-like appearance, the look of a man wise in the ways of business and wise to the ways of sin.

Sin. Sin such as acting, blackmailing . . . why did that carving resting on the massive desk look so familiar?

"Do we?" Tony asked.

"Aye, that we do."

"Do ye wish t' speak t' these folk, Sir Anthony?"

Rosie recognized the rasping voice and turned to see the man with the close-cropped gray hair standing in the doorway. The steward. The man who'd held her down while Tony set her arm, and then sneaked into her nightmares.

"I'll speak to them," Tony replied. "Shut the door behind you."

Hal bowed with every appearance of respect, but Rosie shivered. There was something about Hal, something not quite right. His gray hair, his wrinkles, his expression portrayed an old man bludgeoned by life. But how old was he, really?

Sir Danny joggled her elbow, bringing her attention back to the scene that they must play. "It has come to my attention, sir, that this estate is a grant from Queen Elizabeth."

Tony nodded in austere agreement. "Queen Elizabeth did indeed grant me this estate."

The carving beckoned Rosie, begged for attention. She could almost imagine its weight, the wood smoothed to the grain . . . although it faced Tony, she knew it to be a simple depiction of the Madonna and child, old beyond imagining.

"And all belongings of the Bellot family?" Sir Danny insisted.

"Aye, all belongings of the *extinct* Bellot family."

At that moment, the drama swept Sir Danny up. His hand dropped away from Rosie's arm, his voice gained depth and expression, and he gestured grandly. "The family is not extinct."

"So I've been hearing." Tony rose slowly, his chair scraping the floor as he pushed it back. "Do I have you to thank for those scurrilous rumors?"

"Not rumors, sirrah, but the truth."

Without volition, Rosie's hand crept across the desk and picked up the knickknack. It wasn't as heavy as she expected, and she used such force to swing it up all eyes focused on her.

Tony observed Rosie. She jumped when she turned the faces to her—the faces of the Madonna and child. He asked, "Do you like it? It was one of Edward Lord Sadler's prized possessions, I am told. Saved from the destruction of an abbey on these lands, and created even before the Normans won this fair isle."

Sir Danny placed a steadying hand on her shoulder,

but spoke the words of the script. "Young Rosencrantz probably remembers it from his childhood."

"Ah, now we get to it." Tony's sharp gaze never left Rosie as she placed the statue on the edge of the desk, then skimmed the surface with the fingertips of her good hand, reading it with the concentration of a blind woman. "What are you saying, Sir Danny?"

Tony, too, seemed to have read the script.

With a dramatic flourish, Sir Danny replied, "I'm saying that—"

Rosie cleared a place at the opposite end of the desk and replaced the carving there. That seemed the right place for it.

"—Rosencrantz is the missing heir."

"Nay!" In exaggerated dismay, Tony caught his throat with both hands. "Then I will have to leave Odyssey Manor at once so young Rosencrantz can assume his heritage."

Rosie moved the inkwell, then the sharpened quills. She rearranged a pile of papers and found an old ink-blot. She touched it and looked at her fingers, but no ink stained them. At least, not this time. She adjusted the sealing wax, and looked for the seal which should be in the niche beside it. It wasn't there, and she glanced around. Not on the desk. Kneeling, she searched the floor. Not on the floor.

Where was—

I didn't take it, Dada.

Dada won't be angry, but you must tell me where it is.

I didn't take it for keeps.

Dada needs it. Tell me. Tell me, Rosie.

"Rosie?" Tony crouched beside her. "Are you ill?"

His face was the wrong face, his time was the wrong time. Was she ill? "Nay." Maybe. "Nay, I'm well."

Sir Danny lifted her with his hand under her armpit and brushed the hair back from her forehead. Compassion put a rein on his histrionics; he seemed to have forgotten his lines.

Rosie glanced at Tony, who stood brushing his knees, then at Sir Danny. The eerie sensation of familiarity stifled her, and she wanted out now. Hurriedly, she offered, "We will accept recompense."

Tony's cynicism returned in a hurry. How well she played the part of bewildered child to soften him for the monetary demands! Perching one hip on his desk, he folded his arms across his chest. "Generous of you, considering you have no proof."

"You require proof?" Sir Danny gestured at Rosie. "As you can see, Rosencrantz is the right age to be the heir."

"And his hair is brown, too. Lord Sadler's hair was brown," Tony marveled. "What a resemblance. Why didn't I see it sooner?"

They stood too close together: Sir Danny, Rosie, and Tony. She felt hemmed in, overpowered by the men, a pawn in a chess game they played.

"There's only one problem." Tony grinned into her face. "The heir—"

She braced herself for some unknown shock.

"—was a girl."

She hadn't braced herself enough. "What?" She stepped back, knocking Sir Danny aside.

"A daughter," Tony clarified, watching her for signs of betrayal. "Lord Sadler's only child was a girl. You're not a girl. Are you?"

With her hair pulled back from her forehead and no cosmetics to camouflage her complexion, all of Rosie's face lay pitifully bare. Horror, shock, and a sense of betrayal left it as white as well-milled flour. "A mistake." Rosie caught Sir Danny's arm with her free hand. "There's been a mistake. We'll go now."

"Why hurry?" Tony straightened, towering over Rosie and Sir Danny. "Stay."

"We have to go. Sir Danny." She tugged again at him. "Let's go."

She fluttered frantically, like a pheasant facing the hunter's arrow. Either she truly hadn't known the heir was a female, or she was a magnificent actress, and she'd already proved that to be false.

But what game was Sir Danny playing? Why wasn't *he* backing toward the door? Why was he smiling at Rosie in the manner of a father giving his frightened daughter into the hands of a loving husband?

"Danny, I beg you, Danny . . ."

She whispered hoarsely, clearly choked with some kind of emotion, but Sir Danny took both her cheeks in his hands and kissed her mouth, kissed her as if he bade her farewell. "Trust me," he murmured, and pulled a paper from inside his vest. Handing it to Tony, he said, "If you would read this, sir, you would see the truth of the matter, and this news might be better received if you are sitting firm in a chair."

Taking heed, Tony seated himself. He pressed his back firmly against the cushions to soften the blow, for Rosie's obvious anxiety, Sir Danny's burgeoning air of elation, warned Tony of the truth even before his gaze skimmed the document.

Written in a shaking hand, it consigned the child Lady Rosalyn Elizabeth Ann Katherine Bellot to the care of the actor Danny Plympton. It instructed the reader of this letter to allow and assist said Danny Plympton to place the child Rosalyn in Her Royal Majesty Queen Elizabeth's care. It reminded the reader that the child Rosalyn was heir to a fortune and an estate, and the queen herself would pay most dearly for the return of said child so she could be brought up according to the circumstances of her birth. Finally, it called down the curses of heaven on anyone who dared interfere with Danny Plympton's holy mission or the proper placement of the child Rosalyn.

Tony wanted to shout his skepticism to the skies. This was a forgery. This was part of the plan to dispossess him. This was treachery at its deadliest. This could not be the truth.

So he would play out the scene, stripping Rosie of her disguise and Sir Danny of his falsehoods.

"An interesting document." Tony tossed it contemptuously on the desk. "But to whom does it pertain?"

"Aye." Rosie placed one fist on her hip and arched back like a cocky youth. "What is this document, Sir Danny, and to whom does it pertain?"

"It is the will of a dying man." Sir Danny looked right at her. "And it pertains to you. Dear girl—"

"Girl?" Tony mocked.

"Girl?" Rosie drew an audible breath.

Sir Danny's smile mellowed. "Sir Tony ridicules us. No man ever laid hands on a woman's chest and failed to realize what he held."

Her fist slipped off her hip as if it had been greased.

He wouldn't have believed it possible, but Tony was amused. "Is that what you told her? That I didn't realize I held a woman's breast in my hand?"

With profound significance, Sir Danny explained, "She *is* an innocent."

Her bare face, previously so pale, flushed ruddy with color. Hugging her injured arm, she turned her back to them and swept to the window where she gazed out onto the lands.

Her lands? His lands? What had Sir Danny wrought? And why? Most crucially—

"Why?" Tony demanded aloud. "Why, Sir Danny?"

Sir Danny combed his flowing mustache with his fingertips. "There are many whys in this situation, sir. You'll have to specify—"

"If this document is the truth, and not some wretched forgery, then *why* did you not do as Lord Sadler instructed and take the child Rosalyn to the queen?"

Clearly uncomfortable, Sir Danny confessed, "I . . . do not read, and the gentleman . . . was dying, most horribly. He could speak only a little, and that none too clear, for the fever carried him off repeatedly."

"It was the plague?"

Everyone knew the appearance of the black death; it had made itself a familiar visitor to England, and Tony never doubted Sir Danny when he said, "Most definitely. The gentleman had purple buboes on his neck, and his armpits and groin were swollen."

"And you stayed?" Tony invested his voice with scorn.

Sir Danny stood as tall as his height would allow and looked Tony in the face. "Lord Sadler suffered the agonies of the damned, so worried was he about his daughter. Do you think I would abandon him? Do you think I could leave that child to die?"

"Black death was almost certainly her fate, and hence yours, also. Yet you stayed?"

From the still figure at the window came a soft utterance. "Sir Danny Plympton has always done all that is in his power to be kind, and he will always do what is righteous."

Tony glanced at the figure silhouetted against the sun. Her cheek rested against the diamond-cut panes of glass, and she stared fixedly at something: the sill, the stone wall, the bit of outdoors she could see. Her hunched shoulders, her pinched expression bespoke pain past bearing, but she defended Sir Danny. Not surprisingly, she believed Sir Danny's compassion to be greater than his fear. Tony himself believed it.

Changing his tack, Tony asked, "You stayed until Lord Sadler died?"

"Aye."

"Afterward, why did you not deliver the child to the queen?"

Sir Danny shuffled his feet. "Lord Sadler mumbled about the queen and the child, but I believed his pleas to be the raving of delirium. The coach had no rich trappings, it was built for speed. He had two attendants, and they were dead. I did not believe he knew the queen."

"A racing coach, perhaps?" Tony mused.

"I wondered if he sought to outrun death. But since I had the will read to me, I have tried to remember . . ." Squinting, Sir Danny tried to see into the past. "The coach had *no* rich trappings. None. No blanket warmed the occupants, no gilt decorated the interior."

"Horses?" Tony asked.

"Gone."

Disgusted, Tony stated, "The thieves cozened you, then."

Sir Danny shared his disgust. "I only hope they sickened with the fever as they dangled at the end of a rope."

So far Sir Danny's rescue made a horrible sense, and Tony feared it might continue to do so. Intensifying his interrogation, he asked, "You accepted responsibility for the child?"

"Aye."

"Was she ill?"

"I thought she would die."

The rueful tug of Sir Danny's mouth alerted Tony. "You hoped she would die?"

The rueful grimace grew. "Not hoped, nay. Never hoped. But I was a mere forty years, free and unfettered, and I did not want Rosie for even the short time I deemed I would have her." He glanced at the figure by the window. "She was violently sick and puny and a deterrent to a carefree life."

"When it became clear she would survive, why didn't you make an attempt to take her to London and follow Lord Sadler's directions?"

"London had proved to be an unhealthy environment for me." Sir Danny's gaze shifted from side to side. "The plague, you see."

Rosie once again proved she had been listening. "Was that when you'd been swiving the mayor's wife and got caught?"

Sir Danny's gaze shifted again, this time to glare at Rosie's back. "It might have been. I forget. Once in the provinces, finding someone who could read, and would read, to someone as disreputable as an actor, proved beyond me. I tried, believe me, I tried."

Sir Danny's character became clearer and clearer to Tony; a more lighthearted vagabond he had never met. "For how long?" Tony challenged.

"We-ell." Sir Danny seemed to contemplate the time, then said brightly, "For a long period. But naturally, as time went on, my efforts lessened. Remember, I had no idea Rosie was an heiress. To me, she was only a frightened child who clung to me with flattering desperation."

"For how long did you search?"

"Until . . ." Tilting his head from side to side, Sir Danny searched for an acceptable answer.

"How long?" Rosie asked.

Sir Danny let out his breath with a sigh. "Until you

worked your way into my heart. Until I couldn't think of losing you." He looked from one to the other, waiting for a challenge, but neither said a word. "So, have you faith in me?"

Tony replied for the two of them. "Unfortunately, we do." Pulling a candelabra close, he held the letter close to the flame. "But what's to stop me from burning this paper?"

Sir Danny flinched. "There's nothing to stop you from burning the letter, murdering Rosie and me and all of our troupe and burying us on the grounds of Odyssey Manor. I knew that from the beginning. For that reason, I investigated you thoroughly before I offered our services for your house party."

Investigated him? A cheap half-pence actor had investigated him, head of the Queen's Guard, son of Alfred Lord Spencer? The edge of the letter turned brown, and a faint curl of smoke lifted toward the ceiling.

Sir Danny's gaze never left the paper. "I spoke to the men who served under you in Her Majesty's Guard. I spoke to the servants in your town house, and I slipped onto the grounds of Odyssey Manor and spoke to your servants here. The way a man treats the lesser folk, sir, often provides a clue to his character, and you'll be pleased to know your character passed the test. You have the loyalty of your servants. They assured me you are all that's honorable, and on that honor we now depend."

Tony stared at the hand holding the paper. Closer. Closer. So easy to light it on fire, to send it into oblivion. The proof would be gone. His estate would be his forever. Sir Danny would be once more nothing but a traveling actor and Rosie . . . he'd have to do something for Rosie. Perhaps she could work on his estate as a serving maid or a—

"Curse you, Sir Danny. Curse you to hell." In his rage, Tony knocked the candelabra to the floor. The impact brought Rosie around to watch him as he snuffed each candle with the heel of his boot. Subsiding, he studied the wary woman who would dispossess him. "Why now? Why did you find someone to read this now?"

"Ludovic." Wiping a shaking hand across his brow, Sir Danny tried to hide his relief and fear.

"Ludovic is the cause of this?" Rosie shook, too, but not with fear and not with relief.

Tony didn't understand why they could hear the rasp of her breath, why her whole body tensed as if to flee or fight.

"Ludovic is challenging me for control of you." Sir Danny watched her with a frown of puzzlement. "He wants you, and he's not good enough. Even before I knew who you were, I knew he wasn't good enough."

"So now you're going to replace Tony with me as lady of Odyssey Manor?"

Sir Danny held his palms flat out in a stop signal. "Not at all. I trow, you both misunderstand. Because of my . . . irresponsibility, Rosie, you have no training in the management of an estate such as this. Not to mention the Sadler foundry—"

"Ah, you know about that, too." Tony grimaced.

"—and the Sadler town house. Our blessed queen has granted Tony shares in shipping and the right to sell silken cloth, and the income from that must be considerable."

Tony sneered. "Well, you'll have to advise her on the best way to spend her wealth, won't you?"

Sir Danny chided Tony's skepticism. "It would not be in her best interest for me to advise her, nor can I believe you wish to be removed from all of the privileges which you worked so hard to gain."

"Ah!" Tony opened his arms in mock embrace. "You want to hire me to care for my former possessions."

"Not at all," Sir Danny said sharply. "I want you to marry Rosie."

Somewhere, children played. Somewhere, women laughed. Somewhere, men shouted. But in the study at Odyssey Manor, silence reigned. A silence unbroken by movement, breath, or heartbeat. A silence so complete as to be a hole in time.

Then Tony's arms collapsed, knocking documents to the floor, and Rosie's elbow struck the window. Papers fluttered in a winsome accompaniment to the ringing of the glass.

In one comprehensive glance, Tony absorbed her emotions. Attraction, fear, amazement, and something else. Fury? It could not be. What right had she to be furious?

As an even exchange, he let her absorb his emotions. Fury, fury, and lust. And . . . fury. At being so trapped. At having to marry a lowlife, highborn actress. At losing the status he had slaved so hard to obtain.

At being a bastard with no other prospects.

Slowly, Tony lifted himself to his feet. "As you say, Sir Danny, marriage is the perfect solution to our problem." Strolling over to the window, he wrapped his arms around Rosie's stiff figure and insolently nuzzled her neck. "I will marry the vagabond heiress as soon as possible."

But he'd forgotten that Rosie was a child of the streets. One bony fist split his lip and one sharp shoe bruised his shin. As he cupped his mouth and hopped on one foot, she straightened with disdain.

"If I'm the heir, why do I need Tony? Why do I need to be married? I'll take my lands and my title back, and he can fry in hell."

10

What is wedlock forced but a hell,
An age of discord and continual strife?
—HENRY VI, PART ONE, V, v, 62

Stupid men, gawking at her like pelicans denied a fish.

Stupid Sir Danny, playing the scene with flash and drama and thinking she would thank him for shaping her whole life while abandoning her.

Stupid Tony, imagining he was doing her a favor by marrying her and lifting her from her lowly existence. Making a fool of her by pretending not to know she was a woman, and all the time laughing deep in his chest.

And stupid Rosie, for fantasizing that she might really be the heiress Rosalyn. That she might have lived here in this place with a father who had loved her and servants who adored her. That she might *belong* somewhere other than a cramped gypsy wagon and a different village every week.

Stupid, gullible Rosie.

"Manly smell, indeed," Rosie sneered. "You stink of carnation soap."

Sir Danny looked confused. Tony did not. He lowered his hand and wiped his bloody palm on his canions. "I smell of carnation, and you strike like a warrior. We will be a seemly couple."

Did he think she was jesting when she declared she would not marry? "We will be no couple at all."

"How do you think you will be rid of me? I'm in possession. You might say"—Tony smiled, although she would have sworn he was furious—"I am firmly in the saddle."

Outraged by the innuendo, she snapped, "Why not return to your original plan, with some modification, forsooth. I'll take possession of the Sadler lands, and you can marry into the nobility and live off your wife. Lady Honora has been eyeing your codpiece."

Tony roared like a baited bull, and Sir Danny grabbed her wrist and jerked her aside as if he expected him to charge. But Tony regained control immediately—or perhaps he'd never lost it—and smiled with insolent disdain.

Drawing her stiff figure into his embrace, Sir Danny hugged her tight while keeping an eye on Tony. "You're hurt. You're angry. You're speaking without giving consideration to the advantages for *me*."

"Advantages?" She could scarcely understand him, and didn't care.

Holding her gaze, Tony slid a hand along the sill where she had stood and rubbed the rich brown wood with his palm. "It's still warm," he said.

Sir Danny chatted. "You'll have a title, and with that you'll be able to sponsor my acting troupe."

She watched the caress of Tony's fingertips and remembered that first moment they met. How he had tempted her, taught her, touched her.

"Wouldn't you like to be our benefactor?" Sir Danny coaxed.

"I don't need *him* to be your benefactor."

Sir Danny struggled on, regardless of her aversion. "I'll be able to legitimately act in London, just as Uncle Will does. I'll have money for costumes and when I get too old to go on the road, I'll have a place to come."

"Fine. But all this is mine. I needn't marry."

Observing her unrelenting rejection, Tony asked, "Ungrateful wretch, isn't she?"

She shoved Sir Danny aside and marched right up to the obnoxious, scornful jackanapes. "*You're* out of favor with the queen. I heard that much from your guests at your house party, and as obnoxious as you are, I understand why. I'll present my claim to Her Majesty, and she'll grant it at once."

"How do you propose to get to the queen?" Tony took hold of her shirt strings and reeled her in like a fish. "I have you here, and I will hold you."

She looked down at the knuckles close under her chin, and looked up at him, taller and broader and tougher than any man she knew. He would keep her here, a prisoner? "I've got out of tighter predicaments."

"By yourself? Without the help of Sir Danny?" His beautiful wide eyes narrowed. "With my faithful servants and my faithful soldiers watching your every move?"

Tony thought just because he paid the soldiers and servants they would do as he wished, and she feared he was right. She said, "I trow there are some servants left from the days when young Rosalyn played here, and I trow they would help me."

"That's a thought." Tony nodded. "Thank you for warning me. I'll take steps to thwart that alley of escape."

Defiance, she realized, exacted its own retribution.

It wasn't fair, but the life of an actor had prepared her for injustice. However, nothing could make her like it. Trying to peel his grip off her shirt, she said, "Hold me, but I'll not wed you."

"As you wish." Their fingers grappled, fumbling, straining, slipping, and even with one hand Tony could easily have overcome her. She knew it, and he knew it. She fumed, and he smiled unrelentingly as he insulted her. "You'd be totally inappropriate as my wife. You haven't had the training to be a noblewoman."

Stung, she broke his hold. "I've got noble bloodlines," she cried. "I'm a fast learner and I'm an actress who has many times played the part of a noblewoman. 'Tisn't I who lacks what is necessary to be noble."

"Rosie," Sir Danny warned.

But she rushed on, unheeding. "I've heard rumors about your background. You're a bastard. *You're* not fit to be a nobleman."

Thrusting his head down to her level, he asked, "Are you really a woman?"

Equally aggressive, she thrust her head forward, meeting him nose to nose. "Aye."

"You'd best prove it then, because if you're a man, I'm going to run you through."

"Prove it?" Sir Danny squawked.

"Now," Tony agreed, and grabbed her by the crotch.

Furious, beset, invaded, she grabbed right back. Neither of them jumped; they stared, eyeball-to-eyeball, breathing heavily. Finally, Tony whispered, "Have I proved to your satisfaction that I am a man?"

"Aye," she whispered back. "Have I proved to you I am a woman?"

"Aye."

Did he know how those little pulses fed excitement

to her insides? Did she know exactly what it meant?

"I think," he continued, "we should wed soon."

"Nay."

For the first time in this dreadful interview, his smile was whimsical, a curve of happiness that begged to be kissed. "Pray tell, lady mine, why not?"

"Why not? Why not?" Lady Honora stood in the doorway, bristling with indignation. "Because you're going to wed me!"

Tony and Rosie jumped apart, and Lady Honora swept in, her wide, stiff skirt catching the sides of the door. She freed herself with a jerk. "Explain yourself, Tony." Tony slid behind his desk and seated himself, and Rosie knew why.

"How did you hear of this?" he demanded.

Without inflection, Lady Honora said, "Your steward did his duty and told me."

"Hal?" Tony glanced around, then shouted, "Hal!"

"Sir?" Hal hastened in.

"I have scarce heard the news myself, and you're spreading the word like a royal messenger?"

Bowing repeatedly, Hal stammered, "Nay, sir, I only kept guard at th' door because o' th' faulty latch."

"Faulty latch?" Tony stared, impressive in his fury.

The color slid down Hal's wrinkled brow and found residence in his sagging chins, and he swung the door back and forth, back and forth in nervous little movements. "Aye, th' door developed a problem with th', ah . . ." Giving up, he bowed to Lady Honora. "This lady demanded t' know th' events which transpired within, an' sir, I'm so sorry, but I couldn't withstand her questioning."

"Of course not." Lady Honora dismissed him with a gesture.

"Of course not," Tony agreed. "Justly punished for

your eavesdropping, you are and will be. Get out of my sight and stay out. I'll replace you as steward—"

"Nay, sir," Hal implored.

"—unless you can prove your loyalty to me and Odyssey Manor."

"Aye, I will. I swear I will."

"There are others who vie for your position. Now get out."

Rosie shut her eyes to close out the sight of Tony, still, quiet, and so angry he frightened her. But some sound brought them open again, and she found Hal on his knees before her.

"My lady." He took her limp hand and held it as if it were a holy chalice. "'Tis an honor to serve ye once more. This time—"

"Don't touch her!" Tony was beside her before she could blink, snatching her hand from Hal's grasp, holding it so tightly her knuckles cracked.

"Tony, such violence! He's just ignorant," Lady Honora rebuked as Hal scrambled up and ran. "He believes she is the heir."

"Lady Honora," Sir Danny called, but Lady Honora's high ruff kept her from turning her head. Stepping into Lady Honora's line of vision, he said, "Lady Honora, she *is* the heir."

"You!" Ignoring Tony with impressive disdain, Lady Honora looked down her impressive nose. "You've lied to me about everything."

Sir Danny tossed his impressive mane. "There is another alternative. I could have told you the truth about everything."

"Why should I believe an actor?" she demanded.

"Because"—with impressive courage, Sir Danny laid his finger between her thin, tweezed brows—"you are an excellent judge of character."

She stood still as if she couldn't believe he'd touched her, and he held her gaze until the door slammed against the wall once more.

Jean and Ann elbowed each other like children, both anxious to enter the room first.

"Tony," Jean said. "What's this tale the servants are babbling?"

Ann finished, "That the lost heiress is back, and you're marrying her?"

Tony looked out the door to the milling group of excited servants. "News travels faster than a flash of lightning, I see."

"You mean it's true?" Jean clutched her red wig as if it would blow off in the strong wind of change.

Silently Tony handed Lord Sadler's yellowed will to Jean, and Ann and Lady Honora crowded close, reading it over her shoulder. When they had finished, Jean silently handed it back.

Ann recovered first. "Lady Honora, what think you?"

Lady Honora answered, but not the right question. "Sir Danny was saying I was an excellent judge of character, and that's true."

"Fantastic," Tony murmured. "He's thoroughly charmed her."

Lady Honora continued, "But regardless of the truth of any claim, it's impossible. A woman of low repute cannot become an heiress."

Sir Danny fixed her with his most hypnotic gaze. "Rosie . . . Rosalyn is not a woman of low repute. I've personally supervised her every moment, waking and sleeping. She passes from my hands to the hands of her husband, untouched and unawakened."

Lifting Rosie's hand to his mouth, Tony kissed it with lingering care. "I knew that."

She dug her nails into his hand and he quickly let go.

"Queen Elizabeth is above all a practical monarch, and the truth of Rosalyn's purity, even her heritage, pales beside the disgrace of her upbringing. Nay!" Lady Honora slashed the air. "With sorrow I must inform you, Sir Danny, that she is not suitable. But"—she lifted a finger—"I would be glad to offer her shelter in one of my homes. Sir Edward Sadler's daughter *must* be rescued from the gutters into which she has fallen. She must be trained to behave like a lady."

"I have a better idea." Tony's cheek quirked in amusement. "Teach her to behave like a lady here." Rosie jabbed him in the ribs with her elbow, and he grunted. Rubbing his side, he continued, "Teach her not to attack me. Teach her how to behave at table, how to run a household, how to be a correct wife for a nobleman of my stature." Anchoring her arms with his, Tony picked her up and turned her kicking feet away from him. "'Tis a challenge worthy of you three, is it not?"

He'd read them correctly. Jean avidly examined the struggling girl. "She has possibilities."

Lady Honora listened to the street curses spilling forth. "She needs to be taught when to speak and when to be silent."

"Mostly"—Ann sniffed—"she needs a bath."

"A bath?" Sir Danny shuddered. "Disgusting concept."

"A bath?" Rosie shrieked. "Sir Danny, they want to drown me."

Jean went to the door and ordered a tub of hot water, upstairs in the largest guest room, at once. Ann threw a rug over Rosie's head to subdue her. Lady Honora ordered, "Quiet, girl. We're going to give you a bath." Taking a pinch of Rosie's short, dirty cloak between her fingers, she rubbed it, then dropped it in disgust. "Probably two. Hand her to the serving maids, and be careful of her arm."

Everyone watched—the women and Tony in approval, Sir Danny in consternation—as the transfer was made and the screaming bundle was carried off.

Lady Honora dusted her hands briskly. "We'll let you know when the deed is done."

Tony listened as the howls for Sir Danny and the shouted demands proceeded up the stairs, then went back to the desk and seated himself, prepared to take up the work interrupted by his betrothal. The foundry demanded much of his attention; it should be running soon with improved machinery, and the money which he had so freely invested would at last be returning.

A shaking finger appeared under his nose, and he looked up at the horrified Sir Danny. "You can't do this," Sir Danny said. "She had a bath just last summer, and everyone knows a winter bath will kill a body."

Tony picked up his quill and contemplated it. "A bath will not kill her."

"Likely tale. If you're going to torment the poor lass, I'll take her away and find another method to get her settled." Sir Danny wheeled for the door.

"As you wish," Tony replied. "But if you go up to the bedchamber to rescue her, I think I should warn you—Lady Honora has already mentioned you need a good scrubbing."

Sir Danny wheeled back around and stared in terror. Tony nodded a gentle confirmation. Sir Danny fled, not up to the bedchamber, but outside to safety.

Tony looked out at the line of serving maids who carried steaming buckets. He looked up at the ceiling to the place where he knew Lady Honora and his sisters scoured Rosie. He looked down at his hand, cupped no longer in the shape of Rosie's breast, but in the shape of Rosie's womanhood.

And he grinned.

*   *   *

Sir Danny paced the gallery, hearing Rosie's wails and remembering how, in the past, he'd always raced to her rescue. Sometimes the "other" lads tormented her as a sissy. Sometimes she'd been ill. But most of all, she'd had nightmares. He'd been there for her, always, and now he'd lost that right. Without consulting her, he'd given her up to the past which so frightened her, and now events, and Tony, swept her along.

A particularly loud shriek ended in a splash of water.

When would the torment stop?

Hal stretched his hands out to the red flames of the kitchen fire. They tinted his thin skin scarlet and gave the flesh a transparent glow, and he wondered if the flames of hell would eat him alive. Would he see his flesh consumed throughout eternity to pay for his sins? Would demons dig at him with pitchforks?

Or had he already died, and the devil tormented him with these stabbing pains in his brain? Would he eternally try to redeem himself, and eternally find himself condemned by God, Jesus, Mary, all the saints, and his fellow man?

When would the torment stop?

That old fool Sir Danny had outmaneuvered him. Huddled in the shrubs below the terrace, Ludovic cursed and watched the manor. The old fool and the young lord. Together they'd conspired to establish Rosie so far above Ludovic's status he had as much chance of having her as of touching the stars.

But she wasn't happy. Her screams tore at his heart.

The laughter of the serving maids infuriated him. Even from outside the manor, he could hear the cold, precise tones of those three women, those witches who directed the torture.

What kind of man did Sir Danny and that cocky lord imagine him to be? Not a chivalrous fool like these Englishmen, but a real warrior of the north. He would show them.

Evening fell, lights glowed from the long windows, and still the cruel bath went on.

When would the torment stop?

"I'm not the heir!" Rosie sputtered. She stood in the bathtub as the maids sluiced fresh water over her head.

"Tony is convinced you are." Jean lifted a gown from a trunk. "What think you, Ann? You have an eye for color."

Ann considered the yellow silk, then shook her head. "Nay, 'twill turn her dark complexion sallow. Try to find a really vibrant red."

Jean shook out a crimson velvet gown, trimmed in gold braid loops.

"Aye, that'll be grand," Ann said.

"I have cuffs trimmed with black and red thread that would set off Rosalyn's hands." Lady Honora examined Rosie's nails, then gestured to the maid wielding the well-used brush. "Scrub them."

"I'm not wearing those clothes." Rosie winced as her nails were scoured clean, and she wondered at her own defiance. She'd done everything these three women, these witches, had commanded so far. She'd had no choice.

She'd taken not one, but two baths. She had been sand-scraped, deloused, and washed until she expected to see long strips of skin lying in the tub. Her protests had been ignored, her threats laughed at. Tony's two sisters, she realized, had dealt with recalcitrant children before, and such they considered her. And Lady Honora—it would never occur to Lady Honora to be afraid of anything.

"Of course you'll wear these clothes, or you'll go naked." Jean laid out stomachers until she found one that met Ann's approval. "We burned those other rags you were wearing. Besides, these may be twenty years out of fashion, but they're yours."

A linen towel enveloped Rosie's head, and when she emerged, hair tangled, she asked, "Mine?"

Jean explained, "You're Edward's daughter."

"I'm not."

"The trunks were here when Tony took possession of Odyssey Manor."

Urging Rosie out of the tub, Ann held Rosie's splinted arm out while the maids dried Rosie from head to toe. "Of course you're the heiress. We all knew Edward. He was a favorite of the queen's, and we were Her Majesty's ladies-in-waiting."

Rosie grabbed at the towels, trying to cover herself from what seemed like thousands of eyes. Indeed, she hadn't realized so many women existed on the estate, but everyone wanted to witness the bathing of the new mistress, and the three witches seemed to approve. "Witnesses will quiet any rumors, my dear," Jean had told her when she protested her embarrassment. "They'll all have seen your transformation from actor to heir, and there'll be no talk of a switch."

The maids snatched the towels from Rosie, and she found herself dry and bare as a babe. Mocking to cover her discomfort, she said, "Now you're going to tell me I look like him?"

"Not at all." Lady Honora's deep tones disapproved of her frivolity. "You look like *her*."

"Her?"

"Your mother."

Her mother? She'd never thought about a mother.

"You did have a mother, forsooth." Jean pressed her lips together.

Bewildered by the undercurrents, Rosie asked, "Didn't you like her?"

"She almost ruined Edward." Ann dropped a cambric smock over Rosie's head, helped her pull her splinted arm through, and loosely tied the strings.

"Ruined him?"

"The queen does not like her courtiers to wed," Lady Honora intoned, "and Edward was one of her favorites."

"We never knew what he saw in her." Jean wrapped a silk-covered stomacher around Rosie and when it was approved, a maid laced it to her body. "She was skinny like you."

"And brown like you." One by one, Lady Honora tried caps on Rosie until one, a black cap trimmed in pearls, won approval.

"No charm at all, but Edward couldn't resist her. He built this manor for her. 'Twas called Sadler House then, of course." Ann handed her maid a petticoat of black mockado, followed by one of red serge, and the maid tied the points to the stomacher. "Then he married that woman without the queen's permission."

"Forsooth, she was with child." Jean peered at Rosie. "With you. Edward was quite foolishly pleased when you were born, and presented you to the queen as her future lady-in-waiting."

"He had an insolent charm." Ann sighed and smiled.

"You were in love with him," Jean accused.

"As were you, sister."

Lady Honora put an end to their squabbling. "We all were."

"What happened to my mother?" Rosie queried.

The sisters grinned at each other slyly, realizing she'd laid a claim to the Sadler heritage, but Lady Honora said, "She died."

"Oh." Everyone died. Everyone abandoned Rosie. Why had she even asked?

"Edward never looked at another woman, except the queen, and we all knew he cultivated her for your sake." Jean wrapped a bum roll farthingale around Rosie's hips. "Luckily, Queen Elizabeth never knew how much he adored you, or she would have been jealous of you, too."

"As it was, she searched for you most assiduously when you disappeared, and mourned Edward with real grief." Ann wiped a tear from her cheek. "She said she promised him to care for you should anything happen, and she felt she'd failed in her duty. Your arrival at court should make her very happy."

"If we can make a lady of you," said Jean.

Lady Honora put the period on Rosie's fate. "We *will* make a lady of her, one worthy to wed a nobleman— although not Tony. He's mine."

"For Edward's sake." Jean put out a hand to her conspirators, and each laid a hand atop hers.

"For Edward's sake," they agreed.

11

See where she comes, apparell'd like the spring.

—PERICLES, I, i, 13

"Hey, Sir Danny! Look at this costume." Rosie skipped along the long gallery toward her guardian. Branches of candles sent a glow around the waxed and polished wall paneling and illuminated the vivid colors of the tapestries. The tall glass windows glistened, black and shiny with encroaching night, but at each end of the gallery, a huge fireplace roared with a conflagration that hurled warmth into the cool atmosphere and challenged the darkness.

Sir Danny turned from the flames, and his eyes widened at the spectacle Rosie presented as she whirled before him.

A single hand on her elbow jerked her to a stop.

"Ladies do not run nor do they prance," Lady Honora said in reproof.

"They glide," Jean said.

"Lest their petticoats fly up or they trip on their high heels." Ann minced along on her own heels. "Embarrassing and all too common among women who should know better."

"Nor do they demand admiration from their friends for their clothing." Erect with pomposity, Lady Honora folded her hands in front of her.

Rosie stuck out her lip, and Jean pinched her cheek. "Ladies do not sulk."

"After all, you have a responsibility." Lady Honora nodded a greeting to Sir Danny. "You must acquit yourself well, or you'll be a disgrace to us."

Bowing with a flourish, Sir Danny proclaimed, "These ladies are as fresh as the first buds of spring, bursting forth in color and glory to proclaim, 'Winter is vanquished. Let us frolic in the breeze and dance under the sun.'"

"A bit much," Rosie murmured to him, but Ann tittered, Jean inclined her head, and even Lady Honora smiled cordially.

Sir Danny shot Rosie a triumphant glance, then graciously said, "You do look lovely. I especially like the sling, which matches your gown, Rosie."

Lady Honora cleared her throat and frowned.

"And you do look clean." Sir Danny frowned back at Lady Honora. "I hope this 'bath' has no ill effect on her."

Looking equally severe, Lady Honora intoned, "A bath never hurt anyone, as long as it is administered in a well-heated room with the proper herbal additions, and not more than four times a year. But Sir Danny, I must warn you against calling Rosalyn by that dreadful name."

"Dreadful name?" Sir Danny seemed confused.

"Rosie." Lady Honora made it sound like an insult.

Bewildered, Sir Danny asked, "What else should I call her?"

"Her Christian name is Rosalyn"—Lady Honora pronounced it carefully as if to educate his ear—"and since she is the daughter of an earl, she should be called 'Lady Rosalyn' by all but those closest to her."

Sir Danny and Rosie exchanged eloquent glances.

"Since you are a mere actor," Lady Honora continued, "you should certainly call her by that title."

Rosie realized they were already trying to separate her from the man closest to her heart. She might be angry at him for his high-handed dominion of her fortune, but, damn it, she would decide his punishment, and not because his rank was less than hers. Furious, she demanded, "Does his position as my savior count for nothing?"

Ann clasped Rosie's free hand between her own. "It sounds cold, I know, but you must realize that the tale of your life must be strongly edited. I think we must say that Lady Honora found you living in the care of one of her kindly old aunts."

"I have no kindly aunts," Lady Honora said.

"Why doesn't that surprise me?" Rosie muttered.

Jean was patient with her literal friend. "We'll pretend."

"We do know how to pretend, don't we . . . Rosie?" Sir Danny softened his defiance with a charming smile and offered his arm. Rosie came forward to take it, but Lady Honora stepped in front of her and accepted it as if it were her right.

Ann took it on herself to explain the order of rank to the gaping Rosie. "We go in one at a time in order of the nobility. Lady Honora enters first, forsooth, for she is a dowager duchess and has inherited a barony of her own. Jean goes next. She is a dowager marchioness and the daughter of an earl. You and I are of equal rank, both being daughters of earls. However, I married down. My husband is only a baron, so I am properly known as Lady Ann, the daughter of the earl of Spencer since that is my higher title. Since I'm older than you, and you're unmarried, I will enter next." Observing Rosie's wide-eyed wonder, Ann asked kindly, "Do you have an inquiry?"

Rosie gulped. "How do you remember all that?"

Ann laughed, a tinkling, young sound. "Wait until you go to court. There, you'll have to remember everyone's title and the order of precedence."

"You're going to frighten her away, Ann." Tony's warm voice broke Rosie's horrified trance, and he swung her around with his hand on her waist. "Let me see you."

See her? See him. See all of him, in an elegant black velvet outfit with lace at the neck and lace at the sleeves and red-thread embroidery and a small stiff ruff. Such an outfit would have worn a lesser man, but Tony wore the outfit. Maybe because she remembered how he looked this afternoon—proud and naked.

What did he think of her? She stood still, shoulders back, telling herself that his regard in no way differed from the regard of an audience. If anything, it should be easier to accept with equanimity. But somehow, Tony's regard felt different than the regard of an audience. Her skin was too clean—dry, bare, unprepared to shed its camouflage of dirt and reveal itself. Or perhaps it wasn't her skin, but her spirit which lay exposed to Tony's observation and awaiting his verdict.

But when his verdict came, it was no eloquent soliloquy, but a breathlessly simple, "You're fine as a new-minted fivepence piece."

Rosie gathered comfort from the thought that he failed to realize how he disarmed her. He had the dazed appearance of a man drunk on good fortune and insensate to nuances. She replied with the same simplicity. "Aye. I always thought I made a good-looking woman." Prosaically she tweaked her skirt and made her first bid for freedom. "But I don't intend to dress like a woman all the time."

Ann cried, "But you must! You must. Why not?"

Her high-pitched dismay seemed to knock Tony from his trance, and he gathered his wit with a speed that boded ill for Rosie. "Didn't you have the clothes she was wearing burned, Annie?"

"Oh." Ann laid one hand on her chest, sighing as if her heart tried to escape through the stomacher's ivory cross-bracing. "Burned them. That's true. We burned them. You'll have to wear your skirts, Lady Rosalyn. We burned your nasty actor clothes."

Unable to resist Ann's fluttering goodwill, Rosie begged, "Please, call me Rosie, or at least Rosalyn."

"Oh, my dear." Ann petted Rosie's head, even though that head was taller than her own. "I would be honored, but we must stick with Rosalyn. It's a proper name for a lady of your stature. You call me Sister Ann, even though I suppose you're not going to be my sister."

She looked troubled, but Rosie patted her back in return.

"Why isn't she going to be your sister?" Tony inquired.

"Because Jean and Lady Honora have decided she'll have to wed someone else."

"I have decided she'll wed me." Tony bent down until he was at eye level with Ann. "And who do you think will win?"

"You?" Ann pointed at him. "Or Lady Honora?"

She pointed toward the dining room, then pointed at him, then pointed toward the dining room.

She might have gone on forever, but Rosie took Ann's outstretched index finger and closed it into her palm. "Don't fret about it. No one's counted me yet."

Tony grinned. "I'll get you on my side, then there'll be no stopping us."

Ann squeaked like a mouse. "I don't want to be around when that happens."

"It's not likely to occur." Rosie threw out the challenge casually, hoping Tony took heed.

He bowed his head, according her the respect of a worthy opponent, but if he was worried, he hid it well.

"You smell clean." He sniffed ostentatiously. "I find a clean body under a gown of silk to be a mighty aphrodisiac."

Rosie sniffed right back at him. "If there's a trunk upstairs with ladies' clothing from Lord Sadler's era, I'm sure there's also a trunk with gentlemen's clothing. If the ladies' clothes are mine, so are the gentlemen's, so I'll have no trouble changing back."

Tony openly admired her good sense, then mused, "I wonder what Queen Elizabeth will think when you bow to her, dressed in bean-filled canions and a doublet, and present her the petition for the return of the Sadler estate. I think she'll be amazed, don't you, sister?"

Ann's mouth moved, but no words came out. And if Ann was this agitated, Rosie could imagine the queen's shock. Defiant, she said, "I'll dress like a woman when I present the petition."

But she could almost hear Tony's retort, and he didn't say a word. He just thought very loudly.

To claim Odyssey Manor, she needed the training Lady Honora, Jean, and Ann offered, and they wouldn't give it to a woman dressed like a man.

"Oh dear." Ann wrung her hands. "Oh, dear, this won't do."

"Go in and have a seat." Tony guided his sister toward the dining room. "Rosie and I will be there in a moment."

"But I need to explain to her—"

Tony gave Ann a little push. "*I'll* explain."

"Oh." Ann glanced at him doubtfully, then brightened. "Oh! You'll explain to her."

"Aye."

"Listen to Tony, dear." Ann spoke over her shoulder as she moved into the dining room. "Tony always knows best."

Ann's blind faith in Tony's persuasive abilities irked Rosie almost more than Tony's smug assurance, and she crossed her arms over her chest. "I'm listening."

Moving to the doors, Tony flung them open and moved onto the terrace. The darkness outside was absolute, flowing in on the breeze and almost smothering the candles in the gallery.

So little light. So much darkness.

"Come out," Tony called. "I won't let it get you."

He knew how she hated the dark, but he challenged her with his tone, his words, his action, and she wanted to be and do everything better than Tony. After all, the true heir wouldn't be afraid of anything.

On the other hand, the true heir needed to learn the correct way to behave, and her instructors remained in the dining room. On the other hand, if she left Tony by himself, he might think she shied away from him because of his seductive ability. On the other hand . . . taking a breath, she stepped across the threshold onto the terrace.

Darkness surrounded her like a blanket, blotting thought from her brain.

"I'm over here."

Tony's voice guided her to the corner on her left, and she inched forward, hands outstretched. She didn't want to run into the benches and tables placed to take advantage of the sunshine, when the blessed sun was shining.

"I would be honored by your courage." Tony sounded ironic. "But I know my sisters can be over-whelming, and Lady Honora is . . . Lady Honora."

Rosie's eyes began to adjust to the dark. The light from the windows illuminated the obstacles in her path, and Tony revealed himself to her by blocking the light of the stars.

"Fighting the dark with me has to be more amusing than learning proper table ceremony."

"Aye, you're right." She reached his side without incident, and panted as if she'd traversed a great distance. Her stomacher must cut her too tight. Her heels must be too high. She must be too tense, waiting for Tony to confront her as she dreaded.

But he said nothing. He was nothing but a form beside her. He looked out over the estate, and she looked, too, trying to see what he saw.

There was nothing. Just the dim outlines of the land as it rolled away to the horizon, and then the great, black sky alive with strings of stars that sparkled like Queen Elizabeth's jewels.

"Look out there." Tony whispered as if they were in church. "'Tis the prettiest spot in all England."

"Aye." Aye, it was. It was a dreamscape unlike any other she had imagined, with mists hiding in the hollows and great oaks whispering to the stars.

"Some nights I come out here by myself and just sit. I can almost hear the grass and crops drawing strength from the soil. Some days I come out and each ripple of ground sings with beauty and a sense of timelessness."

His arm slipped around her waist, and she stiffened. Would he start to seduce her now? "Can you hear it?"

"I think so." She heard a siren singing, and while the voice was Tony's, the lyrics and the long-forgotten melody enticed her.

"The land has been here forever, basking beneath the sun and reveling in the rain. To own it is to possess a piece of eternity."

She breathed the night air and her nerves burned with more anticipation than she ever experienced when she stepped on the stage. She, who had never owned anything, who didn't even believe in her claim to this patrimony, reached out and embraced the land.

The hand at her waist tightened. "You want it, don't you?"

She put her claws into his flesh until he yelped and jerked back. "It's mine."

His teeth flashed in the shadows of his face. "It's *mine*, and if you want it, you'll have to marry me to get your part."

Seduction. She'd been worried that he would seduce her body. But no. He'd seduced her senses, exposing the needs she'd hidden even from herself. Naturally, she'd laid claim to Odyssey Manor, but she hadn't craved it, lusted after it, coveted it. Now she did.

The man was clever. Cleverer than she'd ever imagined. She had better never forget it, and she had better discover a way to combat it.

So she kissed him.

As she mashed her lips onto his, she tasted his astonishment, then his amusement. Pulling back, she studied the situation, made corrections to the tilt of their faces and the pressure of their lips, and tried again.

This time she seemed to have got it right. His arms closed around her when she nibbled at his mouth, and he stopped breathing when she slid her tongue between his lips. His knees collapsed; he sat against the wide rail and tried to draw her close. Her bum roll and voluminous petticoats thwarted him, and she allowed herself a moment of triumph.

Seduce her with words, would he? Well, she would seduce him right back. The women in the plays always reduced their men to quivering wrecks of passion, and she wanted to see Tony shaking like a bowl of eel jelly. She wanted him senseless with desire. She wanted him.

"I have to go in now," she said, dismayed when her voice quavered.

"Not yet."

"They'll be wondering—"

"So, let them." Tony blessed his good night vision. Able to see Rosie's face in the dim light of the stars, he realized how her expression vacillated between jubilation and prudence. She hungered for the land, but her craving infuriated her. She wanted him on his knees before her, but she feared the steps that would bring him down. Her passions confused her, and he planned to utilize that confusion.

"You fit at Odyssey Manor because you were born here." He lifted her off her feet, swung her around, and placed her on the rail where he had been sitting. "You fit in my arms because you were born for this."

She struggled when he leaned her out into thin air, but he whispered, "Be careful. I don't want to go over the edge with you." She froze, and he kissed her throat and smiled. "The shrubs would break our fall, but I like it better up here where we can kiss. Don't you?"

Frustration rippled through her. He'd effectively neutralized her gutter combat skills, and he chuckled when she snapped, "I do prefer the terrace to a nasty fall, so put me back on the terrace."

"Your passion holds me in thrall," he answered, and kissed her.

God, she kissed him as if she'd invented kissing at the beginning of time. It proved his theory; that when she fought the force that drew him to her, it retaliated by sucking her into the whirlpool. The stars whipped around them in ever tighter circles; his heart beat in ever faster rhythms.

"Rosie." He tried to touch her all over, but her stiff stomacher inhibited his exploration. "Rosie," he groaned in exasperation, and started grabbing great handfuls of skirt and petticoats.

"What are you doing?" she demanded.

"Trying to get under your skirts."

For some reason, his honesty aggravated her, and when he freed her legs she used the opportunity to kick him in the kneecap. He cursed and grabbed her ankle. "I've never had to fight a woman for her favors."

Sarcastically, she said, "I'm fretting about the damage to your male pride."

He paused. His pride? What about her distress? He didn't lie when he said he'd never had to fight a woman, because he'd always been the one in control. He'd prided himself on his suave protestations of devotion, his smooth methods of seduction. He'd certainly never had to hang a woman over a precipice before to gain her cooperation, nor had he ever induced a woman to violence.

What was Rosie doing to his discipline?

Swinging her off the rail, he set her on her feet. *Suave,* he told himself. *Remember your discipline. She longs for romance, just like any other girl, and perhaps deserves it more.* "My apologies, Lady Rosalyn."

He tried to arrange her skirts, but she knocked him on the shoulder. "Leave me alone."

"I can't." *Suave,* he thought. *Romance.* Dropping onto one knee, he placed a hand over his heart. "Your face, your body, your sweet countenance move me to such ardor I'm no longer in control. I live for a smile, sigh for a glance, dream of your—"

"I've heard passion done better by legions of actors," she said impatiently, "and you've made your ambitions clear to one and all. I heard it from every servant on your estate. You want to take a noble, wealthy virgin to wife, and I've destroyed your plans."

"How so? You are noble, you are wealthy." He caught her hand when she tried to back away from his query. "Are you not a virgin?"

"What difference does it make?" She tugged at her hand. "You wish nothing more from me than a clear title to this estate."

"Have you convinced yourself of that?" Touching the new rings that decorated her long fingers, he said, "Do you think this finery makes any difference to me and you? We are the same people when stripped of our garments."

"I have to go in."

The truth alarmed her, he was pleased to see, because she didn't want to discuss it. "Do you dismiss my passion before I even knew your name? Do you remember the vows I made that day before I saw you on the stage? I begged to know your father's name. I told you we would wed."

She glanced longingly at the doors that led to the gallery. "Nay!"

He pressed his suit. "I was going to sneak into your chamber and teach you the ways of passion."

"You were furious when Sir Danny presented me as the heir," she answered, sure of herself with this, at least.

"I am still furious." Rising, he retained her hand. "I am, as you so gently reminded me, a bastard. One hundred men have insulted me, and one hundred men have I taught respect with my fists and the sharp tip of my sword. When I wed you, it will start again. The sly insinuations, the sidelong glances, the outright slander."

"I don't understand."

She didn't, either. He could see her confusion, and he clarified the situation as calmly as he could. "The gossips will say this estate is not mine, but my wife's, and that I live on your charity."

She shifted away from him as if he menaced her. "You won this estate through your own efforts, so you should take comfort in what is true."

"Truth does not always matter." The injustice of it infuriated him, as it had always infuriated him. "For often falsehoods are more entertaining."

"Then you should deny me my"—she gulped—"heritage."

"It is your heritage. You are the heiress. No matter how much I wish to doubt it, I know you are the heiress, and I live by the truth." He stepped close and smiled into her leery face. "So you see, if I owe you the right to this estate, then you owe me what I desire."

"I owe you nothing."

"You owe me yourself."

She picked up her skirts and whirled to run, and he caught her by the waist and lifted her high. She kicked and shrieked; he laughed and strode toward the door. To hell with control. To hell with romance. To hell with everything except Tony and Rosie, naked on a bed until the next full moon.

Then he heard the twang of a bow, and dived for the floor.

12

My good will is great, though the gift small.
—PERICLES, II, iv, 21

It was a simple arrow, made of a sharpened
ash shaft and a goose feather flight. Every man in
England knew how to make one. But who had made
this one?

Tony stood at the window of his study and twirled
the arrow in the morning sun. This arrow couldn't have
killed anybody. He corrected himself. Probably couldn't
have killed anybody. For the most part an arrow needed
a steel tip to embed itself deep into its victim. So why
fire this arrow?

Last night he'd been frantic with fear that Rosie had
been hit. She'd assured him she was fine, but he'd
wanted to strip her down and examine every inch of
her to assure himself of her good health.

Now he looked at her, seated before his desk in a

modest gown. She had allowed her three mentors to dress her hair, and had come when he summoned her with an obedience that might have boded well for their future, except he knew the reason for her compliance. She wanted answers, and had found none last night.

No answers last night, and none this morning.

Moving to the door, he inspected the latch. It was closed firmly, and he shot the bolt into place. He wanted no repeat of the previous day's "accidental" eavesdropping. "I hope you understood when I asked that you tell no one of the incident last night. I thought it best to keep it between ourselves. We don't want to deal with a panic."

Her eyes glinted with dour humor. "You mean—more panic than my own?"

Panicked? Aye, she'd been panicked, but not at first. First she'd been furious, demanding what madness had seized him, and why he'd thrown her—and himself—to the ground. Then, when he'd shown her the arrow, she'd acted coolly, urging him inside when he would have gone beating the bushes for a man with a weapon. Only when they were safe had she panicked. Her instinct for survival explained more about her upbringing than she would have liked, if she had realized. But she didn't. She thought everyone had experienced life-threatening situations and reacted accordingly. It infuriated him to think of Rosie in danger, yet at the same time he admired her poise. "Who taught you to fight?"

Off-balance by his question, she stammered. "What?"

"You're handy with your fists, good with a kick. Who taught you?"

"Sir Danny, mostly. He feared I'd get into a scuffle with the other . . . boys, and he thought I'd best know how to give them better than I got." She lifted her chin, and her voice grew cold. "Sometimes the fair people of the town would refuse to pay us and, as an added fillip, would try to beat us, kill us, and steal our horses." Without inflection, she said, "If *I'd* shot that arrow, you'd be dead."

He leaned against the door and ruffled the feathers of the flight. "You're the only one I know for sure didn't shoot it."

"What do you mean?"

She very carefully kept expression off of her face, but he surmised she didn't like the trend of his thoughts. He didn't like it, either, but together he and Rosie had to discover the source of this threat. Together. If he had planned it, he couldn't have come up with a better scheme to force them to remain together. "We were out on the terrace, taking our pleasure, for, shall we say, an hour? Then we were out on the terrace, crawling around, trying to stay alive for another few minutes." He grinned at his comrade-in-terror. "It only seemed like another hour, I'm sure. It couldn't have been more than five minutes."

She grinned back at him, as grimly amused by their alarm as he. "Five minutes."

"We limped upstairs as fast as we could, avoiding the dining room and every servant, and went into the master's antechamber, where we recovered ourselves and checked for injuries. Then you went to your bed-chamber and locked yourself in, and I went downstairs to make your excuses to our guests."

She leaned forward. "And?"

"And every one of them had left the room at one time or another."

He watched her as she followed his logic. The dull gold of her plain dress brought out the highlights in her hair and reflected the freshness of her complexion and the glow of her amber eyes. Whether she liked it or not, she was all woman.

Not the kind of woman he'd known before, though. His other marriage prospects would have been worthless consultants in such circumstances. Rosie would face the facts without flinching, help him deduce the scheme, and she'd want to help him deal with the culprit.

She wouldn't leave him to deal with the culprit. He ran his hands through his hair. Therein lay the rub, didn't it? How did he keep Rosie in her womanly place?

"You can't seriously suspect Sir Danny?" she asked.

He countered, "You can't seriously suspect my sisters? And Lady Honora?"

They looked at each other for a long moment, then burst into laughter.

"The thought of Lady Honora skulking through the bushes . . ." Rosie imitated a rigid figure drawing a bow, and he sobered.

"I've seen Lady Honora during a hunt, and she's an expert with the bow." Rosie sobered, too, and he leaned forward. "Don't you see? Every one of them has reasons."

"But who's in danger?"

That *was* the question, and they both knew it. The arrow had struck directly in the place he'd been standing, but without knowing the skill of the bowman, they had no way of knowing at whom he'd been aiming. The dilemma had kept Tony awake through most of the night. Somehow the thought of injury to himself seemed less worrisome than an injury to Rosie. He'd seen her in pain once when she broke her arm; he couldn't bear to see it again.

"You're a popular master. Your servants do whatever you command." Rosie looked at her fingernails. "Could it be that one of your servants or tenants might wish to remove me and my claim on the estate?"

He'd thought of that, too, but he didn't believe it. He could handle Rosie and her claim. Surely everyone knew that. But someone had tried to separate Rosie from him in the crudest way. He suspected the simplest crime of all. The crime of passion. "Are you cursed with some inappropriate suitor?"

She blinked at his brusque query, but she didn't flinch. "Besides you?"

Insolence. She'd almost been killed, and she looked at him through clear, bright eyes and mocked him. Well, she could be insolent, but he could be intimidating. Stalking over to her chair, he stood in front of her, toe to toe, and looked down at her. "A suitor. A lover. Someone who might be jealous enough to take aim at us with a bow and arrow rather than allow you to marry me."

"Is that the best explanation you can think of?" She spoke to his belly rather than acknowledge his height. "That someone was shooting at us out of thwarted love? You flatter me, sir."

So he didn't intimidate her. No surprise. "So you have no suitor?" he insisted.

"How could I have a suitor when until yesterday I was an itinerant actor?" She answered well, but her gaze shifted to the arrow in his hand, and she reached out and removed it from his grasp.

"You're the kind of woman all men love."

"They've been hiding it very well."

Leaning over, he placed his hands on the arms of the chair, trapping her. "It's that Ludovic, isn't it?"

Her start was answer enough, and he remembered the fellow's bold visual claim during the first play Sir Danny's troupe had performed. "I knew it! He challenged me over you before I even knew I would have you."

"You're not having me."

She spoke with conviction, but she answered a man who'd never conceived of defeat. "I'm having you every night in my dreams, and last night I would have had you in truth, but for the arrow." He rejoiced to see her color rise and her breath come more quickly. The stomacher bound her, and he winced when he thought about her breasts mashed against her body. He imagined an expedition to liberate them, and thought of Rosie's gratitude for his concern. She'd cup one for him, and he'd place his mouth on it and suckle until she—

Her hand grabbed his hair and jerked his head up. "Mayhap you've made someone angry enough to kill you." Lifting the arrow in her fist, she aimed it at his heart. "From what you said last night and the way you're acting today, it's possible. More than possible—probable."

He grinned at her threatened violence, and something in him eased. Her mind might be convinced that he wouldn't have her, but her body answered his in perfect accord. "My enemies aren't likely to use an untipped arrow to assassinate me."

"Ah. You have a higher class of assassins." She nodded knowingly and loosened her grip on his hair. "Perhaps I should ask if you have suitors—and of course you do. Mayhap it is not a man who shoots so well, but one of your ladies."

"None of the ladies I know would shoot an arrow at me."

"All of the ladies I know would."

He glanced again at her flushed chest, then into her furious face. "Not after they got to know me." Pulling up a short stool, again directly in front of her, he sat. With his head lower than hers, she would be less threatened. That, combined with his appeal, would surely win him some answers. "Are you sure your arm wasn't hurt when we hit the floor?"

"It was wrenched a little, that's all." Watching him warily, she lifted the splint within her sling. "'Tis you who should be injured."

"I have bruises up and down my side." He tried to coax a smile from her. "Want to inspect them? I'll let you kiss them into health."

She shook her head.

"You don't know what you're missing."

"And not likely to find out."

They stared at each other, then he reached out and smoothed his thumb across her lower lip. "I could kiss you and show you how it's done."

"Ludovic wouldn't have missed."

As a distraction, it worked well. The pleasure in him curdled, and he let his hand drop away.

"He was a soldier on the Continent, and he's the reason we escaped those places where they wanted to rob and murder us. When he fights, he makes no mistakes." She was quite earnest, and clearly relieved that she'd diverted him.

But he could divert her, too. "I have a present for you." He stood and walked to his desk, and she stood, too, moving away from the chair and into the middle of the room, where he had no chance of trapping her.

Foolish woman! She stood no chance against his wiles.

He kept his gaze trained on her, and fumbled for the drawer. The handgrip he sought eluded him, hidden in the intricate carvings of the desk. He had to look before he found the handle, then pulled the drawer out and held up his gift. "A purse."

She looked less than impressed. "A purse?"

Two round pieces of tough tapestry material were sewn together. A sturdy string looped through holes at the top and formed one long strap. "Here." He advanced on her. "Take it."

She smiled politely. "I appreciate your kindness in all things, but I have one." She did indeed, a large and grubby bag that ill matched her splendid attire.

He pressed his more elegant purse into her hand and let go, then grinned when she almost dropped it.

Astonished, she weighed it in her hand. "What's in here?"

"A chunk of marble."

"What do you want me to do with it?"

"Keep it with you at all times."

"Keep it with me?" She looked at him as if he were crazed. "It must weigh twenty stone!"

"You exaggerate. It doesn't weigh more than ten." Reaching out, he ran his palm up the muscle in her arm. "It's one-half stone, and it'll build up your strength."

"What am I supposed to do with this"—she disparaged him with her tone—"purse?"

"If you're threatened, you swing it." He moved behind her so his chest was against her back, then took her wrist and pivoted in a circle.

The purse whipped around, a weapon of ballast, and she understood his purpose without further explanation.

Stepping back, he watched as she took a few practice swings. He'd added to his lady's arsenal, and that gave him a sense of security. With her gifts, she'd not be taken from him by force. But still she remained impassive in the face of his beguilement, and his chagrin knew no bounds. There had to be a way to keep her at his side, at least until her barriers had failed her and she languished at his feet like a proper woman. Baiting the trap with a new tidbit, he suggested, "You're going to be a very rich woman when we marry."

The purse wavered. "I'll be very rich when Her Majesty awards me the estates," she corrected, but two words had caught her attention. "*Very* rich?"

He could have rubbed his hands in glee at the success of his ploy. "Aye. Have you thought what you will do with so much money?"

"I had a strawberry once." Her eyes widened. "Will I be able to afford strawberries?"

"Even in December."

She snorted and in her gutter-girl accent, said, "Ye're chaffin' me."

"Some very clever farmers grow strawberries within doors, with windows all around, and grow them all year long."

Her lips parted, her eyes widened; she looked the picture of a starving waif. "Sir Danny used to buy me honey cakes."

"I'll have the cook make them tonight."

She touched her lower lip with her tongue. "What about . . . ?" She concentrated, but her imagination failed her.

"Almond milk? Stuffed chicken with spiced apples and oatmeal? Oranges? Carp?"

That caught her fancy. "*Fresh* carp?"

His sense of triumph faded beneath her awe and amazement. She adored Sir Danny, and he'd done what he could for her, but there had been lean times. She had gone hungry. Had she choked down day-old fish or eaten beggar's scraps? His own stomach cramped at the thought, and he wanted to grant her every wish. "Fresh carp, certainly, and prepared any way you like."

"Oh." She thrust out her right hand, but her purse was still in it. Laughing at herself, she traded it to the other hand. Snatching his hand, she lifted it to her lips and kissed it. "I hadn't imagined such bounty. I'll be fat as a smokehouse wife in a year!"

His fingers tightened, and she looked up at him: engaging, happy, completely unselfconscious, and kissing him spontaneously. But it was the kind of kiss a servant gave her master, and he brought her hand back to his mouth and returned the salute in reverent tribute. Taking the marble-laden purse, he tied it to her belt, then said, "Come."

"Where?"

He tucked her hand into the crook of his arm. "To the kitchen."

He pulled her along so quickly she was puffing when she reached the lower regions. "Mistress Child?" he called. "I've brought your new mistress to meet you."

A tall, rawboned cook turned from the fire where she supervised the roasting of a joint, and in unison she and her dozen assistants dropped curtsies, bobbing like boats on the waves.

"It's taken ye long enough, ye rascal." Mistress Child bustled forward, welcoming Tony and Rosie with floury, outstretched hands. Catching sight of her fingers, she chuckled deeply and wiped them on her voluminous apron, then clasped Rosie's hand and gave her the salute which Rosie had just given Tony. "'Tis honored I am, m'lady."

"I'm a rascal, and she's m'lady?" Tony teased. "Have you no respect for me?"

"Great respect." Mistress Child poked him in the ribs with her elbow. "I have great respect fer any man who eats as hearty a meal as yerself. M'lady," she cooed, urging Rosie toward a stool, "won't ye sit an' visit a bit?"

"She wants more than that, mistress," Tony said as Rosie wondered at his intention. "She wants to know what you've prepared for dinner."

"Takin' o'er yer duties early, are ye?" Mistress Child winked and smiled at Rosie. "Good thing, too. Young Sir Anthony needs a firm hand on th' reins or he'll be riding roughshod o'er ye."

Tony looked annoyed, although Rosie didn't understand why. "I'm not a horse," he said.

Mistress Child paid him no attention. "We're going t' start wi' clear oxtail soup. Do ye like that, m'lady?"

Embarrassed, Rosie whispered, "I don't know."

"Ye don't know?" Mistress Child looked affronted. "Ye mean ye don't know if my soup measures up? Well, let me get ye a bowl, an' ye'll tell me 'tis th' best ye've ever had."

Appalled, Rosie said, "Nay, 'tis not what I meant at all. I meant"—Mistress Child thrust a full bowl and a silver spoon into Rosie's hands—"I've never had—" The steam rising above the bowl distracted Rosie. Bits of orange carrots and clear onions floated in a rich brown broth dotted with slivers of meat. The mild scent of garlic mingled with the richer scent of peppercorns and cloves, spices Rosie had only dreamed of tasting. Dipping her spoon in, she watched as the broth flowed into the shiny curve, filling and changing it from an expensive ornament to a useful utensil. She sipped the broth and almost fainted from joy. "It's a beautiful spoon," she said, "but it doesn't do justice to the soup."

All the workers in the kitchen let out all their breaths at once, just as if they'd been holding them, waiting for Rosie's verdict. Before Rosie could lift the spoon again, Mistress Child whisked the bowl away.

"Wait!" Rosie protested.

"Get her th' deviled kidneys," Mistress Child ordered, and the kitchen sprang into action. "Th' marrow toast, an' th' cold steak pie."

Before Rosie could speak again, a small platter covered with delicacies was presented to her. Ecstatic, she tasted each one. A mug of ale appeared at her elbow, and she drank it in one long swallow. She'd never dreamed of such heaven—sitting, eating her fill, drinking as much as she wanted, breathing wonderful aromas, surrounded by people who wanted to please her. It was worth taking that torturous bath for this. She paid no attention to Tony as he spoke to Mistress Child; she simply ate as she had learned to—quickly, before someone took it away.

Another plate appeared before her nose. Tony waved it, crooning, "Apple pie and cheese."

She gave up the empty plate to Mistress Child and reached for the new delights, but Tony held it out of reach. "I'll feed you. If you keep eating like that, you'll be ill."

"Didn't ye break yer fast this morn, m'lady?" Mistress Child looked concerned.

"Aye, I did, and wonderful it was." Closing her eyes, Rosie recited, "Grilled sausage, kippers, spiced chestnut cream, and dropped eggs. See?" She opened her eyes and rummaged in her big old bag, then held up filled, turnover-shaped crusts dusted with the previous contents of the sack. "I saved some of the pork pasties for later."

Scandalized, everyone gasped, and Rosie realized she'd made a huge blunder. But before she could do more than blush, Tony broke the crust of the pie and the scent of cinnamon and honey steamed out.

"Eat this," he whispered, "and know you'll never lack again while I am living." With his fingers, he fed her the first bites.

"Eh, Sir Tony." Mistress Child tucked her hands under her apron. "Ye aren't usually so willing t' share yer apple pie."

Tony joked, "It's not often I get to see such a look of ecstasy on a woman's face."

The kitchen crew laughed, but Rosie didn't understand and didn't care. Tony's fingers caressed her lips as he fed her warm pie and chunks of strong yellow cheese. He didn't seem worried about the apple juice that ran toward his wrist or the bits of crust that clung to his skin. When it got too sloppy, he simply held his hand to her mouth, and she licked it.

He trembled and she looked up; he looked back, his gaze hot. "Someday, I'll let you do that to me when we're alone," he murmured. "But I'll wait until I've satisfied your voracious appetite." He smiled whimsically. "I'd hate to have you bite."

That she understood. She pushed the plate away, careful not to touch his skin, but it was too late. She knew what he wanted, and if she weren't careful, he would make her want it, too. Mistress Child offered another mug of ale, and Rosie accepted it, sipping it this time.

Tony used a finger bowl, then dried his hands with such fastidious care she could think of nothing but those hands on her body. Of course, he watched her the whole time, projecting his thoughts into her mind, arousing previously useless instincts.

Mistress Child brought her a finger bowl, and she wet her shaking hands before drying them on a towel offered by an older maid. The maid curtsied and rushed to introduce herself. "I'm Mary, m'lady, an' on behalf o' th' other servants, may I say how gratified we are t' have ye return, Lady Rosalyn, to Odyssey Manor. 'Course, 'tweren't Odyssey Manor when ye left, but Sadler House, but we're gratified."

"Were you here when Lord Sadler and his . . . when Lord Sadler was here?" Rosie inquired.

That seemed all the encouragement Mary needed, and words bubbled from her. "Aye, there's two o' us maids 'twere here when ye was a child, me in th' kitchen, Martha in th' laundry. We stayed fer a bit after they found yer father's body an' while th' queen was lookin' fer ye, but eventually Hal came back an' closed th' house. Told us 'twould be cheaper t' run, an' he took care o' it all fer a bit, he did, an' how a man could do so much, an' alone, I'll never know."

"Nor I," Rosie said, a little dazed by the flood of language.

"'Twere a few men here working th' stable what worked here before, too, but they scarce saw ye before an' ye know men, they're not th' least mawkish. Only glad t' get th' work back when Sir Anthony got th' estate, an' we're all glad ye'll wed him so we'll not be turned off again. I always say life's hard enough without losing th' income from a position like this."

Mary drew breath to speak again, but Mistress Child bumped her out of the way with a swift thrust of the hip. "Ye'll talk th' mistress t' death," she chided Mary.

Not at all offended, Mary beamed. "Aye, it's a talker, I am, an' th' poor lass needs another wee pie t' help her through th' day."

"Nay!" Rosie rubbed her belly. "My spirit is willing, but my stomacher won't allow it."

Again everyone in the kitchen laughed, startling Rosie. But, she observed, it was not necessarily her words which tickled them so much as her own nervous avoidance of Tony's devotion. Love sent some precious instance of itself after the thing it loved, Uncle Will claimed, and Rosie suspected that it also fascinated any stray onlookers.

She wanted to shout that she wouldn't marry this man, but to knock those fond and knowing smiles from the servants' faces seemed a cruelty. Instead she asked, "Mistress Child, were you here before?"

"Alas, I wasn't here when you were a lass," Mistress

Child said. "Sir Anthony stole me from another household."

"Stole you?" Was Mistress Child confessing Tony's dishonesty? "What do you mean, stole you?"

"She was the best cook in London," Tony said. "And I lured her to me with my charm and good looks."

"An' yer money." Mistress Child crushed his pretensions, but she did it with a smile. "Still, I've been happier here than I ever was wi' Lord Bothey."

"I'm better than Lord Bothey?" Tony's voice carried tones of sarcasm. "Flattery like that will turn my head."

Rosie hated it that she liked him. He was almost as charming as he claimed he was. What would she do if he were as good a lover as he claimed he was?

"I've decided what I'm going to do with my wealth. I'm going to be the patron to an acting troupe." Her own words surprised her, coming out of the confusion in her mind, but they surprised everyone else more. But somehow, the phrase—patron to an acting troupe— firmed a resolution she didn't know she'd made. "When I get my money, I mean. I'm going to be like the earl of Southampton or the chamberlain. I'll sponsor Sir Danny's troupe, and Sir Danny can act in London until he's so famous he'll never have to worry about money again."

"That's wonderful." Tony seated himself on a stool opposite her, and lowered his voice to a murmur. As Tony and Rosie put their heads together, Mistress Child gestured and the kitchen help went back to work. They were left in relative privacy, although the servants cast fond glances in their direction. "It'll fulfill Sir Danny's dreams."

"Oh, he didn't really think I'd do it. He just used that to bribe me into accepting"—she gestured—"this."

"Bribe you into accepting . . . ?"

"This. You." She gestured again. "This."

He smiled. "Ah. This." He seemed to meditate. "And you've come to accept this?"

"Accept?" That seemed like a permanent word, and she wanted to avoid permanence. At the same time, she could imagine bringing the world the expertise of Sir Danny's acting revealed by the genius of Uncle Will's plays. "Well, I'm going to be Sir Danny's troupe patron."

"Will you pick out the plays for them?"

He sounded so genial, and he still smiled, but something about him put her on her guard. "I will."

"Can you read?"

"What?"

"Can you read? Many plays are printed. It would greatly help you if you could read."

How true. How logical. How humiliating that he realized she knew less than the youngest yeoman's child. "I can't read." She lifted her child mutinously. "And I'm too old to go to school."

Tony stroked his chin. "True, but mayhap there's another way."

Rosie brightened. "If I were in London, Uncle Will could teach me."

Tony frowned. "Uncle Will?"

"William Shakespeare. He's an actor and playwright," she said, proud of her connection to such a famous man. "A close friend of mine."

"I'm not familiar with him." Tony dismissed William Shakespeare with a wave of his hand. "Nay, I was thinking of teaching you myself."

Himself? Tony wanted to teach her himself? She had thought herself humiliated because he knew she couldn't read. How much more humiliated would she be when he saw how truly ignorant she was?

"Nay."

"You don't want to learn to read?"

"I'll find someone else to teach me."

"Someone else?" He'd kept his temper through this whole, painful day, through all the provocation and all the suspicion, but this was too much. Standing, he pulled her up. "There'll never be someone else for you. Don't you understand yet? You're mine."

He saw that she, too, had been keeping her temper through all his provocation—and he *had* been provoking her. He couldn't help it. Nothing bothered him as much as the indifference of his beloved. But while he tried to overpower her when he was provoked, she tried to escape him and run away. In fact . . . he detected the blur of movement, and pain exploded in his ribs. Doubling over, he saw the purse coming again and somersaulted back off the stool.

"Thank you for the gift," she said, and fled the silent kitchen as he struggled to his feet.

Holding his side, he looked at the shocked and staring kitchen crew, then the place where Rosie had sat. "You're welcome."

13

I had rather have a fool to make me merry than experience to make me sad.

—As You Like It, IV, i, 25

A sweet piping trill from a fife announced Rosie's return to the open area ringed by the troupe's wagons, and she faltered in her stride. The jester had seen her, and she would have to run the gauntlet of his mockery before she could complete her mission.

"Behold, 'tis the lady of Odyssey Manor, queen of all she surveys and mistress of Sir Tony Rycliffe. But hark!" Cedric Lambeth's pliable features achieved an expression of astonishment, and he projected his voice. "Did not yon sun of yesterday shine upon a lad where now the lady of Odyssey Manor stands?"

"Ah, rein your tongue, Cedric." Rosie wasn't in the mood to jest. She'd just bashed Tony with a rock, just refused to learn to read, denying a secret desire, and now she was on an errand that, if it were discovered, would destroy any trust between her and Tony and, mayhap, between her and Sir Danny. But what were her choices?

"Aye, m'lady." Cedric bowed so low his knuckles dragged on the grass. "Whatever you say, m'lady." Then, braying like a donkey, he yelled, "Rosie's back! Rosie's here. Come an' take your pokes at Lady Rosalyn, the actors' patron saint."

Actors leaped out of their wagons, popped up from their conversations, all responding to the chance to roast Rosie over the coals of their insolence. They surrounded her, jostling each other, staring and pointing as if they were an audience expecting a performance.

Cedric pranced around her like a mischievous elf. "Lady Rosalyn, tell us true. What magic potion did you swallow to effect this transformation? 'Twas only yesterday we saw Rosencrantz the man leave on Sir Danny's arm, but Rosencrantz returns not. The heavens blasted Rosencrantz with displeasure, and knocked off the best part of him—that part which made him a man."

The actors groaned in unison, holding their crotches as if they were so wounded.

"The heavens improved me, then," Rosie snapped.

The actors booed.

"Nay, not so. For if the heavens have blasted your best part, then might the heavens not also have endowed you with"—Cedric stood on tiptoe and tried, with elaborate effort, to peek down her bodice—"those parts which cause a man to behave like—"

"A jackass?" Rosie widened her eyes when the actors laughed.

Cedric drew himself up. "A man needs no excuse to behave like a jackass."

The actors groaned, and Rosie laughed, relaxing for

the moment. Here she felt at home. The actors laughed, too, then began to shout, each trying to top the other in wit. A pang of grief struck Rosie as she looked around at the smiling faces.

She'd miss Cedric with his everlasting jests. She'd miss John Barnstaple, their romantic lead and a fellow accorded respect for his sound head and his quick fists. She'd miss Stuart and Francis and George and Nick. She'd even miss Alleyn Brewer, her chief rival for the feminine roles.

The distance between a manor house and a gypsy wagon was the greatest distance in the world, and if she took the estate, as she desired, she would never be one with these men again. She'd never be onstage again. She'd never move an audience to laughter or tears. Another dream denied. Another hope destroyed.

Events were sweeping her away as a stream in flood sweeps away a pitiful twig, and she grappled for footing and handhold.

Then she found it. Arms crossed over his chest, Ludovic watched her from the fringe of the group. 'Twas he she'd sought when she came out here, and she locked eyes with him, then looked toward the garden.

He understood immediately. Feigning the surliness which was so much a part of his personality, he grunted and stomped away as if disgusted by the frolic.

She waited until he was out of sight, then cried to the thespians, "I will share my wealth and my good fortune with you as you have shared your poverty and hardship with me." They chuckled and nudged each other, and she knew they didn't care about her true identity. To them, she was only a comrade who'd fallen into good fortune, and they wished her well. Never again, she knew, would she be accepted so indiscriminately. Her voice faltered and her wit failed. "If ever you have need, call on me. If ever I can help, call on me. I would that you should know me not as woman, nor as man, but as friend. A friend to all of you for all your lives."

No one knew how to reply to her sudden vow of devotion, and the men shuffled their feet and cleared their throats. Alleyn, always sentimental, honked his nose. Then Cedric stepped up to her, and bowed with genuine gallantry. "You offer your friendship now that you are rich, but we had it before, when you did indeed share our poverty, and never have you withdrawn it. 'Tis a treasure which we hold dear, and the only treasure we can return in full. We are your friends, one and all, and should you ever have need of us, come you at once, and we will do all within our power to ease and assist you."

Tears started to her eyes and one escaped to trickle down her cheek.

Incorrigible Cedric grimaced, rubbed his eyes with his fists, and broke into loud boo-hoos. "If I had woke one morning to find myself stripped of my manhood, I would cry also. If I woke one morning and found myself a lady, no longer able to travel the road, I would cry also. If I woke one morning to find myself rich as Croesus"—he paused with swelled breast, then shouted—"I would bid my belly ruffian farewell!" Leaping into the air, he proceeded to tumble in an excess of jubilation.

The actors cheered as he finished and bowed. Clapping her dear old friends on the back, speaking to them one by one, Rosie freed herself from the group. Casually, she strolled toward the garden, stepped onto the flat stone walk, and found her good wrist caught in Ludovic's huge fist.

"This way," he said, and led her deeper into the shrubs. When the trees formed a shadowy disguise and the hedge wrapped them around, he stopped. He looked down at her with an odd expression, anguish and anger mixed in equal parts. "You wished to speak to me . . . Lady Rosalyn?"

The title was insult on his lips, and she faltered before she began. How foolish to be caught in this hidden place with this half-man, half-brute. She'd known him for seven years, yet she knew him not at all. She suspected he'd been guilty of unspeakable crimes. On nights when phantasms had kept her awake, she'd seen him pacing the dark roads as if to escape something, and that something was himself. But he'd been ever kind to her. He'd often saved her from exposure and he'd frequently saved her life. She couldn't condemn a man for what she guessed when his deeds had proved his gallantry.

"Ludovic, there's trouble, and I have to warn you. Someone shot an arrow at us last night while we were on the terrace."

His cold eyes flickered. "On the terrace. Before dinner. You and Sir Anthony Rycliffe were talking, then he held you over the rail and kissed you."

His knowledge chilled her. How came he by it? Had he crouched in the bushes and watched and listened? Had he held the bow and waited for the perfect moment to shoot?

"Tony." Ludovic spit on the ground. "Your betrothed. An arrow shot at him doesn't surprise me. No doubt someone wishes to kill him."

"That's what he thinks." She almost didn't say it, but she forced herself. "And he thinks it's you."

Ludovic stared at her, and his gaze heated until it singed her like a flame. "He's right."

Od's bodkin. She'd misjudged Ludovic. Was he going to kill her first?

"I would love to kill the man who would wed you. But if I had tried to kill your handsome Tony last night, he would now be dead."

She released her breath in a rush and realized she'd been holding it. "That's what I told him." She laughed, a high, mortifying giggle. "I told him that if you had tried to kill him, you'd have done it. Ludovic, I said, was no ordinary man, but a warrior who had much experience in killing men." Damn, what had made her say *that?*

"Your Tony has experience in killing men, too," Ludovic said flatly. "Never doubt that. He has much blood on his hands, even though it's not—" He looked down at his huge paws.

The silence lengthened, and she rushed to fill the void. "I just wanted to tell you so you wouldn't do anything or be anywhere that might cause us grief."

"Us?"

"Sir Danny and I and the other actors. We're all fond of you."

"Especially you?"

Her heart began a heavy pounding. She didn't like the way he stared at her, the way his breath rasped in his throat, the masculine threat he projected. "Me and Sir Danny and Cedric and—"

"You?" he insisted, pointing his stubby finger right between her eyes. "You?"

The birds twittered, laughing at the stupid woman who put herself in such a precarious position. She had to reply to his question. She had to make herself very, very clear.

But she didn't want to. She didn't want to hurt him, and she didn't want him to hurt her. Picking her words carefully, she said, "I am very fond of you, but even if I had never come to this place, even if I had never heard this tale of the lost heir, and even if I had no hope of any existence beyond the actor's life, I would still not be more than fond of you." He stared, his mouth dropped open, his agony throbbing between them. She felt sick to her stomach, like she'd just taken a stick and wounded a dumb badger, and now waited for the badger to return the attack. Ludovic didn't move, and she finally asked, "Do you understand?"

His roar, when it came, terrified her. He spun in a circle, his arms outstretched. He threshed the branches clean of their leaves. He struck at an oak trunk so hard acorns rained down on her head. He galloped in a big circle like a horse out of control. She watched, prepared to run yet afraid that to flee would fire his predatory instincts. When he stood in front of her again, however, she wondered if remaining had signed her death warrant. Her fingers tightened on the weighted purse.

His chest rose and fell. His fists clenched as if he held his fury captive in his hands and planned to release it on her head.

She wanted to tremble, but refused. Wanted to cry, but didn't. Wanted to hit him, but didn't dare. She might be a coward, frightened of pain and death, but she wouldn't show it. Clenching her teeth together so her chin didn't quiver, she vowed not to show it at all.

Ludovic's hands reached out and grabbed her by the hair; her scalp hurt as wisps loosened from her braid, and she reconsidered her bravery. Mayhap a bit of screaming would not be amiss. Maybe she should swing the purse. But he just held her head still and stared into her eyes.

His voice was guttural with pain. "Stay close to your Tony."

"What?" Whatever she expected, that wasn't it.

"Stay close to Rycliffe. Stay close and watch him. You'll be safest when you're near him." He pushed her back so hard she stumbled. She protected her arm when she should have been breaking her fall, and landed in a bed of sharp-leafed holly.

She floundered, trying to save her petticoats from a dozen tiny tears, and when she looked up, Ludovic was gone.

She could scarcely believe she had escaped with her life.

She could scarcely believe how guilty she felt.

Ludovic looked and smelled like a creature that lived under a rock, but it didn't mean his emotions counted for naught. She'd hurt him with her rebuff.

Picking herself out of the bushes, she trudged toward the manor. Ludovic seemed sure someone was trying to kill one of them. So should she do as Ludovic suggested and remain close to Tony, not to protect herself, but to protect him?

Forsooth, she would have to find an excuse, and Tony might misinterpret her sudden interest. But she would have to put up with any inconvenience, for if Tony were killed for her sake, she would never forgive herself.

Of course, she'd feel the same about anyone.

Advancing on the terrace, she mounted the steps before she saw Jean watching her, needle poised above an embroidery frame, mouth puckered in disapproval.

Not surprising, Rosie thought. Jean hadn't unpuckered her muzzle since she'd read the letter the night before.

"That is the ugliest purse I've ever seen," Jean pronounced.

Rosie touched it with one finger. "Tony gave it to me."

Jean's expression altered slightly. "Tony? Tony usually has better taste."

"But I like this purse." Rosie smiled unpleasantly at Jean. "I like it a lot. I feel the style lends me the weight of respectability, so to speak."

Sticking her needle into the tapestry, Jean cocked her head and studied Rosie, and Rosie knew she didn't measure up. What woman could measure up to the family standards for Tony's wife?

"Sit down," Jean ordered. When Rosie didn't immediately obey, Jean patted the stool next to her and said gruffly, "Sit down before you fall down."

Rosie wouldn't have complied, but she found her knees were shaking from Ludovic's assault on the foliage. She had begun to lower herself onto the seat when Jean said, "You've got twigs in your hair and dirt on your skirt. Have you been visiting your lover in the garden?"

There might have been a nail upright on the stool, so quickly did Rosie bound to her feet. She tried to walk away, but Jean snagged her skirt before she'd taken two steps. "I apologize."

Rosie grabbed her skirt with both hands and jerked, but Jean tugged back. "Sit down and accept my apology with good grace," Jean insisted. "I don't say anything so stupid often, and that gives you an advantage. Couldn't you use an advantage over somebody?"

Rosie collapsed onto the stool. "I could."

"I shouldn't have accused you of having a lover. Tony says not, and Tony knows more about women than any man I ever met."

Rosie considered standing again, but decided she didn't have the strength.

"He likes women, too. Tall women, short women, silly women, intelligent women, old women, young women. Do you know how rare that is?"

Remembering the battles she'd seen women wage against rough husbands, against the ravages of soldiers, and against men who considered them less important than dishrags, Rosie had to admit she did know how rare it was. She didn't have to admit she appreciated it, however.

Picking up her needle, Jean straightened the thread. "I've known Tony almost his whole life. When he came to us he was still a babe with a wet nurse, and we had decided—"

"We?"

"My sister Ann, my brother Michael, and I."

Rosie didn't want to be interested. She didn't want to care, but unbearable curiosity prompted her to say, "Go on."

"We had decided we weren't going to like him." Jean placed her stitches prudently, creating a picture in the rough material beneath her hand. "He was my father's bastard, you know, born of a love affair with an aristocratic woman. I thought his whole existence was a slap in my mother's face."

Rosie's curiosity had been piqued, and she wanted to hear the story, but she didn't have to admit that. "I can't blame you."

"My mother didn't agree," Jean rapped out. "She said a baby wasn't responsible for his existence."

"Oh." Rosie brushed at a grass stain on her skirt. "So she blamed your father?"

"My mother didn't blame anyone. She had a disease"— Jean cleared her throat—"that seemed to creep over her limbs and waste her muscles. My father loved her, but he was only a man, and when he saw Lady Margaret, he—"

"Created Tony?"

Jean nodded, accepting Rosie's tact with gratitude. "If Mother was hurt, she never let us know, and when

Lady Margaret refused to care for Tony, Mother insisted on taking him into our home. Then when I wouldn't pick him up, she insisted on picking him up. What was I to do? I was afraid she'd hurt herself."

"So you cared for Tony?"

Affection animated Jean's sharp features, and her face warmed and mellowed. "He was the smartest baby. Did you know he said his first word at nine months? And walked before he got his first tooth. He used to smile up at me and make those big eyes, and I couldn't refuse him anything. I must have carried him everywhere until he got so big I couldn't lift him."

Rosie pulled her braid over her shoulder and took the ribbon from her hair. With her fingers, she combed through the tresses and frowned at the leaves that fell around her skirt. "You spoiled him."

"We all did."

"Surely not the heir, your brother," Rose said, drawing on her experience of young men. "Young men like to fight and shout and drink, not care for a child."

"Michael is a special man. Tony adored him then, and adores him now. And Michael, like the rest of us, spoiled Tony until the time he was six. Toward the end, he was the only one who could make my mother laugh, and he called her 'Mama.'"

Rosie shook her hair, trying to dislodge the last bits of grass. "Your mother died when he was six?"

"Nay. Lady Margaret decided she wanted him when he was six."

"What?" Again Rosie bounded to her feet. "His mother took him when he was six?"

Jean no longer placed her stitches with care, but stabbed the tapestry as if she could stab Lady Margaret. "Kidnapped him."

"Why?"

"There was some criticism of her for her coldness in abandoning her child and returning to court. She didn't really care until she married, and her husband, the earl of Drebred, desired that Tony be raised with his other children."

Rosie didn't understand. She couldn't even begin to comprehend. "Why?"

"I don't know. Because it was the proper thing to do, I suppose, and the earl of Drebred is determined to do all that is proper." Jean no longer even pretended to embroider. She simply stared at the needlework and recited the facts. "We refused to give Tony up. Our father had the right to him, of course, and they could do nothing, we thought."

Wrapped up in the tale, Rosie didn't move from her place on the terrace.

"They took him when he was riding on our estate. His horse was new. He'd got it for his birthday, and when the horse returned without him, we thought he'd been thrown. We searched every inch of every acre, twice. Finally, one of the innkeepers on the route to London came to us and said he'd seen a boy who looked like Tony, crying for his mama."

Rosie couldn't believe it. She couldn't believe that open, cheerful, confident Tony concealed such a disturbance in his past. "Why didn't you demand him back?"

"We did, but while our family is reasonably wealthy and influential, the Spencer family has nothing that could be compared to the Drebred fortune. They're one of the great families of the north." Jean looked as if she tasted something bitter. "And they're cold as ice."

A small boy with Tony's face, crying for his mother in a fortress by the Scottish border. It made Rosie ill to think of it. "He didn't stay with them?"

Jean began to sew again. "Until he was eleven."

"Eleven? Those people kept him until he was eleven?"

"Aye."

"What happened at eleven?"

Jean leaned over into her basket and shuffled through the array of colored threads. "He ran away and came home."

"Came home." Rosie knew about the difficulties of the road better than most, and she asked, "Where is home?"

"In Cornwall."

Rosie caught Jean's hand, and Jean looked up at her. "He came from the north to your estate in Cornwall?" Jean nodded, and Rosie's voice soared. "At age eleven?" Jean nodded again, and Rosie sat down hard on her stool.

"I hate to think of the journey," Jean said. "It took him four months, and when he arrived, the servants didn't recognize him. They tried to feed him in the kitchen and send him on his way."

Rosie knew without asking, but she asked anyway. "Dirty and thin and threadbare?"

"And heartbroken. He'd come all that way for his mama, and his mama—"

Rosie stifled her own cry with her fist.

"I would have thought Lord and Lady Drebred would tell him. God knows they tried everything to break his spirit, but from the few things Tony said, they used Mama as a token against his good behavior." Jean mimicked a falsetto voice. "'If you're good, Anthony, we'll let you go visit your beloved mama.' Mama died within a year of Tony's kidnapping. He cried like an infant when he learned the truth, and I've never seen him cry since."

"Poor Tony."

"And poor Mama. I trow, to be without him broke her

heart." Jean licked her thumb, reached out, and wiped at Rosie's face. "You have dirt on your cheek—and tears."

Something—a noise, a shadow—brought their heads around, and they saw Tony standing in the open doorway. Rosie jumped guiltily; Jean did not.

"Have you come to enjoy the last sunshine before chill winter, brother?"

"I have indeed." He exited the manor and came to stand so that his shadow fell across Rosie's face.

How much had he heard, she wondered. Did he realize she'd been crying for the pain of his childhood? She didn't think he'd like this—that she knew he'd at one time been young, weak, and hurt.

"I've come out to let my ribs heal and to converse with two of the loveliest women in the world." He frowned. "But what happened to you, Rosalyn? Why the dirt and hay in your hair?"

So much for her attempt at grooming. "I . . . fell."

"You . . . fell?" he mimicked. "Well, you'll just have to be more careful when you walk in the garden, won't you?"

Rosie's gaze flew to his, and he lifted his eyebrows. He didn't know what she'd been doing. Did he? How could he, when she'd just got back from her meeting with Ludovic? And why should he care, anyway? She'd done nothing wrong.

Oblivious to the undercurrents, Jean said, "You can't expect the girl to act like a lady when she's been living as a lad—and an uncommon lad at that—for all these years. She probably forgot she was wearing skirts."

"I only wish I could," Rosie muttered.

"I don't think I'm expecting too much from Rosalyn. Do you, Rosalyn?" Tony smiled as if unaware of Rosie's alarm, when all the time she would wager he knew where she'd been and whom she'd seen. "After all, Rosalyn is very intelligent and knows right from wrong. Sir Danny taught her that, and she wouldn't want to betray Sir Danny with a heedless indiscretion. It might result in injury to someone she holds dear, and she wouldn't like that at all."

Jean couldn't be oblivious to *that* intimidation. "Are you holding Sir Danny hostage for Rosie's good behavior?"

"Nay," Tony denied.

"Good, for I doubt that would be good tactics with Lady Rosalyn."

Rosie could have cheered at Jean's defense, and Tony's lip protruded in a genuine sulk.

Then Jean stood and gathered her sewing basket. "I always said that whatever Tony wants, Tony gets."

Rosie's jubilation faded and Tony's sulk became a smirk. "You should listen to my sister, Rosalyn."

Jean continued, "So earlier today I wondered aloud at the result of the battle of the Titans—meaning you and Lady Honora."

"I will not marry Lady Honora." Tony said it as if he'd made the declaration too many times.

"My silly sister Ann said much the same thing, but she also told me I was betting on the wrong fight."

"Oh?" Tony said frostily.

"She says Lady Rosalyn's the one to watch, and my silly sister Ann often displays good instincts about people." She smiled at Rosie. "I'm glad we had this chance to talk, Lady Rosalyn."

Rosie watched Jean leave and wished she could go with her. But something held her in her seat—Tony's hand gripping her arm.

"I want to talk to you," he said.

"And I want to talk to you," she answered.

He cocked his head. "Confession time?"

"Indeed, Sir Rycliffe, it is. I have badly misled you, and wish to beg your pardon."

Tony watched her with a little too much concentration. "Speak, Rosalyn."

"I told you I would find someone else to teach me to read, but that's ridiculous, a result of misplaced pride." She hated to apologize, wishing there was some other way to remain close to him, to protect him from whatever might be threatening him. "I'm sorry for rejecting your kind offer, and if it still stands, I would be grateful for your help."

He flexed his hands, and she watched and wondered what he thought. Did he wish he had his fingers around her neck? Or did he espy the chance to use his hands in other pursuits? Timidly she asked, "What did you wish to discuss with me?"

"We'll talk about that some other time." Standing, he held out his palm. "So you want to learn to read. Wonderful." She put her hand in his. "Let's start now with the alphabet."

14

What a pretty thing man is when he goes in his doublet
and hose and leaves off his wit!

—MUCH ADO ABOUT NOTHING, V, i, 198

Lady Honora leaned over the rail and watched
as Tony and Sir Danny practiced with rapier and dagger on the lawn below the terrace. "He's very handsome, isn't he?"

She seemed to be inquiring of no one except the
evening air, but Rosie stood beside her and Rosie
couldn't ignore the question, nor the tone of admiration with which Lady Honora asked it. With a sinking
sensation, Rosie agreed. "Aye, he is."

"Such flashing eyes, such beautiful hair." Lady
Honora sighed a long fluttery sigh. "Any woman would
feel privileged to be invited to that man's bed."

Rosie looked at Tony, then looked at Lady Honora
and watched as she paid homage to a fine specimen of
man. It sheared years from Lady Honora's appearance,

softened the stiffness of her carriage, made her a woman like any other. "So she would."

"If only he weren't so short."

Short? "Tony?"

"Nay, foolish child." Lady Honora laughed deep in her chest, and it almost sounded like a purr. "Sir Danny."

Rosie set her heel on the hem of her petticoat and stumbled backward, and for the first time in four weeks, since Lady Honora had resolved to teach Rosie the womanly arts, Lady Honora didn't notice her clumsiness. Lady Honora didn't notice anything but Sir Danny, and Rosie couldn't tear her gaze from Lady Honora's enraptured face.

Sir Danny . . . and Lady Honora? Lady Honora, dowager duchess of Burnham and baroness of Rowse . . . and Sir Danny Plympton, Esquire? No matter how she tried to say it, it never sounded less than ludicrous.

But it explained a few things. Like having Sir Danny pat her absently on the head when she tried to complain about Tony's hands-on method of teaching.

Like having him tell her that Tony would take care of everything when she expressed her concern about Ludovic's disappearance.

Like his absolute lack of concern for Essex's plot to overthrow Queen Elizabeth.

Od's bodkin, that had been one of the reasons they'd come to Odyssey Manor in the first place. They'd come right into the household of the master of the Queen's Guard, so why shouldn't they gain his aid? But Sir Danny mumbled and smirked, and now Rosie knew why.

He was in love. Again. She should have recognized the symptoms.

She flexed her arm, newly removed from the splint, to put strength back into it. She would need that strength. She was now on her own.

*   *   *

Sir Danny measured the length of his arm against Tony's, and shook his head. "No wonder you're so good with a sword." He panted, drawing in deep, exhausted breaths. "You can scratch your knee without bending over."

Tony laughed and with the back of his hand wiped the sweat from his brow. "Nothing so fine as that."

"Whew! Such fighting is warm work." Sheathing the sword and dagger, Sir Danny untied the laces of his doublet and lifted it over his head. "I would that I had your reach. I fear I'll have more need of it than just for acting in sword fight scenes."

"I fear so, also." Tony suspected it wasn't just heat that made Sir Danny strip down to his linen shirt. Open at the neck, Sir Danny's almost transparent shirt both hid and displayed the muscles of his chest and arms, teasing the ladies and perhaps whetting their appetites. How ridiculous. How flamboyant.

How clever. Lady Honora hadn't taken her gaze from him.

Slowly, Tony removed his doublet, also, and loosened the lacing at the neck of his fine thin shirt until it opened almost to his waist. Had Rosie noticed? One sly glance proved she hung over the railing, and he strolled casually to Sir Danny's side. "When will you leave?"

"On the morrow." Sir Danny swung his doublet over the stiff branches of a gorse bush.

Tony placed his doublet beside Sir Danny's. The brilliant colors of the shrub accented the rich blacks and reds of the padded fabrics, and they dangled together as symbols of the unlikely partnership. "I cannot lie. I am grateful for your plan, but I dread the moment you tell Rosie."

"*I* tell Rosie?" Sir Danny picked up his sword and the tip of it waved in negative exclamation. "I'll just slip away. *You* can tell Rosie."

"Nay," Tony said decisively. "She'll take it better coming from you."

"Nay, nay. She feels unacknowledged affection for you. 'Twill draw you closer together."

"More likely she will rip off my head."

"You're not afraid of a woman, are you?"

"Are *you?*"

They drew breath and stared at each other, hostile enough to fight, and they touched blades in salute. Then, moving more slowly than he would in real combat, Tony began the lesson once more. "Touch, break, thrust, break." He watched his pupil closely. Sir Danny knew more than the just the bare rudiments of fighting with rapier and dagger. He'd had to learn, Tony guessed, to defend his troupe. But Sir Danny knew less than the lords who made swordwork their career, and Tony had tried, these last weeks, to cram Sir Danny with the skill of years of training.

"Watch for the opening! Stab, stab with the dagger, dammit!"

Sir Danny rushed into the gap Tony had left deliberately and stabbed at his heart.

Tony praised the thrust, then said, "I won't allow it. You go to seek death for love of the queen, and you must say good-bye to the woman who considers you her father."

With a sigh, Sir Danny glanced toward the terrace. "I suppose, but she's going to be angry."

"There is that chance."

"Chance?" Sir Danny snorted. "'Tis a certainty. She's always angry when I put myself in danger. This will make her livid."

"Perhaps I can bring her around after you leave." Tony grinned in anticipation of a furious, out-of-control Rosie. She was easy to incite, and fun to divert.

"Aye." Sir Danny's worried face cleared. "She'll have you and probably won't even notice my departure. After all, she's older now, with concerns of her own. She doesn't need her dada for reassurance. Aye, you'll be able to restrain her."

Sir Danny sounded so apprehensive, Tony asked, "Are you sure you want to do this?" Sir Danny's tale of the earls of Essex and Southampton and their plans for rebellion had come as no surprise. Queen Elizabeth might have temporarily relieved Tony of duties as the master of her guard, but he gathered information from the captain of his men and he knew of the mutterings.

Everyone knew of the mutterings. But did the queen?

Until she found out about this treason and moved to squelch it, the kingdom would be in jeopardy. And Tony couldn't advise her, for she believed him prejudiced against her beloved Essex.

As he was. But a serious situation was rapidly moving toward crisis and, stripped of his power, Tony could do nothing. The queen needed to relent, to allow him to leave his exile and return to his duties before it was too late. For that he needed Sir Danny, and Sir Danny had cheerfully volunteered.

Cheerfully? Nay, enthusiastically.

"Who better than I to go into London and report the nefarious plot to the queen?" Sir Danny held his sword outthrust, curved his arm back, puffed out his chest, raised his chin, and let the wind blow his hair away from his face. "'Tis dangerous, 'tis true. I face a myriad of evil forces allied against me. But I and I alone—"

Tony laid his hand on Sir Danny's arm. "They can't hear you."

"Sir?"

"The women." Tony nodded at the terrace. "The pose is alluring, but they're too far away to hear you. I just want to know if you truly think you can get all the way to the queen before Essex seizes you."

Sir Danny kept the pose, but dropped the rhetoric. "With the help of your letter of safe conduct, I can."

"Essex won't give a damn about my letter of safe conduct, and he has spies in the court. If you're not wary, you may find yourself several inches taller with the assistance of a helpful torturer. Even if you're not wary . . ." Tony trailed off. What was he doing, using a common actor as a pawn in this game of power? Essex would smash Sir Danny heedlessly, cruelly, and send his lifeless body to Tony as a warning.

"Sir Anthony." Sir Danny faced Tony full on and spoke with a candor all the more convincing for its simplicity. "All my life I've been convinced that I would someday fulfill a great destiny. Someday I knew I would be more than a wandering actor. Someday I knew the merit I support within my bosom would find an outlet in some splendid deed. Well, this is it! I feel it! I will save the queen of England, and England herself! Don't try to keep me safe. Don't blame yourself should I die in the undertaking. Know that I bless you for giving me this chance at glory, and mourn me not should I fail."

"As you wish." Tony slashed the air with his sword. "But if I've sent you to your death, it's going to be cold in my bed—after Rosie and I are married, I mean."

Sir Danny studied him with shrewd eyes. "I've heard it's warm in your study right now."

"In my study?"

"Where you're teaching my Rosie to read. She's

complaining that you reward her successes with an embrace and her failures with a kiss."

Defensive at once, Tony said, "Well, she doesn't like my kisses . . . yet."

"I thought you were England's greatest lover." Sir Danny's tone made it clear that if Tony were England's greatest lover, he'd succeeded Sir Danny for the honor.

"I am, but Rosie is a most stubborn woman. She resists wooing so stubbornly I'm forced to dim my brilliance and resort to trickery." Tony waited a beat. "She's loath to allow herself to feel the slightest pleasure, for she fears if she does, all her resistance will crumble."

"Ah, aye. I've had experience with wenches of that ilk." Sir Danny kissed his fingers at some long-distant memory. "But when the resistance does crumble, it's magnificent. In sooth, I remained in the bed of that lady so long, I scarcely escaped London with my life."

"The mayor's wife?" Tony asked.

Sir Danny nodded melodramatically, then slipped his sword under Tony's unready guard and placed the tip at his throat. "However, my exploits differ from yours, for you are trying to seduce the woman I consider my daughter."

Amazing how one could remain still, not even swallowing, when the shining arc of a blade threatened.

"When I leave, I'm leaving everything in your hands and trusting to your honor. I'm leaving you the letter, and I'm leaving you my Rosie, and if I should survive this operation, I would take it ill to discover you have used and discarded her."

"Sir Danny—"

"And even if I should die and you should fulfill your duty and wed Rosie, you'll find my shade haunting you should you not cherish her as she so richly deserves."

Tony didn't mind assuring Sir Danny of his good

intentions, but Sir Anthony Rycliffe did not use women and discard them and he took it ill when so accused. "Rosie will be the wife of my heart and mind, but until she consents to wed me, we'll not indulge in the ultimate pleasure. I'll have no one whispering that my firstborn was a six-months babe and mocking his legitimacy."

Sir Danny stroked his mustache in puzzlement. "Then why such physical methods of teaching?"

"Rosie's skittish as a colt—unlike most women upon whom I've cast my gaze—and I'm trying to break her to my hand." Tony experienced a moment of regret for comparing her to a horse. He well knew his own resentment at such treatment, and he was embarrassed when he recalled his own previous demand for a woman as fecund as a mare. "I'll get her accustomed to me gradually, and when she's malleable to my desires, we'll . . ." Tony broke out in a sweat. When Rosie was malleable to his desires, they'd be lucky to make it to the bed first, much less to the chapel.

Sir Danny seemed to comprehend what Tony didn't say, and surprisingly, he did not take it ill. Withdrawing the sword, he said, "Quite. Do you wish to practice more today?"

Tony eyed him consideringly. Sir Danny would work until he couldn't lift the sword rather than admit his exhaustion, and they'd been practicing for most of the day. "I'm weary. If you don't mind, we'll rest now and give the ladies a chance to say good-bye to you."

Sir Danny grabbed his doublet before Tony had finished speaking. "I don't mind. I'd like a few words with the Lady Honora tonight, and then on the morrow I'll tell Rosie."

"On the morrow? Are you mad? Tell her tonight."

"On the morrow. There's no use worrying the girl unduly tonight"—Sir Danny surmised the objection hovering on Tony's tongue—"and knowing Rosie, she'd stow away in one of the wagons before the morning."

"God forbid." Tony hadn't thought of that. "Tell her on the morrow, then."

"I've told my troupe to pack up, although I've not told them why we return to London."

"Whatever will Mistress Child do if she only has to fix three meals a day?" Tony took his doublet also, and considered. Should he put it on? The night breeze blew cold as the sun began to set, but might he not impress Rosie with his body one last time before he dressed for dinner?

"Are you saying my actors eat too much?" Holding his doublet over his shoulder hooked on one finger, Sir Danny sauntered toward the stairs.

"Too much?" Tony followed Sir Danny's example, strutting for his lady while trying to appear oblivious to his own performance. "Let us say, they consume copious amounts."

"Actors adore a free meal." Lowering his voice, Sir Danny said, "I wish I could tell you different, but Ludovic hasn't returned."

Tony stumbled on the stairs. "Nor has he left the estate."

Sir Danny slowed his ascent. "What have you discovered?"

"The remains of a coney by a fire in our wild wood. A footprint by the stream. And one of the serving women insists she saw a man looking in a window last night."

"Don't tell Rosie," Sir Danny begged. "She spoke with him before he left."

Tony sought Rosie's gaze with his. "I know."

"She's likely to blame herself for his defection. She won't tell me, but I think she rejected him."

Tony *did* know that Rosie had spoken to Ludovic.

Hal had seen them sneaking into the garden together, and reported the matter to his master.

Tony didn't believe Rosie was capable of deceit, but to whom did she owe her loyalty? Would she have warned Ludovic that Tony suspected him of violence? He very much feared she would, and now, despite the efforts of his huntsmen, Ludovic was out of reach, yet only too close.

"Sir Danny." Lady Honora's voice vibrated with enthusiasm. "Your swordsmanship is awe inspiring." As they reached the top step, she added graciously, "As is yours, Anthony."

Tony grimaced. He wanted Rosie's praise, not Lady Honora's.

But Rosie had eyes only for Sir Danny, and those eyes were narrowed in foreboding. "Your swordsmanship *has* improved, Dada." She intercepted Sir Danny before he could go through the doors into the manor. "Why?"

The name she called him staked a claim, the bald query proved she'd noticed their incessant practice, and her hostile stance proved she suspected the cause.

"Ohh." Sir Danny skipped backward a step. "When I have a tutor as proficient as Sir Tony, 'tis a shame not to take advantage."

He tried to go around Rosie, but she thwarted him. "You haven't been practicing *Hamlet* at all. How will the troupe perform when you leave Odyssey Manor?"

"Trying to get rid of me?" Sir Danny pinched her cheek.

She bore it stoically. "When *do* you plan to leave Odyssey Manor?"

Lady Honora came to the rescue. "Lady Rosalyn! One does not invite guests to leave in such a manner. Especially not a guest as cultured as Sir Danny."

"I'm not inviting him to leave," Rosie said through clenched teeth. "I'm wondering when he's planning to leave. Those are two entirely different inquiries."

Lady Honora acknowledged that Rosie might know her guardian. "Sir Danny, is Lady Rosalyn aware of something we should know?"

Tony waited, sure Sir Danny would have to announce his departure now.

But Sir Danny clasped his fists to his breast. "Rosie realizes I cannot remain here forever, for performance is to me what wind is to the wild gull. I cannot fly, I cannot live, I cannot *be* without it, and the time is rapidly approaching when I must take to my wings and soar away." He gazed soulfully at Lady Honora, then in a normal tone of voice, added, "But not tonight." Slipping around Rosie, he took Lady Honora's arm and hustled her inside. "Tonight we feast, drink, and dance while finding pleasure in the company."

"That man is plotting something." Rosie turned to Tony. "What is he plotting?"

Tony loved the look of her—eyes flashing, chest heaving, cheeks aglow with fury. He loved knowing that she'd rage and fume when Sir Danny made his announcement, for in the correct hands, rage could be transformed into desire. With a grin, Tony looked down. Aye, he had the correct hands.

"Why are you grinning?"

He had the right lips, too, and when he kissed Rosie . . .

"Get that look off your face right now." She shook a finger at him, and he caught it and bussed it. She snatched it away with an exclamation of frustration. "You men always collaborate. You're not worth a pence, any of you!"

She marched away and he still grinned. Frustration and rage—a volatile mixture, and one he could exploit for their mutual pleasure. Ah, tomorrow would be an exciting day.

*   *   *

Today was the worst day of his life.

"Lady Rosalyn, this is an improper way for a gentlewoman to behave." Lady Honora looked the image of a stern taskmaster, but her voice wavered slightly.

"Rosalyn, you must come in. The wind is cold and from the look of the sky, 'twill start raining soon." Shivering, Jean stood so her skirt protected Rosie from the chill of the breeze.

"Rosalyn, dear. Rosie, dear." Ann knelt beside the girl's hunched figure and rubbed her back. "You mustn't cry so. It'll make you sick."

It was making Tony sick—sick with worry and self-recrimination. Nothing Sir Danny had said, no assurance he had offered, made an impression on her absolute conviction she would never see him again. She cried the tears of a child abandoned.

"Sir." Hal crept out of the manor and tugged at Tony's cloak. "Aren't ye going t' make her stop?"

Tony turned on him savagely. "Don't you think I would if I could?" His sisters were looking at him, too, and Lady Honora, but what did they expect him to do? He was a man, terrified of any woman's tears, horrified by this check to his plans for Rosie, and vaguely ashamed of his expectations. He thought he understood women, so how could he have failed to understand what Sir Danny meant to her?

"What does she want?" Lady Honora asked. "Is she trying to get you to give her the estate?"

"Oh, Lady Honora!" Ann looked distressed. "Don't be disagreeable."

"I'm not being disagreeable. I just don't understand why she's crying like that." Lady Honora wrapped her cloak tighter around her and stared at Rosie through sightless eyes. "Sir Danny has made himself amenable to all of us, but none of us are crying just because he left. Just because he's a shallow, selfish actor who left us to visit the fleshpots of London."

"You can be the most callous witch." Jean pushed Lady Honora toward the manor. "Go in before you cause more damage."

"She's just trying to get attention." Stumbling toward the door, Lady Honora said, "She's trying to gain our sympathy and persuade us we should allow her to marry Tony."

Standing up, Ann hustled Lady Honora through the entrance. "Leave off."

"I don't care if she is the heir to the estate, she can't marry Tony. I'm going to marry Tony."

"She can't even hear you." Jean sounded exasperated.

"I'm going to marry Tony, and no glib, charming actor is going to change my mind."

Glib, charming actor? Tony rubbed his forehead. Was she referring to Rosie? Or Sir Danny? Why was she so bellicose? So defiant?

Why wouldn't Rosie stop crying?

As if nature aspired to add to the misery, a mist began to fall.

"Fine," Tony said, as if someone had given him instructions. "I'll take care of her."

To his distress, no one argued. He gestured to his sisters to go in, and they shivered and obeyed. Hal shifted from foot to foot, staring at Rosie with miserable eyes. "Go in," Tony commanded. Hal didn't move, and Tony repeated, "Go *in!*"

Shuffling, Hal entered the house, leaving Rosie and Tony alone in the wretched weather.

Kneeling beside her, he called her name. "Rosie." She huddled inside her cloak and he could see nothing but her braid and the pale stem of her neck. "Rosie, sweetheart. We have to go in." Her tears didn't check, and he laid his hand on her back. "Rosie." He stroked his hands through her hair. "Come, dear."

Like a turtle leaving its shell, she lifted her head.

She looked awful. Her puffy eyes and splotchy cheeks too clearly expressed her anguish. The rain soaked her hair, the tears drenched her face, and she badly needed a kerchief. Yet he'd never seen a woman who appealed to him more.

He loved her. There was no other explanation. Beneath the lust and the quick-fire attraction lay a bedrock of affection, admiration, and devotion. She needed comfort; he would provide it. He, and no other. "Sweetheart." He gathered her into his embrace. "Don't cry anymore. I'll take care of you forever."

15

Where is the life that late I led?
—THE TAMING OF THE SHREW, IV, i, 134

The fire burned on the massive hearth, but the heat it produced could not dent the chill of the master's chamber. Tony pushed Rosie within that embrace and, removing her cloak, threw it into the corner, where it subsided in a sodden mass. She stood cold, unmoving, her face still blotched, but blank, as if she did not know where she was or what person served her.

It horrified him. It made him remember a time when he was a boy, alone in a big house in the north, thrust by his beloved family into the bosom of a frigid clan and abandoned.

Oh, it wasn't true. Even as a child, he'd known it wasn't true. The memory of his mama had burned in his mind, keeping his spirit alive when the earl of Drebred and his rod would have murdered it. For days, for weeks, for years he had waited to be rescued from Drebred Castle, and at last he'd come to realize he must rescue himself. He'd done it. Damn, he'd done it, but his exile had been too long and too unhappy. Within himself, he was still as sunny a lad as he'd always been, but for a different reason. He knew only too well how quickly life could lose its savor and become a fight for survival. Now he erected bastions around him—bastions of income, of land, of fighting skill, and relentless charm.

Looking at Rosie, limp, still, and silent, recalled his own old hopelessness, and he'd already fought that battle once for himself. Rather than fight it again for Rosie, he wanted to call a maidservant to wait upon her, a doctor to bleed her, and on heaven to cure her ills—and all he dared to do was call on heaven. Rosie was his responsibility now.

Brisk as Jean, kind as Ann, he stripped off Rosie's overskirt and bodice, and went to work on the strings that supported her petticoats. "I don't blame you for being distraught at Sir Danny's leaving today. 'Tis a miserable day for travel. The roads will be a quagmire, but what are his choices? 'Tis St. Nicholas Day tomorrow, and the winter rains have held off long as they're likely, I suspect. The country folk complain if it's a dry autumn and they complain if it's a wet autumn, but they're predicting a long, wet winter."

She wasn't listening. She turned at his direction, let him remove what he would, but she stared straight ahead as if stunned by events too dreadful to absorb.

He opened the door to the antechamber, a massive room that contained his favorite volumes, a small desk, chests, and tall standing wardrobes filled with clothing, shoes, and anything else he might need. "Come in here and help me find you something to wear." Seeing that she followed him, he moved inside, opened a chest, and rummaged through the contents. "After you've made your choice, I'll call a serving maid to help you."

She made an ugly, broken noise, and he stiffened. Had he erred? "I thought you wouldn't want me to help you, but gladly I will do so, if that pleases you." He glanced at her, then openly stared at the spectacle of Rosie, groping along a table that didn't exist.

She fondled an invisible post and caressed the air with a knowing touch. In a high, childish tone, she said, "Dada, where's your bed? Have you moved it? That is not your desk. What happened to the carpet? I liked to sink my toes into it." Then, in a tearful voice, she added, "I didn't take it, Dada. I only touched it. I didn't lose it. Please don't be angry. Please please please."

Standing, Tony moved slowly toward her. He recognized the dazed expression on her face. He'd seen it many times after the fighting on the Continent. When a soldier had had a leg ripped off by a cannonball, or his best friend had been sliced open before his face, he frequently looked and spoke like Rosie. But what had Rosie done? She'd been upset in the other room, but she'd still been Rosie. Now he didn't know where or who she was. Sliding an arm around her shoulder, lifting her face to his, Tony looked into her eyes. "Rosie?"

"I didn't hide it, Dada."

Scared, questioning her sanity, he shook her a little. "Rosie?"

Rosie—the essence, the being—snapped back into place. She touched her forehead with her hand as if checking the truth of her existence, then stared at him before mouthing, "Tony."

She tried to flee, but he held her and she fought

him. When he wouldn't let her go, she buried her head in his chest as if she could hide in his arms, and he gladly gave her shelter.

"He's not here." Her muffled words sounded as if she were trying to convince herself. "He's not here."

"Who's not here?" he demanded.

She peeked out and started, and her fear and pain vibrated through him. He glanced around, half expecting to see the shade of Lord Sadler, but nothing stirred the tapestries, no sound disturbed the silence except the rain tapping on the window. "What do you see?" he asked.

"Just a room." She pointed at the wardrobe. "Was this here before?"

"I brought it from London with me."

She eased herself away from him. "And the desk."

"It's mine, also."

Gaining confidence, she stepped away—but not too far away—and feathered her hand along a narrow table. "But this was in the room before."

"Aye."

"And this?"

She picked up one of the carvings Lord Sadler had collected, another Madonna and child. She stroked the smooth wood, and he wondered at the memories cradled in her palms. There was no madness here, Tony admitted, only memories so old they tormented Rosie with their flashes of recollection. If this was to be her home, she couldn't continue denying those memories or her heritage.

"Did your father like that carving?"

"I don't remember."

"Was this his table?"

"I don't remember."

She stood absolutely still, yet he sensed the emotion

that roiled beneath her facade. Why was she so angry? So afraid? "Rosie?"

"I don't remember anything. I don't remember this place. I don't remember the man you say is my father." Setting the carving down hard on the table, she insisted, "I don't remember."

"I don't believe you."

"Why not?" She turned on him fiercely. "Why doesn't anyone believe me?"

"Because you are too emphatic."

"I'm not! I'm—" Taking a breath, she gathered her composure around her. "I've already warned you that I lay claim to Odyssey Manor, so what is the point of your questioning?"

"Rosie." Going to her, he stroked her cheek with his fingers. "Talk to me. Tell me what you remember. Don't you know you're Lord Sadler's daughter?"

She smiled at him tightly. "Everyone believes I'm Lord Sadler's daughter. Sir Danny says"—her voice shook—"I'm Lord Sadler's daughter. Even you say I'm Lord Sadler's daughter."

"Aye, so I do."

"Therefore, I must be." In a softer voice, she said, "Maybe that's why Sir Danny left me behind."

Shudders shook her slender frame, and he pulled her into his arms. She shook him off, wanting none of his comfort, and although he understood the strife within her, her rejection hurt.

"Come, then," he said sharply, leading the way toward the light and warmth of the bedchamber. "You're damp, and this chilly antechamber is no place for a woman who has suffered the loss of one father and the discovery of another."

She made no move to follow him. She wilted, sliding back into apathy and anguish, and he couldn't allow that. She had to stay with him, talk to him, become the vivacious woman that lurked beneath the shadow of want and insecurity.

She needed a shock. He glanced around the chamber, seeking he knew not what, and said, "You shouldn't worry about Sir Danny. I sent a letter with him to be delivered to one of my men in the Queen's Guard, and besides, he's as wily an old goshawk as ever I've seen." His knife. He pulled his fighting knife from his belt and thrust it under her nose.

She saw that. She tried to jump back, but he clasped the strings of her shift. "I'm going to remove your stomacher," he said. "Don't move."

"You can't."

"Watch me." He sliced the ribbons at the front in one clean slash, made all the more impressive by the sharp edge he honed on his blade. "Oops!" he exclaimed. "Nicked the material. I must not be as proficient as I thought."

Her eyes widened, and she sucked in her breath.

"I'll have to practice on these." He cut the strings that held the stomacher together, and the whole contraption fell open.

"Are you deranged?"

He'd succeeded. He'd brought her back to life.

Rosie reacted to his exhibition with fury. "A more childish performance of manly prowess I've never seen."

Her damp linen above-the-knee shift revealed as much as his had during the sword fight, and she had more to show. Ah, and he wanted to see, but she turned her back and paced toward the bedchamber. The light shone through the fine material and he followed eagerly, captured by the curve of her silhouette.

He latched the cursed door behind him as she stalked to the fire. "Not that I haven't seen other childish performances. Men are full of them. Once Sir Danny walked the top rail of the Globe and I thought he . . ." She brushed her hand across her eyes, and her voice wobbled. "Sir Danny . . ."

Tony realized that her fury was disintegrating into tears again. But these tears were different. Not tears of mourning, but tears of rage.

"How could he have left me here?"

One of her hose drooped, and with her back to him, she tugged at the loose garter. He saw a peek of curly hair when she bent over. He thought his heart would stop and groped for the big chair set within the ring of warmth.

Not that he needed the warmth. Somehow a coal had dropped into his lap and it was igniting his whole body.

"He knows how I feel about losing him. Didn't he understand that if he dies, I die?"

Tony tested his restraint, and didn't grab for her. He tested her knowledge, and asked, "Why should he die now? Why not yesterday? Or tomorrow?"

"Because today he goes back to London where the earls of Essex and Southampton wait for him like vultures wait for carrion. And that's what Sir Danny is to them. Carrion, just—" She turned on him, and the flames behind her almost banished the straight drape of her shift. He couldn't have seen any more if she'd been naked.

The coal in his lap turned from flaming red to intense blue.

"You know why he's gone," she raged. "You know the danger he's in. How could you encourage him to leave without me?"

How could she fail to notice the glorious agony of his burning? "What possible good would you be to him?"

"I can fight as well as any man!"

"And go to prison as well as any man." The blaze within him dimmed as his mind brought forth pictures that made him cringe.

"If that be what is required."

"But you're not a man, and prison has special tortures for women which it reserves almost solely for the fair sex." Fear stifled his fire, leaving him cool and focused. "And those special tortures would not preserve you from the others which the executioner would call forth."

"Upon Sir Danny's head."

Too late he perceived the trap which he had set for himself, but he couldn't deny the truth. "Sir Danny serves the queen unselfishly, for that is Sir Danny's nature. Would you have him be less than what he is?"

"Nay, but I would serve the queen with like generosity."

"Sir Danny has delayed his service for love of you. He couldn't return to London until he knew you had been settled, for your safety means more to him than his hope of salvation."

"My safety." She wrapped her waist in her arms and hugged herself, pulling the shift into her form and up her legs. "I care nothing for my safety if Sir Danny lives not, and am I not the master of my own fate?"

"Nay, for you are the daughter of Sir Danny's heart."

"You seek to bind me in chains of affection."

"Methinks you are already bound, at least by Sir Danny." His voice deepened as his love and his wanting ignited the spark once more. "And the chains with which I seek to bind you owe little to the paltry emotion of affection."

For the first time, she glanced around and realized they were alone. She glanced down and realized how scantily the shift covered her charms, and tugged the hem of it as if she could stretch it to cover her legs. "What do you intend?"

"What do you think I intend?" He grinned at her trepidation. "I'm going to acquaint you with the running of the estate. *Your* estate. You must know your duties before you present your petition to the queen."

"Now? You wish to tell me about the estate *now*?"

"Nay, 'tis not what I wish to do." He stared meaningfully at her body. "But it's what I must do. There's one of my shirts draped over the fireguard. Why don't you trade your wet shift for it?"

She blushed. "Not likely, varlet!"

"It's considerably longer than the one you're wearing." She still shook her head, and he still smiled. "Think of it as a way to distract me."

She fingered the massive cream-colored shirt that hung on the metal fireguard. "Silk?"

"I indulge myself." The smooth pink roundness of her nipples pressed against her shift. If he held them in his palm, they wouldn't be smooth, regardless of her body heat. They would be tight, puckered, and in his mouth.

He must have made her nervous, for she babbled, "I'm accustomed to men seeing me without my clothes, you comprehend."

He was on his feet without realizing it. "What?"

"I mean that a gentlewoman cannot dress herself without help, and Sir Danny frequently helped me when I prepared for my acting parts."

Sinking down in his chair, he rubbed his cheek with the flat of his hand. "Certes. I knew that was what you meant." How evil a man he was, to be jealous of the man who loved her like a father.

"Turn around," she instructed.

He covered his eyes with his hands.

"That won't do."

"Don't you trust me?"

She laughed, a rather brusque laugh, and when he peeked through his fingers she had disappeared. He heard a scrabbling behind him, then she came into the light and he forgot to pretend he hadn't watched. The shirt had never looked like that on him. The cream color accented her brown hair and amber eyes and made her skin glow. It reached well past her knees in a shimmering fall. The full sleeves covered her hands, and she'd tied the neck tight to inhibit his thoughts.

It didn't work.

Luckily, she had refused to remove her hose, baggy things that they were, and the wool material obscured her ankles and knees.

"You'll catch a chill from those wet hose," he said.

She ignored the hint.

"Just as well to leave them on," he grudgingly admitted. "Throw that pillow over here by my feet and sit."

"Sit at your feet, sir? I will not."

"Bring a comb, too. I'll untangle your hair."

Lifting her hand self-consciously, she touched the wisps that stuck out in wild profusion.

He nodded at her unspoken question. "Aye, it looks like a bird made a nest on your head. The comb's over there."

With a cushion under one arm and the comb in the other, she did his bidding, and he rejoiced at her obedience. She was obviously in a weakened state, and he planned to make inroads on her resistance while he could.

"The parish on this estate supports over three hundred souls." Separating the strands of her braid, he began to work the ivory comb through the damp tangles.

"When I arrived at Odyssey Manor, the estate had been in the queen's hands for thirteen years, and much neglected. The villagers were hovering on the edge of starvation, and I sank my free capital into renovating the manor. Necessary, but also good for the economy of the parish."

"How generous of you." Her obvious interest offset her sarcasm. "I'll see that you're compensated."

"Not at all. I'd been planning my whole life for the moment I acquired an estate of my own, and nothing was more important than the health of my property and my people." The wide-set teeth of the comb bit into the glossy brown, subduing the wildness and leaving sleek wet strands in his hands. "Can you understand that?"

"I think so."

Her cautious answer didn't fool him. He depended on her comprehension to build a longing for the land. "During the spring and summer, we hire an additional six men to work on the grounds. That causes a hardship in the fields, but I discovered early that the villagers would rather be overworked than ignored, and that professional gardeners are sneered at in the country." Up and down the comb worked, massaging her scalp, spreading the individual hairs to dry. "Having Hal as a steward has worked marvelously well, for he's a native and conscientious beyond the bounds of duty. Should you persuade the queen to grant you this estate, you would be well served to keep Hal on."

As he talked and worked his fingers through her hair, he saw her tension dissipate.

"What's the use of learning about the estate when I only wanted it for Sir Danny?"

She loved Sir Danny, true. She loved him above all things, and that mortified Tony, for surely by now the silly woman should have developed fond and lusty feelings for him. But if she had, she hid them well, and he resolved to hold the mirror before her face until she saw herself as she truly was—selfish and considerate, grasping and generous. A human like any other. A human like him.

Turning her to look at him, he said, "You only wanted it for Sir Danny? Who would you have laugh at such a jest? Not me, Lady Rosalyn. I know why you demanded your rights to the estate. You may not like it, but you and I are as alike as two litter mates."

"We are not!"

"Aren't we? Two travelers through the world, never quite as good as the others for no fault of our own, branded by the cruelest of epithets—bastard for me, actor for you."

"Not so," she said faintly, but he persisted.

"You know me, but what's worse for you—I know you. I know how the wandering life left you longing for a place of your own, where you could strip off the disguise and be what you are and not what others expect you to be. You longed for the dirt in which to sink your roots and the time to remain and grow. When you laid claim to this estate, I knew what was in your heart, and you can't tell me that the land will mean any less to you should Sir Danny perish. If anything, it will mean more."

Unnerved by his acute observations, she struggled to speak. "Not so. If Sir Danny should die, I'll have nothing left to live for."

He chuckled, and wrath and hurt struggled for supremacy on her countenance. "When I threatened you with the knife, you struggled against me. If you had no reason to live, you would have let me slit your throat."

She didn't want to admit that life once more coursed

through her veins. He suspected her blossoming fascination seemed like a betrayal of Sir Danny, and she said defensively, "I don't know that he's dead yet."

"Exactly." With his thumb, he traced the tracks of her tears, then rising, wet a cloth and returned. "Think on it, Rosie. Think of the injustice you do Sir Danny by donning mourning black before his death, and think of how proud he'll be when you prove his faith in you by taking control of your responsibilities. He'll know then he made the right decision."

"He won't know if he's dead!"

"Oh, won't he?" He held her gaze until she looked down, then with the expertise of a parent, he scrubbed her tearstained face.

He was done before she could do more than struggle and cry, "Hey!"

He chuckled. "I have experience with rebellious children."

"Yours?" she asked sullenly.

He checked, then hustled her toward the bed. "Nay. Didn't you know? My brother Michael has eight little heirs whom I have undressed and placed in bed, and that is what I plan to do with you now."

As he expected, she clutched the bottom of his shirt. "What?"

"Not for any nefarious reason—yet. But because you've cried and I know the consequence of tears. Also from my experience with my nephews and nieces."

She glanced at the bed, then glared at him. "And what is that?"

"The one who cries is tired, fretful, ill-tempered—"

"I am not!"

"—disagreeable, perverse, contrary." Picking her up, he tossed her onto the mattress. "Obnoxious, cranky, and in need of a nap." He leaned over her, trapping her between his two hands, and he wanted to climb onto the bed with her and kiss her. He wanted to caress her breasts and discover if the shapes he remembered were in sooth their true shape. He wanted to hold her between the legs and probe the depths of her.

She crossed her arms in self-righteous appraisal. "You're looking a little cranky yourself."

"After your nap, the world will look better to you."

She pushed the drape of hair off her eyes. "After my nap, Sir Danny will still be gone."

"Ah, but after your nap, I'll show you another reason to live."

16

Touches so soft still conquer chastity.
—The Passionate Pilgrim, iv, 8

Rosie opened her eyes, and realized she lay on her side in a bed. A hairy, muscled arm extended from under her head, ending in a hand, palm up, blunt fingers curled. It rested among the ripples of white sheets over a feather mattress, directly below a pile of embroidery-trimmed pillows.

Tony's arm. Tony's bed. Her back curled into his front. The thin crackle and the smoky tang of a dying fire hung in the air. The dim light of early evening proved she'd been here for hours, ever since her humiliating collapse on the terrace. She, who'd been so guarded, had revealed her vulnerability to Tony in one traumatic, dramatic scene. She squeezed her eyes shut as if that would help her flee the consequences, yet the scene of the morning came to vivid life.

Ugh.

Her tears. Tony's kindness. And the reason for it all—Sir Danny's defection. He'd gone to meet his death, she knew, and he'd gone without her. He'd abandoned her, and there was no reason to get off this bed.

How long had Tony been beside her? She remembered that final promise of his. Or had it been a threat?

She opened her eyes to see the fingers flexing. Was his arm asleep? Cautiously, she lifted her head, and he spoke close against her ear.

"Awake?"

She jumped. She'd known he was close. It was just that she'd had no experience with having someone *so* close. She hadn't realized how his chest would reverberate with the timbre of his voice, or the way he could tuck his knee against the back of hers. One arm supported her head, but the other lay across her waist, and it moved. Holding her breath, she waited to see where it would light, and when it wrapped across her ribs and pulled her closer still, she whimpered slightly. This damned silk shirt proved no bulwark against Tony's battering ram, and somehow her hose had disappeared while she slept.

"I had promised to show you," he murmured, "another reason to live."

Flinging herself around, she glared at him with what she hoped was stern dignity.

Poor strategy. His halo of spiky golden hair stuck up all around his head, making him appear as innocent as a child. His blue eyes glowed with unholy pleasure, and the warmth of his smile could have melted a plaster saint.

Obviously, sainthood was beyond her.

She held out a restraining hand and cried, "Wait!"

"I've done nothing."

As he spoke, he raised up on his elbow and the sheet

fell away. Maybe he'd done nothing, but he'd done it with nothing on.

He had a muscled chest with crinkly blond hair, but she'd seen that before. He had ripply arms with powerful hands, but she'd seen that before. He had the sheet clinging to the lowest part of his hips . . . but she'd seen everything hidden by the sheet before.

And she remembered it quite clearly.

Amazing how he could distract her mind from her woes.

"I promised to show you another reason to live." He smoothed her hair out of her face, petting her as if she were a wildcat he wished to tame. "But actually, I know of several reasons."

"I'm not interested in any of them." Sadly, she liked the way he stroked her. She wanted to stretch and flex her claws and purr, but it would have been surrendering without a fight. And surrender, she'd just discovered, looked very much like paradise.

"The first reason to live is kissing."

"I don't like to kiss."

"It rhymes with bliss."

"Will Shakespeare's poetry pales before your own," she said sarcastically.

"There's a purpose for kissing."

"We're not right for each other."

"And that's it."

He diverted her with his illogic. It didn't even sound like they were having the same conversation. "What?"

"The purpose of kissing." Leaning forward, he put his face so close against hers, her eyes crossed. "When we think we're not right for each other, we kiss, and we're so close, 'tis impossible to see any disparities." His lips fluttered against hers, tempting her with a physical declaration of devotion and the unspoken lure of delight. "Can you focus on our disparities?" he murmured.

Her lids felt heavy, as heavy as they had before her sleep, but for different reasons. "Nay."

"Close your eyes and put your arms around my shoulders. The important differences will be obvious beneath your fingertips."

Unwisely, she obeyed. The disparities between them—of breeding and upbringing—faded. As he pressed his mouth to hers and her hands quivered across his back, it was the difference she noted. He was a man; she was a woman. He was a teacher; she was a student. He used his tongue as a lure; she rose to the lure as eagerly as a Scottish trout.

Stupid trout.

She shoved against his shoulders, and he backed off immediately.

Forsooth, why shouldn't he? When she had pried her eyelids open, he smiled at her, and she knew that if she were a trout, she would have been cooked to the bone.

No man with his looks would have to demand. He'd just wait, and a woman would beg to give to him.

She determined not to beg. "These differences of which you speak are unimportant when compared to our divergent desires."

"Divergent desires." He stroked his chin and narrowed his eyes thoughtfully. "Aye, we do have divergent desires. 'Tis ever so. Men desire women, and women desire men."

"These light matters matter not when compared to . . . what are you doing?"

Dusting her lips with his fingertips, he murmured, "Rosie lips." With his palm behind her neck, he lifted until her head fell back, and kissed the cord below her jaw. "Rosie throat." Then, through the silk material, he brushed his mouth across her breasts and asked, "Rosie nipples?"

How could he transform her into a wanton with a few words and a touch? How could he make her wish to show him what he hadn't seen before? Her voice shook when she accused, "You have swiving on the brain."

Looking up at her face, he chuckled. "Well, let's see if we can move it down where it belongs."

She almost chuckled, too. Damned seducer! To make her laugh and want at the same time.

He shared the gleam of camaraderie, then in a soothing tone, he promised, "I won't take the jewel of your virginity from you now, but I will show you the pleasures that await us." He stroked her from her shoulder to her knee. "If you like."

Damned seducer, indeed, to banish her suspicions with honesty and tenderness. With Tony, she remembered her girlish curiosity. She remembered how she'd always wondered what it would be like to mate with a man, and how she'd reluctantly dismissed the possibility. With Tony, for just a fleeting moment, she wondered if she should use him to satisfy her curiosity. Not all of her curiosity, for the complications would be too great, but part of it.

There was no doubt, Tony was like a bright spot on her wit, blotting out good sense. "I think . . . I would like."

He grinned in delight. "You'll see. Swiving is the most fun you can have without smiling."

"You're smiling."

He seemed to contemplate, then concluded, "Swiving is the most fun you can have."

She was smiling when he kissed her again, no longer

with delicate finesse, but with relish and skill. When he lowered himself to cover her, light and warm, she drew as much comfort from his weight as she had drawn from her baby blanket. But although the comfort relaxed her, each touch of the tongue, each brush of the lips intensified the feeling of sweet madness. It must be madness, to feel secure yet daring.

She grasped him eagerly, wanting the experience of freedom, but he pushed himself off of her body with one mighty thrust of his arms. He hadn't shown her half his experience, yet already he'd doubled her knowledge.

He panted, his eyes dilated. She wiped her fingers down his chest. "You're sweating."

Catching his breath, he said, "So we won't catch fire."

Delighted, she laughed.

"We dare not do more, or we'll be a conflagration and my promise not to take you will be for naught." But his gaze lingered on her face and dropped to her bosom. "Although, I suppose, we could look more upon each other."

She ran her gaze down his naked body. "How much more is there to see?"

A sheepish grin gave rein to his dimples. "Humor is contagious. Be careful lest you catch it from me."

"Other men than you have thought me droll."

"Other men have thought you . . . another man."

"Would you have them know different?"

"Nay, lady." He reached for the hem of the shirt. "Even now, I mourn the loss of the bold lad who won so many of my serving maids' hearts." Slowly, his fingers pushed the material up her thigh as if he were waiting for her objection.

The objection hovered on the tip of her tongue, but

something about the wonder in his eyes made her quip, "Give a man a free hand, and he'll run it all over you."

His palm cruised over her hipbone, over her ribs, and found her breast.

She gasped. "If you're lucky."

He pushed the silk up and looked, and she knew he didn't really know what she was saying, and probably not even what *he* was saying. He spoke only to relieve her apprehension. It was working; by concentrating, she could pretend the glow on his features was a mundane occurrence.

Well, not mundane, perhaps. Perhaps, no matter how often it occurred, she would still revel in his worship, want to stretch and show off, want to give him more than he had given her.

"I won't take you, but sweet Jesú! you are so beautiful."

He said it, and she believed it. She especially believed it when his head dipped, he took her nipple in his mouth, and suckled as if he wanted to consume her.

She twisted upward, trying to make contact along the length of him. His body pulled her like a magnet. She had to be with him, pressed against him, now. She was still speaking, but the words no longer made sense. They were just sounds created in the kiln of heat and pleasure.

He lay on her once again and rested his head on her chest, panting as if he'd run a long way. "My sisters say that men are creatures with two legs and eight hands, and with you, I know the truth of it. I won't take you. We don't want to make a babe out of wedlock. But if it please you, I would untie the string which strangles your throat."

She touched the shirt string she'd knotted so firmly around her neck. "That would please me beyond all imagining."

Grasping the end, he tugged as if a weight were attached to the opposite end. As he freed the bow, he grimaced. "I won't do more than look," he promised. "I won't do more than . . ." He touched his lips to the hollow of her collarbone. "You don't have to worry about your virtue." His breath whispered across the tender place behind her ear. "I swear you shouldn't worry about your virtue."

"Virtue?" she questioned groggily.

His shirt was constructed simply. That string gathered the fullness of material, and when Tony loosened it, he was able to slip both her shoulders free. He kissed one shoulder, then, as the silk slithered down her arm beneath his urging, he extended the caress all the way to her fingertips. What had been previously revealed from the bottom was now revealed from the top, and she wiggled to free herself from the expanse of cloth.

"Don't," he commanded.

"Why not?"

"You'll be nude."

"Tony." Boldly, she thrust her fingers through his hair. Then because he *seemed* to like it and because she *did* like it, she crooned, "I'm as good as nude now."

"Parts of my body believe that if you are wearing something, no matter how little it covers, you are unattainable."

"Which parts?"

He didn't answer.

"The big parts?"

He caught her questing hand. "Flattery will get you everywhere, but we mustn't."

She slithered out of the shirt and kicked it aside.

"We mustn't . . ." His gaze traveled down. "I won't take you, but might I just give you a sample of pleasure?" Without waiting for permission, he touched her.

Lightly. Barely. Fingers drifting like dandelion seeds on the wind. She stilled, breathless, tensed, waiting, wanting something.

Wanting a chance to learn the whole of the secret. There would be repercussions; Tony would be difficult to deal with once the deed was done. But no other man existed who could take her so far so quickly.

She wanted him. "Tony."

He jumped as if the faint whisper of his name startled him, and he stared at her with wild dismay. "Tell me quickly to leave you, or we are lost."

"Lost"—she stroked the blade of his cheekbone—"together."

He groaned as if she'd stabbed him, and she loved it. She loved having the strong-willed Tony subservient to the needs of her body. She loved being subservient to the needs of his. His chest worked like a bellows, his fingers still strummed a melody on her body, and she reveled in the scent of Tony. The scent of pleasure.

Still he struggled one last time, desperate to maintain control, to keep to his morals, to save her from shame. But she'd been reared without the normal strictures that restrained a woman, and she knew that nothing about this mating could shame her. Calling on her instinct, she sat up and leaned forward so that her head could rest on his shoulder. She kissed his neck, touched the lobe of his ear with her tongue, then, while he waited and trembled, she bravely rushed at his mouth. Mashing her lips on his, she touched him with her tongue, and the conflagration he feared took place. Both of their mouths opened, breath and wet and rapture mingling. She realized, to her delight, that he liked what she taught him quite as much as she liked what he taught her. But before she could discover more to teach him, he took over.

He kissed with the craft and passion of a master. He fondled all the places he'd looked at; he kissed all the places he'd touched. She found herself clutching handfuls of the sheets while she watched him taking joy, giving joy. His eyes glowed when she gasped. "Did you like that?"

She glared, and he chuckled. "If you're not sure, I'll do it again."

"Aye." She closed her eyes, as if that would help contain the sensation. "More. Now."

He repeated the movement, but she caught his hand. Opening her eyes, she insisted, "*Now.*"

"Now?" He looked her up and down. "This moment?"

"Aye."

"By all manner of means, it shall be now. But I swear I'll pull out before I empty my seed. I swear." He bussed her forehead to solemnize the vow; he then snatched one of the pillows from behind her head and slid it beneath her hips. "Let me between, sweeting. Let me in. Let me."

He closed his eyes, and she knew why. He, too, tried to contain the sensation, or did he seek to concentrate it? His fingers touched her intimately, pushed inside her, and he said, "You're ready. You're so ready."

She wanted to say something that proved she could speak and pant at the same time, just as he did. "Are *you* ready?"

His eyes flew open, and he grinned as if he were in pain. "If I were any more ready, you'd miss out on the best part." Arranging himself, he promised, "I'll make it the best part."

He pushed inside her, and her flesh burned. She whimpered, and he said, "Don't worry. I'll pull out when it's time. Trust me, I won't put you in danger."

It was difficult to whimper when she wanted to laugh. He battered her maidenhead in this, the first act, and thought she worried about the final climax. Then he pushed hard, and she forgot all tendency to humor. She didn't scream—she never screamed—but she bit the back of her hand hard.

With his thumbs he wiped the trickle of tears off her temples and murmured, "That's it. That's the worst of it. Now I'll make it good. Rosie"—he looked into her eyes, and made a vow she believed—"I'll make you happy."

He did. She who never screamed, screamed for joy. And he who had never emptied his seed in a woman, gave her his everything.

"I can't believe I did that."

"Pray don't chastise yourself."

"I was weak. How can you respect me when I was so weak?"

"I respect you."

"I thought I would be strong, but at the first sign of temptation, I crumpled."

"I crumpled, too."

Flinging his arm across his eyes, Tony groaned. "People who crumple at temptation are called parents."

Rosie had the odd feeling she was playing the wrong part in this scene. Shouldn't the deflowered virgin be indulging in an agony of guilt?

Tucking the sheet beneath her arms, she stared at the man sprawled across the rumpled bed. Regardless of her sentiments, she couldn't discount Tony's real anguish. She was legitimate, but an orphan, and she had passed from one guardian to another wrapped in an insulating blanket of affection.

Tony was a bastard, torn between his father and his

mother like a bone between two dogs, and he carried the scars on his soul. Ignoring her own disappointment at this ending to an idyllic interlude, she said, "Tony, if we have begotten a child, 'tis not a matter for—"

You, she was going to say.

But he bounded up. "We've got to get married. Now. I'll send for the clergyman, get him from the table if necessary, and we'll wed."

She crumpled the sheet in her fist. "Wed?"

"At once. It's a lucky thing I got a special license, isn't it?" He snatched up his shirt—the silk shirt she'd worn so recently—and jerked it over his head. He efficiently tied it and scrambled among the clothes on the floor. Bringing up a short padded waistcoat, he donned it for warmth. "I'll have the cook prepare a special meal for us tonight. We must celebrate, although my sisters will choke at wedding on such short notice. Ha!" He rubbed his hands together. "'Tis an abrupt finish to Lady Honora's plans. Won't she be disgusted?"

What lunacy made Rosie think she could handle the repercussions of her impulsive mating? Could she handle Tony in a frenzy, or stifle a force of nature?

Starting for the door, he said, "We'll have a celebration tomorrow, roast a sheep and a steer, crack a few barrels of beer and a cask of wine. I'll have Hal notify the parish."

Coldly, she asked, "Aren't you forgetting something?"

He stopped, his hand on the knob. "I can't think of anything." Looking down at his bare legs, he laughed. "Except that. Already you act like a wife. I would look foolish, running down the hall with—"

"I wasn't speaking of your garb. I was speaking of your plans."

He froze. He hadn't imagined another solution to

what he viewed as their dilemma. Until she spoke, he hadn't thought she might have an objection. Now, clearly, he imagined and thought, and it filled him with unanticipated horror. "You cannot still be refusing to wed me."

He came back to the side of the bed and loomed impressively, but Rosie refused to be intimidated. If she let him, he would overwhelm her and she'd find herself married, and she wasn't ready. Some things were easy to grow accustomed to. A warm dry bed. Regular bountiful meals. Even the clothes she wore, although a woman's, and uncomfortable, were beautiful.

None of those amenities could replace a young man's freedom.

Tony knew nothing of her thoughts, but either he realized his looming was fruitless or something in her expression disclosed her plight. Easing his hip onto the mattress, he said, "I didn't plan this."

He looked wretched, but she hadn't even considered that he could have used these circumstances to so manipulate her. At least—not consciously. "Forsooth, I know you did not."

"I have never had to force a woman."

"You didn't force me."

"And I would never trap a woman."

"You would have no need."

He touched her shoulder, and she pulled the sheet up to cover it. "Nor do I wish to marry you only because of our child."

"Nay, you want to marry me *at this moment* because of a babe."

"I *do* want to marry you as soon as possible, but I've always wanted that." His brows crinkled together in worry. "I didn't seduce you for the lands, either."

"You could just cheat me out of them if you chose."

She gave him credit for persisting in the face of her hostility, but while he speculated on every possible reason for her refusal, he hadn't come close to the source of her troubles. For some reason, she expected him to understand her without her explanation, and her anger grew with every reassurance he gave.

"I was selfish and unthinking to tell you my worries rather than hold you close after we finished. I should have told you how much joy you gave me." He touched her cheek, and she scrubbed his touch away. In rapid succession, he touched her other cheek, her forehead, the tip of her nose, and she would have looked foolish if she'd objected to all of them. "You did give me joy," he said, and he smiled so radiantly she warmed in spite of herself. Then he gave her the most dreadful blow of all. "I've never loved a woman before, but I love one now."

"Nay!" She threw out her arm, knocked him aside, and scrambled off the bed.

He struggled to sit up, but she jerked at the sheet beneath him. "What?" Shaking his head, he rolled off the other side of the bed. "Why?"

"You don't love . . . are you saying you love me?"

Her skin shone pale beneath her tan and she shook all over. For a man who thought he was irresistible to women, it proved a sad set down. Worse, it proved he didn't comprehend the female mind, and Rosie's in particular. He had given her a dazzling display of sensual skills and what amounted to his virginity, and she was reluctant. He had offered his heart served on the platter of his estate, and she was repulsed. Shocked, he asked, "Don't you want me to love you?"

"What has love brought me but heartache and worry?"

"You love?" His mind sprang to Ludovic. "Who is this man you love?"

"He's been gone since this morning, and already you dismiss him?"

Sir Danny. She was talking about Sir Danny. He scrambled for footing in a suddenly slippery world. "Of course I don't dismiss him, but what has he to do with me loving you?"

"Don't say that!"

Had he been expecting her to melt at his declaration? He could almost laugh at himself, except that his heart wept. There had been another time when he'd offered love, and it had been laughed at, rejected, ignored. He'd been the bastard member of the earl of Drebred's household, and he didn't like feeling that way again.

Yet his mind knew Rosie didn't reject him because of his illegitimacy. She rejected him because she needed a father's love, not a husband's.

She paced toward the foot of the bed, tripped on the sheet, and recovered. "I have to be able to go find him."

It had never occurred to Tony—or to Sir Danny—that she would be unable to settle into the role required of her because of her anxiety. Of all the things Tony had thought, he'd never considered that his competition was Rosie's father.

Nevertheless, Tony had given her his seed, and it might be growing at this very moment. For him, their babe had a face, a personality, a destiny of bitterness and struggle if born without the protection of its father. Tony could not indulge Rosie, nor could he brood about her rejection. Somehow he had to coerce her into taking the vows.

If only she didn't look so horrified.

"I'm bleeding," she said.

"Oh, sweetheart." He'd hurt her more than he should, and he walked toward her with outstretched arms. "I know you are, but it's nothing to be concerned about. Every maiden—"

"Nay. I mean, I'm bleeding. 'Tis my"—she blushed, and her embarrassment struggled with her horror—"monthly flow."

"Then we didn't . . . ?" Acrid disappointment mixed with relief.

They had failed to make a bastard, thank the blessed Virgin.

They had failed to make a child, damn it. His seed would not find root in her this time.

17

Lovers and madmen have such seething brains,
Such shaping fantasies, that apprehend
More than cool reason ever comprehends.
                              —A MIDSUMMER NIGHT'S DREAM, V, i, 4

Lady Honora was staying.

Tony couldn't believe his sisters would abandon him, leaving such a burden, but they wished—not unnaturally, he admitted—to spend Christmas with their families. Lady Honora had no such family, and she kindly volunteered to stay and continue Rosie's education.

And Rosie had thanked her. Thanked her!

The little coward had been avoiding him ever since the evening in his bedchamber. He'd declared his love, and she'd been indifferent.

Very well. He'd been humuliated when he'd lived at Drebred Castle. The past was dead—let it stay buried.

But he'd also shown Rosie passion. He'd swept her

away on the high waves of desire, and he'd been swept away with her. Together they had scaled the peaks, flown to the stars, swept the heavens. Apparently she considered his magnificent skill at lovemaking insignificant. Tony didn't like feeling insignificant. He knew he was the finest lover in England, and Rosie should realize it, too.

Next time he'd prove it. Next time . . . on their wedding night.

He gnashed his teeth and glared out at the wind-swept morning.

He didn't rue that he'd lost all discipline and given her his seed. He could only regret that it had had no chance to take root, and that he regretted with every breath he took and with every beat of his heart. He wanted his sisters to stay and arrange a hasty marriage and an equally hasty baptism, but the carriage waited on the drive beyond the terrace, and Jean, Lady Honora, and Rosie waited for Ann to finish dressing.

They'd been waiting quite a while.

"Take care of Tony." Warming herself before the long gallery's fire one last time, Jean spoke to Rosie but grinned at her brother. "He's in a delicate humor right now."

"Amusing." Tony glared at Jean, dressed in her traveling clothes and swaddled in a wool cloak, then encompassed Rosie and Lady Honora in his displeasure.

His displeasure focused on Lady Honora when she said, "If anyone should take care of Tony, it should be I. I am, after all, to be his wife."

She seemed to be the only one who believed it any longer, but Lady Honora's belief was a powerful thing, and impossible to discount. She did indeed know about that evening of intimacy in his bedroom, and she had taken it upon herself to make sure it never happened again. Under the guise of preparing Rosie for her life as mistress of the estate, Tony gave her her reading lessons, taught her the necessary accounts, or showed her the duties of the estate, and always, always Lady Honora found a way to interfere.

"Lady Honora." Jean patted her friend's hand. "I don't doubt your ability to overwhelm Tony, or to overwhelm Rosalyn, but I think you'll find them impossible to defeat together."

"We're not together," Rosie answered quickly.

Jean patted her hand, too. "You're together in a way I had forgotten existed."

Did she really think so? Tony lifted an inquiring brow at Jean, and Jean nodded reassuringly. He'd begun to doubt his own instincts, and having his rational sister say so bolstered his flagging confidence. He turned a fierce stare at Rosie.

"Excuse me," Jean said to Lady Honora and Rosie. "I need to say something private to my brother." Jean took Tony's arm and led him close to the portraits at the center of the gallery. "If you keep looking at Rosalyn as if you're going to devour her, she's going to give up pretending she's dauntless and take to her heels."

"I don't look like that," Tony protested.

"Tony, you're shooting blue flames at the poor girl, and she's already frightened enough. Ann is convinced that Rosalyn is seeing her father's ghost, and that must explain her skittish behavior, but Ann's never stood between you and Rosalyn when you recall your preferred evening activity."

Heat climbed from his ruff to his forehead. It was one thing that his sister knew what he did, another thing that she knew what he thought. "Am I so obvious?"

"Stubby used to look at me like that." She sighed in remembrance. "I wish the old dear could still do so."

"He's watching you in just such a manner," Tony

said, recalling his pudgy brother-in-law and his undying devotion to Jean. "From heaven."

Jean blinked hard. "I do miss the old goat." She nodded at Hal who shuffled along the wall toward them. "Does your crazed steward wish to speak to you?"

Puzzled by Jean's comment, Tony observed the man as he carefully avoided the carpet runner, keeping on the hardwood with religious intensity. "Hal doesn't feel the servants should wear out the carpet, but really, he's as steady as a beached boat."

Jean snorted.

"Am I not a good judge of character?" Tony asked.

"You always have been before." Jean glanced at Hal's stooped figure. "But this time . . ."

When Hal came within speaking distance, Tony asked, "Are the ladies' bags loaded?"

"Aye, Sir Anthony." Hal kept his gaze fixed to the clean, fine design on the carpet. "All is ready fer yer sisters' departure."

"Except my sisters."

"*I'm* ready," Jean answered. "'Tis a long journey we make, but Ann is ever tardy."

Tony glared up the stairs. "Where *is* Ann?"

"In a hurry to be rid of us?" Jean teased. "You behave as if we've overstayed our welcome."

"My home is ever open to my *family*."

"It'll take more than that subtle insult to unseat Lady Honora."

With a sigh, Tony agreed.

"If there'll be nothing else, Sir Anthony," Hal said, "I'll just go cipher on figures fer th' year's harvest."

"'Tis a good day for ciphering." Away from the fire, Tony could feel the drafts that crept in around the doors. Jean moved toward the warmth once more and he followed, adjusting the short cloak he wore even inside.

"Where is Sister Ann?" Jean burst out. "We'll scarcely make London this day, and we had hoped to shop for gifts."

Tony commanded, "Be careful in London."

"Always," Jean said.

"Why?" Rosie demanded.

He should have known Rosie would notice the serious note of warning in his voice. He thought of the steadily increasing stream of messages coming from Wart-Nose Harry, his guard commander, and the warnings and worries they contained. Then he thought of the news he'd received this morning. He'd hidden that communication in a pile on his desk. He wanted no one to know of it, least of all Rosie.

So with pointed intent, he said, "London is a wicked town filled with pickpockets, cheats, and *actors.*"

Rosie flounced over to examine a portrait, and he hastily changed the subject. "Jean, will you visit Her Majesty and take her a gift from me?"

"We hadn't planned to go to the court, but if you wish we will."

Tony snapped his fingers, and one of the footmen went running.

"What do you send?" Lady Honora asked.

"A cambric smock, wrought with silk at the collar and sleeves, with ruff wrought of Venice gold and edged with a small, bone lace of Venice gold. And I send a message."

"Write it down," Jean commanded rudely.

"I have, but I would that you repeat it so I may catch the tenor of her mood in her reply."

Jean groaned. "What is it?"

"Say that I send a smock for her to wear close to her heart so that I may imagine 'tis I who am so honored."

Rosie proved she'd been listening when she cried,

"Od's bodkin, the queen'll not tolerate such rubbish."
Tony, Lady Honora, and Jean were silent, and suddenly
uncertain, Rosie asked, "Will she?"

"The queen thrives on such expressions of fondness,
especially from her most charming courtiers," Jean told
her.

"The queen is no longer in the first blush of youth,
and it profits all when a man professes admiration for
her beauty," Lady Honora said.

"How old is she?" Rosie asked.

"She wears her sixty-seven years as lightly as if they
were sixty-seven snowflakes," Tony answered.

"Sixty-seven?" Sixty-seven was an unheard-of age.
Rosie didn't think she'd ever seen someone that old.
And she had always thought of Queen Elizabeth as
being young. Tales abounded in England of Elizabeth's
beauty, her wisdom, her modesty, but now it seemed
she was none of those. "Is she very—"

"Last fall I rode on a hunt with her." Lady Honora
rubbed her posterior. "I couldn't keep up with Her Majesty."

"Aye," Jean agreed. "Her Majesty dances all through
the night, wearing out her young courtiers and discard-
ing one for another."

"That's why she likes me." Tony grinned. "I can
dance all night and ride all day."

Lady Honora and Jean cried out in mock disdain,
but Tony watched Rosie keenly. He was giving her a
message, she realized, and that message was twofold.
The servants listened, and these members of Elizabeth's court dedicated themselves to maintaining the
fable of her mastery. From the smiles on their faces and
the worship in their voices, Rosie surmised the queen
had truly captured their hearts.

"Sixty-seven," Rosie whispered in wonder. At age

sixty-seven, Queen Elizabeth commanded Tony's devotion. Would he be as devoted to his wife at sixty-seven? Would he still see her with the eyes of a lover, and flirt as if she were the most beautiful creature on earth? When that great age weighed on his shoulders, would he still seek his wife's bed and lavish amorous intentions on her receptive body? Rosie quashed that thought and every thought that paraded through her head like temptations taking flesh.

Since the evening in his room, she'd been wary of temptation. 'Twas too easy to remember his magnificent passion, and not easy enough to remember the chains hidden beneath it. She said, "Tell me of the queen."

"She wears dark red wigs"—Jean touched her own red wig as illustration—"and has radiant white skin."

"She has beautiful deep eyes, and a voice worthy of a queen," Lady Honora said.

"She has a fine figure, beautiful long fingers, and a magnificent bosom," Tony added.

Rosie shook her head. "You would notice that."

Glancing up the stairs once more, Jean mourned, "'Twill be evening before we leave." She sank down on one of the straight-backed chairs pulled close to the fire, and waved Rosie into one at her right. "We've obviously neglected your education in royal matters, and that could prove fatal when you meet our dread and sovereign lady. Although Queen Elizabeth teases until the men are half-mad, she likes it not when her favorite courtiers flaunt their attachments, and 'tis better to pretend to wish to marry for the continuation of the line, or for wealth, or for any reason other than fondness."

Realizing Jean spoke for a reason, Rosie sat and occupied herself with arranging her skirts. "You said Her Most Gracious Majesty remembers Lord Sadler fondly."

"She still speaks of him with tears in her eyes." Lady Honora sat on Rosie's other side.

"Is there then a good way to present my petition for the return of my estate?"

Tony propped his foot on the bench opposite them. "Aye, ladies, tell her how to take my property from me."

Lady Honora and Jean exchanged glances. Then Jean said, "Entertain her."

"Flatter her," Lady Honora said.

"And duck if she boxes your ears." Tony rubbed his own ears as if recalling similar treatment. Noticing Rosie's wide-eyed astonishment, he said, "Her Majesty does not like to be told she's wrong, and if she is, she's likely to take action. My lord Essex found that out to his fury."

"He tried to draw his sword on her, did he not?" Jean asked.

"He would have drawn it, but the earl of Nottingham stopped him." Disdain rolled off Lady Honora like fog off the ocean. "I was there. I saw it. Essex screamed he would not take such insult from even King Henry, her father, and ran from Her Majesty without permission."

"He is a stupid boy," Jean said.

"He is a dangerous boy," Rosie corrected. "He must be stopped. I wish I could be the one to stop him. Tony?" She wanted to ask about Sir Danny. Had he been successful in his quest to assist the queen? Where was he now, and what was he doing?

But Tony would tell her nothing; she'd already discovered that, to her dismay. It wasn't meanness nor the patronizing superiority of a man to a woman, but the ingrained caution of a man on whose shoulders rested the security of the queen of England. Tony told no one the contents of the dispatches which arrived every day from London, although he had promised to inform Rosie if Sir Danny were in danger.

Clearly Tony realized the drift of Rosie's thoughts, for he attempted to distract her. "If our sovereign queen rewards you custody of these lands before I've secured your hand in marriage, Rosie, will you pension me off like a faithful servant or leave me to starve?"

He sounded innocently curious, but any reply could be hazardous. Rosie said, "Lady Honora wishes to wed you. You'll have no need of a pension."

Watching Lady Honora from the corner of his eye, Tony said, "Lady Honora has high standards, and kindly overlooks my illegitimacy when claiming me for a husband. Would she also overlook my poverty? For if the queen bestows Odyssey Manor on Lady Rosalyn, I will be as penniless as the day I was born."

Lady Honora's jaw dropped with such dramatic emphasis, Rosie almost laughed. She'd seen actors use more subtlety, but Lady Honora could not act.

"You've no fortune, no other lands?" Lady Honora demanded.

"I started with a goodly fortune, and invested it in the estate, which was much neglected, and the foundry, which in a few years will produce a fortune again. As for other lands—nay, these lands were sufficient for my purpose."

"The queen will reward you should she remove the estate from your jurisdiction," Lady Honora decided.

"Lady Honora, you know the state of the queen's finances," Tony chided. "Her household is ever growing and she likes not to call Parliament to adjust her allowance. And let us not mention the queen's own stinginess."

"And let us also not mention the queen's displeasure with Tony," Jean added helpfully. "We know not for certain if she'll forgive him."

"Certes, 'tis true." He examined his fingernails.

"Nay, I would imagine I'd come to a marriage shorn of wealth."

"But he's still a mighty stallion," Jean said helpfully. "Capable of producing many children. Although, forsooth, should a woman decide to wed a penniless man, I'd think she'd prefer to wed one who's elegant and courtly. Someone like Sir Danny."

"I couldn't wed Sir Danny." Lady Honora leaped up and paced across the floor. "He's as common as dirt."

"I never linked your name with Sir Danny's." Jean stared in assumed surprise. "I never suggested you should wed Sir Danny. Why should you think that's what I meant?"

The one thing Rosie never imagined could happen, did happen. Lady Honora blushed from the top of her stomacher to the top of her plucked forehead.

Rosie hid a smile, and Jean answered her own question. "He's a charming man, and one would never know he's an actor should he decide to act the part of a nobleman."

"That's true," Lady Honora said, obviously much struck.

Jean said, "In sooth, he's probably related to my family in Cornwall."

Astounded, Lady Honora asked, "He is?"

Patient with Lady Honora's gullibility, Jean said, "Just as Rosalyn was brought up by your aunt in seclusion and in perfect respectability."

"I don't have an aunt," Lady Honora said, then stopped. "You mean, *lie?*"

"It wouldn't be the first time the gentry has added relatives in such a manner." Jean rose as Ann's bright voice sounded on the stairs. "Ah, my sister arrives at last. There's hope we'll make London this day."

Dressed in her traveling clothes, Ann rushed into

the long gallery, riding a wave of violet scent. "Forgive me, good people. Have you been waiting long?"

Speechless, Jean could only stare, but Tony took Ann's fluttering hand and patted it. "Not at all. My sister Jean would probably like to have a bit of speech with Rosie before she leaves, anyway."

"Oh, Jean." Disgusted, Ann placed her fists on her waist. "I hurried because I thought you'd be angry, and you want to sit and chat?"

"I—"

Ann rushed on before Jean could complete her sentence. "It's not possible, I tell you. We must leave at once, or we'll not make London this day, and you know how we hate the inns between here and there. Tony, you should send a gift to Queen Elizabeth." The footman handed Tony a package wrapped in brown paper and ribbon, and Tony handed it to Ann. "Excellent!" Ann cried, weighing it in her hand. "'Tis clothing. Shall I tell her she should think of you when she wears it?"

Jean grabbed Ann's arm and pulled. "Let us begone before you repeat our entire conversation."

Lady Honora accepted a cloak from her hovering maid, but Tony took Rosie's cloak and wrapped her in it himself. He seemed very concerned that it remain close about her; he tied it at the neck, tucked it close around her arms, pulled the front shut, and brushed Rosie's skin a dozen times in the process. She remained aloof.

At least she thought she did, but Tony chuckled with deep satisfaction and released her only when a footman opened the door onto the terrace and the winter wind whistled through.

"What a day to travel." Tony accepted his long cloak and pulled it over the top of his short one and stepped out into the cold.

Rosie held back, watching him as he welcomed the winter with an exuberant shout. That was his secret, she mused. Everyone liked Tony, even Old Man Winter, because he liked everyone. He wasn't a stupid man; he judged everyone astutely, but he reveled in their differences, their personalities—them.

Rosie *had* to convince herself that Tony was nothing more than a good-looking man whose conceit was perfectly justified and perfectly odious. Just because he shone like a sun god with his golden halo of hair and his relentlessly radiant personality didn't mean she should waver like a willow in the wind. She was stronger than that.

Ann scurried after him, chatting with animation, adoring him with her gaze. Lady Honora followed with more dignity, but just as much eagerness. Jean hurriedly pulled on her leather gloves and stepped out into the wind with a fond smile at her brother.

And Rosie? How did Rosie feel about him? She'd been avoiding the subject for weeks, blaming her own adoration on lust, on madness, on just about anything but the truth.

She idolized him just as much as Ann, admired him just as much as Lady Honora, and loved him . . . Od's bodkin, she loved him more than Jean, more than any sister, different from any sister. She loved him like those lovestruck fools in Uncle Will's plays, and she wanted to know if he loved her. He said he did, but she hadn't been ready to listen. Now, dared she ask him?

Aye, she did. Puffing out her chest, she stepped out on the terrace and caught sight of him.

Nay, she didn't. She stopped short and was bumped by the door as a footman shut it behind her.

Aye, she dared. She'd do it now. Right now. In front of everyone.

Then Ann cried, "My hat!" as it lifted off her head and sailed over the edge of the terrace.

Rosie sighed in relief. Not now.

A footman ran down the steps after Ann's hat, Lady Honora and the sisters hurried to the railing and peered over, and Tony laughed and chased a few steps after the footman.

Rosie watched them, trying to catch her breath and watching Tony. He stood halfway down the stairs, encouraging the footman with shouts, then looking back at his sisters and teasing Ann. He grinned at his sisters and even at Lady Honora, then turned and saw her. His smile softened; he looked as if the mere sight of her tantalized him. His smile invited her to reply, and she almost answered. Almost.

Then the sky fell.

18

Times goes on crutches till love have all his rites.
—MUCH ADO ABOUT NOTHING, II, i, 352

Thunder battered Tony's ear. Dust rushed up in a whirlwind. Women screamed, and windows shattered.

"Rosie!" Tony leaped up the steps in two bounds, darted into the cloud, and tripped over a piece of the sky. A tall stone statue from the roof's trim lay shattered in the crater of the ruined terrace floor. He leaped it, skidded on the chips, and ran into Rosie, rushing at him.

She was alive. She was on her feet. He could see no more, for the wind, like a giant broom, whisked the dust aloft. Grabbing her by the shoulders, he coughed, then gasped, "Hurt? Are you hurt?"

His hands ran over her as he spoke, and he found her doing the same thing to him. "I'm fine. You?"

"Fine. Move!" He glanced up through the cloud, and

silhouetted against the cloudy sky, he saw a hole gaping among the finials at the edge of the roof. "God's love." He pushed Rosie out of the center of destruction, and wanted to keep pushing her until she was safe.

But valiant Rosie choked, "Your sisters. Lady Honora."

His sisters. He stumbled, trying to find them, then the dust swirled away as if it had never been. The three women were huddled at the rail, their faces shielded by their cloaks. They were not crushed. All was right.

"Away, ladies," Rosie cried, and she and Tony rushed to them.

Ann sobbed, and Jean's ominous silence worried him. Wrapping his sisters in his grasp, he gave the shattered statue a wide berth. He spared a thought to Lady Honora, but knew he could depend on Rosie to care for her. They reached the manor as the servants spilled out the door.

Inside, the cacophony of many voices assaulted his ears. Eager hands took charge of his sisters. Ann was untouched, although shock had bleached her swarthy skin to white. Or was it covered with a fine coating of dust? Jean lowered her cloak, and he inspected her. She seemed hale, although she coughed into her handkerchief.

Then he heard gasps from many throats and spun to the door. Lady Honora swayed there, propped up by a white-faced Rosie. Blood flowed from a long gash on Lady Honora's temple and dripped from tiny wounds on her cheeks and chin.

The footman stood behind them, holding Ann's squashed hat. The serving maids hovered, and Tony realized with a wrench they were too much in awe of Lady Honora to touch her. Springing forward, he caught Lady Honora as she toppled, unconscious. He staggered beneath her weight, but Rosie helped steady them.

She said, "Flying fragments slashed her. Gravel may be in the wounds. If you'll take her upstairs to a bed, I'll see to her."

Tony started for the stairs. "I'll get a surgeon."

"You will not!" Rosie hurried ahead of him. "We'll not leave her to one of those butchers."

"But you—"

"I've acquired some skills in my travels, skills a lady might not have." She called for the maids as they reached the hall and ordered hot water, towels, needle, and thin sheep gut thread. Seeing his horror, she explained, "I had to stitch wounds when the actors got into fights."

"Stitch? You want to stitch?" He stopped and clasped Lady Honora. For the life of him, all he could remember were the simple skills Rosie had had to be taught—how to use a handkerchief, how to eat at a leisurely pace. And she wanted to sew Lady Honora's face? When Lady Honora had been her primary instructor, and she'd resented every minute of her education?

"Sir Danny taught me. He is a most excellent healer, and that big gash must be stitched." Rosie adjusted Lady Honora's lolling head and peered into her unconscious face. "Or it will heal poorly."

"I'll send for a surgeon," Tony said firmly.

"If it'll comfort you, do so." Rosie held the door to Lady Honora's room while he maneuvered her inside. "But I'll try to finish before she wakes."

Laying Lady Honora on her bed, he turned to speak firmly to Rosie, but Rosie was directing the maids, and capably, too. With a minimum of fuss, she prepared a needle, thrusting the limp brown sheep gut through the tiny eye with dispatch. Climbing on a stool, she leaned over Lady Honora and examined her. Tony edged forward, fascinated by this exhibition of efficiency from the woman he had considered, well, primordial clay for his molding. She called for a warm wet cloth, then carefully bathed the wound. He crept so close that when she turned again, she knocked his head with her elbow. Exasperated, she cried, "Move, Tony! I can't work with you there."

"Better yet, leave," Lady Honora said.

She was awake, and glaring at him. "Go away, Tony. I don't want you here."

He found himself backing away. Even wounded, Lady Honora was formidable, and if she wanted him gone . . . he found himself in the hall, but not alone. Jean waited for him, a serious expression on her grubby face. "Is it Ann?" he asked, alarmed.

"Ann's fine." Using the end of her skirt, Jean scrubbed at his face and showed him the dirt. He shrugged, but she said, "Come into this room and I'll wash your face."

He opened his mouth to protest, but she glanced around at the milling servants. "Ah." He nodded, understanding. "Whatever you wish, madam."

Jean led him to one of the empty rooms and shut the door. Leaning against it, she whispered, "I'm not sure, but Tony—I would swear I saw a man on the roof."

Visible through the windows, an occasional tendril of mist swirled like a flaw in the diamond-cut ebony of night. Inside the study, the dark, polished paneling reflected the glow of candlelight, and the air smelled of beeswax. Only the crackle of the fire broke the profound silence which matched Tony's solemn mood.

He had a murderer on the estate.

He'd spent the afternoon on the slippery slate roof, examining the evidence. Stone chips littered the area where the statue had been; some maniac had worked very hard to push it over.

But on whom? The arrow had been aimed at either him or Rosie, but this attempt could have killed everyone on the terrace. In fact, it was a miracle no one had died. The servants who'd been employed to clean up the shattered remnants had chattered about the extraordinary depth of the crater left in the marble floor of the terrace. The statue had weighed perhaps a ton, and they'd found chips in the grass, in the bushes, and inside the house mixed with the shattered glass of three large windows.

Despite Jean's discretion, everyone in the manor seemed to know the accident was no accident. Everyone buzzed about their fear of Ludovic and how he must be caught, and Tony had immediately put his best huntsmen on Ludovic's trail. But how had a man of Ludovic's size and appearance entered the house and reached the rooftop without someone—*anyone*—seeing him? Unless he had an accomplice, it seemed an impossible feat, and an accomplice placed a whole new light on the situation. He, or she, would have to be a member of the household, and why would a member of the household want to kill anybody? More than that, why would a member of the household need Ludovic to do the killing?

Rosie, when she heard the rumors, insisted Ludovic would never take the chance of hurting her, but she looked troubled.

So where did that leave them?

With an unknown murderer who sought an unknown victim. Or was it victims?

A faint knock sounded and he turned away from the window to stare at the door. He didn't know if he could bear more excited servants giving him clues which meant nothing and led nowhere.

Before he could respond, the handle turned and the door slowly opened. A head popped around the edge. "Rosie."

He must have sounded welcoming, for her solemn expression lightened, and she slipped into the room. She'd washed off the dust of the afternoon, for she smelled of soap and flowers. She wore a demure white gown of a style so old-fashioned and informal, it was made with a bodice instead of a stiff stomacher. Her damp hair was caught back in a ribbon, and a faint dark hue smudged the skin beneatxh her eyes.

She looked lovely.

"Am I disturbing you?" she asked.

He walked toward her. "You are the only person I want to see right now." Taking her hand, he kissed the cold fingers and marveled at the quick squeeze she gave him. Then she blushed as if she'd been bold and tried to recover her hand. Hastily he asked, "Is Lady Honora sleeping?"

Serious at once, she answered, "Aye, but not well. She's in pain, and when she sleeps, she dreams horrible dreams." She glanced around the chamber. "I've experienced that."

He glanced around, too, remembering her reaction the first time she'd seen the room. Rosie had too many secrets, and when he uncovered one, he found ten more. She was a mystery, and he loved mysteries—except when they threatened Rosie's life. And his craft had to be ten times greater than her stealth, for she liked to keep her secrets, so he casually inquired, "Have you spoken to Jean and Ann?"

"They're retiring early tonight and plan to stay until Lady Honora is better. Perhaps even through the holidays, for they say they'll scarcely make Cornwall in this vile weather."

He knew that. He knew it all, but he didn't want her to leave, and he struggled to think of something else to discuss, something comforting, something not related to the horrible events of the day.

She glanced down at their still-entwined hands, then up at him. "May we continue with my reading lessons?"

Her reading lessons? She'd come for her reading lessons? "Certes!" He looked for the materials he'd used to teach her her letters, but didn't see a quill. Had one of the servants cleaned his study again?

He frowned, and she said, "If you're too busy . . ."

"Not at all." Not for her. Thinking fast, he said, "I think we'll read a real book." Tugging her by the hand, he pulled her along until she stood beside his desk, and he picked up his Bible. "'Tis a gloomy, vaporous night, and we'll sit by the fire and read."

She caught her lower lip in her teeth and gazed at the massive Bible. "Read a book?"

"Exciting, isn't it?"

She accepted it, and her hands trembled as she touched the leather binding.

She seemed almost reluctant, and he promised, "I'll help you." She nodded and sat on one of the straight-backed chairs. He dragged a table beside and behind her, placed a candelabra on it, then drew his chair close. Seating himself, he said brightly, "There. That's cozy."

The room grew very quiet. The gilt edges of the pages seemed to fascinate her. She ran her finger along them many times, then took a breath.

At last he realized the problem.

The big Bible intimidated her. She knew sections of it by heart. But to read it . . . ah, that would surely frighten her. Perhaps she feared that she would make a mistake, or that he'd laugh at her, or that the great mystery of written speech would not open for her.

"I know you anticipate your first chance to read a book," he said. Anticipation didn't seem to correctly describe her expression, but he plowed valiantly on. "You know the letters and many, many words. I've never met a pupil as clever as you."

Her gaze flashed to his. "You've never met a pupil as old as I."

Ignoring that, he continued, "I had wondered if someone taught you your letters years ago, for you seem to know them almost without my telling."

She looked around at the room with that expression she sometimes wore when the ghosts of the house were speaking to her. "Who would have taught me my letters?"

"Perhaps your father?" She didn't answer, and he said, "In fact, I've actually put off allowing you to read a book for fear you'll decide you don't need me anymore, and these quiet hours will stop."

She smiled. "Really?"

"I've enjoyed it." He smiled back at her. "Have you?"

She watched him from beneath her lashes. "Very much."

Her shy admission quickened his heartbeat, and he almost reached for her. He wanted to hug her, to hold her against him, to assure himself that she still breathed, that the blood still coursed through her veins, that her skin still flushed with warmth, that her lips still guarded paradise. . . .

"Tony, are you sure you wish to read tonight?" She cocked her head like a kitten unsure of its welcome.

"Read?"

"You seem far away."

Waking to the dangerous trek of his thoughts, he subdued them. "Nay, I am too close."

Her lashes fluttered again. "Tony?"

"We'll read," he said firmly. Taking her hands in his, he helped her open the book. "This is Cranmer's Great Bible, published after our beloved King Henry declared himself head of the Church of England. Look at the illustrations." He helped her stroke the pages back. "Aren't they colorful? When I learned to read, 'twas with this very book. 'Twas given to me by the lady I called 'Mama,' and she told me when I couldn't decipher a word, I should rest my mind by studying the illustrations."

She glanced up at him. "You can't decipher all the words?"

"I can now." He guided her to turn another page. "But I couldn't when I was learning to read. My tutor used to complain that I was a difficult student to teach. That's because I wanted to be outside, riding with my father and brother. You put me to shame with your eagerness."

She turned a page on her own, and he slowly released her hands. He contemplated her as she studied the page. She'd never looked lovelier, with her hair swept back and her expression intense. She squealed suddenly and pointed. "Look! 'Tis the word 'and.'"

"So it is."

"And 'the.'" She pointed again and again. "'Thou,' 'time.'" She paused, then announced triumphantly, "'Borders.'"

He sighed in feigned despair. "I knew your ability would make a mockery of mine. Can you read a sentence?"

Flipping the pages, she looked until she found one she liked. *"Ten fat oxen, and twenty oxen out of the—"*

He leaned over and looked. "Pastures."

"—Pastures, and—" Growing bored, she bravely flipped through until she found another she liked. "'Tis a song. We should like this."

"A song?" Craning his neck, he tried to see what she read, then suggested, "Why don't you sit on a stool here, where I can see the book?" Today, death had been close. Tonight, he craved her proximity.

She seemed of like mind, for she pulled up a stool and seated herself at his knee. She even leaned against him, warming his leg with her back. He liked the fine, short wisps of hair that grew along her neckline, the tracery of veins that outlined the shell of her ear, the scent of carnation that rose in waves to stimulate him.

How he loved her! He wanted to hold her close, whisper of his love, lie down with her, breast to breast, stomach to stomach. . . .

"'Tis called the song of songs, which is"—she faltered, then sounded it out—"Sol-o-mon's."

He sat up straight. The Song of Solomon? She'd found the Song of Solomon? He'd always taken pleasure in the proof of such lusty delight in those long-dead patriarchs of the Bible, but to have Rosie read it aloud . . . Nay, he should not allow it.

"Let him kiss me with the kisses of his mouth: for thy love is better than wine." She stopped and stared at the page, then looked up at Tony. "Is that right?"

She wasn't asking if she'd read it correctly, and he ought to stop her.

In a voice warm with approval, he said, "Exactly. Go on."

She turned the page. *"He brought me to the—"*

He helped her when she faltered. "Banqueting."

"—Banqueting house, and his banner over me was—" She hesitated again, but not because she didn't know the word.

"Was?" he encouraged.

"Love."

The word dropped into the quiet like a pearl into a cup of rich, intoxicating wine. She waited for his reaction, and he whispered, "You said it just right."

"Stay me with flagons, comfort me with apples; for I am sick of love." She turned her head slightly, presenting her profile, and watched him from the corner of her eye. "Does it mean 'I am sick *with* love'?"

"So am I."

She turned all the way to face him, her amber eyes wide and softly glowing like heated coals. "I meant . . ."

He smiled, and he saw the movement of her throat as she swallowed. "Read this," he instructed, pointing at the page.

"How much better is thy love than wine! and the smell of thine ointments than all spices! Thy lips, O my spouse, drop as the honeycomb; honey and milk are under thy tongue. . . ."

She paused and when he leaned forward to look at the word, she turned her head. They were nose to nose, and with a little adjustment . . . but it was a long distance, he reminded himself. A very long distance indeed. If he closed it, he would have leaped, wide-eyed, into the canyon of desire, and he'd already proved himself too weak to leave without tasting every delight.

Her breath, scented sweet with mint jelly, fanned his face. "That reminds me of you."

"What do you mean?"

"Your tongue is honey when you speak. You say the most wonderful things." She looked into his eyes. "As when you told me the reason for kissing was for lovers to get so close they couldn't see their differences."

"Did I say that?"

"You did. And it works. Like this." Tilting her head, she closed that very long distance between them. She pressed her dry, soft lips to his.

It was a gesture of trust, and he treasured it, not seeking to deepen it at all. He let her take the lead, willing to let her guide him along the edge of the canyon.

Then she pressed her tongue into his mouth and shoved him off the cliff.

He tried to jerk back, but she caught his head in her hands and kissed him again.

Cotzooks, she remembered every trick he'd used to pleasure her, and she applied them to him without a shred of conscience. She licked and probed at his mouth, matching the rhythm of her tongue with the pressure of her hand on his groin.

How the hell did her hand get on his groin?

He jerked his head back and glared at her. "We can't do this."

She opened her eyes slowly, and her swollen lips parted in a smile. "I only wanted to express my admiration for your heroism today." Her hand lingered on his groin, testing the heat and length of him before he picked up her fingers and removed them.

"Are you always so big?" she asked.

"What?"

"You're straining your codpiece."

He was, but he didn't want to acknowledge it. He just wanted to pretend that that part of him in his canions didn't dictate his actions. He could scarcely articulate, but he managed to say, "Read."

Picking the book off the floor, she opened it again. "Where was I? I can't remember exactly."

She tapped her lower lip with her finger, and he looked at that lip and that finger, imagining how they would feel on his bare skin. He'd taught her to kiss; had he taught her how to caress with hand and mouth?

"This thy stature is like to a palm tree, and thy breasts to clusters of grapes."

He closed his eyes and imagined taking one of her grapes in his hand, in his mouth.

"I am my beloved's, and his desire is toward me."

It was. He wanted Rosie so much that when she laid her arm across his lap, his hips shifted to press the length of him against her. Somehow, that part of his body believed he'd gain relief if she touched him—but he didn't. It only made him want her more.

"Let us get up early to the vineyards: there will I give thee my loves."

Making love with Rosie outdoors in the spring. What a fantasy that was. Warm sun on his back, warm Rosie beneath him, and the earth beneath them shaking with exaltation as he planted his seed.

"I like this."

So did he.

She read, *"Let me see thy countenance, let me hear thy voice; for sweet is thy voice, and thy countenance is comely.* Tony, you are comely, and the sound of your voice makes shivers run up and down my spine."

Only one relief existed for his condition, and it was so close. She could hike up her skirts and he could open his canions and she could face him. He could hold her legs over the arms of the chair, and thrust until he'd buried himself deep inside her.

"Tony?"

"What?"

She placed the book on the table and stood up. "Would you mind if I sat in your lap?"

"Do—"

She sat.

"Not." He grasped her waist to push her off and realized she wore no stiffening at all beneath her bodice.

Laying her head on his shoulder, she said, "I just wanted to be close to you. Today I thought"—her voice quavered—"that you'd been killed. I imagined how lonely the world would be if we could never touch again, and I just want to touch you."

Her fingers traced the outer shell of his ear while she snuggled closer. And closer. And he discovered she wore no petticoats beneath her skirt.

Except for her gown, she was as good as naked in his arms.

Such a stupid thought! She still wore stockings . . . didn't she?

He tried to look, but he dared not turn his head, and his rigid neck ached with the effort of stillness. By moving only his eyes, he located her foot, and saw she did indeed wear a stocking. A red stocking. A red stocking which glistened, catching the light.

Where had she located such fine silk? How would it feel beneath his palm? Would it be a short stocking, or a long stocking? Would it be tied at her knee, or would he have to seek the garter closer to her downyshire? And would he wish to remove it at all, or would he prefer to experience the smooth frictions against his arms while he moved her hips up and down, up and down.

Her bottom, warm and lush, stroked him with small restless movements. Her arms circled his neck, and she kissed his jaw. Again he swiveled his eyes, not daring to look into her face for fear he'd have to kiss her, and kiss her, and never let her go.

"Tony, you're stiff all over," she crooned. "Let me massage you. 'Twill relax you."

She stood up and Tony experienced the relief of pressure—until his manhood stretched toward her. Then she hiked up her skirt.

The red stockings went to her thighs.

She straddled his knees.

He pushed her off.

She landed with a thump and a cry, and Tony shook his finger in her face. "Don't you know the danger you're courting? If you continue as you are, I'll have your skirts over your head and your legs wrapped—"

His finger waved too close, and she bit it. He tried to jerk it back, but she caught it in her hands and pulled it back to her mouth—and sucked it.

His heart and respiration stopped. He was aware of only two things; the wet, hot mouth suckling his finger, and how it would feel around his man-root. Then she pushed his hand aside, leaned forward into his lap, and placed her lips there. She blew gently, and the fire fed on her breath and raged out of control.

"That's it." With his arms beneath her armpits, he jerked her to her feet. "I'm going to—" On tiptoe, she kissed him, and when she released his lips, he said, "Aye, I'll do that, too."

He picked her up and looked for the bed.

Ridiculous notion. There was no bed. But there was a desk, broad, long, covered with papers. He sat her on a clear corner, and with a sweep of his arm, disposed of everything in their way. He didn't know why Rosie was so insistent, but he hadn't been able to resist her when he'd made the advances. What manner of man could resist when she did?

She laughed quietly when he lifted her skirts. The sound infuriated him. Toy with him, would she? Take control, would she? She'd learned the art of seduction quickly, but he'd been born with the knowledge and, through hours of practice, had mastered each technique. With a stroke of his tongue, he could steal her superiority and reduce her to the same witlessness that affected him. With several strokes of his tongue . . . he slid her bottom to the edge of the desk and knelt.

"What are you doing? Tony?" She tried to walk backward on her elbows. "Tony?"

He listened for her first gasp when he licked her and chuckled when it came. Then he listened for the frantic objections, the faint screams, then the swelling moans. He liked it all. He especially liked when she began to struggle against, not him, but herself. He tasted her, he tested her temperature; then he loosened his canions and stood. She clung to the edge of sanity; he pushed inside and drove her over the edge. Her body spasmed around him and, leaning his hands on the desk, he waited until she finished. "Rosie," he called, and when she opened her eyes, he demanded, "Again."

19

'Tis in my memory lock'd,
And you yourself shall keep the key of it.

—HAMLET, I, iii, 85

"*Sir Anthony!*"

The door handle rattled and Rosie groaned. The rug lent little softness to the floor, the room was chilly, but Tony held her in his arms and she'd never been so comfortable.

"*Sir Anthony!*"

Tony stirred and his grip on her tightened. "Damn," he whispered. "'Tis scarcely dawn. Couldn't they leave us alone one more hour?"

The dying fire licked his hair with red highlights and gave his complexion a golden glow. His beard shadowed his chin, but no shadow marred the satisfaction in his eyes.

She'd done that. Last night when she'd come in,

he'd been so serious she scarcely recognized him. Now he was Tony again.

Her Tony.

A few weeks ago, he'd made love to her. Last night, she'd made love to him. It made all the difference in the world to be the aggressor, yet the result was the same. They'd both found pleasure—on the desk, then on the floor, then on the chair, facing each other, with her legs over the chair arms and Tony's hands on her hips. He'd seemed to enjoy that quite a lot, although he assured her that with her, the worst was wonderful.

"Sir Anthony, I beg of you." Hal's frantic voice hissed through the keyhole. "There's a messenger here. 'Tis from the queen."

Tony stiffened. "Now?" he whispered, then louder, "Make the messenger comfortable. I hear and come at once."

There was a silence, then they heard Hal shuffling away.

"Queen Elizabeth must have planned to interrupt," Tony said.

"She must truly be a jealous woman."

"For good reason."

Rosie licked her finger and ran it across his lower lip. He sucked the tip inside his mouth, and she quoted, *"My beloved is white and ruddy, the chiefest among ten thousand. His head is as the most fine gold—"*

The truth dawned on him, and his eyes narrowed. "Why, you little snoke-horn."

"His locks are bushy, and black as a raven." She grinned at him insolently. "Only *your* locks are blond as a finch."

"I was gently encouraging you, nursing you along, and you weren't reading. You had every word memorized."

He seemed truly insulted, and she said, "I did read

the words at first, but the Song of Solomon is one of Sir Danny's favorite parts of the Bible. I've heard him quote it to every ladybird he's courted."

Raising himself, he leaned over her. "I ought to punish you."

Wrapping her arms around his neck, she asked with anticipation, "How?"

"By getting up and putting on my clothes."

Action followed his words, and she sighed in gusty disappointment.

"Serves you right," he said, plucking one of his hose off the candelabra, one off the bookshelf. "To so deceive me."

Sitting up, she wrapped her arms around her bare knees. *"His cheeks are as a bed of spices, as sweet flowers: his lips like lilies, dropping sweet smelling myrrh."*

"Flattery will not replace you in my good graces." He pulled his waistcoat out from under the desk, and his doublet off the rod that supported the tapestry.

"His hands are as gold rings set with the beryl: his belly is as bright ivory overlaid with sapphires."

Looking down at his flat stomach, he declared, "There are no sapphires on my belly."

"A little lower, 'tis as hard as sapphires."

He threw her shift at her head. "Put your clothes on, woman, and stop trying to tempt me."

Dragging the shift away from her face, she quoted, *"His legs are as pillars of marble, set upon sockets of fine gold: his countenance is as Lebanon, excellent as the cedars."* Standing, she slowly shimmied into the shift.

He watched and proved himself ready as a stallion, but he ignored his condition. Undaunted, he found her skirt and bodice stuffed under the chair and tossed them at her, and she wasn't surprised. Tony might appear to be nothing more than lively and handsome, but she knew without a doubt his loyalties ran deep. He would go when his queen called, and for her he would shed each drop of his blood.

Did his loyalties to his queen run deeper than his loyalties to her? She didn't know, nor did she want to know. Did her loyalty to Sir Danny run deeper than her loyalty to Tony? She didn't know, and she couldn't bear to seek the answer.

As Tony lifted his shirt off the bronze andiron, she realized one sleeve hung in black tatters. It had fallen too close to the fire and smoldered.

He looked at her. She looked at him. She tried to contain her amusement, she really did, but when he glared a snigger escaped her. She covered her mouth, but it was too late. Tossing the shirt away, he donned his waistcoat and doublet, found his canions beneath the edge of the rug and pulled them on.

He held his hose in his fist and glanced around, and she asked, "Looking for these?" She dangled his garters.

"Give them to me."

"Certes." She grinned. "When you come and get them."

His eyes narrowed, and he considered her. "I see I have been led astray by a temptress." Approaching her with the dexterity of a duelist, he reached for the garters, but she put them behind her back. "A temptress," he repeated, and caught her around the waist. Smiling, he kissed her. Kissed her until her mind clouded with a fog as thick as the mist outside. As he drew back, she opened her eyes.

"Steady?" he asked, and when she nodded, he snatched his garters and stepped away. His shoes he retrieved from two separate corners of the room, and he watched her suspiciously as he finished dressing.

"You're looking rather rumpled," she observed.

"Good enough for the queen's messenger," he answered. Fully clothed, he came to her and lifted her chin. She pursed her mouth and closed her eyes, but he chuckled. "Nay, I can have no more of that this morning, or Her Majesty would have to wait."

Pouting, Rosie opened her eyes. "Then she'll wait."

He shook his head. "She was furious when she ordered me from court, and if she sends me a message now, it can mean only one thing. She needs someone she can trust, and she needs him desperately. 'Tis I, Rosie, and I'll go to her at once."

"You'll do what you must, and I send you gladly," Rosie said. "But the queen treasures you for more than your reliability, I think. Don't forget to come back."

"How can I?" He stroked her cheek and pushed back her hair as if he had to touch her. "We were lucky before, but this time you are surely carrying my child. I take full responsibility for the time in my bedroom, Rosie, but I recognize a seduction when I see one, and last night you seduced me."

"You were in a weakened state," she said solemnly.

He reared back in indignation. "Weak? Cotzooks, a man would have to be a gelding to ignore—" He saw the twinkle in her eye, and cuffed her softly on the chin. "When we're wed, I promise always to be so weak." She said nothing, and he said anxiously, "We must wed, and wed before I leave. Will you so agree?"

She thought of her childhood dream—to move an audience to laughter and tears. She thought of her new dream—to possess Odyssey Manor all on her own. Then she thought of the dream she'd never dared to dream—to have a family, a place to put down roots, and a man to grow old with. With Tony, that dream could come true, and in such generous portions she knew herself blessed. Did she carry Tony's child? She hoped so. She prayed so. And she would marry him regardless.

He must have read her reply in her face, for he picked her up and swung her around. "I'll call for Parson Selwyn at once. We'll wed this evening after supper, and I'll leave in the dawn." Putting her down, he kissed her hands and walked to the door. "You do me too much honor. And for God's sake, woman, brush your hair. You look like a wanton."

Her hair? She touched the tangled locks. She stood clad in a shift, and he thought her hair looked wanton?

Opening the door just a slit, he blew her a kiss.

"Wait!" she cried, remembering her other worries.

Looking like a felon awaiting sentencing, he stepped back into the room. "Aye?"

"When you go to London, will you take me with you?"

"Not if there's danger, as I suspect there must be."

"Is there not danger here, where arrows fly through the air and rocks drop from the sky?"

"Aye, that is why I'll ask my sisters to take you with them when they leave."

She sucked in a breath of dismay. "Leave Odyssey Manor, and go to some foreign place where Sir Danny cannot find me?"

A strange expression crossed his face, and he looked almost ill. She hadn't been tactful, she realized, but she didn't want to leave Odyssey Manor, not without Tony—because of Sir Danny, and because this place had become a haven. "I'll know no one," she faltered.

"You'll know Jean and Ann, and I imagine Lady Honora will go, too. You'll meet my brother and his family, and my father."

Although she understood Tony's concern, she didn't want to go. She didn't want to meet more strangers, be left alone again.

"I would be more at ease," he said, "if you would go."

"You must promise me one thing."

He relaxed. "Anything."

"You must promise you will find Sir Danny and keep him safe."

Something changed in him. He seemed intense, quiet, determined. "I had already resolved to do that."

She thought he wanted to say something else. She waited, obscurely anxious, while he struggled to speak. "In the short time I knew him, I realized how precious Sir Danny is to you. You have the heart of a lion, and if Sir Danny were in danger, I know you would go rescue him."

"Certes, I would."

Her fervency seemed to answer a question in his mind, and he said, "I can do no less." Keeping his hands to his sides, he leaned over her and kissed her mouth. "Lady Rosalyn, you honor me by accepting my proposal. I'll do everything in my power to be worthy of you, to make ours a happy union. Do you believe me?"

She liked the way his hands half rose as if he wanted to pull her close again. She wanted to wipe the troubled expression from his face. She wanted to reassure him of her love. But how did one express love? Sir Danny had never said he loved her, although she knew he did. Uncle Will's characters expressed love eloquently, but somehow she thought she should be original. She struggled to say something, something wonderful, but by the time she'd found the words, he'd slipped out.

She looked at the door until she was sure he wouldn't return, then used the ancient words so many people had used before her. *"His mouth is most sweet: yea, he is altogether lovely. This is my beloved, and this is my friend, O daughters of Jerusalem."*

So she was to be married, and married to Tony. Most women would be jubilant, but what did a former actor-gypsy know about marriage? She wasn't jubilant, she was worried.

She laughed softly. Who was she trying to chicane? She *was* jubilant. Singing an off-key, off-color ballad, she dressed in her wrinkled gown and looked for her shoes and hose. She couldn't find either, but it wasn't the shoes that concerned her. She'd found the red silk hose in one of the old trunks she'd explored, and she knew without consulting anyone that they were wicked and likely to tempt a man. Perhaps Lady Sadler had used them to entice Lord Sadler. Perhaps they'd made love in this very study.

She glanced around and shivered.

Spooky, to think of the long dead making love, maybe making a baby . . . maybe making her.

She shivered again. Silk hose. She wanted her silk hose. They were rare commodities, and were hidden, no doubt, somewhere beneath the papers strewn across the floor. With a sigh, she picked up a pile of papers and set them on the desk. Then another pile, then another. While she worked, she entertained herself by reading a word here, a word there. Then she tried whole sentences, then whole letters.

The urgency of the correspondence captured her interest first. Here at Odyssey Manor, Tony seemed like nothing more than a country gentleman of leisure. But she held proof he was more than that. He was the master of the Queen's Guard, and a man named Wart-Nose kept him constantly apprised of any threat to the safety of the kingdom.

Rosie recognized many of the names of the trouble-makers who roamed the streets. The theater attracted that sort.

But the more she straightened Tony's office, the more she came upon the names of Essex and Southampton. Tony had been watching them before she and Sir Danny had come to the estate, and his efforts doubled after their arrival—after Sir Danny had told him what they'd heard, she supposed. She avidly read the letters containing their names, finding the words difficult at first. Her fascination helped her comprehend more, and quickly.

Since she'd left London, the situation had disintegrated. Essex House proved a magnet for every dissatisfied subject of Her Majesty, and with Southampton's encouragement, Essex himself raged like a madman against the queen.

As the letters became current, she read eagerly, looking for one specific name. Looking for Sir Danny.

And she found him—in Newgate Prison, condemned to death for treason against the queen.

Nay, she must have read the letter wrong. Her skill must be at fault. Sir Danny couldn't be in the Tower. He couldn't be condemned to death. If something so dreadful had happened, Tony would tell her. He wouldn't keep such news from her.

Would he?

Taking the paper to the window, she held it close to her face and slowly read it again. She lowered it and closed her eyes.

It was true. Sir Danny had gone to Whitehall Palace, given up a letter of recommendation from Tony, demanded to speak to the queen, and had been taken by Essex's men. With a little political finagling, Essex had managed to have Sir Danny declared a traitor and condemned to death. An effective way—indeed, the only way—to quiet Sir Danny.

With a whimper, Rosie dropped to her knees, crushing the letter as if that would crush the villains who had taken him. Sir Danny would die. No one could save him now. The torturers of Newgate Prison were famed for extracting a confession. Closing her eyes, she dropped the letter and clutched her stomach. Sir Danny was famed for fearing pain. He would confess to anything, and he would hang—if he were lucky.

She'd seen the traitors' heads rotting on spikes on London Bridge. She'd seen them splash into the Thames when the wind blew. But she never imagined her beloved Sir Danny, her honorable Sir Danny . . . She whimpered again.

Like an infant seeking comfort at her mother's breast, she crawled toward the desk, toward the desk kneehole. Tony's chair was pushed in; she shoved it out of the way.

Dim and warm and close. Hugging herself, she listened. Where was the deep, loving voice? Why didn't he call for his Rosie anymore? Hot tears leaked from her eyes and burned her cheeks. Had she lost him? "Dada," she whimpered. "Please, Dada, come back."

But he didn't. She couldn't even hear the echoes of his speech.

It was her fault he was gone. She'd taken something of his. Something he wanted very much. What was it?

Closing her eyes, she tried to remember. She saw a babyish hand reaching out and grasping a shiny ring. A special gold ring. Dada's precious ring, decorated with two entwined 'Es' and set with a sparkling red stone. She saw the chubby fingers decorated, one at a time, with the ring. She saw it roll back and forth, too big for the fingers, and she saw the young child's hand clutch it tight in a fist.

In the darkness under the desk was her hiding place. There she kept her own precious possessions.

She knew Dada didn't want his special ring sitting out. Even though he'd warned her never to touch it, he'd be happy if she kept it safe while they went to London to visit the queen.

Rosie's eyes popped open. Her secret hiding place. She watched as her adult hand reached out and fumbled among the ornate carvings and knobs. Dust feathered to the floor as she searched, not truly knowing what she sought and not believing it was there.

But it was. Her fingertips touched a loose, cool, round object. Carefully, she lifted it from its protected position and crawled free of the kneehole. Raising it to her face, she looked at it.

She held a gold signet ring, embossed with two 'Es' and set with a bloodred ruby.

She *was* Lady Rosalyn Bellot, daughter of the earl of Sadler. She was the heir to Odyssey Manor.

Had she ever really doubted it? Doubling her fist over the ring, she held it over her heart. Aye, she remembered the manor, the lands, the servants. She remembered Hal and his betrayal. She remembered everything.

Had she ever really doubted that Lord Sadler was her father? That he was the man whose voice spoke in her dreams?

The child Rosalyn had taken his ring because it was his, because she adored everything about him, and when he'd wanted it back, she'd been too scared and embarrassed to admit she had it. Then he'd died, and the child had blamed herself. Like the ring, the knowledge of his death and her own culpability had been stored away, hidden and unacknowledged.

Another man had come into the child Rosalyn's life. Another man different from her true father in wealth and rank, yet so alike in his capacity to love she had transferred her affection to Sir Danny. Her first "Dada" had become a lifeless body that walked only in the halls of midnight. If she didn't rescue Sir Danny, he would walk, also.

It was Tony's fault. All Tony's fault. Why hadn't he rushed to rescue Sir Danny? She wiped her nose on her sleeve. Even now, the torturers of Newgate might be stretching him on the rack, and she stood here because she hadn't known. Why hadn't Tony told her of Sir Danny's imprisonment so she could rush to his assistance? Why . . . ?

She laughed, a bitter, unhappy laugh.

Of course. She knew why Tony hadn't told her. Because she *would* rush to Sir Danny's assistance. She wasn't a youth anymore, free to roam the roads, free to fight for a cause. She was a woman. Nay, worse, a noblewoman, good for nothing but breeding and sewing.

Why had Tony withheld the information? Why, to protect her, of a certainty.

Snatching the wadded up letter from the floor, she smoothed it out and read it again. It was dated yesterday. Tony received a package every morning from London, and this had been in it. This explained his serious mien as he vowed to find Sir Danny and keep him safe. This explained his eagerness to send her as far away from London as possible.

But nothing could explain his deception, and in no way could she explain her need to him. She only knew she couldn't proceed to a new life, a new love, if she lost the man she considered her father—again.

Moving quickly, smoothly, she tied the ring around her neck with the ribbon from her hair. Opening the door, she slipped out and went in search of the trunk in which was stored a young man's clothing.

She had been protected long enough.

*   *   *

"Sir Anthony, Parson Selwyn has arrived."

Tony turned from his contemplation of the laden dining room table and greeted the parish clergyman. "Ah, Parson, how good of you to come at such short notice."

"'Tis a pleasure, Sir Anthony, to serve you." Removing his cape, the little man handed it to Hal without a glance. "Although I found myself quite astonished at your request that I wed you to Lady Rosalyn Bellot tonight."

"A sudden request," Tony acknowledged. He watched as Hal fumbled with the cape, holding it with shaking hands, staring at it as if he'd never seen such a costume in his life. "But not completely unexpected."

Parson Selwyn folded his hands over his protruding belly and lifted his nose into the air. The younger son of lesser nobility, he obviously found it painful to serve the bastard of an earl. "Not completely unexpected, but as your clergyman I must counsel you before you proceed on such a course. Such unseemly haste ill befits the lord of Odyssey Manor."

As long as the man kept a civil tongue in his head, Parson Selwyn's opinion mattered little to Tony. What mattered was Hal. He crumpled the cape into a ball and placed it on the laden side table in the midst of a platter of golden lamb pastry. His shoulders stooped, his lined face was gaunt with distress. Like a man pursued, he constantly shot glances behind him. What disaster, Tony wondered, had been visited on Hal?

Oblivious to Hal's distress or Tony's concern, Parson Selwyn blathered, "If you will recall, Sir Anthony, one of my Sunday sermons pertained to the evils of a rapid matrimony and the results thereof."

Hal whimpered, shrinking beneath Tony's gaze like a slug exposed to caustic salt.

Parson Selwyn droned on. "Lady Rosalyn is the daughter of Edward Bellot, earl of Sadler, a noble house of impeccable ancestry, and when Her Majesty discovers Lady Rosalyn's existence, she might wish a different union for her."

Was Hal about to collapse? Tony held out his palm and walked toward the steward.

Emboldened by Tony's inattention, Parson Selwyn rocked back and forth on his heels and said in a stern tone, "Although it is a sensitive issue, I feel I must speak freely. You are a bastard, and as such are damned by the Almighty to a lesser—"

"What?" Tony spun around and glared at the parson.

"I was saying"—Parson Selwyn frowned, the staff of his self-importance propping him up—"that you are a bastard and since Lady Rosalyn can trace her ancestry back to the Conqueror, it would be inappropriate—"

"For you to finish the sentence."

The parson lowered the lofty tip of his nose. Tony stood stiff and still, one hand on his sword, one hand on his dagger, and the willingness to use them etched on his brow. Parson Selwyn blanched. "I meant no disrespect, Sir Anthony."

"If I did not need you to perform the ceremony, and perform it now, my good man, you would not live to see another dawn." Tony stalked toward Parson Selwyn with murder on his mind while the parson backed up with cowardly dispatch.

"Sir Anthony, I simply tried to do my duty by playing devil's advocate." Parson Selwyn put a chair between himself and Tony. "I wouldn't have you surprised when others say what I have said." He skidded around the edge of the laden dining table. "'Tis sad, but true, this union has the appearance of a marriage forced on Lady Rosalyn by a man who holds her captive."

Tony stopped stalking the absurd little man. It was true. Others would say he had forced Rosie to be his wife. It was true. When he discovered her heritage, he determined to marry her, and would have married her if she'd been one hundred years old. It was true. If Rosie were allowed to take the fruits of her heritage to court, she might find a man she could better love.

But she would never find a man who could love her better.

Tonight, Mistress Child had done just as he requested. Every one of Rosie's favorite foods was represented in this sumptuous supper. Wild fowl and venison steamed in rich gravies. The rich odor of wheaten bread warmed the air, and conserves and marmalades waited to be laden thereon. The pinnacle of the cook's artistry was the rainbow of jellies that glistened, mixed with a variety of flowers and herbs and formed to represent the manor itself.

It was a wedding supper to remember.

He would make the wedding night one to remember also. He would make every day of their lives one to treasure. She would never regret her marriage to him.

If only the queen hadn't chosen this moment to summon him, just when he needed to rescue Sir Danny. Her letter had been vague: a gracious forgiving for his previous insolence, an invitation to join the Christmas court at Whitehall, and a casual mention of his continued position as master of the Queen's Guard. His enduring good fortune was contained within the letter, but more important, beneath the cordiality ran a thread, tight with tension. Something worried the queen, something serious enough for her to forgive Tony his effrontery about Essex. While the queen was old, Tony had total respect for her keen mind. If she perceived danger, if she suspected Essex of rebellion, then to her side Tony would fly.

But without Rosie. Without his bride.

Wanting to see her, wanting to marry her, he bellowed, "Hal!" No one answered him, and he realized Hal had slipped away. "Hal," he called again, striding through the door and into the gallery.

A strange scene met his eye. Hal and all his servants stood as motionless as stone statues. His sisters sat before the fire, also frozen by the spell which held his servants enthralled. No one moved, no one looked at him, and the chill of foreboding shuddered down his spine. "What is it?" he asked.

No one answered.

He stepped closer to his sisters. "Ann? Jean? What's wrong?"

Ann turned her head away. Jean looked at him, then looked at the tips of her slippers that peeked from beneath her skirts.

Spinning around, he searched the room. "Rosie?"

Jean croaked rather than spoke. "She's gone."

"Gone? Gone where?"

Jean shook her head. "Just gone."

He waited to hear the joke. "She can't be gone."

"She packed her bags."

"Impossible." He started for the grand stairway, moving as quickly as he could, yet not quickly enough. Shoving open the door of her chamber, he sprang inside. "Rosie?" Her dresses had been laid neatly across the bed, but in the middle of the room a trunk gaped open, showing its remaining contents. He knelt and tossed through them, seeing the young men's clothing, knowing what it meant, yet refusing to believe the truth. He remembered the night before, the morning after, Rosie's bright and shining pledge to marry him.

She couldn't be gone.

Battered and bruised, Lady Honora came from her room to lean against the door frame. She observed him through her one good eye. "She's gone."

"Someone kidnapped her," he declared. Absurd, he knew, but he couldn't stand to admit that Rosie would seduce him, lie to him, take his seed with every expression of gladness, then flee him.

"No one kidnapped her." Lady Honora enunciated her words carefully, her face so swollen even her lips were affected. "She's only an actress, cut from the same cloth as Sir Danny. He pledged to send me word of his travels, and I've heard only once. She's treating you as he treated me."

"Sir Danny?" Tony rose to his feet as the idea surged through his mind. "Sir Danny!"

He rushed toward the door and tried to step around Lady Honora, but she caught his arm. "What about Sir Danny?"

He shook her off, and in her weakness she let him, but she slowly followed him as he rushed down the stairs and into his office. A single glance revealed that his papers had been returned to his desk, placed in stacks—read, perhaps, by a woman desperate for news of London and her father.

Frantically he sought the letter he knew should be there. He found it nowhere.

"What are you seeking?" Lady Honora had reached his office at last, and her weakness made her no less formidable.

"A letter."

"With news of Sir Danny?"

He didn't answer, but she took that as an affirmation.

"What has he done?" she asked. "Is he dead?"

"Not dead. Not yet."

"He's in danger?" Lady Honora's face flushed with distress. "My God, I have to go to him!"

Her cuts and bruises shone on the pale palette of her face, and Tony cried, "Doesn't anyone trust me to handle this? I will handle this. I'll take care of him. Trust me." Going to Lady Honora, he took her hands and found them shaking. More gently, he said, "Just trust me. You can't go to London in your condition. You can barely stand. I promise I'll beg the queen. I'll bribe the jailers."

"He's in the Tower?"

"In Newgate Prison with the rest of the common prisoners." He took a breath. "You must realize I'll do all in my power to get Sir Danny released."

She searched his face for reassurance. "Aye, I know you will." Staggering to a chair, she lowered herself. "Is that what you seek?"

A crumpled wad of paper lay by the window, and with a cry he sprang for it. Smoothing it with shaking hands, he saw what he dreaded. The communication which relayed the news of Sir Danny's capture, and the stains of tears that blurred the ink.

Aye, Rosie was gone. Gone to London to rescue Sir Danny. Gone because she believed Tony had betrayed her by keeping her in ignorance. She would never forgive him for seeking her safety.

"Rosie!" The anguish of his cry sounded through the room and rose to the heavens, and on the dark road that wound away from Odyssey Manor, Rosie heard its echo.

Inside the padded doublet, her father's signet ring hung by its ribbon around her neck. Shivering from cold and fear of the night, she pulled it from its place in her bosom and held it in her hand.

She remembered it all now. The study, the manor, the grounds, the servants, Hal . . . Hal. She understood his dedication to the manor now, the awe and fright he exuded when he looked at her. She ought to tell of his crime, but she clutched the ring tight and the sharp edges dug into her palm, reminding her of her own shame. How could she destroy a fellow prisoner of Purgatory when she so well comprehended the wretched guilt that haunted Hal's sunken eyes?

Her thoughts made her stumble in the ruts hidden by the night. They made her wish to turn back, yet urged her on. Real guilt for hiding the ring, imagined guilt in the cause of her father's death, guilt for leaving Tony. Aye, she knew she had plunged Tony into a maelstrom of rage and grief. She valued herself, and he valued her, too. He didn't just want her for her property, she knew that, but a man like Tony could always find another woman. A man like Tony had only to crook his little finger, and women would be on him like flies on honey.

But she suspected his need to lay claim to his child transcended every other need. The child she probably carried. The child she was taking away from him with every step she took.

How would he react when he realized she was gone? Would he search for her, or would he go to answer the queen's summons? She thought he might comprehend the bent of her mind in much the same manner as she comprehended his, and seek her in London while fulfilling his duty to the queen and the nation.

And that, too, would be disaster. He needed to concentrate his whole mind on the queen's business. Would he still have the confidence of the finest swordsman in England, yet maintain the wariness of a man marked by greatness for an assassin's blade?

As if in answer to her questions, she heard the thunder of a horse's hooves behind her. It was Tony. She knew it was Tony, and she fled toward the thicket that lay just ahead. Just in the nick of time. As she sprang into the bushes, she felt the tremble in the loam beneath her. She flung herself face first onto the ground and clasped the tough grass. She had to hang on tight, for when the horse and its rider drew close to the thicket, their rapid pace slowed. She turned her head and saw Tony silhouetted against the moonlit horizon.

"Rosie!" he called. "I beg you, Rosie, don't go by yourself. Come to me. I swear I'll take you with me. I swear." His voice broke, and he spurred his horse on. "Rosie" he called again.

She rubbed her forehead in the cold dirt, trying to convince herself she was doing the right thing. Sir Danny needed her. Tony would only try to protect her, and thus endanger himself. He'd get in her way; she didn't want to be an ornament on Tony's chain. She needed to be in the midst of the action, and Tony— damn him, damn him—had betrayed her by keeping Sir Danny's imprisonment a secret. She hated him for that, and understood why he'd done it, and wished she didn't need to be brave and strong, to vanquish the dark and the phantoms that lurked there.

Holding her head against the ground, she listened as the vibration of the hooves died away, then pushed herself onto her hands and knees. Squinting at the vague forest forms, she thought she didn't remember the tree planted so close to her nose. She looked up and realized the massive presence didn't extend to the heavens, but only to the height of a man. With a shriek, she fell back.

Ludovic said, "You've come out to me at last."

II

It is well done, and fitting for a princess
Descended of so many royal kings.
—ANTONY AND CLEOPATRA, V, ii, 326

20

London
February 1601

"I will not have my tooth pulled." Queen Elizabeth plunked out a tune at her virginal, in too much pain to play with her usual skill. "There's nothing wrong with it. I'm healthy as an English war-horse."

Tony exchanged glances with Robert Cecil, secretary of state, and realized again how glad he was not to hold that post. As Elizabeth's adviser, Cecil held a position of power, glory, and wealth. Unfortunately, it included the task of persuading the queen that one of her rotting teeth would have to go. A thankless job, but one which no one else had the stomach to perform. Within the confines of Elizabeth's antechamber, Cecil had to bear the brunt of the royal displeasure. Still, he spoke without flinching. "The tooth drawer says we can dress it with fenugreek, and it will fall out."

"Excellent!" Elizabeth's long, thin face accentuated the puffiness of her cheek, and she pursed her thin lips as if hiding her problem would somehow vanquish it.

"But that might make the neighboring teeth fall out as well."

The queen's deep-set eyes had circles beneath them, for toothache had kept her sleepless for two nights, but they flashed with vibrant royal displeasure, and Tony wished he were elsewhere. But since his arrival in London, Elizabeth had kept him close at her side. Fruitlessly, he had begged to be told of the concern which brought him to her. Imperiously she declared he was the master of Her Guard, and as such, he should guard her.

"What have I done to deserve such trials?" she cried petulantly. "I vigilantly use the tooth cloths, but to no avail. Still am I cursed with this pain."

Tony contemplated her with a knitted and serious brow. "I think, Your Majesty, that the gods fear your perfection."

Her shrill voice deepened and smoothed. "Why are you prating of perfection?"

"When I look upon you, I see perfection. Your long hands, your white skin, the beauty of your eyes, the sharp wit of your mind. I fear the gods punish you for daring to be a woman of extraordinary gifts."

Queen Elizabeth plucked at her ruff, striving for modesty while acknowledging the truth of Tony's sentiments. Robert Cecil thanked Tony with a nod, although they both knew the queen's blackened teeth owed more to her fondness for sweets than the gods' displeasure.

Wrapping his hunched body deep in his cloak, Cecil returned to the fray. "Your Majesty, you've had teeth extracted before."

"I didn't like it." Queen Elizabeth peered at the two

men. "The last time, the archbishop of London had one of his teeth extracted to show me it didn't hurt."

Tony and Robert Cecil both shut their mouths with a snap and remained silent. Satisfied with muffling her two tormentors, Queen Elizabeth turned back to the virginal and picked out a plaintive, haunting tune.

Did she regret summoning Tony from Odyssey Manor? He didn't think so. He was the weapon she concealed until she needed the use of him. While flattered by her trust, he chafed at her caution. She refused to speak to him of Essex, for she still retained a fondness for the handsome young man. She believed, and rightly, Tony admitted, that Tony despised Essex and wished for his downfall. Despite the application of Tony's finest tact, she took any mention of Essex's perfidy as criticism of her previous foolishness.

But he desperately needed to discuss Sir Danny, and she, in her wiliness, had evaded his every attempt. He had guarded her through Christmas and Twelfth Night, cajoling her, playing cards with her, searching for Rosie at every opportunity, and all the while Rosie's beloved dada had been suffering in prison.

Sir Danny hadn't died—yet. The winter cold bit deep, even in Whitehall Palace, and Tony cringed when he thought of the damp cold of prison seeping into Sir Danny's bones. Worse, for all his bold gallantry, Sir Danny couldn't remain immune to the exquisitely skillful tortures. Tony had done what he could with liberal bribes, but he woke every day afraid he'd hear the news—the news that Sir Danny had died.

And if Sir Danny died, Tony would never get Rosie back. He had tried to find her, but she'd slipped into the London acting world without a ripple. She had the connections to remain hidden, and had chosen to do so. If he could rescue Sir Danny, Rosie would come back to him. It was a guarantee for his future happiness, and desperation made him gauche. "Your Majesty, the tooth pains you. Miasma flows from it and poisons your blood and, therefore, must be withdrawn, just as the earl of Essex pains you and must be plucked forth."

The melody ended in a clash of chords, and Robert Cecil coughed in dismay. He'd never heard Tony fail in tact, and the queen seemed to realize it at the same moment as Cecil. "I know what ails me, my dear Tony. Now what ails you?"

"A heartache, madam, at the injustice which is perpetrated in your kingdom. Right now one of your most loyal subjects lies in Newgate Prison, accused of treason by the earl of Essex."

"Have you run mad?" Cecil murmured.

Tony ignored him. "Your subject came to me—the master of the Queen's Guard—with information concerning the traitorous activities of Essex and Southampton. I sent him to you with a letter, recommending you listen to his story, and before he could even reach you, Essex intercepted him, charged *him* with traitorous activities, and had him incarcerated."

Queen Elizabeth leaped off the padded stool. "I know that. Do you think Essex runs this country?"

"Never, Madam."

"You're jealous of him."

"I just want to know why you ignored my letter."

Grabbing his doublet in both her hands, she pulled his face down to hers. "Are you demanding answers from me?"

She might be old, she might be a woman, but she was the queen. His queen. And this time she was wrong. "Did you ever see my letter?"

"Are you demanding answers from your queen?"

"My letter told you—"

She boxed his ears.

He hadn't had his ears boxed since Jean did it when he was a boy. He wanted to roar and shout. Instead he smiled with all his charm and determination. "If you won't listen to me, perhaps you'll listen to your subject."

"My subject. An actor! Do you think I don't know about the actor?" Her knuckles turned a bony white as she clenched her fists tighter. "Sir Daniel Plympton is his name, and he confessed to being a troublemaker even before the torturer began his work."

"He fears pain. So he's a coward. Yet he dared to return to London after Essex had marked him for death, for love of Your Majesty and the peace of her kingdom. He came like a tiger and you imprisoned him like a kitten. And why? Because Essex wanted you to. Because you wanted to try to appease that pretty spoiled boy with his honeyed tongue."

She boxed Tony's ears again. "You could take lessons from him."

"In betraying my queen? I think not."

She boxed his ears again. And again. He flinched beneath the assault, for she had a strong arm and a wicked temper, but he wouldn't lift his hand to his queen, as Essex had tried to do when she treated him with similar disrespect. Tony hoped she remembered and made the comparison. He hoped she would follow the instinct that had protected her kingdom for the forty-two years of her sovereignty.

If she did, he didn't see it.

"Get out!" she shouted. "Get out of my sight, and don't come back."

He bowed. "Sir Danny Plympton will die happy if he can help the captain of this ship we call England steer a safe course through these shoals. He is your most faithful admirer."

Picking up a gold enamel pot, she shouted, "Go!"

He bowed again and backed toward the door. "Call him before you. Hear what he has to say. I beg of you, madam. Listen to his words."

She let fly with the pot as he shut the door, and it smashed at the place where his head had been. "Insolent baggage," she raged. "How dare he speak to me in such a manner?"

Bobbing and weaving like a Christian facing an enraged lioness, Sir Robert Cecil declared, "Sir Anthony Rycliffe is an insolent fool."

"Fool? Fool?" Queen Elizabeth snatched up a vase and threw it at Cecil's head. Cecil didn't dodge as well as Tony and took the blow in the chest. "Sir Anthony Rycliffe is no fool."

"Nay, madam, he's a rogue."

Her rage temporarily expunged, she sank onto a pile of cushions arranged for her comfort. "Aye, he's a rogue."

"A knave," Cecil suggested.

"Not a knave." Exhausted by her tantrum, she closed her eyes.

"Madam, shall can I call your ladies-in-waiting?"

"Nay." She flapped a limp hand. "Call the tooth drawer."

Cecil bowed, although she couldn't see him, and hastened to the door. As he opened it, she said, "And Cecil?"

"Aye, Your Majesty?"

"Bring me Sir Danny Plympton. Immediately. I wish to question him."

The Chamberlain's Men and the members of Sir Danny's troupe laughed and quarreled as they drank the evening away at Cross Keys Inn in Gracechurch Street. This was their place; it had always been their place, just as the Queen's Men gathered at the Bull in Bishopgate Street and the Earl of Worcester's Men gathered at the Boar's Head in Whitechapel. When the winter grew too bitter to perform their plays in the open-roofed Globe Theater, they came and performed in the inn. The innkeeper found it a draw for customers, and for the most part the actors behaved in a seemly manner.

But now he kept a weather eye on them as they debated the most outrageous event in the history of theater.

Lady Rosalyn Bellot wanted to perform with the Chamberlain's Men, and before the queen, no less.

Richard Burbage, leading player for the Chamberlain's Men, peered gloomily into his tankard of beer. "Rosencrantz is a woman now, they say."

"Aye, she's a woman now." Cedric Lambeth, fool for Sir Danny's troupe, pulled his fife from a flap inside his doublet and played a tune, one that ranged from deep and masculine to high and feminine, with a confusion of notes in the middle. "We saw her, me and Sir Danny's boys, and she's a woman. Sir Anthony Rycliffe knew she was a woman from the moment he laid eyes on her, I trow, but then he's the greatest lover in all England."

Dickie Justin McBride, the handsome actor who had been Rosie's childhood torment, stopped drinking in mid-swig. "Who says?"

Cedric wrinkled his brow. "Think 'twas him that told me."

A blast of laughter from the men on the benches tossed him in a somersault, and he came up grinning.

Richard Burbage shouted, "Sir Anthony sounds like a man with his mind in his codpiece—just where it belongs."

Finishing his drink, Dickie thumped his tankard hard on the table. "Sir Anthony Rycliffe may be a boasting bastard, but he's master of the Queen's Guard. What's he going to say if we let his woman play the part of Ophelia? Not just play the part, but do it before Her Majesty."

The merriment faded; then a voice from the back, timid and unsure, called, "It's not as if she hasn't played the part before."

"Aye, but we didn't know before." John Barnstaple of Sir Danny's troupe excused their previous actions.

"Do you think our ignorance would matter to the Puritan bullyboys if they ever found out?" Dickie leaped onto the plank table and stomped from end to end, shaking the tankards. The men snatched up their drinks as he passed and brayed for him to jump down. Instead, he swirled his short cape and projected his voice. "'Tis the infraction they've been waiting for. They've been saying the theater is the storehouse of sin for all England. If they found out a woman performed the women's roles, they'd point and say that it proved our wickedness." He glared into each man's eyes as he circled the table. "Verily, 'twould be the truth."

The speaker in the back sounded curious. "What's so dreadful about a woman playing women's roles?"

Richard Burbage stared into the shadows and said dolefully, "Don't be daft, man. 'Tisn't done."

"She's made fools of us for years." Alleyn Brewer, Rosie's principal rival for the lady's roles, stood on a bucket before the fire and waved a tankard of ale. "Why should we help her make a fool of the queen?"

"*She* made a fool of us?" Cedric stood on a bucket behind Alleyn, doing an imitation of the effeminate young man. "She made no fool of me. I made a fool of myself, and I'm sure every man here will second that boastfully." Alleyn spun around on his bucket and glared, and Cedric said soothingly, "Except you, of course, Alleyn."

The actors who perched on the tables in the taproom made little attempt to muffle their merriment as Alleyn spoke. "If the queen should discover that Ophelia's role is played by a woman, we'll lose everything. Our patron, our playhouse, and our livelihood."

"If Rosie doesn't play Ophelia, we'll lose the man who guided our faltering feet along the path of performing." Cedric hopped off the bucket and scampered along, mimicking an actor's difficult voyage.

Dickie snorted. "But what can Rosie do for Sir Danny?"

"She'll play Ophelia, and Queen Elizabeth will be so moved she'll grant her a boon." The soft voice spoke from the shadows at the back. "Rosie will ask for the life of Sir Danny, and he'll be saved."

Voices hummed as everyone nodded, satisfied with this prediction of the future. Everyone but Dickie.

"Rosie's going to do this? Rosie? The same Rosie who can't act her way out of a sheep's bladder?" Dickie held his ribs. "Ha. Ha. Ha."

The room fell silent. Gazes slid from one side to the other, touching, sidling away. No one wanted to admit the truth of it, but Cedric took the temperature of the room.

"So for fear of the stocks, we should slink away like rat-eating weasels and let Sir Danny die?" He spit in the fire, and it sizzled with a yellow flare. "You're a babe, mewling and puking in craven dismay at the first hint of danger."

Dickie knocked over a tankard, splattering his shoes. "I'm a wise man. I know when we go to Newgate and pay for Sir Danny to be fed and given blankets, and the jailers—as greedy a bunch of bastards who ever drew breath—refuse to even accept the money, I know that Sir Danny has been nipped by a great lord, and we're marking ourselves by trying to help him. 'Tis *you* who is a babe, reaching for the sharp edge of the executioner's blade and pulling away bloody fingers."

In the battle of eloquent phrases, Dickie had won, and that counted for much with the actors. But Cedric expressed his own conviction in an equally eloquent gastric event. He bowed amid cheers and applause.

In desperation, Alleyn said, "Let someone else do it."

Cedric closed one eye and pressed his finger to his nose. "What?"

"Aye. Let *anyone* else do it," Dickie said. "Let anyone else play Ophelia. If we let Rosie do it, we're condemning Sir Danny."

"We could do that," Cedric agreed. "'Twould be safer."

A draft whistled through the room, and William Shakespeare stood in the doorway, his cape wrapped close around his ears. He asked, "But when have we ever done what is safe?"

"Rosie's got to have her chance," that shy one called from the back.

Will Shakespeare whipped his head around and stared into the shadows. Did he recognize that voice?

"'*Tis* fitting that she should be the one to rescue Sir Danny." John Barnstaple sounded thoughtful.

Trying to lure further comments from the back, Will said, "I came to tell you. The date is affixed." Actually, two dates were affixed, but he hesitated to tell them he planned to refuse moneys for a performance of his most notorious, most treacherous play. "The Chamberlain's Men will perform *Hamlet* for Her Majesty on the evening of February eighth, three days hence. We must decide who will play the part of Ophelia for Queen Elizabeth's pleasure, and decide it now."

"I say Alleyn should play Ophelia." Dickie waved at Alleyn, posed on the overturned bucket and still as a stone effigy.

"I say Rosie should play Ophelia," Cedric declared.

"Rosie's not here to present her own case. In sooth, Rosie seems to be nowhere and everywhere, all at the same time." Shakespeare glanced around intently. "Has anyone here actually seen Rosie?"

One by one the men shook their heads.

"I thought I saw her on London Bridge," one said. "But she disappeared before I could catch her."

"I saw something more real than Rosie," John Barnstaple said. "I saw Ludovic."

"Ludovic?" Alleyn paled. "That foreign ape is present in London?"

"He is," John Barnstaple confirmed.

"You aren't afraid of Ludovic, are you, Alleyn?" The voice at the back strengthened and taunted.

"He has a dagger," Alleyn said, as if that explained everything.

"And a rapier, too." John Barnstaple spoke in a cajoling tone. "So does everyone else in this city. So what?"

"He'll skin me alive if I take that part from Rosie," Alleyn said.

"What are you saying?" Will asked. "That you don't want to play the part of Ophelia for the queen?"

Dickie strode to Alleyn and shook him so hard he fell off the stool and landed on his bum. In disgust, Dickie kicked at the shivering bundle. "Get up and declare your desire to act the part."

"Let Rosie have it," Alleyn declared, clinging to the leg of a bench. "I would not play it if Queen Elizabeth herself begged me."

Will swept the room with an all-encompassing stare. In the manner of a judge passing a sentence, he declared, "If Rosie's in London, I say she must present herself to me before tomorrow at noon, or Alleyn will play Ophelia."

Alleyn moaned.

Everyone started talking at once, and William Shakespeare listened until he heard the door open and close, and knew the bait had been taken. Then he stepped outside into the dark courtyard where thin snakes of fog had begun to slither. The half-moon provided a bit of light, and he'd taken only a few steps when two figures, one slight and one tall, stepped out from beneath the eaves and confronted him.

The large man's very stance bespoke challenge, but William Shakespeare concentrated on the shorter one. A voluminous cape and a large floppy cap made identification difficult. Then she spoke in the diffident tones of the player in the back of the taproom, and her words made him laugh in exultation.

"Uncle Will, I've come to tell you I'm going to act the part of Ophelia."

The sodden atmosphere clung to Tony, but he pulled his hat over his ears and strode along the street. He didn't fear the darkness, so thick he had to rely on senses other than sight. This was what he'd wished for—the opportunity to seek the queen's enemies in the stews and palaces of Londontown. His return had relieved his captain, for although Wart-Nose Harry could handle trouble among the citizens, trouble from the gentry required discretion. Tony protested that his own discretion consisted of a sharp edge on his blade, but Wart-Nose claimed it was a discreet sword point. Now he trotted up Gracechurch Street with Tony, giving his report in troubled tones. "I tell ye, Master, th' lord o' Essex has run wild, an' all th' discontents o' London have run wi' him."

"That's no news." Tony sniffed the air, which lightened a little as they moved farther away from the Thames. He should have been perfectly happy. Perfectly happy, except Queen Elizabeth had banished him, prison had swallowed Sir Danny, and London had swallowed Rosie. On the few times he'd been out, he'd questioned some of Sir Danny's troupe about Rosie's whereabouts, but they all claimed ignorance. He didn't believe them. They seemed to be telling the truth, but they were actors, after all. He'd set spies on them, but he'd had no results as yet, so Tony resolved to check at Cross Keys Inn for his lady. She had to be there. She had to be *somewhere*.

Unless her throat had been slit on her trip to London, or some dockfront madam had captured her and placed her in stock.

Tony shuddered and realized Wart-Nose was talking. "I have a man in Essex House."

"In Essex House?" Amazed anew at Wart-Nose's ingenuity, Tony asked, "How did you do that?"

"'Twas not hard. Every malcontent in London resides there. Lord Essex, with Lord Southampton, Sir Christopher Blount, and Sir Charles Davers, have determined to surprise the court and the queen's person."

"Surprise them?" It was no more than Tony expected. "To what purpose?"

"To rescue the queen from evil advisers."

A glint of white light shimmered across Wart-Nose's grim features, and Tony glanced up. The patchy fog stuck fast across the sky in some places, while in others it drifted, playing dodge with the half-moon. "A traditional formula for English rebels."

"Essex, with all duty, will tell the queen she must dismiss his enemies."

"Sir Robert Cecil first, I trow."

Patient with Tony's interruptions, Wart-Nose agreed. "No doubt. After they are dismissed, and Queen Elizabeth has appointed Essex Lord Protector, Essex will put his enemies on trial for their lives and afterward summon a Parliament and alter the government."

"Damn." The incoming fog gathered on Tony's lashes and brows and trickled down his face. "Is that all?"

"If need be, they will shed Queen Elizabeth's blood."

The words and the flat tone in which he spoke them froze Tony's feet to the ground. "May they burn in hell, and may I be the one to send them there." He contemplated the gratifying picture of Essex doused in eternity's fire, then sighed. He feared, even now, that Essex would somehow escape the torment due him. It was true, London adored Essex, but it venerated Queen Elizabeth and had from the day of her ascension to the throne. Might not good sense—not Essex's, Tony never apprehended that—but the good sense of one of his advisers dissuade Essex from open revolt at the last moment? Until Elizabeth's trust in Essex had been completely destroyed, her sovereignty would never be completely sturdy. "Is that all?" Tony asked, half-wistful, half-joking.

"I thought 'twere plenty, Master."

Wart-Nose sounded stricken, and Tony sighed. He had forgotten the soldier had no sense of humor. "That's more than enough. You've done well, my friend." Clapping his hand on Wart-Nose's shoulder, Tony continued, "I'll have to find a way to send Queen Elizabeth a message from someone she could not fail to trust."

A man swirled out of the mist. Tony grabbed his shoulder and slammed him against a wall. Slivers of light slipped through the shutters, revealing Hal, haggard and hollow-eyed. "God's blood, Hal, what are you doing here?" He clutched Hal tighter. "Is something wrong at the manor?"

"Master, please Master." Hal struggled against Tony's grip. "Ye're hurtin' me."

Reluctantly, Tony loosened his fingers.

"All is well at Sadler House, but—"

"Odyssey Manor," Tony corrected.

"Aye, Master." Hal bobbed up and down. "But I accompanied Lady Honora an' yer sisters."

"Lady Honora?" Tony remembered the cut and swollen face he'd last seen at Odyssey Manor. Regardless of good sense, he felt responsible for her wounds, and with sincere concern, he asked, "How is that dear lady? Has she recovered from her injuries?"

Hal wiped a drop of moisture off the end of his pointed nose and smeared it on his doublet. "Lady Honora seems t' have returned t' her former self."

"Ah." Tony grinned. "Excellent. In sooth, I expected her to rush to Sir Danny's rescue sooner."

"She got a fever," Hal reported.

"Poor lady. Have there been any other incidents at Odyssey Manor? Has anyone else been injured?"

"Nay, Master." Hal sniffled. "Must be ye who causes them. Do ye think ye'll be giving it up?"

"Giving what up? Odyssey Manor?" Tony was shocked. "Never. 'Tis mine until I die. But why are you here? Tonight? In this night of chill and unsavory vapor?"

"The ladies sent me out t' tell ye they'd arrived, an' th' men in th' guardhouse suggested ye'd be here." Hal's flaming gaze seemed to pierce the mist and see the environs of Gracechurch Street. "Int' this cesspool o' sin." He tucked his chin down onto his chest and closed his eyes. "I had hoped never t' see it again."

"Ah, ye're an old London blade." Wart-Nose sounded sanguine. "I thought I amembered ye, but it's been so many years I doubted me recollections."

An unhealthy effulgence pocked Hal's complexion with quivering shadows, and he swung on Wart-Nose like an offended saint. "I know scarce about London."

"Ah." Wart-Nose nodded, winked, and grinned. "Ye don't want t' recall yer youthful extravagances."

Hal's breath rasped in his chest. "I had no youthful extravagances."

"'Twasn't ye, then, who bought a room an' a whore at Tiny Mary's fer a whole month? 'Twasn't ye who raced his horses from one end o' Cheapside t' th' other an' defeated that gentleman-dandy, Raleigh?" Wart-Nose slapped his knee and snorted. "'Twasn't ye who got whittled as a fiddler's bitch when we stole a new barrel o' Frenchie wine an' almost drowned in Hounds-ditch in an inch o' water?"

"It . . . wasn't . . . me."

Hal loomed over the shorter man, and Wart-Nose said hastily, "Nay, o' course not. 'Tweren't ye. 'Tweren't ye at all." Hal still hovered, and Wart-Nose cleared his throat. "I've realized me mistake. Stand aside now."

Recognizing the warning in Wart-Nose's tone and realizing that the younger captain of the guard could easily trounce this unwary steward, Tony laid a calming hand on Hal's shoulder. "You might want to go back now. Lady Honora and my sisters are staying at my town house, aren't they?"

Hal backed away cautiously, as if Wart-Nose were a snarling wild animal. Actually, the reverse seemed true, with Hal harboring a savage torment brought on by Wart-Nose and his jolly memories.

He continued to stare with unblinking intensity until Tony shook him gently. "Where are my sisters and Lady Honora staying?"

Gulping audibly, Hal turned his attention to Tony. "At th' court."

"The queen will think I set this up," Tony said glumly. "She'll think I brought my sisters to soften her anger at me."

"Oh?" Hal brightened. "Is Her Majesty angry with ye again?"

"You sound like a courtier," Tony grumbled. "Always thinking you'll advance on my trampled body."

"Nay, sir." Hal's damp gray hair hung in lanky strands beneath his cap. "I cannot advance in th' queen's affections even after yer fall. I'd have t' be mad t' imagine such a thing."

Tony wanted to explain that Hal's boorishness would never find favor with the queen, but in the last few months, Hal had aged before his eyes, trembling in a constant palsy and muttering to some unseen companion. Nay, Tony had no wish to distress Hal. He would have to retire him to the stables soon, and that would torment Hal enough.

In the silence, Tony heard a distant conversation. Although the saturated air muffled most of it, he could occasionally pick out a word, a tone, a voice, and he stiffened.

It sounded like Rosie.

"Did you hear that?" he whispered.

"Woulda sworn ye were th' man," Wart-Nose murmured.

"Am not!" Hal flared.

"Sh." Tony strained to hear, and once again detected the clear bright tones that beckoned like a lighthouse through the fog.

"Wonder where ye got th' money," Wart-Nose mused.

"It wasn't me!" Hal sprang at him, and they hit the ground fighting.

Abandoning them to their quarrel, Tony ran silently down the street toward Cross Keys Inn. The voices he followed faded in and out, wafting on the breeze, then sinking with the mist. He entered the courtyard of the inn, but its emptiness mocked him. He'd overshot, he realized, and he returned to the street and stopped to listen. At first he heard only the noise of merriment and quarrel that leaked through the shutters at the inn. Then, beneath the carefree sounds, he heard the scurry of stealth, and his suspicions multiplied. Using the skills honed in Her Majesty's service, he scanned the area with an instinct that depended on nothing more than a scent on the wind and a touch of faith.

He prowled back up Gracechurch Street. He could hear nothing from Hal and Wart-Nose, but he saw—or felt—a presence lurking in the shadows of the herb market. Casually he strolled by, inviting attack.

Nothing happened, and his conviction that he'd found Rosie soared. Doubling back again, he crept up to a large and shadowy figure, and with dagger drawn, he pounced.

The arm he caught was heavy with muscle, and the figure was as tall as Tony. "Help! Thief!" the man called, and his deep voice brought forth a curse from Tony.

"Shut your maw, you silly sot. I'm not going to steal from you. I'm the master of the Queen's Guard."

"That's no promise." His prisoner stumbled as if drunk. "You could be the worst of the bunch, and no one to catch you when honest folk complain."

Again he stumbled, and Tony smelled his breath. No bitter scent of beer or ale stained his exhalations, and a stinging suspicion pricked Tony by the neck.

Someone was behind him. Whirling around, he again stretched out his senses, seeking his quarry, wanting Rosie more than safety or duty or desire.

"The master of the Queen's Guard?"

The man behind him spoke, and Tony shushed him harshly.

"Aren't you Sir Anthony Rycliffe, the famous soldier for Her Majesty?"

Tony reached around and grabbed the loquacious fellow by the throat.

The stranger choked, then freed himself with a twist. "I've information about the earls of Essex and Southampton."

"Curse your eyes!" Furious with the mischance that brought him the only information capable of staying him from his pursuit, he called, "Wart-Nose." No one answered, and he cursed again. Had Hal and Wart-Nose murdered each other? A likeness of Hal, face pasty and eyes aflame, passed through his uneasy mind, but he couldn't abandon his duty to rescue Wart-Nose, if he needed rescuing, any more than he could chase Rosie, if Rosie was whom he chased.

To the man huddled against the wall, he commanded, "Tell me."

"My name is William Shakespeare."

Tony remembered Rosie's praise. "The playwright and actor."

With smug self-consciousness, he said, "You've heard of me."

More suspicious than ever, Tony agreed. "I've heard of you. Have you heard of me?"

"Aye, sir."

"Have you heard that I will rip off the head of the man who distracts me from my pursuit of Lady Rosalyn Bellot?"

The craven fellow stammered, "Sir, I assure you, I do not seek to distract you from any pursuit."

"Ha."

"I didn't know whom to approach with this development, and you simply appeared like a gift from God to the stability of the kingdom. If you must go, I beg of you, then go. I'll seek out another."

William Shakespeare straightened his cape and prepared to depart. Gritting his teeth, Tony stopped him. "Tell me."

Shakespeare capitulated with suspicious ease. "I had a message from my patron, Lord Southampton, that the Chamberlain's Men should perform my play, *Richard II*, on Saturday, and I have reason to know they wish it performed, not for its brilliant prose, but for its seditious material."

"You wrote a seditious play?"

"I wrote a historical play," William Shakespeare corrected. "It simply tells of the circumstances in which King Richard was deposed by his cousin, Bolingbroke. When I wrote it, I wrote it for the glory of England, to exult in the line which produced our beloved Queen Elizabeth. Od's bodkin, man, it passed the censor, but now . . . would to God I had never written it. It's caused me nothing but trouble."

"And landed your friend in prison."

Tony watched William Shakespeare for any sign of discomfort, but Shakespeare confounded him by crying, "Sir Danny Plympton? Do you know the plight of Sir Danny Plympton?"

"How could I not? 'Twas my plan which led Sir Danny to Newgate."

"*Your* plan?" Shakespeare looked puzzled, then shook his head. "I assure you, Sir Danny landed himself in Newgate. He blew into London with all the discretion of a blizzard. He roared and bragged, telling everyone—on their promise of secrecy, of course—that he was Essex's downfall and the queen's savior."

"Certes, that's Sir Danny for you." What manner of man would hug the secret of Rosie's inheritance to his bosom, yet sacrifice his own safety for brief, bombastic glory?

Shakespeare answered Tony's unspoken questions

when he said, "I've known Sir Danny for years, and I assure you, he ever has played the part of a beneficent god."

Tony hadn't known Sir Danny for years, but he'd glimpsed the vision which drove the man, and he corrected Shakespeare firmly. "Nay, 'tis not a part he plays, but a dazzling belief in his own purpose on this earth. God grant he fulfills it."

"Amen." But Shakespeare sighed dolorously.

"I also know Lady Rosalyn Bellot, daughter of the late earl of Sadler."

Shakespeare cocked his head back and forth, curious as a sea gull served grubs on a silver platter. "I don't know Lady Rosalyn. Who is she?"

Skeptically, Tony added, "You would perhaps know her as Rosencrantz."

"Rosencrantz is Sir Danny's adopted son. He is not—" Shakespeare did his sea gull act again. "Are you trying to tell me Rosencrantz is a girl?"

"Not a girl," Tony corrected. "A woman. My betrothed. The woman who agreed to marry me, then ran off." He watched Shakespeare closely. "The woman who may carry my babe."

The bird act stopped. Everything stopped. Shakespeare stared at him unblinkingly. "Your babe?"

"Whom I'd like to see born in wedlock."

"Your babe?" Shakespeare dropped his head back and banged it on the wall behind. Under his breath, he muttered, "She never said . . ."

Tony could have jumped for joy. Here was proof. She was alive. Rosie was alive. She'd been in communication with her Uncle Will, and would be again, no doubt. He'd set his men to watching the London theaters and all the inns frequented by actors, and he planned to have Rosie in his custody before Essex made his move. Then Tony could concentrate on arresting Essex and freeing Sir Danny. Then he could be wed and his son would be born in the big bed in his bedchamber. Or on the desk where he had been conceived.

Meanwhile, Shakespeare looked so stiff it seemed his sea gull had swallowed a piece of splintered driftwood. "If I see Rosencrantz, I will certainly pass on the message you're looking for her."

"If you see Rosencrantz"—Tony threatened with a smile—"tell her the world will be minus one playwright if she doesn't return to me."

Shakespeare grimaced and stirred uncomfortably. "You may be sure I won't forget. But Sir Anthony, none of this treats with my problem, which is—what excuse should I give Southampton for refusing to perform the play? He sent a decent sum of cash, forty shillings, and actors never refuse cash. He knows that very well."

"Do the play, then."

Shakespeare laughed briefly with bitter humor. "Nay, I'll not help provoke an insurrection."

"But it would be a most important provocation," Tony said. "Don't you see? Until Essex and Southampton break into open rebellion, the queen will continue to tie my hands and refuse to let me act. But if all signs point to a successful uprising, Essex and Southampton will take the bits in their teeth and gallop toward the Tower of their own accord." Tony chuckled softly at his uncontrived analogy. "Perhaps the women are right. Perhaps all men *are* divided into geldings and stallions."

Crouched tight against the rough plaster wall, Rosie wanted to laugh. If men were divided into geldings and stallions, she knew in which group to place Tony. She placed her hand on her belly. He'd done his work too well, and damn him for being so certain of it. Damn him for bragging to Uncle Will about it. At the moment of Tony's grand unveiling, she'd thought her secrecy was lost. She'd thought Uncle Will would reveal her hiding place and insist on marriage, here and now.

Only the brotherhood of the actors protected her, and she knew when next she saw Uncle Will he'd be furious at being so manipulated. Her only excuse *was* her pregnancy. Now when she needed all her well-being, all her wit, fatigue and nausea plagued her. Their babe grew within her, and she blamed the babe for these moments of doubt.

Why else, when all her plans were coming to fruition, did she want to run into Tony's arms? Why did she want to tell him about their child, rejoice with him, and do the easy thing rather than the right thing?

Beside her, Ludovic stirred. He suspected her sentiments, she knew. Since the moment he'd found her on the road, he'd been the rock on which she leaned. He'd helped her get to London, engaged separate quarters for them at the Bull Inn, scouted out Sir Danny's situation, and supported her when she hatched her plan to perform for Queen Elizabeth. It had been Ludovic who had spread the word among the acting community that she wanted to play the part of Ophelia, and Ludovic who accompanied her to the Cross Keys Inn so she could participate in the debate.

It had been Ludovic who realized Tony approached, and Ludovic who had concealed her and persuaded Uncle Will to distract Tony—although persuaded seemed to be too mild a word.

Ludovic had been silent and stoic about her relationship to Tony, and she'd been too wary to ask if he knew the cause behind the accidents at Odyssey Manor. If he *were* the cause of the accidents at Odyssey Manor.

It had been odd, to depend on a man she suspected of attempted murder, but more than once she'd caught him looking at her as if she were his last chance of redemption. She tried to be worthy of his worship; she tried not to encourage him to love her.

Both causes were hopeless.

Behind her, Ludovic tensed when they once more heard the sound of hurrying feet.

"Wart-Nose!" Tony exclaimed. "Did you teach Hal a lesson, or did he teach you?"

Hal? The steward Hal? Rosie could have groaned. Was all of Odyssey Manor traveling to London to plague her?

"That man stinks o' deceit," Wart-Nose said. "That face o' his looks well lived-in, but I'd swear he abided in London fer a few glorious months fifteen, twenty years ago."

Rosie hung her head and shrank, shivering, against the wall.

"Let's find out," Tony said, his tone chillingly calm. "Where is he?"

"Dashing his arse toward the river, last time I saw him," Wart-Nose said, and he sounded very pleased with himself.

"Returning to Whitehall Palace, I trow." Tony's voice moved down Gracechurch Street toward the Thames. "I'll find him there."

"*If* Her Majesty invites ye back."

"Oh, Her Majesty will invite me back."

Rosie frowned. How pleasant to note her defection hadn't dented Tony's conceit.

"From the report you and this worthy playwright have given me, there'll be work for the master of the Queen's Guard, and very soon."

Uncle Will's voice sounded faint. "So you do believe

the lords will stage an insurrection after we perform the play?"

"I do."

"My heart swells with shame that my work can be used for harm." Uncle Will repeated, "My heart swells with shame."

Then Rosie heard nothing. She waited until she knew no one remained within earshot. Rising slowly, she shook the kinks out of her limbs and whispered, "I think they're gone. Don't you?"

No one answered, and she said, "Ludovic?"

Still no answer, and the hairs rose on the back of her neck. "Ludovic." She whirled around, groping in the dark, but Ludovic was nowhere to be found, and Rosie was all alone in Londontown.

21

I have seen a medicine
That's able to breathe life into a stone.
—ALL'S WELL THAT ENDS WELL, II, i, 74

Sir Danny's shriek rose through the air like a living thing, pleading for mercy in its very intensity. "No more." He sobbed. "No more."

"Ye have t' have a bath afore ye see Her Majesty." The rough soldier repeated the same thing he'd been saying for the last hour. "If ye'd stop struggling, we'd be done by now."

"You're lying." Three burly men-at-arms pushed Sir Danny under the water to wash the soap from his hair, and Sir Danny knew this time they would hold him under too long. But they let him up, and he screamed, "You're lying. This is just another torture you're inflicting before you take me to the gallows."

"Her Majesty doesn't like evil odors. She has a very sensitive nostril, ye understand, an' ye smelled o'

Newgate Prison." The rough soldier nodded at his compatriots, and they lifted Sir Danny free of the tub and set him on his feet.

Sir Danny collapsed, too weak with hunger and fear to stand. His rump missed the reeds scattered on the floor and hit cold stone, and he suddenly found the strength to rise. "Hark!" he croaked. "I serve Her Majesty Queen Elizabeth however she demands, and if my life is forfeit, I give it gladly to preserve her."

"Hell, man, 'tis only a bath, an' a warm bath at that." The commander looked disgusted. "Don't ye even bathe on yer name day?"

"Ugh." One of the men-at-arms shuddered. "No one bathes willingly."

"I do," the commander said. "That's why I'm th' commander an' ye're just a soldier."

"Bet ye don't bathe in winter," the soldier retorted.

"Scarcely." The commander glanced around the bare gatehouse room where he and his men slept on pallets. "But I'm not going t' visit th' queen. Best wrap th' skinny bugger. He's turnin' blue."

Sir Danny had been cold and hungry, tormented and in prison, for too long. No one had come to his assistance. Not one of his friends had sent blankets or food. Sir Anthony Rycliffe had not even tried to use his influence to free him. The torturers had assured him of that when they'd made him confess to treason.

And Rosie, his dear Rosie, probably didn't even know of his misery.

So when these soldiers had plucked him from his cell and carried him through the night, he assumed the worst. This talk of Her Majesty and the palace was nothing but more empty promises produced by a torturer who wanted him to confess to vile treachery. Shivering, Sir Danny watched as the men-at-arms approached him with a large sheet of linen, and he moaned. "My shroud."

"Ye're a yellow-backed coward, aren't ye?" the commander commented as his men rubbed Sir Danny from top to toe. "Bring th' clothes Sir Cecil sent, an' let's get him up t' th' palace afore Her Majesty has another one o' her royal fits."

"Will you send word to my daughter, the dearest daughter in all England, that I've gone to my death unfairly accused of treason?" The soldiers handed a shirt to Sir Danny, and the material was soft as butter and twice as slippery. He fingered it as he pulled it over his head. "Tell her I died bravely." While he donned hose and garters, he mused, "Possibly you shouldn't say I died bravely. I fear my Rosie knows me too well for that." Picturing himself dangling at the end of a rope, his feet kicking while children threw stones, he shuddered. "Nay, tell her I died for the safety of the kingdom." The soldiers jerked him in a circle as they dressed him in a waistcoat, canions, and doublet and finished him off with a stylish cap.

The commander marched in front, the soldiers on either side of Sir Danny as they left the gatehouse. When they realized he couldn't keep up with their rapid pace, the commander cursed and gave an order, and the soldiers formed a chair with their hands and carried him.

Odd behavior, Sir Danny mused, but perhaps they always so assisted the condemned.

"Don't like this," one of them complained. "They say there's a crazy old man on th' grounds, an' his eyes burn like fire. Might be he could attack us, an' we've got no hands free."

"I'll protect ye from any old men, crazed or otherwise," the commander said. "Ye'd best be more worried about getting th' prisoner t' th' palace."

A low fog swirled around the garden paths, and Sir Danny longed for one last glimpse of the world. If he looked straight up, he could see stars, bright and friendly as ever. The half-moon, too, grinned with partial amusement, and this evidence of eternity gave him the courage. "Oh, lighthouses of heaven, twinkling in a globe of nothingness. Eternal lights, eternal night, eternal death, and precious life, snuffed like a candle by men who, gripped by the madness of treachery, do attempt to wrench England's rudder from the hand of her oil-anointed captain."

"Thirteen years I been workin' at Whitehall, an' I've never spoke t' th' queen," the commander mourned. "An' this sheep's head is complainin' in his fancy talk."

Wrenched from his poetic haven, Sir Danny asked, "Is this Whitehall Palace?"

"Ain't ye been listenin'?" one of the soldiers demanded.

The commander rapped on a tiny door set in a looming stone wall. The door opened slightly, and a bony hand grabbed Sir Danny's wrist and jerked him inside. A hunchbacked man, all in black, held a single candle and whispered hoarsely, "Hurry."

Sir Danny hurried.

Despite the man's unprepossessing appearance, he wore his air of command with confidence. He led Sir Danny up stairs and through halls and rooms furnished in tapestries and woods and ivories. Sir Danny was, he realized, actually in Whitehall Palace, and he moved closer to the stranger and asked, "Is it only those condemned of treason that you treat with such grace?"

The gentleman looked at him oddly.

"I've never been executed before." Sir Danny excused himself. "I don't know the protocol."

"Didn't they tell you why they were bringing you here?" The man spoke softly, as if he wished to avoid detection.

Sir Danny chuckled, and found himself surprised he could still laugh. "To see the queen, they said."

"Then play not the fool. Bow when you enter the room, speak only when spoken to, and answer the questions in a forthright manner, but with the proper reverence." The stranger opened a narrow door set into the wooden paneling and shoved Sir Danny ahead of him.

The richly appointed chamber blazed with candles. The flames reflected off the diamond-shaped windowpanes, the waxed woods, the mirrors, the wrought gold, and the polished silver. Tapestries draped the walls and a carpet of dazzling color and intricacy covered the glossy wood floor. Beside an immense blazing fire stood a massive, carved chair. Surrounding it, like disciples waiting for enlightenment, squatted benches and stools. The chair drew Sir Danny's eye, and for the first time, awe prickled along his spine.

The childish sense of wonder which had never abandoned him drew him now, and he almost expected to see a regal figure materialize in the chair.

Instead, a querulous voice jerked him around to the pile of cushions thrown in the corner. "What have you brought me, Master Cecil?"

The black-robed figure bowed deeply and in tones of reverence, announced, "Your Majesty, I bring you Sir Daniel Plympton, Esquire."

Sir Danny gaped. It was the queen. Of course he recognized her from the coins that circulated with her likeness etched on them.

The cushions that surrounded and supported her were silk, satin, wool. Embroidered, woven, sewn. Cobalt, scarlet, amethyst. Likewise, the queen's clothes were magnificent creations, overwhelming in their opulence. And the queen herself seemed insignificant. Nothing but a skinny old woman.

Until Sir Danny looked into her eyes.

The color had been muddied by age, but they glittered with interest and acumen.

Conquered, Sir Danny fell to his knees. "God save Your Majesty!"

"Want me to pardon you, do you?"

Her shrill voice fell on his ears like water on the parched earth. "There is no need." Removing his cap, Sir Danny worshiped her with his gaze. "Simply seeing Your Majesty's beauty one time before I die makes my sacrifice worthwhile. In sooth, all call you Gloriana, monarch of England and chosen of the gods, and verily, it is true."

"He's a charmer, isn't he?" She spoke to Cecil, but she watched Sir Danny steadily, and her mouth had curved into a slight, closed-mouth smile. Then the smile disappeared. She winced and pressed her hand to her cheek. "Have you questioned him?"

Cecil tucked his hands in his wide sleeves and watched Sir Danny's homage with approval. "Nay, madam, I waited for you."

She pointed a long, clawed finger at Sir Danny. "We want to know about you and Essex."

"Your Majesty, I will tell you whatever you require." Sir Danny noted the lines of stress between her brows, the tension in the hand she still held against her jaw. Tentatively, he said, "However, if you would forgive my imprudence, you seem to be in pain."

Her hand fell away from her face, and she said, "I'm healthy as an English war-horse." She said it as if she'd said it before, many times.

"Your Majesty, again forgive me, but you look nothing like an English war-horse." Slowly, Sir Danny approached, walking on his knees. He'd always known the safety of his sovereign was his destiny. Was it also his destiny to give her ease? "Your magnificent health glows from you like a fire that warms you from the inside. You are a morning rose, protected by the thorns of duty and nobility as you open to delight your subjects with vigorous beauty and sweet perfumes."

Queen Elizabeth relaxed even as he spoke. She lifted her chin, the lines smoothed from her fair complexion, and he caught a glimpse of the young goddess who had captivated the hearts of her subjects even before her coronation.

The cushions bumped his knees now; he bent to keep the top of his head below hers and gazed at her most earnestly. "Yet the rose, if not tended by the loving gardener, might be harmed by the overzealous sun or the attentions of greedy parasites."

"Too true," the queen murmured, and she glared at Cecil.

Primming his mouth, Cecil retorted, "If you would allow me, Your Majesty, I would call the tooth drawer back. He thought to relieve your pain, but you changed your mind before he'd even entered the door."

She sat up with all the vigor she claimed. "Am I not the queen? May I not send a charlatan away if I see fit?"

Cecil drew breath to retort, but Sir Danny placed one hand behind his back and made a gesture. A rude gesture, and Cecil saw it, for he moved in a huff to the fireplace, there to fold his arms across his chest.

When Sir Danny looked back at Queen Elizabeth, he realized with a jolt she had seen it, too. She looked as satisfied as a peahen presented with a strutting display of feathers. "Good," she said. "He's offended."

"He is young," Sir Danny said soothingly. "He'll learn the correct manner to treat his monarch."

"He is not his father. I do miss my dear Burghley, the greatest statesman of my reign."

Sir Danny bowed his head in respect.

"You remind me of him."

He looked up.

"Not in your appearance, of course, but in your tact and good sense." Plucking at the silk tufting that decorated her massive puffed sleeve, she asked fretfully, "Do *you* think I should summon the tooth drawer?"

Picking his words with caution, Sir Danny said, "Your Majesty, you are a glorious monarch with the resources of all England at your feet, but might not so many resources be as big a problem as not enough? Might the selection of physicians and barbers who long to serve you be so large, you are unable to find the best among the crowd?"

Cecil proved he had been listening. "What are you babbling about, man?"

Elizabeth pointed a restraining finger at her secretary of state. "I want to hear what he has to say."

"Why, simply, madam, that I have a reputation as a physician among my lowly compatriots."

"Lowly indeed," Cecil snapped.

"Shut your maw, Cecil." The queen leaned forward and looked into Sir Danny's eyes. "Tell me more."

"Among the actors I am known for my skills at physicking, and if you would perhaps allow me to try, I might be able to draw the tooth without pain to Your Majesty."

"Madam, I must object!" Cecil strode forward. "This man is under suspicion of treason. He can't be allowed to give you some magic potion which turns out to be poison!"

"I see no obstacle. I'll have you taste it first." Elizabeth burst into unrestrained laughter at Cecil's expression, laughter so wild Sir Danny flinched.

She had been too long without sleep. She was balanced

on the edge of madness, and she needed him in a way he'd never imagined. If he could not serve England with his knowledge of Essex, he could at least serve her with his skill.

"I use no potions, madam, but I will have to touch you." He glanced apologetically at Cecil. "There's no other way."

"This is outrageous," Cecil fumed. "Dismiss him at once."

Elizabeth ignored Cecil with all the stubbornness of her sixty-seven years. "What do you have to do?"

"Just touch your face and hands," Sir Danny said reassuringly. "However, if the tooth pains you, it must be drawn, and for that I'll need the tools of a tooth drawer."

"Cecil." Elizabeth snapped her fingers. "Get the tools from the tooth drawer."

Stiffly, Cecil said, "Madam, he has gone home."

She scorned his falsehood. "Nonsense, he remains within the palace on your pleasure until he's done the deed. Now get his tools."

"I can't leave you alone with this charlatan."

"I'm not giving you a choice." Regally, she drew herself up. "Sir Cecil, seek the tooth drawer. It is your queen's command."

Cecil didn't like it, but neither did he have the presumption to defy a direct order. In a softer tone, he begged, "Might I at least have a guard remain within?"

"You may station one directly outside the door. Should this treasonous actor attack me, your conscience will be clear. Now be off, and shut the door behind you." She watched until he had gone and Sir Danny remained alone with her, then said, "You realize if you fail to draw my tooth painlessly, I'll have your head cut off."

Sir Danny permitted himself a smile. "Your Majesty,

if you cut off my head, it'll be an improvement over the hanging you have planned for me right now. What have I to lose?"

An answering smile played around Elizabeth's mouth. "Aye, what indeed? So tell me what you heard from Essex that proves his treason."

She had changed the subject so quickly, Sir Danny's head spun before he realized her brilliant tactics. She'd relaxed him, given him the illusion of control, then slapped him with a sharp query designed to knock the truth from him. More than that, she'd removed Cecil from the room, so no audience gawked with smug delight as she listened to the proof of treason by her favorite courtier.

It was a totally understandable desire, and Sir Danny told his story quickly, explaining how Essex had boasted of his plan to overthrow the queen and wished to have the play *Richard II* played by the Chamberlain's Men to induce an atmosphere of rebellion.

His fellow actors would not recognize him, Sir Danny thought, as his very restraint lent a veracity to his words and Elizabeth's head sank onto her chest.

Distressed, he wrung his hands. "Madam, I have given you pain when I thought to ease it."

"Nay, 'tis not you who gives me pain." She touched her fingertips to her papery eyelids. "'Tis the sunset of my reign, and all around me I see death and betrayal as my powers fade into nothingness. 'Tis a bitter thing to grow old, Sir Danny, a bitter thing."

"I see no sunset. I see no peacock display of colors that announces the approach of night, nor could I ever perceive the anguish of such a fading. When future generations remember Queen Elizabeth, they'll still bask in the warmth of your legacy. What you have wrought can never fail."

"You are a funny little man, and you comfort me." She stretched. "Can you really draw my tooth, or was that simply a tale to put Cecil out of the room?"

"I have references, madam, if you chose to call upon my fellows who act with the Chamberlain's Men."

"The Chamberlain's Men?" The queen lifted her brows. "The company is performing a play for me on Sunday."

"A play?" Forgetting himself, Sir Danny leaped to his feet. "Which play?"

She watched him curiously. "'Tis called *Hamlet,* I believe."

"I wonder if . . . I hope that . . . oh, Your Majesty, do you have the list of the players?"

"Not at all. Should I?"

"It's just that my child might play one of the parts. But nay, my son wouldn't be here in the city. She's safe now." He had always concealed Rosie's gender with such practiced proficiency, he didn't even realize when he failed. His shoulders sagged. He wanted to weep and instead cursed his weakness. He'd refused to allow himself to think of Rosie, to wonder how she was faring in her new role as mistress of the manor. He'd refused to think of the marriage performed, no doubt, while he languished in prison. He'd felt only joy in her safety.

But he'd missed her. Od's bodkin, how he'd missed her.

The queen watched him fidget, her bright eyes seeing more than he liked, but before she could question him further, someone rapped on the door. "Enter," Queen Elizabeth called.

The door swung wide to reveal Cecil with the tooth drawer close behind him.

"I'm still alive," Queen Elizabeth said. "More travail to you."

"'Tis care for you which causes me concern." Cecil led the tooth drawer into the room by the hand.

By the terrified looks the tooth drawer cast toward the queen, Sir Danny supposed she had quite intimidated him. "Let me see your tools," he commanded.

The tooth drawer sidled forward and handed Sir Danny the bag, then retreated with great haste to the wall opposite.

"He begs Your Majesty for another chance to assist you," Cecil said, glaring meaningfully at the quivering dentist.

"He's a maggot." Queen Elizabeth dismissed the tooth drawer with scorn. Glancing at the tools and the herbs Sir Danny was laying out, her voice turned shrill. "Cecil, I want you to send word to Sir Anthony Rycliffe. He's to present himself to me tomorrow morning, and no more of this shirking of his duties."

"Aye, Your Majesty."

"His first duty will be to go to Essex House tomorrow, and tell my lord Essex that I command he come before the Privy Council and give an accounting of his activities." She clenched a pillow in her fist. "His treasonous activities."

"Aye, Your Majesty." Cecil bowed deeply.

"I thought that'd please you. Well, come on, come on." She snapped her fingers at Sir Danny. "If you're going to do it, do it at once."

Sir Danny again crept forward. He'd done this so many times. With Rosie, with Will, with the other members of his troupe. But to the queen? To the lady he'd always worshiped from afar?

"Well?" Cecil said loudly. "What are you going to do?"

"Cecil," Queen Elizabeth barked. "Either shut your maw or get out."

Then Sir Danny realized she couldn't help him, because she was more frightened than he. Her need gave him courage, and using his satin-smooth tone, he said, "With your permission?" She nodded graciously, but he could see her tense as he touched her hand. "You have a beautiful hand," he murmured. "Such long fingers, such fair skin." He stroked the back of her hand, then her palm and stared into her eyes. She stared back, but she couldn't keep her eyes open as long as he could, and she blinked. "Pain is exhausting, and you are very tired. So tired that as I touch you, you can think only of sleep."

"That's very relaxing," she admitted.

"May I touch your face?" He reached out with his fingertips and grazed the skin. Slowly, he accustomed her to his touch. "Such beautiful skin. Such regular features. How much it must pain you to have a tooth causing puffiness."

"It does." She slurred her words.

"Show me the tooth."

She opened her mouth. He touched the tooth, and she winced.

"Think of the pleasure sleep would bring you. Think of how sleep will lessen your uneasiness." He kept his tones low and regular. "Think of how sleep would lessen any discomfort as I remove it."

"Aye." Her lids dropped, but she brought them up again.

He stroked her cheek. "You can sleep now. In your sleep you'll know that I'm helping you with your tooth, but you'll still sleep until you wish to wake. You are in command. I am just helping you achieve your desire."

"Aye."

Her eyes had closed, and Sir Danny reached for the cloth and pinchers, taking care not to clang metal against metal. The tooth drawer had slipped closer, fascinated by Sir Danny's performance. Cecil stood by the fire with his mouth spread as wide as the queen's. Using the most exquisite care and speed, Sir Danny extracted the tooth which was so rotten it slipped from the gum with ease. He packed the cavity with a poultice of willow bark and cobwebs and whispered, "Sleep, gracious queen."

With her eyes still closed, she murmured. "Stay in the palace. See your actor friends once more. See if your child is among the players."

Sir Danny could scarcely believe it. He'd come to die, and now the queen commanded life. But had she? With hands clasped in silent prayer, Sir Danny asked, "And my death sentence?"

Head resting against a cushion, she waved a slender, dismissing hand. "I'll decide later. After all"—she yawned and snuggled down—"I might need another tooth drawn."

22

A nest of traitors!
—THE WINTER'S TALE, II, iii, 80

"Never seen a man fall as hard an' as fast as ye have," Wart-Nose observed.

"What do you mean?" Tony stepped off the boat landing on the Strand and glared at the elegant cluster of buildings that constituted Essex House. Damn Essex for subjecting Her Majesty to such suffering, and damn him for so interrupting Tony's own wooing.

"Got a good, bright, cold mornin'. Got th' queen callin' ye back t' yer duties." Wart-Nose paid the boat-man sixpence and promised him another nine if he'd wait for them. Hurrying to catch up with Tony, he said, "Got th' earl o' Essex finally showin' his hand, an' all ye can think about is yer woman."

"Have you ever thought about having that growth on your nose removed?"

Wart-Nose touched the protuberance that gave him

his name. "Nay, sir, don't trust no surgeon with a razor."

With gentle intent, Tony said, "You won't need a surgeon if you don't stuff a clam in your mouth."

Wart-Nose cocked his head and thought, then decided. "That 'twere a threat. Very well, I can stuff a clam in it."

Tony nodded and walked on along the path lined with trimmed shrubs. On the street side, Essex House faced the Strand, the area east of Whitehall Palace where the most exclusive homes in London had been built. No expense had been spared when building Essex House. The grounds were well tended, the stables were the finest, and the house itself rose to three stories of pretension.

It wasn't nearly as impressive as Odyssey Manor.

Following close behind Tony, Wart-Nose said, "Just seems like ye're always lookin' behind ye, expectin' t' see her. An' when I talk, ye seem t' listen, but all th' time I've can't shake th' feelin' ye're listenin' fer her voice."

Drawing his dagger, Tony turned and stalked toward Wart-Nose, who backed off, cackling.

"Now, now, Sir Anthony, ye might need me in there." He pointed at Essex House. "Got enemies within, ye do."

"Do I need a fool guarding my back?"

"Don't know. Want me t' see if I can find ye one?"

Wart-Nose's cheeky, gap-toothed grin eased a little of the tension in Tony. "My thanks, but I have one." He sheathed his dagger and silently acknowledged the truth of Wart-Nose's accusation. He did look for Rosie, listen for Rosie, no matter where he was. He kept thinking that if he wanted her badly enough, she would come to him.

But that hadn't proved the case, for he wanted her very badly, and she remained elusive.

Last night after he'd bid farewell to Wart-Nose and the playwright, he'd visited every inn that housed actors, looking for Rosie, but he'd accomplished nothing. He wanted to finish his duty quickly today, so he could once more continue on his quest.

"Damned cold day t' leave th' door open," Wart-Nose observed.

It was true. The massive door stood wide open and no one guarded it. Tony stepped inside and blinked as his sight adjusted to the shadows. From inside, he heard the babble of many voices. Men's voices.

No footmen asked his business nor did any servants greet him, so he and Wart-Nose walked toward the gallery as if they belonged there. No one stopped them. Indeed, no man there—no women were in sight—really looked at the master of the Queen's Guard and his aide.

"Blast me ballocks," Wart-Nose exclaimed when they paused in the doorway. "'Tis nothin' but a bunch o' lads playin' with swords."

"A dangerous bunch of lads," Tony said, but Wart-Nose was right. Bravado clogged the air so thickly that nothing but the swing of a sword could cut it. And the swords were swinging on every side. Tony would have liked to hawk linen bandage strips to this gathering. He'd make his fortune.

"Do you see Essex?" Tony asked.

"Nay, sir, but I see every other lordly rebel." Wart-Nose tipped his hat constantly, showing proper respect with his gesture if not his expression.

The shining auburn hair and flowing beard which were Essex's trademarks were nowhere to be seen, and Tony interrupted an animated debate. "I beg your pardon, can you gentlemen tell me where I might find the earl of Essex?"

A wild-eyed Welshman with a bared sword looked

Tony up and down. "We all want to talk to him, but he's busy planning the rebellion. Tell me, don't you think Sunday is a good day to rouse London?"

Tony found himself speechless.

"Because of the apprentices, you see. Sunday is their day off," the Welshman explained. "If we call on London to rebel, and the apprentices are out from under the thumbs of their masters, they'll join us freely."

Tony nodded, dumbfounded at this madness of reason. "Essex?" he asked again.

"He's over there by the fire." The Welshman pointed at a large assembly of men clustered in a circle. "But you'll have to take your turn just like the rest of us."

Coldly confident, Tony said, "Essex will see me."

As he moved away, he heard the whisper behind him, "Don't you know who that is? Sir Anthony Rycliffe, master of the Queen's Guard."

"Stay close," Tony murmured to Wart-Nose. "The flesh between my shoulder blades is itching."

"Aye, sir. An' look, they're clearin' ye a path."

In sooth, the whisper must have outrun them, for as Tony walked toward the merry, confident group around Essex, the jocularity died. He walked a silent path cleared for him. Pleased to know that his name and commission inspired deference, Tony walked right to the bench upon which rested Essex and Southampton.

Both men were elegant creatures, dressed in blazing silks and adorned with feathers and jewels. Both smiled a mocking welcome, their austere faces powdered and their thin lips rouged. Their pointed teeth shone, proclaiming them to be night-hunting carnivores who skulked in the shadows until unwary prey displayed a weakness.

Which of them was worse? Essex, with his rebellious ingratitude, or Southampton, with his furtive ambitions?

Tony didn't know. He only knew he would display no such weakness. He'd give them no excuse to hunt him. "My lord Essex. My lord Southampton." Removing his cap, he bowed with an elegant sweep.

"Sir Anthony." Essex stood and replied with a like bow, then added, "Look, gentlemen, 'tis Her Majesty's trained bastard."

Southampton shouted with laughter, but he was the only one.

Perhaps Tony's reputation as a fighter had preceded him. Perhaps Tony's pleasant smile contained something less than amusement and more than a threat. But the circle around Essex widened as the others edged away.

Essex sneered when he noticed. "Surely you gentlemen aren't afraid of this pathetic, dispossessed son of a whore? Why, even the estate Her Majesty gave to him is in jeopardy because the true heir has returned. And while God only knows she's been tossing up her skirts all these years, at least she's legitimate."

Tony leaped and smashed Essex to the floor. Sitting atop his chest, Tony mashed his forearm into Essex's throat, and said, "Do not ever call me a bastard again, or I will be forced to teach you respect for your betters."

Essex's face grew red from lack of air. He struggled against Tony's grip, but he was a commander with only lordly experience in combat and in courtly duels. He was no match for a man who'd fought for his life with steel, fist, and claw in countless Continental battles.

"And don't ever mention Lady Rosalyn again. You're not worthy to clean her jakes." Essex's eyes bulged, but still Tony clamped him to the floor and kept him breathless.

But Essex had friends, and this was Essex's camp.

"Sir Anthony!"

Wart-Nose's alarm warned Tony. Still kneeling on Essex's chest, Tony caught a glimpse of Southampton's fine hose stepping toward him. With the point of his dagger, he nicked the earl's leg, and chortled when Southampton yelped and jumped back. "Be off," Tony warned Southampton, then looked around at the watching crowd. "Be off. There are better causes to die for. There are better leaders to follow."

Essex fumbled for his sword. "Get off of me."

Tony pointed the tip of his dagger between Essex's eyes, and Essex froze. In his most cordial, respectful voice, Tony said, "I do as you command, my lord Essex, but first, I have been sent by the queen to tell you her will."

"What does the old—" The point of the dagger came closer, and Essex hastily revised his query. "What does Her Majesty desire?"

"That's better." Tony sheathed his dagger.

Essex's black eyes glittered with cold and shiny hatred.

"Let . . . me . . . up."

He sounded fierce, and Tony grinned. "You're damned bony and uncomfortable, anyway." He stood, then watched as Essex slowly rose. Picking up his cap, Essex dusted it against his knee, watching Tony all the while.

"I hope I didn't hurt you, my lord," Tony said. "I would be most distressed if you were unable to answer Her Majesty's summons."

"Has she returned to her senses at last?" Essex snapped, but his hand half rose as if he wanted to rub his aching skull.

"She?" Tony feigned puzzlement. "She? Do you mean Her Majesty, Queen Elizabeth?"

"That's who I mean." Essex curled his mouth in an elegant sneer. "That is her title—for the moment."

That was blunt speaking, indeed, and Tony wished he'd never let him off the floor. He made a move toward Essex, who pulled his dagger in hasty self-defense.

A collective growl issued from Essex's retinue, and Wart-Nose caught Tony's arm. "We might consider a timely retreat an' live t' fight another day."

Wart-Nose was right. Tony hated to admit it, but he was right. All around them stood Welsh swordsmen, Irish soldiers, Puritan ministers, Catholic priests, and lords who'd failed to make their marks at court. And men who deluded themselves into thinking the queen's sovereignty was open to debate were men who might decide the queen's herald was ripe for murder.

Solemnly, as befitting a royal command, Tony said, "My lord Essex, the Privy Council summons you to attend it immediately and give an account of your actions and your intentions."

Essex glanced at Southampton, but Southampton was examining the notch where Tony had removed both hose and skin. "I cannot attend the Privy Council today," he said.

Tony contained both his jubilation and his scorn. "What excuse should I give?"

"I . . . am in ill health. Aye!" Essex warmed to his theme. "I can't answer Her Majesty's summons because of you, Sir Anthony Rycliffe."

"How so, my lord?"

"You hurt me when you attacked me."

It was all Tony could do not to laugh. "I hadn't realized a minor romp could so impair the commander of the English forces in Ireland."

"Ah, well." Essex rubbed his neck where the bruises of Tony's assault darkened, then glanced at the dagger he still held in his hand. "I was already ill, and your attack exacerbated my weakness."

"That would explain why I was able to bring you down so easily," Tony said.

"Indeed, 'tis true." Then Essex realized Tony was laughing at him, and lunged.

Throwing up his arm, Tony turned aside, and just in time. The dagger sliced through the material of his cape into unready flesh.

Blood dripped from Tony's arm, splattering his boots as it struck the polished floor, but he didn't notice as he drew his dagger. With look and gesture, he and Essex challenged each other.

"Live t' fight another day." Wart-Nose broke their concentration.

Tony turned on him in a fury.

"Are ye willin' t' die?" Keeping his voice low, Wart-Nose took Tony's arm and wrapped it in his sash. "Ah, he got ye, but only opened th' skin directly over the bone. A few stitches will close that, an' if ye fight him here an' he wins, ye'll die. If ye win, his men'll kill ye. Don't ye want t' bed that woman o' yers again?"

Subduing his fury, Tony said sarcastically, "Well done, my lord."

Essex glared at the wound with a mixture of shame and defiance. "A just punishment for a bastard's insolence."

"A just punishment for a bastard's carelessness," Tony corrected. "Shall I tell the queen that you are too ill to obey her summons?"

"Tell the queen it is so." Looking relieved, Essex sheathed his dagger. "I command you, tell the queen it is so."

Again Tony doffed his hat. "I will do as you wish, my lord, but I doubt she desires your excuses."

*   *   *

Queen Elizabeth walked rapidly through the gardens of Whitehall Palace, her ladies-in-waiting trailing behind her like color-dipped cygnets behind a great, graceful white swan. The cold, sunny afternoon invited participation, and Sir Danny had been at first flattered when she invited him to accompany her. Now he could only puff along beside her as she said, "I have checked on the list of players for *Hamlet.* The actor who performs Ophelia is called Rosencrantz. Do you know Rosencrantz?"

Sir Danny clasped his hands to his breast. He'd been in an ardor of gratitude to the queen for the three-course breakfast he'd been served that morning and the seven-course dinner at noon. Now she gave him Rosie. "'Tis my Rosencrantz! My son. Your Majesty, you are too good to me."

"I hope not."

She kept walking, and he scurried to catch up. "I both feared and hoped my son would be in London. He shouldn't be, certes, but the news of my incarceration must have drawn him from . . . from . . ." He couldn't think of a likely lie. Perhaps the exhaustion of an emotional evening drained him. Perhaps two exquisite meals weren't enough to revive him. Or perhaps the cynical gaze of Queen Elizabeth drained him of wit.

"Your son, you say?"

Her gait was strong, her skin looked fresh, and the dark rings of sleeplessness which marred her eyes last night had vanished. He congratulated himself on the miracle of her good health, and at the same time wondered if by freeing her from pain he'd also turned her keen vision on him and his feeble contrivances.

"How old is your son?"

Frantically, he tried to discern a trap, but saw none. "He has twenty-two years."

"How long has your son played a woman's role?"

"Since he followed in my footsteps and became an actor. You see, the younger men always play the ladies' roles because their youthful appearance makes them more believable." He flushed and faltered when she tossed him a scornful smile. She knew that. Of course she knew that. He wished she'd stop walking so fast. After the month in prison, he could scarcely keep up, but never could he admit it to Queen Elizabeth. Not to Gloriana herself.

"At what age did you play only men's roles?"

Panting, he pressed his hand to the stitch in his side. "At eighteen, madam. 'Tis the most likely age." Then he perceived the trap, and babbled, "But Rosie—"

"Rosie is a woman's name."

"Rosencrantz—"

"Rosencrantz is a stupid name." She stopped so suddenly he tripped on the train of her skirt. "Sir Danny, is there something you wish to tell your queen about your child?"

The queen's sharp tone brooked no defiance, and Sir Danny's unexpected frail defenses failed. "She's a woman. I dressed her up like a lad and she played the women's parts."

Queen Elizabeth rapped him across his knuckles with her fan. "You're a bold one, Sir Danny Plympton."

"A foolish one, more like, but what other choice had I? I found her orphaned and had no one to care for her." And he cringed as he remembered Lord Sadler's instructions. *Take the child to Queen Elizabeth,* Lord Sadler had said. This muddle was the result of Sir Danny's disobedience and ignorance, and if—nay, when—the queen discovered, she'd do more than stretch his neck. She'd have him drawn and quartered, too.

He trod on thin ice, and knew not how to extricate himself without betraying Rosie, or himself, or both. He tried to remember the tale Tony's sisters had conceived to make her upbringing credible. "Rosie wasn't always with me. A kind lady helped me by raising her in perfect gentility."

"The lady's name?" Queen Elizabeth rapped.

"Lady Honora, dowager duchess of Burnham and baroness of Rowse." He almost rolled his eyes at the clumsy lie, but Queen Elizabeth rubbed her chin thoughtfully.

"Lady Honora was at one time my lady-in-waiting. I'll have to inquire about this."

Fond of Lady Honora as he was, he was under no illusion about her ability to manufacture a tale which coincided with his. In desperation, he said, "It might have been one of her aunts."

"You don't know the identity of the woman who raised your adopted daughter?" She sounded incredulous.

When in doubt, he decided, bluff. "Virile men care nothing about such things."

Queen Elizabeth faced him, chin up, nostrils flaring in disdain. "You disappoint me, Sir Danny Plympton. I had not thought you were one of those 'virile men.'"

She made it sound like a curse, and he realized with a sinking heart he had destroyed something fragile between them. Was it the masculine histrionics of Essex that soured her on such posings, or was it something older, something that reached into the depths of her past? He longed to ask, to offer the comfort and understanding which had won him so many women's hearts, but they had reached the tennis court.

Stiff and dimissive, Elizabeth sank onto a spectator's

stone seat. "At this moment, Sir Danny, your life hangs in the balance. Perhaps it depends upon your daughter's performance tomorrow. Perhaps it depends on the proof that she loves you. You may leave me now. I won't require your services any further this day."

Unhappy, frustrated, and almost in tears—his weakness embarrassed him greatly—Sir Danny fell to his knees before the queen. From that abject position he bowed, and when she waved her hand, he scrambled to his feet and backed away. He backed and backed until the flock of panting ladies-in-waiting passed him and surrounded her. Then he turned and dragged himself back to the palace, not seeing the lurking figure that watched him from the shadows.

23

Bell, book, and candle shall not drive me back
When gold and silver becks me to come on.
—KING JOHN, III, ii, 22

Lady Honora, Ann, and Jean found the queen
sitting by the tennis courts, staring at the courts as if
she watched some long-vanished players participate in
a rousing game. Her ladies-in-waiting stood shivering
in the sun not far away, and after making the proper
obeisance to the queen, Lady Honora said, "Let me
send the girls inside, Your Majesty. They're cold, and I
will attend you if you should need anything."

Queen Elizabeth looked up as if just noticing them.
"Lady Jean, Lady Ann, Lady Honora, how good to see
you. Aye, send the silly baggages back to the palace. I'll
be happier with you." The maidens fled while the queen
demanded, "Lady Honora, what marred your face?"

Self-conscious, Lady Honora touched the still pink
scar. "Is it very ugly?"

"Nay, nay." Queen Elizabeth waved a dismissing hand. "What difference does it make? You're not some young girl wanting to attract every man, and I'm not some young girl who cries at a cruel word." She stared at the packed grass with its poles for the nets. "Do any of you remember the king, my father?"

The queen's melancholy tone worried the women, and they exchanged glances. Lady Honora answered, although the answer was the same for all of them. "Glorious though King Henry's monarchy was, madam, I have lived all my life in the sunshine of your reign."

Queen Elizabeth still didn't look at them. "You don't remember my sister's reign, in which I almost lost my life? Or the brief reign of Lady Jane Grey? You don't remember my brother Edward, and, therefore, you're certainly too young to remember my father and the manner of his dealings with me."

"I didn't remember personally," Jean said, "but our mother was at King Henry's court."

"I remember your mother." The pinched look on Elizabeth's face relaxed a little. "In fact, your mother was one of my ladies when I was only the lady Elizabeth, and not the queen."

"She spoke of it often, madam."

Ann's gentle voice made it sound as if their mother recounted it a pleasant memory, when in fact she had not. Both Jean and Ann remembered what their mother had told them of King Henry's dealings with his daughters. A colder despot had never existed, conceiving children—two daughters—then rejecting them for their gender. Dealing kindly with them if they behaved exactly as he liked, and banishing them when they didn't. The lady Elizabeth had herself been banished from court for most of her twelfth year. During that time, she had often been cold and hungry, without adequate clothing, and in fear of her life, for she knew what happened to women who displeased King Henry.

Elizabeth's mother had been beheaded for displeasing King Henry.

Aye, King Henry's dealings with his daughters were indeed a good reason for melancholy.

"Sometimes you look at a man and glimpse what you think is a heart and a soul dedicated to kindness. The light of pride and anxiety twinkled in his eyes when he spoke of his daughter, and I thought he loved me not only because I was the queen, but because I was a woman." Queen Elizabeth cackled, an unpleasant, disconsolate noise. "Because he liked all women. But I'm afraid he proved me wrong."

Obviously bewildered, Ann asked, "King Henry?"

Startled, Queen Elizabeth laughed, this time with amusement. "Nay, dear, not King Henry. A nobody who deserves my mercy for all he has done and my contempt for the way he has treated his daughter."

"I found my father always indifferent to my wishes." Lady Honora looked into the past, remembering her first two husbands and their weaknesses.

"Aye, your father cared nothing for you." Queen Elizabeth was brutal in her honesty. "Are all men cool to their daughters?"

"You know they are not," Jean said. "Our father was most generous with his affection to us."

Ann nodded. "And our brother adores his daughters."

"Tony loves women, and will be a like father." Jean decided to brave the stormy waters and prepare the queen for the resurrection of the Sadler heiress—if they ever found her again. "You remember how Lord Sadler was with his tiny daughter, Rosalyn? He adored her every manner."

"Aye." The queen nodded. "I do indeed remember Lord Sadler. A finer lord never lived, and there's a rumor afloat his heir had been found." Glancing at them sharply, she asked, "What do you know about it?"

Lady Honora answered. "She *is* alive. My maiden aunt found the child on the road and, recognizing her quality, took her in and raised her as a lady." She might claim she didn't know how to lie, but when she got started, she proved steady as a rock. "Unfortunately, I didn't realize her identity until recently, when I took her to Odyssey Manor."

"Odyssey Manor?" Queen Elizabeth played with the long strand of pearls around her neck. "Why would you take her there rather than bring her to me?"

"Forgive me, madam, but I felt I needed to return her to her original setting before I could in all certainty say she was the lost child."

"And what convinced you?" the queen asked sharply.

In her high, piping voice, Ann said, "The ghosts haunted her."

Queen Elizabeth began to speak, but held her tongue out of liking for the scatter-witted Ann.

"What Ann means," Jean said, "is that Rosie—"

"Rosie?" Queen Elizabeth bent a scowl on Jean. "You call her Rosie?"

Discomfited by Her Majesty's keen query, Jean said, "'Tis only a pet name for Lady Rosalyn."

"A pet name I've heard recently." Queen Elizabeth looked at each of the ladies as if divining their subterfuge. "The morning, which began so inauspiciously, grows more interesting." She smiled at their thinly concealed horror. "Sit down. You make me nervous when you hover."

What else could they do? Jean sat on the bench in front of the queen, and Lady Honora and Ann joined her, lined up like children before a stern taskmaster. Their uneasiness seemed to entertain the queen. She pointed at Jean and ordered, "Tell me more about Rosie's ghosts."

Obediently, Jean said, "Lady Rosalyn found she knew her way through the manor, as well as knowing how the manor had been arranged during Lord Brewer's time. In addition, some of the older servants claimed they remembered her."

"Did she remember her father?" she asked.

Looking sad and lost, Ann whispered, "That was the ghost."

Jean tried to explain, but Queen Elizabeth waved Jean to silence. "It's more interesting when your sister tells it." To Ann, she asked, "Does Edward walk?"

"In Rosie's mind," Ann said. "Rosie says she doesn't remember, but the whole horrible tale is there, lurking in the sadness in her eyes."

Dissatisfied with such intangible details, Queen Elizabeth asked, "What kind of woman is Rosie?"

"Oh, she's lovely." The cloud which hung over Ann vanished, replaced by vivacious pleasure. "She's modest and kind, and learned quickly everything we taught her. She's beautiful and talented, with a lovely smile and big amber eyes."

"Talented?"

Queen Elizabeth's question seemed innocent enough, and it drew the truth from Ann like a poultice drew evil humors. "She's a wonderful actress."

Jean elbowed Ann so hard she fell off the end of the bench. In the flurry of apologies and assistance, the subject was dismissed, although Jean noted a glow of satisfaction about the queen.

"So it was Rosie's familiarity with the manor which convinced you of her identity?"

The queen played skepticism like bait on a string,

and she caught Lady Honora. "There was a letter from Lord Sadler."

Queen Elizabeth's skepticism failed with her genuine eagerness. "Did it have the seal? The mark of the ring I gave him?"

"It did not."

Jean said, "The ring was lost, we suspect, when the thief stripped Lord Sadler's traveling coach."

The queen pressed her gloved fingers to her eyes. "I trow 'tis true, always I have hoped to see that ring once more. It would have refreshed my memories of dear Edward." She looked up again, and her sentimentality vanished. "What did the letter say?"

Lady Honora got a rather pinched expression on her face, and Jean sympathized with her friend's dilemma. She couldn't lie about the contents of the letter, for the queen could, and would, ask to see it. Reluctantly, Lady Honora said, "It instructed the bearer to bring the child to you for proper placement."

"Why didn't your maiden aunt do as the letter instructed?" Queen Elizabeth asked.

Reluctantly, Lady Honora said, "She is a very old aunt."

"I've met every peer in the country," Queen Elizabeth said, "and I don't remember your aunt."

"You don't remember Lady Honora's aunt?" A bold audacious voice spoke. "But Your Majesty, that is because, compared to Lady Honora, no one in her family bears remembering."

"Tony!" Jean ran to her brother with Ann on her heels. "Your presence fair graces my senses."

He looked as fair, as handsome, as elegant as ever he had been when he leaned down as if to kiss her cheek and murmured close against her ear, "Her Majesty has you trapped, doesn't she?"

"Aye," Jean murmured back, "and I want you to distract her."

"God's blood!" Queen Elizabeth put her hand to her forehead and groaned. "If the Sadler heir has returned, what are we going to do about Sir Anthony and Odyssey Manor?"

"Am I not clever at distraction?" Tony congratulated himself as if the success were his, but he was well aware of the traps which hid in every turn of the maze. "Your Majesty"—with a flourish, he knelt before her while his sisters and Lady Honora arranged themselves behind—"I thank you for your generosity in returning me to my duties. If I could not serve Your Majesty, I would languish in the darkest cell of the darkest prison of my mind, longing always for the sunshine of your presence. In future, disregard my foolish tongue, I beg, and allow this poor, rough soldier to guard you from the knaves who envy you."

Her fingers pinched the ear she'd previously boxed. "Aye, aye. But how will we resolve this quandary? You hold Odyssey Manor—"

"By your grace," Tony interjected.

"—and the Sadler heir has returned!" She put her face down to his. "What shall we do?"

Not even for Rosie could he give up his claim. "Odyssey Manor is mine."

"But the Sadler heir?"

"I'll marry the silly wench if necessary."

He flinched when Queen Elizabeth crooned, "Silly wench? Your sisters and Lady Honora have been singing her praises."

"She is as naught compared with you," he said, wondering what else his sisters and Lady Honora had revealed.

"Then you've met her?"

"Certes, Your Majesty," Jean said. "'Twas his home she visited. Tony was most gracious, indeed, marvelously gracious, until he realized her true identity."

"I am still gracious," Tony snapped.

"You were like a bull, charging at every rival," Jean corrected. To the queen, she said, "He liked not this threat to what he perceived as his."

She meant Rosie, Tony realized, but it sounded as if she meant the property. God bless Jean.

Queen Elizabeth tilted his head in her hand so she could look into his eyes. "Did you kiss her, Sir Anthony?"

"Madam, you know I did." Tony tossed his blond locks off his forehead. "I kiss them all, but no kiss is as resplendent as the one I press upon this fair hand." He caught her free hand and bussed it.

With a faint smile, Queen Elizabeth watched his performance. "You remind me of someone I just met. Full of himself, and full of . . ."

"Of?" He cocked a brow.

"Kindness," she said unexpectedly. "Did I not hear Lady Honora had plans to wed you?"

A gust of fury rocked him back on his heels, but Lady Honora seemed equally dismayed when she said, "I have decided that won't do."

"Forsooth, why not?" The queen looked from one to the other, assessing them as potential mates.

"Without Odyssey Manor, he has no wealth," Lady Honora said.

"I'll give him a dowry," Queen Elizabeth answered.

Tony realized the true weight of Lady Honora's feelings for Sir Danny when she folded her hands together in a silent plea to him. Rescue me, her gesture said, but how was he supposed to do that?

Had the queen caught wind of his scheme to wed a young woman and start a dynasty? Or had she with the mention of Rosie's name detected the constantly burning incense of his passion? In either case, she feared to lose one of her favorite courtiers.

Obviously, she thought he would never desert her for Lady Honora. Obviously, she was right.

Leering, he leaned close to Queen Elizabeth. "A dowry? You'll put a value on my precious carcass?"

Amused at his audacity, the queen tapped his head with her fur muff. "A value of my setting, Sir Anthony."

"A value on my success in begetting," he rhymed outrageously.

Queen Elizabeth shrieked with laughter, but Lady Honora winced.

Dammit, she'd placed them in this predicament. She should get them out.

Then he sighed. If it were up to unimaginative Lady Honora, they'd be trapped in holy matrimony before spring had cracked the earth with the first hint of green.

Donning a sober mien, Tony said, "I adore Lady Honora, and when she came to me with her proposal to wed, I thought it would be a most appropriate union."

Behind Her Majesty, Jean and Ann rolled their eyes. Lady Honora winced.

"But I see no solution to this quandary with the Sadler heir except to wed her so I may keep Odyssey Manor. Odyssey is mine, and I'll not give it up for a wisp of a girl with a long-unpressed claim."

Queen Elizabeth lost her pleasant facade. "*I* gave you Odyssey Manor."

"Aye, madam, you gave it to me, and you can take it away." He wanted Rosie, and he wanted his lands, and he didn't even know which he was fighting for now. "When you gave it to me, everyone assumed I would continue to call it Sadler Manor. Everyone assumed I would seek some link between that family and mine, or change my name, or somehow lay claim to the nobility of that ancient family. Instead I changed the name of the estate, and do you know why?"

Mute beneath his outburst, the queen shook her head, and behind her, his sisters and Lady Honora did likewise.

"Like Odysseus, I have wandered the world, from Scotland to Cornwall, from the barren Continent to the teeming London streets. I've fought monsters of jealousy, prejudice, and envy, as well as real men who would have killed me for the pleasure of it, or the challenge of it, or simply because I was an enemy." He thumped his chest with his fist. "That manor, that estate, is the pinnacle of my personal odyssey. My reward for serving my queen and country well, for defeating all the monsters, is that estate. It is the end of my odyssey, the pinnacle of every cliff I've climbed. There'll never be another Odyssey Manor for me, and I pray you, madam, do not break my heart by depriving me of my home."

The small group seemed frozen in the sunlight, like Italian statues carved for the garden. Then Queen Elizabeth stirred and sighed. "You present your case eloquently. I will consider."

Tony became aware of the ache in his knees, but he didn't dare move. "I beg you, madam."

"I said I would consider." A smile quirked the queen's lips. "After all, Lady Rosalyn—or should I call her Rosie?—hasn't presented her petition to me yet." Standing, she arranged her cloak. "Perhaps you should send for this fair and accomplished maiden so I may speak to her. You *do* know where she is, don't you?" But she didn't wait for an answer. She made her stately way toward Whitehall Palace. After one horrified moment, Jean, Ann, and Lady Honora scurried to catch up.

Tony rose, pleased the queen had forgotten Essex, for Tony didn't wish to report Essex's defiance.

"Sir Anthony."

Queen Elizabeth returned and interrupted his self-congratulations, and he could have groaned. "Aye, madam?"

She stood with her profile to him, not looking him in the eye, denying him the sight of her still-lively optimism. "When does my lord Essex present himself before the Privy Council?"

So blessed forgetfulness had eluded her, and Tony had to say, "He is not coming, Your Majesty. He claims illness."

"Did he send me a message?"

His heart ached for her, but he allowed no pity to color his tone. "Nay, madam."

"Then I will have to deal with him. Did you know the Chamberlain's Men performed *Richard II* today on Essex's command?"

"I did *not* know that, madam."

"On the morrow, send my Privy Council to wait upon him at ten o' the clock to demand an explanation for this offense."

Torn between his desire to search for Rosie and his need to do his duty, he asked, "Shall I go with them, madam?"

"I think not, Sir Anthony." She turned her full gaze on him, and it seared him with its intensity. "I suspect you are a bad influence on my lord Essex and his compliance to my orders."

He acknowledged that with a small bow. "I suspect you are right, madam."

"Escort the gentlemen there, but remain without for their security."

"Aye, madam." Later, he would free Sir Danny from prison, convince Rosie they must wed, and convince the queen of the fitness of his suit. A lesser man might cringe, but while he'd overcome greater obstacles, he'd never overcome more important obstacles.

"When Essex comes out, escort him back." Elizabeth turned away, then turned back. "And Sir Anthony?"

"Madam?"

"Swear you will not harm him."

24

Men's judgements are
A parcel of their fortunes.

—ANTONY AND CLEOPATRA, III, xi, 31

"Essex imprisoned the Privy Council?" Tony stared at Wart-Nose in amazement and dismay. As instructed by the queen, Tony had escorted the delegation of her foremost and trusted advisers to Essex House, but stopped short of the front gate. This was Essex's final chance to redeem himself, and he had failed. Tony cursed him soundly. "And I swore to the queen I would not harm him! Damn! Send a man to Sir Robert Cecil and tell him these developments. Perhaps he will send someone who has not so sworn."

As he spoke, the front doors of Essex House swung wide. The great gates opened, and like water overflowing a kettle, two hundred men boiled out onto the Strand. In the lead was the earl of Essex, his gaze fevered, his gestures extravagant. His dark hat with its white plume bobbed above the heads of the rebels.

"To the court!" the rebels roared, rattling their bare swords. The majority of Tony's men remained on guard in Whitehall Palace, but Tony thought of Queen Elizabeth's age and dignity, and, with a flourish, he planted himself before Essex.

Essex stopped. Tossing the tails of his crimson silk cloak over his shoulders, he said, "Stand aside, varlet! You can no more stop this holy delegation than you may stop the tides of the ocean."

"I have no wish to stop you." Tony kept his gaze steady on Essex and ignored the angry calls of the rebels. "I offer a challenge. Let us join in battle, for in battle, the bastard and the lord will be equal. There we will truly see who is the greater warrior."

Essex was tempted, licking his thin, painted lips like a cat presented with a plump mouse.

Tony raised his voice so all could hear. "Or are you a coward, who fears my weight on your chest and my knife at your throat?"

With a roar, Essex pulled his sword and his dagger. Tony pulled his blades and met Essex's first sword lunge. Essex tried to bury his glittering knife in Tony's chest. Tony slipped under the sword and knocked Essex's dagger hand with his arm.

A mistake, for pain shot through his elbow where the fleshy stitches tore. Essex laughed at Tony's exclamation of agony and swung his sword. It caught in the folds of his own billowing cloak.

Tony laughed back and cut the strings of the offending cape with a quick slice of his knife. "My lord, I dressed for fighting. You dressed for conquest. See now how I help your cause." He leaped back as the crimson silk fluttered to the ground like a flamboyant symbol of defeat.

Essex's face contorted with rage. "Bastard boy, I'll teach you respect at last." In a fury of slashing, he drove Tony back toward the wall surrounding Essex House.

Cotzooks, Essex was good! And he was willing—nay, eager—to kill Tony, while Queen Elizabeth's promise limited Tony to a single blooding.

Tony had no chance, he feared, unless he could move in close enough to use his street skills. One good blow to the groin, and Essex would topple like a tree.

A damned long-armed tree.

Tony ducked a dagger thrust.

Essex was smirking, his white-plumed hat still firm on his head. His hat . . .

Tony flicked the tip of his sword up. Essex flinched back, tossing his head. The hat tumbled, then sailed on the breeze, and Tony whirled past Essex's lowered guard. He gained the open street, then leaped high, exulting in his own prowess. His foot caught his opponent's sword hand. The sword went flying. His dagger flicked Essex's dagger hand, cutting the skin. Essex jerked back, and smacked his arm into the wall. Knocked loose of his grip, the dagger skidded across the street. Tony jumped into him, using his good elbow to knock the queen's pet off his feet.

Essex landed in the soft dirt unharmed, but before Tony could put his blade to Essex's throat, another body catapulted out of the air and knocked him sideways.

Tony rolled and came up, knife seeking the varlet who'd ruined his fun, but Wart-Nose was already racing away. "Run," he called over his shoulder. "Run!"

One look around him sufficed. The rebels had taken the defeat of their leader with no humor and less grace, and the array of steel coming toward Tony convinced him.

He ran.

He ran to Fleet Street, then turned west toward White-hall Palace. He ran until he heard no more footsteps behind him, then he turned.

Essex's disciples had returned to their master, and Tony, too, crept back toward the Strand, staying against the buildings, hearing the babble of belligerent voices.

Then Essex strode onto Fleet Street. Filth streaked his crimson cloak. A strip of linen, dotted with red, wrapped his hand. The white plume of his hat was bent, and he limped just a little.

His rebels were yelling, "To the court!" with almost as much gusto as before.

But without a glance toward Whitehall Palace, Essex turned east and marched through Ludgate, going right to the heart of the City, crying, "For the queen! For the queen! A plot is laid against my life! Good people of London, follow me to save the queen!"

"You're going to have his child?" Uncle Will kept his voice down, so none of the other actors heard, but his vehement tone made his opinion clear. "You're going to have Sir Anthony's child and you ran off before you married him?"

"Sh." Rosie glanced around at the other actors who milled about in the large room in Whitehall Palace. They were preparing for the performance before the queen: helping each other into costumes, putting on their paint before tiny mirrors, practicing their lines in the quiet desperation born before every royal presentation. But Rosie suspected none had been more desperate than this one, and she was the cause. Every actor, regardless of his feelings for her, kept well away as if she might contaminate him with her treason.

If any one of them heard Uncle Will exclaiming about her pregnancy, she'd not perform this day, or ever again.

"I won't be silent," Uncle Will raged as he wiped white powder across her face. "I want to know why you lied to me."

"I didn't lie." She adjusted the stomacher and wondered if breathlessness plagued all women when they were with child. And wished she could ask someone. "I just didn't tell you everything."

Dotting color along her cheekbones, he said, "I shudder to think what might have happened if you hadn't had Ludovic protecting you."

She said nothing, and he smoothed the colors together and stepped back to look at her. Something about her expression must have alerted him, for he asked, "Are you not telling me everything again?"

"Ludovic has disappeared."

Uncle Will groaned. "When?"

"The night Tony found us. I don't know whether it was Tony, or the child, or"—she shook her head, honestly bewildered—"something I said. I don't know, but I haven't seen him or heard from him since."

"You're unprotected." It sounded like an accusation.

She patted the unwieldy purse hanging from her belt. The purse Tony had given her. The purse she went nowhere without. "I wouldn't say that."

"You're alone in London."

Placing the brown wig on her coiled hair, she said, "Only until I'm done with the play."

"And then what?"

Then what? Would God she knew the answer to that. Would God she could see Tony once more. Sometimes she thought she could feel him, feel his gaze searching for her. Sometimes she thought all she needed to do was jump up and yell, "Here I am!" and he would be with her, picking her up and carrying her to safety.

But then who would redeem the soul of her father? The father who now spoke to her every night in her dreams. "When I'm done with the play, I'll be with Sir Danny."

"Rosie." Uncle Will caught her arm. "You're putting too much reliance in this one performance. You cannot truly believe—"

She placed her hand over his mouth. "I'll make Her Majesty laugh at Ophelia's silly belief in true love, and cry at Hamlet's betrayal. I'll win a boon and free my dada—and free Sir Danny."

Her resolution had become a living thing, the most important thing in her life. Touching the ring which hung on its chain around her neck, she whispered, "'Tis the only way I'll ever be free of my ghosts."

Hamlet. Act one, Scene three.

"Your first scene, Rosie." In a quiet tone, Uncle Will gave Rosie direction, and she listened in a state of fatalistic terror. "Remember, you're not Rosie. You're Ophelia. You're a lovely, star-crossed woman who loves a prince and who believes her prince loves her."

The other actors rushed off the stage, flowing around them in frantic haste. Rigged like a ship in full sail, Alleyn Brewer sparkled with lush sensuality as Gertrude, Hamlet's mother. With convincing corruption, Dickie Justin McBride played the part of Claudius. Richard Burbage, the star of the Chamberlain's Men, performed the role of Hamlet as if he'd been born to it. A few actors, like Cedric, played multiple minor parts and shed clothes, then redressed to fit the new scene.

"John Barnstaple will be out there with you, so

you'll not be alone, and I'll be on soon." With gray powder on his face and hair, Uncle Will gave Rosie a numbing slap on the shoulder. "Now go out there and rend every heart."

Would to God that I could, she wanted to say, but he put the flat of his hand in her back and shoved her through the curtains onto the stage, and she couldn't say anything at all.

But she had to. She had a line. Oh, God, what was her line? John Barnstaple—no, wait, he was her brother Laertes—spoke first, four lines.

She had four words. "'Do you doubt that?'"

Not difficult. She'd delivered it well.

But John Barnstaple—no, Laertes—spoke, and she had another line coming up.

Four words. "'No more but so?'"

The temporary boards creaked when she stepped on them. Massive candles stood in stands around the stage, lighting the players, but leaving most of the cavernous room in darkness. And the utter silence sucked the air from the room. Sweat trickled down her back, causing such a chill she shuddered. The stage sickness had come again.

But it couldn't come to her this time. This time was special. This time she needed to be perfect. She needed to be, had to be Ophelia.

Instead, she was only Rosie, and she was afraid.

In a rush she spoke the seven lines reproving her brother for his worry; then Uncle Will himself stumped onto the stage. It seemed right he should play Polonius, Ophelia's father, for after Sir Danny he was the man who had treasured her childhood affection and encouraged her growth. Her eyes misted over, and she frantically blinked to clear them.

Uncle Will—nay, Polonius—lectured her about accepting Prince Hamlet's tenders of affection, and he sounded so much like Sir Danny lecturing her for her own good that her protestations of Hamlet's fidelity came out with the proper indignation. Uncle Will smiled, and as they finished the scene and exited, a few of the actors clasped her hands and pressed them with approval.

The gates of Essex House hung open, the chimneys puffed with smoke, but the manor had an air of abandonment. The mighty company which had before occupied the grounds had dispersed, blown away by the winds of adversity. It seemed not even a servant remained.

Cautiously, Tony entered the gates and picked his way through the litter left by two hundred men.

"Sir!"

A woman's voice hailed him, and he glanced around.

"Sir, we've heard only rumors here. Can you tell us what has transpired with my lord Essex?"

Tony looked up through the gathering dusk, and out of a second story window hung Lady Rich, Essex's sister. For her he had no sympathy; she had ever encouraged her brother in his vanity and ambition. But for Lady Essex, who peeked over her shoulder, unwilling compassion tugged at his heart. She was the wife of a man whose career had begun so brightly and which now lay ruined by his own hand, the wife of the foremost traitor in the land.

The wife of a dead man, if Tony had anything to say about it.

He bowed. "I hadn't realized ladies remained within the house."

Lady Rich leaned out farther, and even from here he could see her sum him up. "You're Sir Anthony Rycliffe, the master of the Queen's Guard. You should know very well the events of the day."

Her callous inquiry and the shrill voice with which she issued it strengthened him. "So I do, my lady, but first I would know if the men of the Privy Council are still imprisoned."

Lady Rich understood the necessity of bartering information for information. "They were released hours ago in perfect health."

Tony could scarcely refrain from wiping his brow. "For you the news is not good. All is lost. London rejected Lord Essex. His troops flee the city. The Archbishop of London has fired on him, and Essex even now flees."

With a wail, Lady Essex turned away from the window, but Lady Rich demanded, "To where, Sir Anthony?"

"To here, I hope, my lady."

She whipped her head inside and slammed the window, and without seeing, he knew she flew to pack her bags and abandon her brother to his fate. It was fitting that all should abandon Essex.

All except his captors. Essex wanted to escape, but Tony wanted him for the queen. Skirting the main house and the stables, Tony strode through the garden to the water gate and looked up the darkening Thames. The usually busy river rippled along, its traffic beached by the rebellion. One boat struggled against the current; one boatman put his back to the oars while his passenger huddled in the stern. A tall, red-bearded passenger feeling a warrior's satisfaction, Tony concealed himself in the bushes and waited.

Soon he heard the slap of the oars on the water, then the thump of wet wood as the boat struck the dock. Essex spoke to the boatman, coins clinked as they changed from one hand to another, and his boots dragged as he started up the path.

His bright head passed the place where Tony hid, and Tony followed as Essex trod slowly toward the house.

Tony didn't blame Essex for his reluctance. To return alone to the place which he'd left this morning surrounded by supporters, a defeated man, marked for death, to return and face Lady Rich and his wife—the two women who would suffer from his downfall—must be the greatest humiliation a man could face.

Too damned bad. Tony hoped Essex wallowed in misery. He hoped he swam in mortification. He hoped his wife and sister spit on him, and his dogs bit him.

He wished on Essex the just results of every stupid, self-serving act he'd ever committed, and when Essex looked behind him in alarm, Tony jumped out, cape spread high, and said softly, "Boo!"

For one moment, Essex stared. His lips curled back from his teeth. "You lowlife bastard," he said viciously. His fingers curled into claws, and Tony thought he would attack with the maddened fury of a wolf.

But when Tony met his narrowed gaze, the wolf realized he had become the prey. "You bastard. You bastard!" he cried, but it was a cry of defeat. Racing into the house, he slammed the door behind him.

Tony heard the bar drop, but he just grinned in sour triumph. Essex might dream he was keeping Tony out, but actually he was keeping himself in.

Behind him on the river, Tony heard the shouts of men and the scrape of boats against the dock. Retracing his steps, he found Sir Robert Sidney, Elizabeth's Lord Admiral, making his way up the walk.

"Sir Anthony!" Grim, yet relieved, Sidney asked, "Is he here?"

"Lord Essex, do you mean?" Tony grinned unpleasantly. Looking beyond Sidney, Tony saw the earl of

Nottingham directing the unloading of a large contingent of armed men. "Aye, he's inside with the door barred. Do you mind if I take one of your boats to Whitehall Palace? I need to report to the queen."

Sidney just stared at Tony. "Report to the queen? God's blood, how will I get him out?"

"Send to the Tower for cannon and kegs of powder and threaten to blow Essex House into splinters." After a last, savage glance at the house, Tony strode toward the boat he had decided to commandeer. "With any luck, you'll have to do it."

25

The play's the thing
Wherein I'll catch the conscience of the king.
                                                                    —HAMLET, II, ii, 616

Hamlet. *Act three, Scene one.*

They were almost halfway through the play, and a quiet sort of triumph permeated backstage. No major blunders had occurred, no misspoken lines, and, despite the traditional actors' wish, no one had broken a leg. Rosie prepared to go on again, knowing that with each scene she had relaxed into her role. Ophelia's clothes fit her as if they'd been sewn for her. Ophelia's personality fit her as if it had been written for her. For the first time in her life, Rosie lived within a character's skin, and for the first time today, she allowed herself truly to believe she would rescue Sir Danny.

"My friend Polonius fears Prince Hamlet is mad for love of you, and he wants me to eavesdrop with him while you meet him." Secure in his role as the evil King

Claudius, Dickie Justin McBride spoke to Rosie as if she were, in fact, Ophelia. "But the next scene will be a revelation for everyone."

In the next scene, Hamlet passionately rejected Ophelia and ordered her to a nunnery. It was the first scene in which Rosie and Dickie were onstage together, and within the fragile partnership of acting, Dickie could destroy her. He would enjoy that, for Dickie had always loathed Rosie, and he seemed to think that she'd taken special pleasure in duping him. Not even for Sir Danny would he subdue his hatred.

But as the play had proceeded smoothly, the other actors had lost their earlier wariness and made their support of her, and her mission, clear. He couldn't harm her without harming the performance, and she warned, "Dickie, if you try to ruin me, I swear . . ."

"Me?" Dickie flashed a toothy white grin. "I would do no such thing. Not out of love for you, but because the Chamberlain's Men would banish me from the boards. Nay, *I'll* not trip you up."

She didn't trust him. She didn't trust the way his eyes danced, and the way he leaned closer to whisper, "Did you see her?"

"Who?"

"Why, Her Majesty, Queen Elizabeth."

Rosie had deliberately shut out any thought of the queen. Oh, she knew Queen Elizabeth was out there. That was the whole purpose of her performance. But the presence of a royal spectator added weight to Rosie's already overloaded mind.

"Her Majesty sits right in the front row." Dickie peeked through the curtain. "In the middle."

"I expected . . ." She'd expected the queen to be seated above them in a box of noble proportions.

Maliciously, he dropped the rest of his poison in

Rosie's ear. "She hasn't taken her eyes off of you yet. When you are onstage, she sees no one but you."

"You jest."

"Nay, I do not. Look when you go out. It's dark out there, but you can see her. You can see the glitter of her eyes as she follows your every move."

Uncle Will, Alleyn Brewer, and the actors who played Rosencrantz and Guildenstern gathered around them, preparing to walk out together, and Rosie realized how cleverly Dickie had planned this. Nay, he had to do nothing to demolish her resolve; with one simple phrase he'd planted in her the seeds of her destruction. All she could think about was the queen's presence. The others moved forward on their cue, but her feet stuck fast to the boards until Dickie jerked her forward by her wrist.

Aye, he knew well what he had done.

She had no lines at first, and her eyes adjusted to the light. She didn't want to look, but her gaze turned unwillingly to the front row.

Dear God, it *was* the queen.

Dickie hadn't lied. Queen Elizabeth sat in a tall, canopied chair on a dais in the center of the first aisle, surrounded by her ladies-in-waiting. She did not move, and as Dickie had promised, the queen's eyes glittered. She never took her gaze off of Rosie.

All the dizziness, all the nervousness, all the stage sickness returned with a rush. Rosie couldn't hear, couldn't see.

When Gertrude spoke, everyone waited, staring at Rosie until she remembered she had a line.

What line?

At last, in an undertone, Uncle Will prompted her, and she repeated, "'Madam, I wish it may.'"

That was all she had to say for a long time, but people were leaving her. Rosencrantz and Guildenstern had already gone. Gertrude exited on her line. Polonius spoke to her and gave her a book, then Claudius spoke, then, oh God, she was alone.

She was supposed to hold the book before her face and pretend to read, but her hands shook too much. She was supposed to retire to the back of the stage; that she did with haste. Hamlet—Richard Burbage—entered and began his soliloquy. Unobtrusively, Rosie wiped her damp palms on her gown, and offered up a prayer to St. Genesius, the patron saint of actors. It was a prayer not for herself, but for Sir Danny.

She had to remember her lines. She had to display Ophelia's emotion. She couldn't fail, for if she did, Sir Danny would die.

As he had taught her, she took deep breaths.

So the queen was out there. So she watched Ophelia. She was no different than any other person in the audience. She wanted to be entertained, she wanted to be sucked into the drama on the stage. Rosie owed her a good performance. She owed everyone here a good performance, and she could almost hear Sir Danny telling her, "They are an audience like any other."

Except they weren't. This was the queen's own court, and they didn't scratch, or call out insults to the characters, or whistle their appreciation of a witty line. The eerie silence was not in spite of them. It emanated from them, and nothing, not even the appearance of the ghost, had drawn a sigh.

"An audience like any other," Sir Danny's voice insisted, and the memory of him gave her strength and pleasure.

Sir Danny had given her Tony. He'd shamelessly schemed and manipulated to unite them. If she was going to lose Sir Danny, it wouldn't be because of that worm

Dickie and his evil stratagem. If she was going to lose Tony, it wasn't going to be because she failed to be what Sir Danny had taught her to be.

There had been many good times with Sir Danny, and many bad times, and she'd survived them all. That was what he'd taught her; to survive, to take the best of life and laugh at the worst.

On cue, she stepped forward and spoke her lines. The vast room echoed when she lifted her voice, intensifying every quaver and crack, and Richard Burbage's quick nod surprised her.

Did that mean he liked her delivery?

Quickly she reviewed the scene in her mind. Aye, Ophelia might be afraid here. She was returning Hamlet's tokens of affection, while he descended into what appeared to be madness.

Aye, by accident, she'd played the scene right, and warmth coursed through her veins. Neither Dickie's mischief nor the queen's steadfast observation could distract her. She might be performing the part of Ophelia, feeling her emotions, but Rosie wasn't torn between her lover and her father. Rosie would do her damnedest to have them both.

"Her Majesty is watching a play."

"A play?" Tony glared at Sir Robert Cecil as if he were personally responsible for such nonsense. "Why is she watching a play?"

"It was planned for today, and it seemed a right good thing to take Her Majesty's mind off of the Essex situation."

Running his hand through his hair, trying to loosen some of the dirt that caked it, Tony nodded. "Of course. How did Her Majesty fare during this difficulty?"

"She displayed no more concern than she would have with a report of an affray in Fleet Street. She knew London would stand by her." Cecil might have his quarrels with Queen Elizabeth, but right now his devotion and admiration triumphed. "Yet at the same time she disregarded the food that came to the table, eating nothing but manchet bread and succory pottage all day. If she hadn't had that posturing actor to entertain her, I doubt she would have eaten that."

"Her jester, do you mean?"

Cecil tucked his lips tight with annoyance, and his eyes shifted away from Tony's as if he'd just revealed a state secret. "In a manner of speaking."

"Should I wait until after the play to give my report?"

"Her Majesty left instructions that you should be shown into her presence at once upon your return." Futilely, Cecil brushed at the soil and gunpowder that stained Tony's clothing, then shoved him toward the dining hall. "You'll have to go as you are."

Tony stepped inside, then closed the door quickly when the noble audience cursed him in annoyance. He stood uncertainly in the aisle and blinked, trying to see his way. The stage blazed with light, but any latecomers to the audience had to stumble around and find a seat—or in his case, find Queen Elizabeth.

He crept forward, but every time he stepped in front of someone they hissed at him, so involved were they in the play. Occasionally he heard a sob, and rolled his eyes.

A tragedy. The actors were performing a tragedy. How fitting. How he wished he'd arrived later, or earlier, or any time but now when women wept and men snuffled.

Damn fools. They should have been with him, and they'd understand real tragedy. Glancing at the stage, he saw one man dressed as a warrior, one man dressed as a man and—he looked more closely than he ever had before—a man dressed as a woman. King and queen, he surmised, since both wore crowns.

The warrior was questioning the king and queen about the death of his father, and his elaborate gestures made it clear he was ready to take his revenge. The king promised he should have it . . . and a hand smacked Tony on the rump. "Move on, you big lout!"

Tony moved.

Seeing an elaborate, canopied chair towering over the front row, Tony worked his way along the jagged rows to reach the queen, stepping on toes and jostling arms. "Your pardon, m'lady. Pardon, m'lord. I beg you, let—"

"'They bore him barefaced on the bier.'" A high sweet voice from the stage stopped him in midstep, and he jerked his gaze around to the stage.

Rosie!

Had he shouted it out loud? But nay, for none of the courtiers turned to hush him. No one did more than push him at him as they craned their necks to see around him.

Rosie—*his* Rosie—stood on the stage. White flowers draped her unkempt brown hair and fluttered from her fingers, her gown was soiled, the weight of sorrow broke the regularity of her features.

She was the sister of the warrior. It was her father who had earlier died on that stage, and the irony of it smote Tony a crushing blow.

How could she act such a part when she'd lost one father and would likely lose another?

Or was she acting?

She sang, but her voice quavered with each note. *"'And in his grave rain'd many a tear—Fare you well,* my dove.'" Her voice broke on the last, and a tear glistened on her cheek.

The warrior who played her brother looked horrified as only an actor who fears another's breakdown can look. He boomed out his line, no doubt hoping to shake Rosie from her anguish.

She replied, apparently as she should, for he calmed a little, but then she handed him some of her flowers and looked deep into his eyes. "'There's rosemary, that's for remembrance—pray you, love, remember: and there's pansies, that's for thoughts.'"

And the warrior who played her brother seemed suddenly struck by the same blight that so aggrieved her. His hands shook and when he answered, his voice quavered, laden with tears.

The king seemed more furious than anguished when she gave him flowers, but the queen sobbed—a loud, manly, hiccuping sob—when Rosie said, "'I would give you some violets, but they withered all when my father died.'"

Someone shoved Tony hard and knocked him through the first row onto his knees. There he knelt, absorbing the sight and sound of his woman as she sang, "'*His beard as white as snow, All flaxen was his poll. He is gone, he is gone.*'"

She opened her hands and tossed the remaining flowers away, and simply watched as they fluttered to the ground. The audience waited, breathless, pitying. Behind him, Tony could hear an occasional muffled sob. Within him, he experienced once more the agony of losing the woman he thought of as his mother. He experienced the grief of losing his father. Her performance resurrected the anguish he'd thought long dissipated, and the tears slipped down his cheeks unheeded.

And still Rosie stood there, quiescent as one whose

life has been sucked from her by the death of another.

When she finally finished the song—*"God ha' mercy on his soul'"*—and walked to the curtain, a blast of weeping sounded through the chamber. She drew the curtain back and faced the audience again. With the faith and grace of a martyr about to burn, she said, "'And of all Christian souls I pray God. God be wi' you.'"

Rosie drew the curtain closed behind her and collapsed onto her knees. She'd done it. She'd moved an audience to tears, but at what price to herself? Her heart thrummed with mourning for the father whose ghost had haunted her for so many years.

Tugging at the chain around her neck, she freed the signet ring. Wiping the tears from her eyes, she looked at the entwined "Es" impressed in the gold. Aye, she mourned him at last, just as she should, and with that he was laid to rest. But mixed with that mourning was her need for Sir Danny. She wanted to hug him. She wanted him to stand as her father at her wedding and dandle her babe on her knee. She wanted to know he was onstage, doing what he loved.

She wanted to know he was alive.

"Rosie." Uncle Will clasped her shoulder. "The other actors will step on you when they come offstage."

Wearily, she rose. No wonder she'd never given herself to a role as Sir Danny demanded. Instinctively she realized that it would tear her soul apart and open the dark places for the world to see. She tried to rub the tears off her cheeks, but Uncle Will caught her hands. "Leave be. You'll truly look like a corpse on the bier."

Rosie laughed, a chuckle that cracked in the middle. "Trust you, Uncle, to always think of the play."

He swallowed as if tears clogged his throat. "You made me proud." He led her to the bier in the corner and helped her lie down. "You made Sir Danny proud."

"I wish he knew." Her tears flowed again as she arranged her gown and hands. "I wish somehow he could have seen this."

Onstage the action went on. Gertrude announced that Ophelia had drowned. Hamlet came to a fresh-dug grave and spoke with the gravedigger. Then Claudius, Gertrude, Laertes, Cedric as the priest, and every spare actor gathered around Rosie as part of Ophelia's funeral procession.

"We're going out now, Rosie," Cedric whispered. They lifted the bier, and her prostrate form swayed with their stately steps as they entered the stage.

As the corpse of Ophelia, Rosie had only to lie perfectly still with her eyes closed while Laertes and Hamlet fought over the right to be chief mourner at her funeral. She listened as the priest spoke, then Laertes. Off to the side, Hamlet spoke not at all, although he was supposed to come closer and speak.

But no one said a word. The silence loomed loud, then Rosie felt it—a ripple of interest flowing through the audience like a draft of fresh air. Footsteps echoed across the boards, coming closer. Rosie couldn't understand the anticipation that flowed from the cast, nor the feeling of suspense which prickled along her skin.

Someone stood over her. She tried to peek through the tiniest slit in her eyelids, but shadow concealed his face. Then he spoke Hamlet's line in familiar, beloved tones. "'What, the fair Ophelia!'"

Emotions—amazement, jubilation, exultation—burst forth inside her. She sat up on the bier and reached out. "Dada!"

Sir Danny fell to his knees and clutched her as if she were the most precious thing in the world. They hugged and kissed, father and daughter united again, laughing and crying, rocking together.

Onstage, Uncle Will blew his nose on a big kerchief. Alleyn knocked his wig and crown off wiping the tears off his face. The others nudged each other and sniffled, and Dickie . . . Rosie didn't care about Dickie.

Grabbing Sir Danny by the hair, she looked for bruises on his face, then picked up his hands and examined them. He looked thin, but healthy, and she demanded, "How?"

"Her Majesty Queen Elizabeth." He nodded toward the canopied throne. "She arranged it."

"You're here? You're free?"

"With her good grace."

Rosie looked toward the row of chairs and half rose in thankfulness, then realized—the play! But no one seemed to care. The audience was crying, laughing, and clapping, involved in the story unfolding before their eyes and forgetting the fiction that had earlier absorbed them. All sense of tragedy had vanished, and nothing would restore it now.

With a smile, Rosie chided Sir Danny. "You disrupted my performance, Dada."

"And a stellar job you were doing, too." He beamed proudly, then added softly, "I always knew you had grand emotions welling inside you, begging for release. You've proved yourself the equal of every actor here."

"And proved you were right."

"There is that."

He tossed his hair back, and Rosie thanked God that prison hadn't killed the vanity in him.

Footmen flung open the doors and lit candles on the wall, and the glow extended throughout the room. Sir Danny assisted Rosie off the stage and toward the canopied chair where Her Majesty sat, a smile curving her thin lips. Jean, Ann, and Lady Honora surrounded her. With gestures and smiles, Jean and Ann tried to indicate what Rosie should do, but Rosie didn't need to be instructed. She fell to her knees before the queen and bowed her head in total reverence. "Your Majesty, my deepest thanks for releasing Sir Danny from that prison."

"Thank Sir Danny." Queen Elizabeth's voice surprised Rosie. Rosie had expected depth and majesty, and instead she heard a thin, old woman quaver. "He bought his life with his honesty, and his liberty with his medical skill."

Rosie slanted a look at Sir Danny, beside her on his knees. Adoration, confusion, and conceit warred on his countenance. Whatever Sir Danny had done, he'd done well, and Rosie's heart swelled with pride for him. He'd always believed in his own magnificent destiny, and he'd proved himself at last.

"But I let him watch the play and sent him onstage to surprise you." Queen Elizabeth sounded smug. "For that you may thank me."

She extended one long, slender hand, and Rosie pressed a fervent kiss on the knuckles. "My gratitude shall never fail, and I will serve you to the end of my days."

Queen Elizabeth tilted Rosie's face up. The famous, heavy-lidded eyes examined Rosie thoroughly. "You *are* Lady Rosalyn Bellot."

Taken aback, Rosie didn't know what to say. Perhaps rumor had told Queen Elizabeth of the return of the Bellot heir, but who had pointed the finger at Rosie? Was it Sir Danny? But nay, he stared in astonishment at the queen, then glanced at Lady Honora.

A faint, fond smile curved Lady Honora's lips, and she nodded at Sir Danny.

The queen's narrow lips pinched together, creasing her upper lip into a multitude of wrinkles. "You look a great deal like your mother, and I see nothing of your father in you."

Her Majesty's tone conveyed disapproval and rancor, and something in Rosie rose to the challenge. Staring directly at the queen, she said, "I have much of my father in me. I would never have proved my right to Odyssey Manor without the memories my father left me."

"Proved?" Queen Elizabeth lifted one narrow brow haughtily. "No one has proved your right to Odyssey Manor to *me*."

Sir Danny seemed to have trouble shifting his attention from Lady Honora to the conversation at hand, but at last he stammered, "Lord Sadler's letter is not here, but I beg Your Majesty to believe in its reality."

"I don't need the letter." Rosie lifted the chain from her neck and held it out to the queen. "I have my father's ring."

Queen Elizabeth snatched it out of her hand.

Sir Danny exclaimed, "Where did you get that?"

Gathering in a wide circle around the throne, the nobles craned their necks to see and hushed each other to hear.

And off to the side, Rosie heard a sound of shock or awe or dismay. Something made her take her attention from the queen, and look—and she saw Tony.

Tony! He knelt not ten feet from her, and he stared at her as if her very presence fed him joy.

As much joy as his presence gave her. She hadn't realized, until she saw him, how much she'd needed him, but now she worshiped him with all of her pent-up yearning. He stood, and she watched each magnificent ripple of muscle. He walked toward her, and she tensed, prepared to run to his arms. He knelt beside her, and she lifted her lips for his kiss.

And he faced Queen Elizabeth and said, "Your Majesty, I have saved your kingdom from disaster this day, and in return I would have a boon. I want you to reaffirm my ownership of Odyssey Manor for me and my heirs forever."

26

Thou art sad; get thee a wife, get thee a wife!
—Much Ado About Nothing, V, iv, 122

Rosie's jaw dropped, but Tony couldn't allow himself to feel compassion. He wanted Odyssey Manor, and he wanted Rosie, and what claim did he have on Rosie if Queen Elizabeth awarded her the estate?

"Essex is vanquished?" Queen Elizabeth was as calm as Cecil had claimed.

Tony nodded. "I chased him into Essex House myself."

The nobles who stood about and the servants who mingled to serve them, applauded his feat, and he bowed his head in acknowledgment.

"I performed my duty to Her Glorious Majesty, good people, nothing more." Tony bent and kissed the hem of Queen's Elizabeth's skirt.

She accepted his tribute with a gracious smile.

He continued, "Nottingham will have him in custody before the night is over."

The queen grasped Tony's shoulder as if to congratulate him, then pulled her hand back and dusted the soil from her fingers.

"Forgive the dirt and the blood, Your Majesty, but I came to you today without having my wound stitched or my clothes and body cleaned." He exaggerated about the wound, of course. It did need to be stitched again, and it ached, but it was yesterday's injury. Still, he wanted to work on the queen's sympathies and remind her of his loyalty. "I wanted to report as soon as possible."

Queen Elizabeth slanted a look at Rosie. "But you've been watching the play for some moments."

She'd seen him. Damn. He'd hoped that she hadn't, for he feared she had seen what he could not hide—his adoration of Rosie. Worse still, he feared she had seen what he had seen—Rosie's adoration of him. Rosie expressed such pleasure in his appearance, such longing for his arms, he had scarcely been able to restrain himself. She did love him, he knew it, and he knew nothing was guaranteed to infuriate the queen more. He tried to excuse himself. "Your Majesty, I saw your enjoyment of the performance, and I dared not interrupt you, but now I beg—"

"Aye, aye." Irritation etched a frown on Queen Elizabeth's face. "I gave you Odyssey Manor before, and I see no reason to change my mind."

"Your Majesty!" Rosie sounded shocked, and Tony elbowed her hard.

"You do not interrupt your monarch," Queen Elizabeth said severely.

"But the ring—" Rosie tried again, and Sir Danny elbowed her from the other side.

"This ring"—Queen Elizabeth stroked her thumb across the ruby—"combined with Lady Rosalyn's appearance, proves her heritage, but I cannot deprive Sir Anthony of the gift I presented him so many years ago." She stroked the ring one last time, then opened Rosie's hand and pressed it into the palm. "Therefore—"

A howl of bloodcurdling rage arrested her. A gray-haired man broke through the surrounding nobles near Sir Danny and hurled himself at the queen.

She raised her hands to protect her face. Tony grabbed for him, but a huge man leaped from behind the throne, knocking the intruder back into the crowd. Pandemonium erupted as aristocrats tumbled like ninepins. The two men hit the floor fighting. The gray-haired man shrieked and pummeled the larger man, pushing him over and over. Drawing his dagger, Tony vaulted toward them, but someone knocked him from behind. He smashed, face first, into a floor.

"'Tis Ludovic," Sir Danny yelled. "Leave him be."

Sir Danny had gone mad. The whole world had gone mad, filled with women's screams and men's shouts and a struggle before him that he could not reach.

But Rosie could. With one swing of her weighted purse, she bashed the gray head that loomed above Ludovic. The intruder went limp and silence fell so suddenly Tony's ears ached.

"Your Majesty?" He heard Jean's shaking voice.

"I'm untouched." The queen sounded calm, calmer than Tony felt. Coming to the scene, she looked down at the two men. "Does anyone know these people?"

Shaking off Sir Danny, Tony crawled to his feet and limped to the two combatants. Ludovic pushed the intruder off and sat up, rubbing his head, while Tony stared at the unconscious form. "Hal?"

"What's he doing here?" Sir Danny asked.

Jean pushed her way to the front. "He came from Odyssey Manor with us."

"But why?" Tony touched Hal with his toe.

"Because he's the man who robbed my father and left me to die." Rosie hooked her purse back on her belt.

Everyone gaped at her, and Queen Elizabeth imperiously demanded, "Explain yourself, Lady Rosalyn."

"He was my father's ostler. He went with us to London to care for the horses, and fled with us when the plague broke out. When the coachman and my nursemaid died, he stripped the coach and left us." Rosie looked down at Hal and saw that his eyes were open and anguished. "When I met him at Odyssey Manor, he frightened me. When I found the ring, I remembered why. When I found the ring, I remembered everything."

"But why attack Her Majesty?" Tony asked.

Rosie shook her head. "Why, Hal?"

"Ye got t' have yer lands back." Hal tried to sit up, but fell back as if he'd been struck again. "Ye got t' have everything due ye, an' I have t' get it fer ye. I owe ye."

Kneeling beside him, Rosie rubbed his shoulder with her hand. "You can't bring him back. You can't change the past. Make peace with yourself and try to forget."

"I can't forget. I left ye in that coach wi' yer father, an' he cursed me. He said he'd haunt me 'til my dying day an' after, too. He promised I'd go t' hell, an' he's made sure I did. I went t' Londontown an' sold yer belongings an' lived high, an' all th' time I could see yer big eyes accusing me." Gingerly, he touched her hand with one finger and pleaded with his rheumy eyes. "When ye came back, I tried t' make it right. I tried t' get those that stood in yer way fer th' estate, but I guess I can't win salvation no matter how hard I try."

"You tried to kill . . .?" Tony grabbed Hal by the throat. "It was you?"

"Aye, 'twas him." Ludovic's accent deepened, and he spread his hands wide as he explained. "I watched the manor all the time after I left the troupe. Waited for my chance with Rosencrantz. Didn't take me long to realize something evil touched your steward."

"Why didn't you come and tell me?" Tony demanded.

Ludovic laughed bitterly. "You'd have believed me? Believed a foreign mercenary that your steward plotted to kill you and your family?"

Tony's gaze fell away. "I would have put you in the stocks."

"Never doubted it," Ludovic said. "But I have always followed after Rosencrantz to take care of her. Even when I realized that she . . . preferred you, I could not leave her with this crazy one roaming your estate."

"I would never have hurt Lady Rosalyn." Again Hal tried to sit up, but Tony pushed him down.

"I didn't know that," Ludovic said. "Didn't know who you hated."

"I didn't hate any o' them," Hal said. "I just had t' help Lady Rosalyn."

"Enough." Ludovic lumbered to his feet, bodily picked up Hal, and flung him over his shoulder. Hal squawked and kicked, but with one squeeze Ludovic dissuaded him.

"Where are you taking him?" Queen Elizabeth demanded.

Ludovic blinked at her, then bowed, flopping Hal from side to side. "Bethlehem Hospital."

"Quite right," the queen decided.

She stepped aside, but Rosie laid a hand on Ludovic's arm. Ludovic jumped as if he'd been burned and lowered his head. "Ludovic, won't you look at me?"

He glanced up, then down again.

"I thank you for your kindness to me. You have ever been my friend, and Sir Anthony has a position to offer you."

Tony raised his eyebrows at Rosie, and she glared at him meaningfully.

He glared back. He didn't want Ludovic at Odyssey Manor. He didn't want Ludovic around Rosie ever again, but Ludovic did deserve a reward for his vigilance, instincts, and fighting skill. Tony *did* have a position to offer Ludovic. "This day has proved I need men who have an eye for mischief and the skill to deal with it. When you've dropped off your burden, find Wart-Nose Harry of the Queen's Guard and tell him I sent you. He'll know what to do."

"What about me?" Sir Danny pushed his luxurious hair out of his face. "Ludovic works for me."

A strange sound emitted from deep down in Ludovic's chest.

"What's wrong with him?" Queen Elizabeth looked alarmed.

"I think"—Rosie grinned at Sir Danny—"he's laughing."

"Ah."

"Never had anybody want me before." Ludovic snorted. "Now I've got two."

He stumped out of the room, and Queen Elizabeth said, "Quite an interesting man. He'll be part of my guard, of course."

"Certes," Tony said.

"Well." Queen Elizabeth straightened her puffed sleeves. "I would enjoy a little clear soup before I retire. Ladies?"

Rosie watched with amazement and dismay as the queen walked to the door. Jean and Ann, then her young ladies-in-waiting fell in behind. The queen was going to leave the matter of Odyssey Manor and her heritage like this? She started after Her Majesty, but Lady Honora caught her arm and hissed a warning.

While Rosie struggled, Tony slipped through the crowd and reached Queen Elizabeth's side. "Your Majesty, what shall we do with Lady Rosalyn?"

"Do?" The queen kept walking down the hall toward her bedchamber. "Why should you *do* anything? Lady Rosalyn is my concern now."

Rosie jerked away from Lady Honora and ran after them. "What about my estate?"

"I thought I'd made that clear." Queen Elizabeth glided along, graceful and unperturbed. "'Tis Tony's estate now. Your title is restored, of course, and I'll find you a rich husband to wed, and with that you'll be satisfied."

"But I thought she'd have to wed me!" Tony objected.

"Not at all. You'll wed Lady Honora."

Grabbing Sir Danny's wrist, Lady Honora dragged him along as she galloped past Rosie and elbowed Tony out of the way. "I can't marry Sir Anthony."

"That was your desire, last time I spoke with you." Queen Elizabeth kept walking. "I wish only to give you your desire."

"It's not possible for me to marry Sir Anthony. I"— Lady Honora took a deep breath—"I love another."

That stopped Queen Elizabeth in her tracks. Facing Lady Honora, distaste oozing from every pore, she questioned, "Love? You would wed for love?"

Rosie hadn't believed it possible, but Lady Honora squirmed beneath Queen Elizabeth's austere gaze. "I know it's contrary to everything I've ever believed, but haven't I done my duty for my entire life? Haven't I always married the proper men? And what's the use of being dowager duchess of Burnham and baroness of Rowse in my own right, of being one of the wealthiest women in England, if I can't wed the man who will make me happy?" Rushing along like a brook in spring flood, she declared, "I'm going to wed Sir Danny Plympton, Esquire."

The queen stumbled backward. Jean gasped and Ann whimpered. The young ladies-in-waiting broke into unrestrained giggles. And one of Sir Danny's knees collapsed as if it had been struck from behind.

Tony said something—it sounded like, "Praise God"—while Rosie reached for Sir Danny's arm.

Lady Honora brushed her aside, helped him to stand, and faced the queen defiantly. The silence in the hall thickened until Ann piped, "Actually, Sir Danny is a . . . long-lost cousin on my mother's side." Everyone stared at her. "From Cornwall," she added helpfully. "Jean knows more about the details than I do."

All eyes turned to Jean, who smiled tightly. "'Tis a long tale. A most intricate, lengthy tale, too long to tell in the hallway when Her Majesty is hungry."

Reminded of her quest, Queen Elizabeth moved along and everyone followed her as closely as they could. She said, "Amazing. Sir Danny is related to the nobility, and Lady Rosalyn was raised by Lady Honora's aunt in perfect respectability. Who knows what further miracles my reign hath wrought?" She inspected Sir Danny and his imminent state of disintegration. "You're undoubtedly the family's fallen angel. What think you of this proposed marriage with Lady Honora?"

Sir Danny ran his fingers inside his ruff and swallowed. "It is more than I ever dreamed."

The queen stopped at a door, and one of the ladies-in-waiting hastened to open it. A sumptuous bedchamber lay within, but clearly the conversation fascinated Queen Elizabeth. How could she abandon it to sit alone, brooding on Essex and his heedless betrayal? Indecisive, she stood there until Sir Danny smiled at her, a smile so sickly her wicked spirit was captivated.

She led the way to the royal study where a brisk fire burned, books lined one wall, a magnificent desk sat close against the window, and a comfortable, well-proportioned chair awaited her. While she seated herself, the people in her train squeezed through the door, elbowing each other, ignoring the rules of priority which Ann had expounded, ignoring everything but their avid curiosity.

"So have I your permission to wed Sir Danny?" Lady Honora asked anxiously.

"I have often forbidden marriages between my young ladies-in-waiting and a reprobate—even if he is the long-lost cousin of a noble family conveniently living in far-off Cornwall—and I've often forbidden marriages among unsuitable members of the nobility, but when the ladies are no longer in the first blush of youth and the nobility lives far from my jurisdiction, weddings happen with or without my blessing." She looked down her nose at Lady Honora. "If you understand me."

Lady Honora did, and squeezed Sir Danny's hand with enthusiasm. "Aye, madam."

Queen Elizabeth watched with heavy-lidded amusement, then said to Sir Danny, "You'll be the husband of a wealthy wife."

Offended at the charge of fortune hunting, Sir Danny said, "I've had that chance before, Your Majesty, and never taken advantage of it."

Queen Elizabeth looked at the crowd which squeezed

into the chamber and seemed to understand their fascination. "So you love Lady Honora as much as she loves you?"

"I . . ." Sir Danny looked at Lady Honora. "She . . ."

Lady Honora looked back at him with her heart in her gaze. Rosie realized how arid Lady Honora's life must have been, to find the attentions of Sir Danny enthralling enough to sink her reputation and her code of conduct to marry him. To marry an *actor*.

Sir Danny must have realized the same thing, and if his affections were not involved as Lady Honora's, he still wanted her, and loved her as much as every woman he'd ever loved. Taking both her hands in his, he looked into her eyes. "You have made me the happiest man in all Christendom. I am in love, a love I thought secret until this day. My ear is enamored of my lady's voice, my eye is enamored of my lady's countenance, my heart is enamored of my lady's soul, and I find this love which consumes me is consecrated by the love returned by my goddess! Forgive my momentary hesitation. 'Twas nothing more than astonishment at the reward which God hath given me, a reward so great it should be conferred on a lord of the blood, or a hero of mythical proportions."

Rosie empathized with Sir Danny's dilemma, understanding more than anyone else in the room what he surrendered—the long days on the road, the great moments on the boards.

"Lady Rosalyn, you have such an expression on your face," Lady Honora said. "Do you not approve of this marriage?"

Rosie understood she was seeking Rosie's blessing, for Rosie was the nearest thing to family for Sir Danny, and Rosie saw the chance to help her beloved guardian. "I could never have imagined such a turn of events." She certainly wasn't lying. "It fulfills my greatest dreams for Sir Danny, yet I wonder, will he miss his acting?"

Lady Honora's eyes lit with zeal. "We'll have revels," she promised. "He'll star in them."

"Or mayhap he could sponsor a theater company," Rosie suggested. "That was my plan."

"Aye." Lady Honora clasped her hands. "A theater company of his own, like the Chamberlain's Men. I believe I might be some assistance in organizing and directing such a company, for I am an orderly person."

Orderly? Rosie almost laughed. Orderly Lady Honora loved ramshackle Sir Danny, and what the result would be, Rosie couldn't imagine.

Slumped against the wall, Tony drawled a challenge. "I understood, Lady Honora, you were seeking the finest stud in England to father your children. I must assume you've given that up."

The ladies-in-waiting were so overcome with laughter Queen Elizabeth ordered them to one corner of the study.

Sir Danny strode to Tony and flipped him under the chin. "Lady Honora now *has* the finest stud in England to father her children."

Tony straightened and towered over Sir Danny. "She's abandoned the finest stud in England for you, my man, and left me without a bride."

"Accept her judgment and cease your whining."

Queen Elizabeth rose and said hastily, "I must rest now."

She wanted to avoid this confrontation, but if she slipped away now, it might be months before Tony could pin her down again, and in those months Rosie could bear his child alone, without the benefit of his name, a hanger-on at court awaiting justice. Moving to intercept the queen, he said, "A man's not complete until he's married, madam."

"And then he's finished," Queen Elizabeth said sourly. "You cannot marry."

"Madam, like Solomon, you are wise, and you must see there is no other fair conclusion to Lady Rosalyn Bellot, heir to Odyssey manor, or to myself, except marriage between us."

"I *must* see? Your queen must not *see* anything." As if her rancor rode her like a burr beneath the saddle, Queen Elizabeth shook her finger in his face. "When men marry, they forget their duties, and I can't lose my master of the guard. You're too important to the kingdom. You've just proved it by defeating Essex. Trust me. I'll find the Sadler heiress a husband, and you a wife, if you really want one."

He stared, stunned at his tactlessness. He knew Queen Elizabeth hated to see her courtiers fall in love and lavish devotion on one another. He knew she preferred polite, formal marriages to those based on passion. Yet he had fallen to his knees when he saw Rosie, argued for their wedding with obvious desire, and all but ordered Her Majesty to do his bidding. What should he do?

But Rosie stepped up to the queen and curtsied deeply. "I have always heard Your Majesty is the fount of wisdom, and you have just proved it."

Tony stared at Rosie as she stood, hands demurely folded before her. Had she gone mad? Had she lost her affection for him?

Or had she a plan?

Queen Elizabeth half turned her head. "Lady Rosalyn, what is your meaning?"

"It has weighed heavy on me that I should marry Sir Anthony when he so obviously loves another." Rosie slumped as if a great weight oppressed her.

The queen looked at her fully. "He loves another? Who so commands his affections?"

"Madam, he ever speaks of her, and while he cannot have her, I think he would be happiest with one who resembles her."

"Who?" Queen Elizabeth struck a table with her fist. "Tell me, I command you."

"The lady whom you choose as his wife should be fair and white, with crimson hair like unto the sunset. She should have long fingers and hands that, when weighed with rings, overshadow the finest jewels with their beauty."

Queen Elizabeth touched her red wig with her long fingers.

Rosie continued, "Sir Anthony's wife should be straight and tall, and be light of foot when dancing and clever of mind when conversing. She should speak many languages fluently, and have fine gray eyes."

Rosie batted her own amber eyes, and Tony almost fainted with relief. His Rosie was a clever minx. He needed to remember he could depend on her in a pinch. He needed to remember her intelligence, too, when marriage pitted them against one another.

"The lady whom Tony weds should wear fine clothes, yet be so elegant the clothes wear not her."

Queen Elizabeth straightened the pearls that looped around her neck, and fluffed the silk that puffed from the slashing in her sleeves.

"She should ride to the hounds and never tire, dance all night and never falter. She should, in fact, be a likeness of Your Majesty, and that is the wife Sir Anthony should wed. Not I, who am so drab and ignorant." Dressed in Ophelia's tattered, white dress, with a garland hanging over one eye and the marks of tears still on her face, Rosie fit none of her own description, and her plea sounded all the more pathetic for her appearance. "Please, madam, out of kindness for me, find him a wife as beautiful as yourself."

Elizabeth extended her hand to Tony. "Is what she says true, my dearest courtier?"

He was overcome with admiration for Rosie, but not so overcome he didn't recognize his cue. He knelt at Queen Elizabeth's feet. "Madam, I have told you so often enough. 'Tis you who hold my heart, and all others pale in comparison."

Elizabeth basked in his admiration as a cat basks in the warmth of the sun.

Assuming a contrite attitude, he said, "Forgive me for appearing to doubt your judgment. I simply thought that if Lady Rosalyn and I were to wed, it would save you much money."

"Save?" Queen Elizabeth said cautiously. "Money?"

"Aye, madam, there is the matter of payment to Lady Rosalyn for the loss of her estate."

If horror had a face, Queen Elizabeth wore it. "I owe Lady Rosalyn nothing for the loss of her estate."

"Surely you don't think *I* can afford to recompense her." His indignation might have earned him a place in the Chamberlain's Men. "Of course, you'll be providing her with a dowry suitable for the earl of Sadler's daughter, which will repay the loss of her estate."

Queen Elizabeth developed that faraway look, the one she wore when budget problems troubled her. "If you married her, there wouldn't be any dowry to be paid."

"Madam, if I married her, she would still be a brown drab of a girl." Tony glanced at Rosie and lowered his voice. "Would a red wig improve her, do you think?"

The queen looked at Rosie and sagged. Tony felt the wind of change whistle through the chamber. The long day, the anxiety about the rebellion, and the changes which every day taxed an old woman seemed to catch up with her, and she tossed her head and said petulantly, "Do as you like. Marry the girl if you wish. I wash my hands of the matter." Standing, she drew a breath. "But don't come to me for a dowry, and don't come crying if she looks like a doxie in a red wig."

Tony had learned his lesson, and showed no enthusiasm. "Nay, madam, I won't. Not the dowry, nor the wig."

"And don't think you're shamming me, either." Queen Elizabeth glared at Rosie. "You really wish to wed her."

Tony nodded as if penitent. "I could not sham you, madam. I do wish to wed her. I wish to start my dynasty, and she's the kind of wife every man wants. She has no other place to go, so she'll be obedient." He hoped lightning didn't strike him. "She's plain, so I know the children born in our bed will be mine." She was beautiful, and he'd be a jealous husband. "And most important, my people at Odyssey Manor believe the lands belong to her. She will seal my claim to the manor, and that's all that matters to me."

Queen Elizabeth understood dynastic matters, and his explanation soothed her. "Marry her, then, but I need my master of the Queen's Guard by my side."

"I live to serve you."

She swept from the room on his assurance and her ladies dragged out with many a backward glance. Tony rose to his feet and shut the door. Silence reigned as he looked at Jean and Ann, Lady Honora and Sir Danny, and finally at Rosie. They stood frozen in place, then slowly, their paralysis melted. Jean laughed softly and with relish. Ann rushed from Rosie to Tony to Lady Honora to Sir Danny, hugging each one. Lady Honora clung to Sir Danny as if she couldn't believe her good fortune. Sir Danny clung to Lady Honora as if not sure he could stand by himself.

And Tony stared at Rosie and wondered how many years it had been since he'd held her. He wanted to lift her onto this desk and find out if it was sturdy enough to hold two bodies. He wanted to sweep her away to his bedchamber and bar the door. He wanted to take her to Odyssey Manor and be with her in every way a man could be with a woman.

But the time they'd spent apart, the things he wanted to say, the frustration, the fury, the desire, kept him from saying anything at all. The greatest lover in all England—*and* the finest stud—had no plan and no words.

Jean snatched at Ann when she floated by on her rounds, and said loudly, "Sister, we have much to do."

"Oh, nothing we need to do could be as important as this." Ann waved a hand at the loving couples. "We've got to help them plan their nuptials. Have you no romance in your soul?"

"*I* do." Jean dragged Ann toward the door. "And so do they." On the way, she pecked Rosie on the cheek, pecked Tony on the cheek. "Once for me, Tony."

Tony didn't remember the last time he'd blushed, but he did it now, and he prayed Rosie hadn't noticed.

Trying to cover his embarrassment, he asked, "Why are you clucking like that, Lady Honora?"

Lady Honora had her hand on Sir Danny's forehead. "My little lambkin is warm. I think he's just over-whelmed with his good fortune, but I'm going to take him to Rowse Manor and help him adjust."

As she led Sir Danny from the room, Tony caught the look in Sir Danny's eyes. Half-smug, half-panicked, and all anticipation.

Tony knew how he felt.

"Plain and obedient, eh?"

He jumped and turned, and there stood Rosie right behind him. He grinned feebly. "I was just trying to convince Her Majesty that I didn't want to wed you. I mean"—he closed his eyes—"I do want to wed you, but if Her Majesty thinks I do, 'twill never happen."

"Aye, so I gathered." She wandered toward the door. "She's a jealous, possessive woman, and she thinks you're charming and handsome." She glanced over her shoulder. "Verily, 'tis a valid concept."

He stood transfixed until she disappeared through the door, then he rushed after her. "You think I'm charming and handsome?"

She chuckled. "You don't need me to feed your vanity."

He stopped, and after she'd walked on a few steps, she stopped as well. "In sooth, you're the only woman I need feeding my vanity."

They looked at each other across the width of the hall. Really looked at each other for the first time in too long, and it all came back to them. The familiarity, the friendship, the passion, the laughter.

Cotzooks, how he loved this woman! In a sudden hurry, he began opening doors up and down the hallway. Most doors opened onto fine chambers, empty but ready for occupancy, but in one a lady screamed, and he exclaimed, "Wrong room."

"What are you looking for?" Rosie asked.

"There's a storage room along here somewhere." One door opened into darkness, and he exclaimed in delight. Taking a branch of candles from the table in the hall, he waved her inside.

She came cautiously, but she came. "Privacy," he explained. "It's long and narrow, a scrap of the palace, so the servants use it for storage. I'd heard"—he wiggled his eyebrows—"they also use it for assignations."

He placed the candles on the floor. They illuminated

the undersides of the shelves piled with linens and blankets and cast elongated shadows along the narrow ceiling. Their light barely reached all the way back where a clutter of broken furniture waved uneven limbs.

Rosie backed up against the shelves, and he followed, eager now, excitement bubbling in him. That gown she wore would be difficult to get her out of, but when were gowns ever easy? The touch of her bare flesh against his would heal every wound, body and soul, this last month had inflicted. He leaned his elbow close to her head, then leaned his head close to her face. "Now tell me again about my charm and good looks."

She ducked out from under his arm. "You're dirty."

"I've been a hero this day." He tossed off his cap, cape, and doublet. "Are you impressed?"

"Impressed? That you threw yourself into danger? Impressed is not quite the word I would use." Her eyes sparked as she crept further from the light. "Do you often bring your ladies here?"

"I've never brought a lady here." He followed. "Most ladies would be disgusted."

"Most ladies would follow you anywhere."

"Because I'm so charming and good-looking?"

"Because you're so modest."

"Is that another one of my virtues which attracted you?"

She swung around to see if he was jesting, and relaxed when she realized he was. A smile nudged at her mouth, and he murmured, "That's better." He dragged two piles of blankets down off a shelf. Extending his hand, he offered it, palm up. "Would you like to sit down?"

She looked at the hand, then at him, then at the

hand. Slowly, she extended her own hand and put it in his. Sensitive as a whisper, her skin slid across his, over the calluses, over the lines and the mounts. Her fingers curled around his, slipping between in an act of mating. Like a connoisseur of Spanish sherry, he closed his eyes fully to appreciate the sensation, then opened them to see she had closed hers. Her head was thrown back, her lips parted, and each deep breath brought her breasts close.

Her magnificent, unmanly breasts, which had first betrayed her to him. How cocksure he'd been at that first meeting! How easy he had thought her seduction would be! And how she'd taken him apart, piece by piece, and then put him together into a different man. A better man.

A man who planned to seduce her in a storage chamber.

"We should talk," he said hoarsely.

"We should."

She sank onto her pile of blankets, and he sank onto his. He took her other hand in his, expecting that the reaction would be less—more like holding hands and less like making love.

Again, it was like the first time they'd touched. Their gazes met and clung. It seemed as intimate as a kiss.

"Talk," he said.

"Aye."

What did he want to talk about? Oh . . . "You left me."

She tried to take her hands back, but he tightened his fingers.

"Talk," he urged.

"You lied to me."

"Never."

"You didn't tell me about Sir Danny."

He didn't need her reproach to feel guilty. "I wanted you to be safe."

"Sometimes there are more important things than safety."

"I knew that. I know it now." He took a breath because he didn't want to tell her, but he had to. She had to know. "If I had it to do over, I'd do the same thing."

Her laughter almost knocked him over. Her body did as she skimmed her arms around his neck and leaned forward. He landed on the blankets with her on his chest. "I know that." She laughed again, hugging him close. "And I'd do what I did. Do you think our baby will be as stubborn as we are?"

She suddenly weighed as much as a horse. A big horse. He couldn't get his breath to speak, and when he did, it sounded more like a howl. "You're . . . going . . . to . . ."

"Nay. *We're* going to."

"Have a babe?"

"Didn't you always know it?"

Did he know it? "Aye." Tears leaked from the corners of his eyes and she wiped them with her sleeve. "I never doubted we had made a babe. Somehow I knew the babe would precede the marriage."

She tried to sit up, but he pulled her back down. "Do you mind?"

"That people will talk?" He held her nose to nose. "People will talk about me marrying an actress. They'll talk that I married Lady Rosalyn Bellot to secure my lands. They'll talk about me as long as I'm a favorite of the queen's, and they'll talk about you because you're beautiful, because you act like a dream, and you're the lost heir. They're going to talk about us all our lives. An early babe will be as a mere nothing."

"But what about you? 'Tis you who feared an early

child, not for what people would say, not even for the child, but for the proof that you carried blood tainted by your birth."

She knew him too well. He had loved his father, yet at the same time, Tony despised his father for his weakness and had sworn never to emulate him. He'd despised his father for allowing himself to be seduced by a woman as cold and ruthless as the north wind. His father had been a fool, and Tony had feared being one, too.

But to be seduced by Rosie . . . ah, that was not a seduction, but a feast of the senses. To be seduced by Rosie was not weakness, but good taste. "I'm proud to be the father of your child."

"*Our* child."

"*Our* child." The slender body atop his relaxed, and he added, "But we'll wed in the morning."

The vibration of her laughter warmed him. "Aye, we'll wed in the morning." She gently touched her lips to his, and each breath gave him life, each contact moved his blood, and the quick, shy stroke of her tongue unlaced her bodice without his volition. Rosie's kiss was a mighty instrument.

When the buzzing in his ears cleared, he heard her say, "Where will we sleep tonight?"

His hearing was impaired and his eyeballs fogged from their combined heat, but his fingers seemed nimble enough as he removed layer after layer of her clothing. "*Will* we sleep tonight?"

She shivered. "It's cold in here."

"We have blankets."

"Someone might come in."

"I have my sword and dagger." He grinned as he freed her breasts at last. They'd changed with the advancement of pregnancy, but he'd always recognize Rosie's nipples. "And you have your purse."

"True." Leaning over, she blew out the candles one by one, but he stopped her when she would have blown out the last one. "Aren't you afraid of the dark anymore?"

"Nay, I have my talismans. My father's ring." She touched the chain around her neck. "The babe in my belly." She took his hand and laid it on the slight mound. "And my cavalier, the second-greatest lover in all England."

Furious at this challenge, he demanded, "Who's the first?"

She slid into his arms, smooth and slow, then leaned forward to blow out the last candle. "Me."

Epilogue

Lord Nottingham and Sir Robert Sidney did indeed have to bring cannon and kegs of powder from the Tower and threaten to blow up Essex House before the earl of Essex would surrender. A trial followed. Essex and Southampton were, of course, found guilty.

Although Queen Elizabeth allowed the earl of Southampton to be condemned to life in the Tower, Essex was condemned to death. On the morning of February 25, Essex was beheaded.

The queen was playing the virginals when a messenger brought the news. She stopped playing. No one said a word. After a time she began to play again.

Lady Rosalyn, daughter of the earl of Sadler, and her husband, Sir Anthony Rycliffe, were blessed with a large, healthy baby girl on September 29, 1601, after eight months of wedded bliss. They named her Elizabeth

Honora Jean Ann Rycliffe, and only one man ever commented about her early arrival.

Lord Bothey recovered from the blow on the head with no ill effects, although it was noted that, in the future, he avoided the company of Lady Rosalyn, especially when she carried her purse.

Honor, riches, marriage-blessing,
Long continuance, and increasing,
Hourly joys be still upon you!

—THE TEMPEST, IV, i, 106